INITIATE

INITIATE
ANIMUS™ BOOK ONE

JOSHUA ANDERLE

MICHAEL ANDERLE

Initiate (this book) is a work of fiction.
All of the characters, organizations, and events portrayed in this novel are either products of the author's imagination or are used fictitiously. Sometimes both.

Copyright © 2018 Joshua Anderle and Michael Anderle
Cover Art by Jake @ J Caleb Design
http://jcalebdesign.com / jcalebdesign@gmail.com
Cover copyright © LMBPN Publishing
A Michael Anderle Production

LMBPN Publishing supports the right to free expression and the value of copyright. The purpose of copyright is to encourage writers and artists to produce the creative works that enrich our culture.

The distribution of this book without permission is a theft of the author's intellectual property. If you would like permission to use material from the book (other than for review purposes), please contact support@lmbpn.com. Thank you for your support of the author's rights.

LMBPN Publishing
PMB 196, 2540 South Maryland Pkwy
Las Vegas, NV 89109

First US edition, September 2018
Version 1.02, September 2018

THE INITATE TEAM

Thanks to the JIT Readers

Angel LaVey
Mary Morris
John Ashmore
Kelly O'Donnell
Kelly Bowerman
Larry Omans
Tim Bischoff
Mickey Cocker

If I've missed anyone, please let me know!

Editor
Lynne Stiegler

*To Family, Friends and
Those Who Love
to Read.
May We All Enjoy Grace
to Live the Life We Are
Called.*

CHAPTER ONE

He made it in time, though with scant minutes to spare. The wispy hum echoed through the streets as Seattle's biosphere activated, and the lively blue skies morphed into a foreboding gray.

Kaiden looked up as hexagonal patterns of white shimmered through the sky, leaving trace amounts of element-seeds that were sown unnaturally into the air. Rainfall would start in about five minutes.

The streets cleared rapidly, and he followed suit, heading to his destination and possible place of employment.

The smooth sounds of saxophones accented with electro-ambiance greeted him when he stepped into the Emerald Lounge and took a cursory look at the interior. Chairs, tables, and walls shared a dull dark-green color, and a retro neon-green sign proudly declared the establishment's name over the bar.

He walked over to the bartender, a Hispanic man with a

thick mustache and comb-over who leaned against the counter. The luxuriant strands were surprisingly novel in a time where hair-loss remedies could be bought for five credits and droned over to the purchaser in less than an hour.

Is this man making a statement or is he merely out of shits to give?

"Hey, *hombre*, I'm looking for Julio…" His voice trailed off. He was conflicted as to whether he should feel stupid for making assumptions or because he hadn't made the connection.

"Looking at him." The bartender's gaze made a slow up and down scrutiny, and Kaiden willed himself to remain outwardly unmoved. "Also, buddy, pal, or dude works just fine." He chuckled, his voice the sound of gravel and dust as he dropped the towel he held. "How can I help you?"

"Ricky set up an interview for me." Kaiden looked in the mirror, then back at the bartender. "My name is Kaiden. Kaiden Jericho."

The man sized him up once more and nodded. "Can I see your…*ID*?" He placed a knowing emphasis on the last word.

Kaiden nodded and pulled his long sleeve up over his shoulder to reveal the tattoo of a skull and longhorns. Old-time Peacemaker gun barrels replaced the horns, and a lone star almost filled the right eye.

Julio nodded and motioned for him to put his sleeve down. "Good to see you out here, Kaiden. Ricky tried to set a few of you up over the last few months." He retrieved the towel and picked a glass up to wipe it. "You're the only one who's shown up so far."

Kaiden nodded and removed a credit chip from the security pouch on his waistband.

He made a drinking motion with his free hand. "Put that away." Julio gestured to the chip. "Considering all that went down, it's nice to see another Dead-Eye breathing." He chuckled. "Just don't drink me under."

He brought out a couple of shot glasses and showed him a bottle of Devil's Cut whiskey, Kaiden nodded as he put the chip back and Julio filled both glasses. They saluted one another and downed the smoky liquid.

"Nice place." Kaiden looked around. "Is it yours?" he asked as Julio refilled the glasses.

The bartender nodded. "Is now. Previous owner kicked the bucket and his kid didn't want to run it, so I got it for a steal." They each took another shot. "Poor bastard accidentally slit his throat while shaving. Tragic."

Kaiden chuckled. "Always sad when that happens. The old proprietor didn't happen to have any friends in the aquarium, did he?"

Julio smirked. "Nah, it wasn't the Blues. They're into illegal modding and EI cracking now. He probably pissed some gamblers off or scuffed the shoes of a Zaibatsu leader or something. I ain't gonna complain. It's probably why the kid didn't want to run the bar—thought they would go for him next."

"Did ya check the books for anything suspicious before putting your savings down?"

Julio gave him a wry look. "Ricky really make me sound that foolish?" He huffed as he pulled the collar of his dress shirt down to reveal a similar tattoo to Kaiden's but with an added bullet looming between the horns.

"A division leader, huh?" Kaiden took the whiskey bottle and poured two more shots.

Julio raised an eyebrow. "He really didn't tell you?"

Kaiden considered his response as he raised his glass and downed it before he replied. "Not unless 'Mi Tio' is a codename now."

Julio let out an annoyed sigh and chased down his shot. "Little punk always did try to flex his lineage. I'm surprised he didn't get his ass booted with all his mouthing off."

"Ricky is—was—a good runner. I expected him to come here himself. I don't know what he's up to now," Kaiden said, then heard both a boisterous laugh and the pounding sounds of rain.

He looked behind him to see a group of four men tumble into the bar, all dressed in black leather jackets with silver and white circular accents. Their haircuts were stylized versions of punk and slaver cuts.

Kaiden grimaced. They were obviously slummer-gangers, rich kids and artsy bastards wanting the edgiest looks Daddy could buy.

Harmless to most, but they made his stomach turn.

Julio poured two more shots as he nodded in the direction of the rich punks. "Don't worry about them. They may cause a fuss, but Papa always pays for anything they break."

Kaiden studied the new arrivals, the attention deliberately casual to avoid notice. "Ya seem pretty laid back for a guy Ricky said was looking for a bouncer," he commented and turned away from the newcomers.

Julio shrugged. "I believe the term nowadays is 'doorman.' It adds a sort of class to the gig. Besides, someone like you would probably get bored with just standing around and giving the stink-eye now and again. Once you get set up, I'll see about some side jobs that are more your type of fun."

Kaiden considered this for a moment.

Ever since he left Fresno, he had received calls and requests for various odd jobs, the kind he might have jumped at back when Jake asked for takers. But in the aftermath of that day…

He placed his hand on his tattoo, and his jaw went tight. "Perhaps, but considering what went down? Maybe ya shouldn't have me be anyone's guardian angel for a bit."

Julio gave him a somber look. "I get it, kid, but you can't —" Wood snapping and angry yells pierced their grim mood.

Julio, Kaiden, and the few patrons in the lounge looked over to the top left section of the bar. The four slummers crowded around another man, blond with a green jacket, who looked to be in his early twenties and was clearly frightened.

Kaiden scowled as he watched the scene unfold.

One of the slummers pushed the blond to the floor. Another put his boot on the downed man's chest and seemed to be hurling insults through gritted but perfectly aligned teeth.

Kaiden rapped his fingers against the bar for a few moments. He wondered if it would seem unprofessional to physically blow off some steam in front of his potential employer.

Julio, to his credit, picked up the signal. "Hey, if you still want the job…" he began with a wry smile and a nod to the assholes. "I'll need a demonstration of your skills." Kaiden gave him a bemused look. "Ricky said you were a damn good fighter, but he'll say anything to make him and his pals look good. So, if you can back it up, show me. The slummers' papa will reimburse me for damages. After all, it's not like you're on the clock just yet."

Kaiden nodded, picked up his still full whiskey glass, and gave him a brief salute. "If ya catch it on the cams, save me a copy, will ya?" With that, he walked over to the stairs.

"You think…you can just…leave us, you damn coward?" one of the slummers growled between each booted kick. The downed man lay immobile.

Kaiden took a good look at the jackasses once he reached the summit of the staircase. The man kicking the helpless patron had several chains around his neck and wrist and a shaved head with a blue Saturn ring of hair—quite immaculately done, as well.

He was shadowed by two others with half-shaved heads and long bangs on opposite sides—platinum and rose hair, along with other designer shades.

The one in the back who'd pushed the man down was the biggest of the bunch, standing around six and a half feet with a head of spiked white hair and neck that looked like a spark plug.

Kaiden let out a sharp whistle as he swirled his shot glass. The four glanced at him as he leaned against the railing, "You know, I'm trying to enjoy an evening of whiskey and wit, but you are making that a damn chore. Your horrible fashion makes my eyes water, but I can ignore that." He shook his head. "The castrato war cries? Not so much."

He had their attention. "None of us gives a *shit*, crank," the one with the chains retorted. "As far as you're concerned, we *own* this bar, and if you don't beat it"—he jerked a thumb over his shoulder—"Moxy here will be happy to blackjack your head into a bowl to piss in."

The big one in the back cracked his neck dramatically to back up the threat.

"Moxy?" Kaiden's eyes half-closed, and he pinched the bridge of his nose with his free hand. "A bit of advice for you dickheads. Don't get inspiration for your face names from your childhood dog."

"He took it in his dog's honor," the platinum-haired one responded with open belligerence.

Kaiden let the moment linger, a bemused smile creeping slowly onto his face as the others turned to glare at him.

"Dammit, Zed, shut the hell up," the blue-haired one commanded, followed by an annoyed growl.

"Oh, uh, sorry, Barry."

"It's Czar, you fucking idiot!"

"Seriously, bro, shut the hell up," the rose-haired one interjected.

Kaiden chuckled. *This might be too unfair.* "So Moxy, Zed, and Czar, and you are..." He pointed to the last one. "Rosie the slaughterer, I'm guessing?"

"It's Zane, shithead," he replied, tapping his fingers against his forehead in frustration.

Kaiden waved his hand in a circle. "You guys are precious. Now, I'm sure you're late for racquetball practice or whatever the hell you need to go do, so how about you let your friend here go and leave before your hair gel melts all over your nice jackets?"

Czar gave the man on the floor a final kick. Kaiden's grip tightened around his drink in anger as the bully stepped over to him and stared right into his eyes.

"He isn't a *friend* anymore. He left us to go to that academy, and we don't take kindly to deserters."

Kaiden shrugged. "Yeah, I'm sure. You take away all their membership benefits—like twenty percent off hair dye and free chardonnay on Wednesdays."

Czar gripped Kaiden's collar. "Shut up. If you keep making jokes, we will pummel the shit out of you right into the floor. I'll see to it that my lawyers make sure you pay for any smudges on my jacket while I'm at it."

Kaiden lifted a finger and tapped the tip of the man's nose. "Well, at least you acknowledge your affluence-induced stupidity," he said as he downed his shot. "But you're probably gonna have to wait to identify me until your jaw heals up."

With that, he flicked his shot glass into the air. Czar looked up momentarily while Kaiden balled his fist and slammed it into the underside of the man's nose. A painful cracking noise resounded as he crumpled to the floor.

Kaiden caught the glass as it fell, smiling at the other slummers.

He flung the glass at Moxy, shattering it against his head and flinging shards into his eyes. The man's tough persona disintegrated as he fell to his knees and screamed, trying to dig out the glass.

Zane rushed forward, with Zed following a few steps behind.

Kaiden kicked a chair into the brothers' path. They stumbled over it and each other, and he dashed toward Zed as he began to stagger up and sent his knee flying into the platinum-haired punk's chest.

Zane stood behind him and threw a punch, which Kaiden caught and then twisted the boy's arm. Zane emitted a few pained grunts before the would-be bouncer threw a real punch into his right cheek.

By this time, Moxy had recovered and charged Kaiden with fury and one eye closed. He dodged around the larger man and kicked his knees, causing him to tumble forward.

He jumped on Moxy's back and put him in a chokehold, holding him there until the big bastard finally passed out.

Kaiden walked over to the victim of the gang's beatings and pulled him to his feet.

"Thank you, I…" he began. Kaiden saw Czar stumbling back to his feet, blood pouring from his mouth and his teeth not quite as nicely aligned as before.

"Hold that for a moment." Kaiden shook his head as the punk yanked out an ornate knife handle and flicked open a six-inch blade.

He charged at Kaiden, who grabbed the knife-wielding arm and twisted it. Czar's hand opened and dropped the blade. "How's your health plan?" he asked, looking into the slummer's shocked eyes. "Time you get some practical use out of it." He finished the statement with a smirk as he flung Czar over both his shoulder and the railing to the floor below.

The slummer landed with a heavy thud.

"That's gotta hurt…"

Kaiden looked down at Czar. His head was bent to one side, and his eyes were closed.

He couldn't tell if the man was unconscious, but he seemed smart enough to at least pretend to be.

Kaiden looked at Zed and Zane, who were conscious, but after seeing that display, they looked at him, then at each other, and simply placed their heads on the ground. He smiled as he turned back to the blond man. "Don't worry about it. Not to sound like an ass, but that was more for my pleasure than heroism."

"I suppose I'm lucky you have such volatile hobbies, then," the man said with some caution in his voice. "Nevertheless, thank you, My name is Ben, and that was my cousin you sent over the railing."

"Genetics can be a bitch like that," Kaiden joked as he crossed his arms and leaned against the railing. "No hard feelings, yeah? Don't really feel like being sued."

"None—at least none toward you." Ben sighed as he reached into his jacket and brought out a silver box. It bore an insignia engraved with an N inside a triangle. "I thought the Academy would be my way of actually making a name for myself instead of merely pretending to be a bigshot like they do, but I couldn't even fight back against these idiots with no real martial training." He looked at Kaiden, then back at the box. "I suppose I should be looking elsewhere to find a profession. Something tells me I wouldn't last too long there with my skills."

"You all kept talking about the Academy. What academy?" Kaiden asked, which drew a shocked response from Ben.

"Nexus Academy? How do you not know about that? I thought you were going there, considering how good a fighter you are."

Not sure I had to be good to take these guys out, but I'll just shut up and take the compliment. Kaiden smiled at the thought. "Yeah, I knew of it, but there is more than one academy, you know."

"Perhaps, but not one as refined, advanced, and reputable as ours," a studious voice replied from behind them. Kaiden and Ben looked over to see a tall man with slicked-back white hair and a goatee. He wore a white-and-black jacket with the same insignia that was on Ben's box on the left breast. Some kind of apparatus around his head connected to the black-shaded oculus that obscured his eyes.

"Commander Sasha?" Ben asked incredulously.

"Indeed"—Kaiden was able to make out dim lights dancing in his glasses—"Initiate Benjamin Hargrove. It is also 'professor,' considering my station at the Academy now." The professor looked at the two younger men. "Well fought, I must say, though I do not think those slummers were much of a challenge to someone with real fighting ability."

"Actually, I was just thinking that," Kaiden replied. "So you know this guy here, and you didn't do anything to help him?"

"Initiate Hargrove is an academy hopeful, and that comes with expectations. When such occasions as this arise, he should be able to handle himself. If the situation had escalated, I would have stepped in.

"Repeated curb-stomping is pretty damn escalated,"

Kaiden quipped, drawing a bemused smirk from the professor.

"Not by our standard. Stomping requires you to be on the ground and submit to your opponent's whim. Perhaps that might be your desire in your free time, but not while on duty."

Kaiden chuckled at this and then heard a low groan from Moxy. It seemed he was coming round. The professor noticed it too and began walking toward him. "Nexus Academy welcomes and trains potential recruits from all walks of life and of many different disciplines, but one must be skilled, knowledgeable, and hardened. However, when the time calls for it…" As Moxy began to push himself off the floor and turned to see who stood over him, he was greeted by the professor's boot slamming against his temple. He slid instantly back to the floor. "All must be ready to back up those talents with a bit of force."

"I see." Ben acknowledged with some dejection in his voice. "I was just telling myself that I might not be cut out for the Academy after what happened. Maybe it was foolish to try in the first place."

"Do not be so self-pitying, Initiate Hargrove. Perhaps you are not cut out for the Academy, but if you give in to that feeling now, you may do so forever. You had the grades and means to pass initial selection. Those criteria will carry you farther than most," Sasha rebuked as he returned to stand in front of the two, his hands clasped behind his back. "If that is what you choose, I believe you have made the right choice for yourself. However, I see you have one of the Nexus' EIs. You will have to return it or pass it along to another initiate. It cannot be used by civilians."

Ben looked at the box and back at Sasha. Then, his head turned slowly until he looked at Kaiden. "Professor, may I make a recommendation?" he asked.

"Go ahead. But I have an inkling that it is the same proposition I intended to make." Kaiden gave them a quizzical look. Both men now looked at him with fixed expressions, and he felt like he was being sized up like a horse preparing for a race he wasn't aware of.

"You, um… I'm sorry, I don't believe I caught your name." Ben spoke hesitantly, still looking alternately at him and the professor.

"Kaiden…Jericho," he replied, raising an eyebrow to indicate his puzzlement.

"I wanted to thank you, Kaiden, for helping me, and I do think the Academy is a wonderful opportunity, even if I don't go there myself." Ben stood straight and reached out to Kaiden with the box in his hand. "I believe you have what it takes to make use of what the Academy offers. If the professor will sanction it, you can have my EI and take my spot in the initiate class."

"Do what? You can just pass that along?" Kaiden asked incredulously.

"Speaking with the authority of the Nexus Board and as someone who can testify that you show promise due to field experience, I can transfer Benjamin's place to you. But this only allows you access to take the initiate's trial. Whether you pass and continue your stay at the Academy is all up to how you perform," Sasha explained. "If you accept, you will learn about the rules and terms on the day of initiation…which, I should inform you, is tomorrow."

"Not really a lot of time to think out my options," Kaiden deadpanned.

"Not really an opportunity you had until a minute ago," Sasha answered with a smirk.

"I know it is sudden, and you would probably like to think it through or talk to someone, but if it means anything from a grateful stranger, I think you could do it." Ben's smile was wide and honest.

Kaiden took the box and examined it, then looked at Ben and Sasha. "To hell with it. I just got one thing I need to do."

"And what is that?" Sasha asked.

Kaiden glanced at the bar. Julio saw him and waved, giving him a thumbs-up as he pointed at the still-fetal Czar. "I need to tell someone he won't have a doorman."

CHAPTER TWO

As Kaiden looked out his window, the sparkling waters of Elliot Bay came into view. The screen on the back of the headrest in front of him came to life, capturing his attention. It displayed the Rainier Hyperloop logo, a silver RH surrounded by a golden circle. The logo shrank quickly and went to the top-left corner of the screen as a message popped up.

Please prepare for submersion, Nexus class of 2196. Wouldn't want to lose any of you in a panic.

He raised an eyebrow. That was most likely merely a humorous comment drummed up by a PR intern, but if it was an honest concern, he should probably identify potential escape routes. Common sense spurred him to take a quick moment to look around.

He could hear the clicks and hums of the hyperloop train's propulsion systems rearranging and felt the shocks as it activated to prepare for the dive. Kaiden looked out the window once more to see the water coming up fast and heard the loud splash as the lead compartment of the hyperloop barreled into the bay. Glow strips activated along the sides and top of the tube as it went beneath the water, and a soft blue light illuminated the surroundings.

Kaiden clicked on the ETA tab of the screen. Twelve minutes until arrival. He scanned the cabin to see the other passengers talking animatedly among themselves, each dressed in the same uniform—white jacket, slacks, and black trainers. The only differences he noted were differently colored strips circling the left arm.

Sasha had messaged him that morning to tell him he would receive the same uniform upon his arrival—the initiate's formal garb—but didn't mention what the colored rings symbolized. If he had to guess, they were some sort of distinction denoting the services or pedigree of the wearer. If you went to a training school, you'd get a gold circle. If you won a dog show, you'd get polka dots.

He grinned at the ridiculous thought and wondered if he would get a special color for being recruited directly by a board member. Perhaps, he mused, a clean silver or royal purple, something nice and obvious that would be a little subtler than a target on his back.

He reached into his jeans pocket to bring out the EI box Ben had given him. With a practiced gesture, he flicked the lock open and looked at the chip. Besides the holographic coating around the perimeter of the chip, there seemed to be nothing unusual about it.

They were officially called hybrid EIs, though he'd heard some of the students call them N-Chips. He was told they were a mixture of the commercial EIs most metropolitans had and professional EIs.

"Mental butler" was the unofficial term, coined because of its primary purpose.

The chips were, in fact, tiny computers with programmed personalities and potentially thousands of functions and applications, depending on what you sprang for. They could only be run through specific devices like that odd contraption around Sasha's head—a stylish neural lens, as he had put it. Others used special wrist-mounted devices or tablets, and he had even seen some goofy-looking hats that had the capability to process and manage an EI.

He had never used one himself, but a few other Dead-Eyes had them. He could never see the point. Playing a game of solitaire in his head while on the job didn't seem very professional, even to him. He could, however, recall one unfortunate instance he had heard of from a division leader who had come in from Baton Rouge.

There weren't many professional EIs currently on the market, and there had been even less back then. Pro-EIs were the top class, and not only offered all the bells and whistles of normal commercial EIs but had the ability to integrate with other devices. This allowed the user to link up all their devices to the Pro-EI and control them from one location. It made them extremely valuable among businessmen, scientists, and mercenary leaders alike.

The leader who related the story said that one of his men had gotten his hands on a cracked Pro-EI. Almost all high-level tech was bound to its user in some way, so even if it was stolen or hacked, the device would usually be near useless to anyone who was not the owner.

Most saw this as a valuable failsafe for their property. Others saw it as a valuable opportunity.

Cracking became big business in the seedier worlds. Gangs and hacker collectives saw the potential in being able to find a way around this supposed failsafe. With some careful tampering and/or less careful physical force, they found a way to access these devices.

Unfortunately, it was far from perfect. Those methods did not negate the failsafe, merely slipped between many of the defenses and created new ways to unlock or force the activation of the device.

This came with a new set of problems. The devices could potentially be used, but not with one-hundred-percent effectiveness. On top of that, the methods were specific. When something was cracked, it was for a specific purpose. If you wanted access to a program on a computer you might get it, but if you even accidentally clicked on the recycle bin, it might literally blow up in your face.

The Dead-Eye with the cracked EI had sadly learned this the fatal way.

According to his one-time leader, he got the EI cracked and loaded into a neural lens he'd obtained from the black market so he could use the link function in a limited capacity. He would supposedly have access to his Hacker Suite in the field, but the dumbass decided to test out the Pro-EI's Hacker Suite to see the difference.

The device short-circuited, and not only shocked him and fried his lens, but the turret he had been able to deactivate just fine with his normal suite was reactivated. It shot, as the leader put it, an obscene number of holes into him.

Kaiden believed any number more than zero would probably qualify, but the image was still clear.

A blinking light alerted him, and Kaiden snapped out of his thoughts. The screen now flashed a countdown—fifty-one seconds until arrival.

He left his seat and began walking to the line that had formed in front of the door to the tube. Another loud splash sounded as the hyperloop breached the water and the glow strips faded away.

The others' excitement was palpable, and he had to admit that his own nervous energy had grown.

He didn't know what this would bring, but dealing with the unknown was kind of his forte. With outward calm, he exited the train and looked around the station, seeing older men and women in jackets like Sasha's waving the students down and loading them onto buses.

Initiates were separated by the colors of their rings, but a small group with no uniforms had gathered beside a bus on the far end. He walked over to them, and, upon closer inspection, noticed something rather odd. A few near the back talked to each other in hushed voices, concern and surprise evident on their faces.

Kaiden didn't pay them much mind—just nerves, he reasoned—but then noticed a slightly larger group who were all rather bizarre-looking. They were all dressed in full-body one-pieces with intricate patterns and some sort of cylinder on their back. The only exposed parts of their body were their heads.

Skin colors were varying shades of blue, from light cyan to dark purple. Ripples and patterns wove through their flesh, and they all wore some sort of mask covering either their full face or only their mouth. These were attached to some sort of apparatus around their neck filled with a dark liquid.

Kaiden wondered whether they were part of some flamboyant gang, or perhaps a special division of some kind. As he drew closer, not hiding the fact he was trying to get a closer look, one of them turned to look at him. He was periwinkle and interlocking triangle patterns in the shape of a crescent bordered his eyes, which were large dark pools of an inky color. *Holy shit, they're aliens!*

He now understood the hushed but amazed whispers from the other humans.

Kaiden had never seen an alien this close before since they were quite rare in the outside world. Ever since the first contact and war at the beginning of the twenty-second century and the ceasefire in 2134, alien beings that came to Earth were usually closely guarded and generally stayed among the cloud cities in the stratosphere or in the few orbitals in space.

Seeing one face to face rather than on a screen at whatever alliance-come-lately shindig was quite something.

He…she…the alien raised a hand in the air, the five fingers held apart like an exaggerated high-five. Kaiden looked it over with more detailed scrutiny. Its anatomy seemed mostly humanoid, but he couldn't tell too much due to the body suit it wore and the scuba-like mouth mask on its face. He did note, though, that this one was bald, while the ones behind it had some sort of leaf-like material protruding from their heads—or perhaps feature-less tentacles—either wrapped into sections or bundled together. Their ears were concave holes in the sides of their heads.

Kaiden looked at the alien in front of him again, its hand still raised. He raised his own hand slowly, hoping he understood the situation and that the alien wasn't flipping him off in some sort of cultural gesture and he'd unwittingly returned the favor.

If that was the case and the alien suddenly got bent out of shape, he might have to punch an alien in its stupid facemask.

"Hey, man." The alien greeted him in a low, mechanical voice. Kaiden saw a light blink on its mask on as it spoke.

"Howdy," Kaiden replied as he put his hand down, the alien following suit. "You got a translator in that bear-trap?"

"I do. It is an EI with a translator function, although it does not register what 'howdy' means."

"It's a way people say hello where I'm from," Kaiden replied.

"I see. Interesting. The man who gave me this device said it was loaded with all words and languages of importance and intelligence on Earth. He said if I should hear a word that the translator does not know, talking to that person would be a waste of time."

Kaiden's eyes narrowed. "Do you happen to know where that guy was from?"

"California. That's what the doctorate on his wall said."

"That's about right," Kaiden muttered. "My name is Kaiden Jericho. Can you tell me yours or is that some sort of sacred thing over yonder?"

"What is a 'yonder?'"

"Goddammit, you got a name?" Kaiden huffed.

"I do, although I have been told that I should tell others my name is Geno."

"Doesn't sound too exotic. Why were you told that?"

"My species' language is not truly compatible with most phonetic languages. A proper translation of my name, though it is quite short, would be the equivalent of 244 letters in English."

Kaiden's head tilted to the side. "Sweet and salty messiah, how do you speak naturally?"

"It's somewhat equivalent to your sonar, using sounds of various pitches, tones, and length. It's almost inaudible to normal human ears, but I have been told it is quite pleasant when listened to through audio equipment."

Kaiden stared at the alien for a moment, trying to come to grips with what he had said. "Really, now?"

"Yes, some of my people have actually made recordings and sold them through the internet. Amusing to me, considering it is mostly gibberish. One of the more popular tracks is about how humans enjoy eating fruit cups while sitting on Martian rocks."

Kaiden chuckled. "Was that creative choice or some weird stereotype?"

"It is a battle song, I believe."

"You guys have peculiar insults."

"Does it help to know that the man had the rocks in his rectum?"

Kaiden scratched his head and chuckled. "Closer, yeah."

A voice interrupted their conversation. The proctor bellowed, "Everybody, get in single file and prepare to board. Human initiates to Carrier Five, and Tsuna to

Carrier Six." The group formed a line to the doors of the buses. The proctor had a tablet and began asking for identification before each one boarded.

"I believe you humans go through different processing than we do, but I hope to see you again," Geno said quickly.

"Hope so too, man. Gotta say, it was a pretty cool experience to meet my first alien," Kaiden replied with a smirk.

"You seem to have taken to it quickly, which is a welcome change. I shall have to learn more stupid words from you." With that, he departed, leaving Kaiden to ponder whether he actually knew what he was saying.

He walked over to his designated carrier and showed the proctor his ID. "Kaiden Jericho."

"I see, got a recommendation less than twenty-four hours ago from former commander Sasha, no less. Must have been an impressive display. Sasha isn't exactly the hand-out type."

"He said you guys could use some fighters. I can do *that*."

"Good to know." The proctor punched something into his pad. "It'll probably give you a lot of profession options, and you'll be out of your contract in no time."

"Do what now?" Kaiden asked, taken aback. He didn't remember signing anything. Had the whiskey hit him hard at some point? Had he made deals he didn't mean and done things he probably enjoyed but would regret and cause him to wake up in cold sweats? Was yesterday Thursday? Shit!

"I don't remember signing a contract. All I got was this." Kaiden showed the proctor his EI box.

"When a Nexus EI is transferred to you, you agree to at least come to the school and go through processing. Don't worry, the real deal will be explained to you by a guidance counselor. After that, you will have a physical and EI integration," the man explained as he closed his tablet and pointed to his right. "Go onto the carrier and choose an open seat."

Kaiden huffed as he put the box away and got onto the bus. He chose a seat near the back and surveyed the carrier, a double-decker with room for at least forty on the bottom half. While he waited, he saw about fifty humans gather in his group during boarding call and probably the same number of aliens. If this was everyone, there were around three hundred people going in. There were probably some people who had gotten in early or driven themselves, so he guessed the final count would be around five hundred.

He looked out the window to see a sign that read Welcome to Bellingham. The city sprawled over the hillside reminded him of Fresno, a modest city at one point that had become a metropolis as time and fortunes moved forward. He leaned back and tried to drift off for a bit, pondering what the Academy would look like, what it would *be* like, and what this contract they wanted to sucker him into contained.

Should he have tried to do more research in the hours before he got there so he wouldn't be so much in the dark?

Perhaps, but then again, he always had liked working with the unknown.

CHAPTER THREE

Good God, this place—this *island*—was huge. The carrier made its final pass around the mountain, and Kaiden was slack-jawed.

It was a literal island. Man-made obviously, but it was a massive circular structure in Bellingham Bay. The Academy was almost its own small city.

Around the island were a couple dozen smaller buildings. They all had a streamlined, militaristic design accented with modern flourishes or eccentric accompaniment. Silver, black, white, and blue were the main colors, but what appeared to be several dormitories had different color schemes.

Kaiden guessed those were the buildings where the students stayed. Accommodations would be designated by the distinct colors on their jackets, whatever those entailed. He pondered whether he and the others who didn't have those special rings also had their own dorm, or if they would all simply huddle together in a kennel.

His gaze finally settled on the central structure which he assumed was the main building and titular Nexus Academy. A central monolith rose proudly at the front of the building, reaching into the sky and towering over the buildings around it. The cylindrical structure bore the same triangular crest engraved on his EI case.

The rest of the building fanned out behind the monolith. It had the appearance of an opera hall—a large half-dome with various long wings jutting out from the back and sides. Ornate glass and mirrored surfaces circled the top like a reflective halo or crown above the pearl-white building, which was accented with blue and silver patterns.

Kaiden had to admit he rather liked the look of it.

He checked his fingers for stains or sticky substances. If some uppity professor saw him accidentally smudge the tiniest amount of wallpaper, his ass was likely grass, no questions asked.

They finally descended the mountain and drove onto the long bridge that led to the entrance. It was roughly two miles from the land to the gates, and as they drove up, Kaiden could almost feel the grandeur that the designers had no doubt had in mind when they built this Goliath. He also figured a two-mile-plus-long bridge deterred fence-jumpers.

He looked down to see if he could get a view of the water but was just barely able to see it from the edge of the window. He figured they had to be at least thirty feet in the air.

The carrier pulled up behind the others and the caravan bisected into two rows of three, then the driver placed his palm onto a scanner on the dashboard and punched something into a tablet.

The other passengers began chatting excitedly, and he heard a girl ask a proctor if they would see the whole thing or if only a portion of it would be open.

It was a little difficult to ignore the peculiar phrasing of the question when he didn't know what "it" was, but as he tried to get a better view of the walls surrounding the entrance to the island, he saw the faintest shimmer. As he watched, fascinated, the water of the bay splashed against something.

That was enough for him to realize that there was some sort of shield in place. It must have taken some intricate and immaculate work to design it, since most fields produced at least some sort of haze or fractal impression once you got close enough.

White blocks formed from the water and sky melded together and met to reveal a giant dome that covered the entire island.

Kaiden straightened in his seat as he studied the barrier. Tech that focused on defense wasn't a particular area of interest—not, at least, until he needed a way to breach it. But even with his casual knowledge, he could understand the power something like this had. If you dropped a nuclear bomb on the island while this thing was active, it was probably the city on the outskirts that had to worry. He doubted anyone beneath it would feel a thing. Maybe a slight shaking that interrupted their nap, while those on the outside would either be roasted alive or have to contend with the various effects and complications of mutation. He was pretty sure the only other place in the world that had something like this was the World Alliance headquarters.

The carrier once again began to move, driving through a small opening that had been formed for them. He noticed that the entrance had no physical barrier, but he didn't wonder why all that much, given the protective dome.

He noticed that his carrier pulled away from the others, and the one carrying the Tsuna stayed behind them. He'd no sooner begun to wonder where they were headed than the proctor who had taken his info before he boarded walked down the aisle and addressed the initiates.

"We are about to arrive at the resources office. Get used to the layout and services there, since I'm sure most of you will visit a lot," he suggested, taking out his tablet. "For your sakes, I hope you do."

"Nice forbidding delivery," Kaiden muttered, earning a chuckle from the guy behind him.

"You have each been assigned a guidance counselor who will explain the practices of the Academy and the expectations you will be held to. They will offer you one last chance to back out when all matters have been explained." He continued as the carrier began to slow, "However, in my opinion, if you have any remaining qualms at this point in time, you shouldn't waste their time or yours. Simply thank the counselor for the opportunity and leave."

"Don't you think you could have told us this before we boarded?" Kaiden asked aloud, causing the others to nod or giggle.

"We've found that most of you punks like to talk that good shit right up to this point. As it turns out, the moment it gets real is when we activate the dome. We've had a few people realize they left their spine at the house after that," the proctor retorted, and Kaiden shrugged his understanding.

"On that note, let me say that the lot of you are special, at least to me," he added. "I've been assigned to looking after the so-called special cases for a decade, and all of you got here by trial or circumstance. Perhaps you were able to make it through the wildcard competitions, or maybe you had that special something that caught one of our professors' eyes. Either way, there is a difference between you and our ranked students."

The bus had now come to a full stop, and the proctor tapped on his tablet and nodded to the driver, who opened the doors behind him. "The others who got here through schooling, connections, or other traditional channels have wanted this all their lives, or maybe their parents did. All of you, I'm guessing, either didn't have the means, didn't have a plan, and maybe didn't even have a clue."

Got me there. Kaiden acknowledged another truth, though it didn't bother him too much.

"But you had an opportunity, and you at least had the smarts to seize it. What you do now is in your hands. If you ever have a moment of weakness or doubt, just remember the courage, willpower, or tenacity that brought you here in the first place, and you might find yourself with a leg up that others don't have."

As he finished, the others on the bus began nodding and smiling in agreement. The proctor nodded in response and looked down at his tablet. "When I call your name, come to the front of the bus. I will give you the name of your counselor and send you off to them."

He began calling names alphabetically. Kaiden looked out the window on the other side of the bus. The building that awaited them was three stories tall, charcoal-colored with silver trim. He made a mental note to see if he could find a map of the campus or at least a pamphlet of the resources building. One thing he could apply from his previous life was that resources were always a good thing, no matter what their form, but guns, food, and warm bodies were preferred.

"Kaiden Jericho," the proctor announced. He stood and straightened his jacket. It was time to see where all this would lead.

Kaiden examined the tiny plaques on each door, looking for his designated counselor.

"I. Asimov…no. D. Webber…uh-uh. C. Lupus…that's unfortunate. Ah." He stopped in front of a door that read 'M. Vodello' and knocked on the door.

"Come in." a wistful feminine voice called. The door slid into the wall, and Kaiden saw a surprisingly large room with plants near the window and hanging from the ceiling. He took a seat on a red leather chair in front of the counselor's desk.

She had tanned skin and long brown hair and wore a red suit with a light-green shirt underneath. After a minute or so, she finished typing something into her computer and then looked up and smiled at him. "Welcome. I'm Mya, and you must be Kaiden Jericho, correct?"

"Ah no, completely different guy," Kaiden joked, trying to ease himself into the formal setting.

"Well then..." Her eyes flicked to him and away, a small smirk playing on her face. "I can deal with that. Chou?" Kaiden saw a small magenta orb appear from a circular device on the desk, a holographic preset of a pro-level EI.

"Yes, madam?" the orb asked in a comically cliché French accent, glowing slightly with each word.

"It appears that we have a troublemaker. Please be rid of him." She waved a hand negligently toward Kaiden, her words not varying from a delighted tone despite the intended threat.

"Understood, madam," the sphere acknowledged and disappeared back into the device. Kaiden then heard a mechanical whir and click, and he looked up to see a double-barreled turret descend from a hidden spot on the ceiling. Uncomfortable flashbacks of the Dead-Eye with the cracked EI rushed through his head.

"Sweet and salty Christ, lady! Yeah, yeah, I'm Kaiden. Turn it off!" Kaiden said in a sudden panic. He had a cold realization that he had no weapon on him. He'd really trusted these suits way too much. If Jake were there, he would smack the back of his neck hard enough to make a crater.

She pointed to her eyes, which glimmered with the identifiable signs of operator contacts. "Just my fun way of greeting. I actually have your file and picture up in my optics."

"The gun is still pointing at me," Kaiden grumbled, and

tried swaying to the left so that the turret would be directed at them both.

"Chou, deactivate defenses and bring up Nexus initiate presentation," Mya requested.

"At once, madam," the artificial French voice stated. Kaiden noticed a magenta-colored light on the turret deactivate as the gun slid back into its hiding spot, allowing Kaiden to breathe easier and check to see if he felt any wetness on his lower half.

The circular device lit up again, this time with a holographic display of his personal info—or at least what official info the government had that the techies back in the gang hadn't tampered with. Alongside it were a number of screens the counselor flipped through.

"So, Mr. Jericho, how long were you in a gang?" she asked nonchalantly.

"Huh, never. Why ya sayin' that?" he asked, trying to play dumb.

"Honesty is one of the best traits a breathing person can have," she mused, pointing to the spot the turret had dropped from.

Dammit, this was a sting, wasn't it? Kaiden's breath hitched, and he cracked his knuckles beneath his crossed arms. He had to give them points. It was quite elaborate— the old promise of going to a prestigious academy, only to be bullet-riddled by a bubbly woman and her vaguely pink blob buddy.

"Yeah, I was in a gang back in Texas. Didn't do anything too bad, though," Kaiden lied. It was the default option in this case—reveal the small pile of bones in your closet and hope to God they didn't check the suspicious hole in the basement.

"Well, good. That probably means you can actually handle yourself when you get started," she said sweetly.

That was not the reaction he was used to. He should have liked the oddly positive spin, but he somehow felt closer to death.

"You're okay with that? Does the Academy know?" he asked.

"Of course. Your forgery was admirable. Or perhaps it was someone in your group's handiwork? But if we fell for something as simple as that it wouldn't make a very good impression, would it?" she stated, seemingly more to remind herself than convince him.

"I guess, but you're all right with it? I wouldn't think a place like this would be thrilled to have a felon in its midst." Kaiden leaned back into his chair, scanning between the open doorway and the turret's hiding hole.

"If that was the case, I wouldn't be employed here," she replied.

"Wait, what did you do?" he asked.

"I was a part of the hacker collective, 9 Circulos. We broke into the servers of a weapons manufacturing company. Karna Munitions. The others were eventually caught, but I got the opportunity to train here." She eased back in her seat, her eyes looking to the side as she seemed to wander into her memories. "They were trying to steal some files or get a delivery manifest or something, but I only wanted blueprints that I could blow-up into posters. Since I was the one who devised the scheme and got the rest in, I was offered a spot here as an SC like you."

"Huh, well, you just found your way onto my decent person list," Kaiden said with a grin.

"Glad to put you at ease, but I brought it up to tell you that upon acceptance, your criminal file will officially be wiped clear." She smiled, her hands now folded in her lap.

"Just like that? No other strings?" Kaiden asked, bewildered. She looked away and rolled her thumbs, and his mood soured. *Of course, here comes the fine print.*

"Professor Sasha called me and gave a little info about how you got his recommendation. It seems that you are not familiar with how one gets into the Academy." She flicked through a few screens before landing on the one she wanted and enlarged it.

"I was told at the station that there's some sort of contract?" Kaiden asked as he looked at the display, which showed several files to choose from.

"Indeed. Every initiate, regardless of how they got here, is contracted to the Academy. It is through that contract that the initiate is allowed access to the Academy and all its classes and technology, along with room, board, and utilities. The student does not pay for these during their training. After graduation, this contract is transferred to a corporation or business that needs the skills and abilities of the graduate for all their accumulated incidentals, plus a fee. The graduate then works for that company until their debt is paid. It helps us continue our research and development and have positive cash flow at the same time."

"Wait…" Kaiden shook his head, thinking back to the first part of her explanation. "So I'll be trained here at this so-called prestigious academy just to become a slave at the end of it all? What good is that?" He fumed. This sounded like a pyramid scheme where he *knowingly* agreed to be the sucker.

"Of course not. A slave would not have an option," she answered with a wink. "Furthermore, the value of the contract is dependent on the student: what they require during their years of training, and their set-up fee. What you do while training—the skills you accumulate, the drive you show, and your standing rank at the end of your studies—will provide a long list of options and many potential employers who would pay handsomely for you. Then, depending on how you negotiate with your employer about salary and how much you owe, you could pay off your debt quite quickly. Some have managed it in as little as a year."

Kaiden leaned forward and tapped his fingers on the desk. "How much would I have to pay?"

"Well, since this includes all fees accrued throughout your potential three years here, plus set-up items—like an integration unit for your EI—over and above the physical training, I would guess a ballpark figure of around five million credits," Mya summarized calmly.

Kaiden could feel a sharp sting in his left arm. He wondered if the gun had been turned back on and had shot clean through him. Distracted now, he took a deep breath and checked his arm and chest. His quick examination showed no discernible holes, but his asshole tightened.

"Doesn't…seem…too…bad," he replied. He tried to sound confident, but his voice had become ragged, and his teeth wouldn't unclench.

"I should inform you that approximately one million of that is the slate-wiping add-on," she teased, giving him what looked like a warm smile but which came across as mockery.

She seriously needs to work on her friendly demeanor.

"Nice…nice to know that even a place like this is willing to take bribes," Kaiden quipped, trying to get his breathing back to normal.

"We prefer to think of it as a cleaning fee," Mya explained, now leaning back into her chair and tapping her thumbs to a cheery rhythm Kaiden struggled to focus on at that moment.

He was conflicted. On the one hand, holy *hell*, that was a lot of credits. He had saved around two hundred and fifty thousand during his time with the Dead-Eyes. Jake always let him skim a bit more than most after a job, but this was ridiculous. He already had skills, and he already had other jobs lined up if Julio could get him those gigs he spoke of. Why did he need this?

You ain't gonna get shit that way. Those words rang in his mind. He remembered being in a small room, his guns on the table next to a medical bag. Jake was patching him up, wrapping his wounds tighter than necessary.

"You ain't keepin' up with your training, you barely think about what your next move is, and I swear to God, you're the sole reason we're constantly low on meds.

He remembered giving a smartass retort, causing Jake to press down on a wound on his knee. He tried to pay him back by headbutting him, but Jake grabbed him mid-lunge and then looked him straight in the eye. *Look, Kai, you're a talented little bastard. That's why I take you along for the fights and the gigs, but you can't keep thinking you can half-ass these things. You keep this up, and one day you're gonna meet someone who actually gave a damn and worked their ass off, and you're gonna realize all you could have been just before he kills your lights. Never settle.*

Mya's voice pulled him out of his daze. "You can think on it more if you wish, but I have other things I need to discuss with you, so I'm going to—"

"Nah, sign me up," Kaiden announced. He affected nonchalance, leaning back and clasping his hands together.

"Well, I admire your sudden confidence, but perhaps I should finish—"

"Do whatever, but I got this." He smiled as he looked at the contract displayed on the holo. "If this place can make me better, then I'll do it and pay off that shitty fee in a blink. But I should probably give you a fair warning."

"About what?" Mya inquired.

"That if this place isn't up to snuff, I'm gonna get my fee back in blood," he replied with a smirk.

He expected a shocked look, even a frown. Maybe he'd messed up and would have to out-run security.

Instead, he heard, "You weren't even prepared for the ceiling turret." She reinforced the truth with a quizzical look and a finger pointing up.

"Just finish the damn presentation and give me a pen." He huffed as his head rolled back. Couldn't he have at least started his tenure on a more *badass* note?

CHAPTER FOUR

Kaiden held the cotton swab against his arm. He could feel the blood beneath it, eager to spill. Gritting his teeth, he looked at the half-dozen vials of blood they'd already drawn and could feel the anemia swell within. The doctor was giving instruction to a nurse as a medical aide picked up the tray holding the vials of blood and other bodily fluids and took it out of the room.

He lay back on the cot as he scanned the medical bay. Six other initiates were in there with him, and he had seen a few others leave while he finished his exam.

It was certainly fewer than those who had arrived with him, so he figured that some must still be in their meetings or had decided to bid the Academy a hasty farewell. He didn't blame them, but he certainly felt a warm satisfaction that he had been able to take on the challenge when others slunk away.

Pity he couldn't get a chart showing the healthiness of his ego, because *there* he would break records.

He reached carefully for his EI box and popped it open. Along with the EI, there was now a smaller translucent chip that held all his academy info.

Mya had gone over the essentials toward the end of their meeting, but he'd been in something of a haze at the time. His bravado mixed with the swirl of new information and possibilities for the future had put him in a near mental-overload, something the counselor had evidently noticed.

Before she'd sent him to the medical department, she'd given him the clear gadget and told him it had all his basic info, and that he should, A) not lose it and B) load it into his EI device once he had received it and had it calibrated after his physical.

He looked up as the lady doctor who took his blood came back over, bandaged the injection site, and helped him stand.

"That should do it. We have your medical history up to this point. You are green for EI processing, and if anything develops from today's physical, we will alert you," she stated, her tone clipped and professional.

"Probably should have gotten a little liver check-up while I was here. It's one of the harder working organs in my body," Kaiden replied as he rolled his shoulders and stretched his arms.

"Well, that merely means your brain may not be up to normal standards, but you are in good company among the SCs," the doctor retorted.

Kaiden grimaced. Was everyone in this place a smartass?

She patted him on the shoulder. "Farewell, Initiate Jericho. Hopefully, you won't need my services too much while you are here, but if you would like, you can request Dr. Saluja if you found my work to your satisfaction."

"I'll be sure to bring a tip next time," Kaiden quipped as he started toward the exit. He flung a hand up over his shoulder. "Nice meeting ya, Doc."

"It was a pleasure, and if I may give you some parting advice," she began, and he paused to turn back toward her. "EI processing is that way," she finished with a smirk as she jerked a thumb to the exit behind her across the room.

"Uh…gotcha. I'm a bit woozy," Kaiden mumbled in a half-hearted cover-up as he doubled back and walked past the doctor. She nodded and shook her head as she went to attend to another patient.

He walked past the enclosed cubicles he had seen some of the Tsuna walk into.

Kaiden couldn't hear any talking, but there were some odd noises that signified medical instruments and machines he hadn't had to deal with during his exam. He felt an ambivalent sense of curiosity and fear as he pondered what the aliens looked like under their body-coverings and what they went through in their physicals.

He wondered if they were treated by human physicians or other aliens.

Another alien had been at the reception when he entered, though this one was unlike those he'd met at the hyperloop station. It had an egg-shaped head with round black eyes like the Tsuna, but a lanky charcoal-colored body with three digits on the ends of its long arms.

It reminded him of how aliens supposedly had looked according to history documentaries detailing popular culture during the middle and second half of the twentieth century. He recalled that people had claimed to see UFOs dart through the sky and abduct people and do…things he preferred not to think about.

They were called the Mirus, though most people called them grays or probes due to their similarity to those old descriptions. Not the nicest of nicknames, but he had never seen one bothered by it. Then again, he had never actually seen one until now.

In fact, along with never seeing one, he had never heard one speak, probably because they didn't have mouths. Supposedly, they created some sort of frequency or energy or something that could be directly translated by the mind of the listener. Most called this telepathy, although that wasn't exactly right. To be honest, he was more curious whether they could do this right away with a new race or if there had been some unfortunate and messy initial trials.

Kind of hard to convince someone you came in peace when you exploded their head saying hello.

Kaiden left the medical bay and saw an interactive map. He pressed a label for "EI Center" and saw a blue light illuminate above him. It was a glow strip that followed the walls and turned the corner about twenty-five feet away. He looked back at the map and read, Please follow the blue path, Initiate Jericho.

Convenient, sure, but he still hadn't fully adjusted to the fact that everything down to the glorified help desk knew him.

Kaiden followed the illumination until he reached a long hallway with arched doors. The light from the glow strip seemed to flow into the door, and a message appeared in the blue light.

Please place the front of your EI case on the scanner to the right of the doors.

He looked over to see a rectangular panel that lit up, took his EI case, and pressed it against it. A line of green light moved across the screen, then the entire rectangle went green and the doors slid open.

The room was a huge cubicle separated into three floors, and it had dark carpet and walls. As he walked in, he was approached by a man whose pin read, Tech. J. Arvin.

"Initiate Kaiden," he greeted him as he scanned information on a tablet. "Welcome. I will be your technician for EI integration and processing. It would appear that you have not had much experience with EI, is that correct?" He looked up for Kaiden's answer.

He shrugged. "I've used a commercial model a couple of times, but nothing professional or higher," he explained as he continued to look around the busy offices. Plenty of humans and a handful of aliens scurried around. He could make some initiates out among the masses, either talking with other technicians or led to other rooms, holding cases in their arms.

"I promise, it is no big deal...well, maybe a little at first, but with our guidance and a little time, you will see the boons our Nexus EIs can grant you. It is a fundamental part of your training, after all," he said, a cheerful chirp in his tone. "Now then, do you have a preferred— Hold on a moment, something came in from medical."

Already? Damn, had he picked up some sort of supervirus he was unaware of in the last few hours? *What did happen after those drinks yesterday?*

Technician Arvin looked over his notes, his brow furrowed, and his green eyes began to squint. Then, he went wide-eyed and looked up at him, back down at his notes, and back at Kaiden, staring at him like he had sent him some sort of prank mail.

"Initiate, would you please follow me?" he asked, though it seemed more of a command than a request as he turned abruptly and hurried away. Not wanting to be left alone in frenzied speculation, Kaiden followed briskly, wondering what Tech Arvin had received to suddenly quench his happier temperament.

"What they tell ya? Am I dying? Growing a new arm?" he asked.

The technician typed something without answering, and Kaiden could see the images signifying a note being sent on the tablet screen. "Hmm? Oh, no, no, you're fine—at least unless something else is found." He added the last statement hastily as if the mysterious something required qualification.

That's comforting.

They approached an elevator. He swiped a card across the pad on the wall next to it, and the doors opened. "It would appear that… Well, I'll let Professor Laurie tell you once we get there. Step into the elevator, please." He placed his hand on Kaiden's back and began pushing him gently.

Kaiden shook him off. "I can walk, it's cool. I just wanna know what's going on." He grunted in displeasure as he stepped into the box and leaned back against the railing as the technician followed. The elevator doors closed without him pressing a floor.

"We are going to see Professor Laurie. He has his own office above these offices, and he'll explain everything," he told him in a flurry, his fingers again tapping on his tablet.

"Well, you seem excited. Did I win a prize?" Kaiden asked as he observed the tech. It looked like he was bobbing in place.

"More like *we* did, potentially," Arvin answered unhelpfully.

Before Kaiden could ask him to clarify, the elevator stopped and the doors opened.

The room was surprisingly stark for what Kaiden had assumed was a guy with high rank. White walls and a matching carpet gave it a cold look. A few decorative holopictures, painted artifacts, and a pristine white desk with a couple of chairs in front did little to soften the overall impression.

When they approached the desk, Kaiden observed a large pearl-colored chair with a curved back facing away from them.

"Professor, I'm sorry to come in on such short notice, but—"

"I got your message. My thanks for your professionalism, dear Arvin," a man replied in what seemed like a smooth, posh accent from beyond the chair back. "Does our friend know?"

"I don't think so. He doesn't seem to, at least. It wasn't in his records, and medical just found it in preliminaries," Arvin said as he placed his tablet on the desk. "I'm sure they would have sent the information to you beforehand, otherwise."

"See here, I'm excited that y'all are excited, but could you please tell me what is going on?" Kaiden asked as he pushed one of the chairs out with his boot and sprawled on the seat.

"Why, certainly, my new friend." The man turned his chair to face him. His hair seemed artfully messy, more feathered than ruffled. Its color matched his sharp silver eyes in an odd way that defied description. His face, narrow with a cutting jaw, curled into an amused smile. He wore a lavender two-piece suit with a white shirt beneath, accented with a silver tie that bore the Nexus Academy crest on the knot.

"My name is Alexander Laurie, former head of Anima Technologies and now lead developer of EI technologies here at Nexus," he announced with a flourish of his hand. Kaiden noted frills edging his cuffs and suppressed a grin.

His eyes narrowed. "Wait, I know you! Aren't you dead or a hermit or something?" he asked.

Kaiden recalled stories in the news about Laurie leaving his position at Anima—one of the first corporations to develop EI technology around the beginning of the century—about ten years before and then disappearing off the face of the earth.

"I gotta admit, if you *are* dead, you look pretty damn good."

"I look damn good regardless," Laurie quipped as he took Arvin's tablet and looked it over. "However, dead isn't my particular style. Developing the technologies and advances of the future is. I was offered the position here and accepted, given that I was granted access to work on projects that would have been...a bit more difficult in a commercial field."

"You left one of the biggest corporations to work at a school?" Kaiden asked incredulously, trying to add mocking disbelief to his tone.

"*Au contraire*, my friend. Nexus is more than a school, though it is the best, I must say, in that field and others." Laurie gave Arvin a nod and returned the tablet. The tech nodded and turned to leave.

"Hey, tech, what about my EI stuff?" Kaiden asked.

"Why, dear initiate, would you bother with a seed when you have a blooming flower?" Laurie asked as he leaned forward in his chair. "It would appear you have something quite special within you, and I can offer something that *may* just interest you."

Kaiden raised an eyebrow, turning from Arvin to Laurie. "What's so special about me?"

Laurie's smile widened. "You see, one of the technologies we have here that grants our students such advanced skills at such a quick pace is our special EIs." He pressed on a switch on his desk, and a silver bottle with a logo of what appeared to be two faces with different features morphing into one appeared. He took out a glass and offered it to Kaiden.

He should probably have been a little more suspicious, but he was thirsty and that stuff looked fancy. He nodded, and Laurie filled a glass and handed it to him.

"Using a combination of what we call hybrid EIs and devices that offer more power and capability than the typical EI gear, the EIs can actually integrate with the user themselves to a small degree."

Kaiden sat back and drank in this information—along with the actual drink, which was as crisp as spring water. It was a bit fruity for his taste, but damn if he wasn't feeling it.

"And this does what, exactly? Pro-EIs give people access to multiple devices and functions, so what makes this so knee-slappin' good?"

Laurie's eyes narrowed a moment before he grasped the nature of his question. "You misunderstand. It doesn't integrate the user with technologies you can use. The EI *itself* integrates with the user. They *become* the technology," Laurie explained, tapping thoughtfully on his chin. "So to speak, anyway."

This caught Kaiden's attention. "Wait, what? We become cyborgs or—" Kaiden couldn't come up with a second option.

"Oh, don't be so silly. You're making something grand and intricate sound not only wrong but *banal*." Laurie huffed, clearly indignant. "Throughout the virtual reality lessons you will undertake, the gear will leave imprints on the brain that the EI helps the user integrate within their natural memories. We call this synapse-connection, or simply, synapse."

Kaiden nodded. It began to dawn on him how and why this place was so sought after and why those who graduated were so advanced among their peers.

It also dawned on him that whatever he was drinking was good as hell. He needed to figure out what it was when this was over.

"Typically, the human mind can only take in so much of this new information at a time, which is why the lessons are gradual. The user builds up resilience to this, and eventually can learn faster as time goes on and improve their skills considerably—assuming they apply themselves correctly and practice regularly," Laurie explained.

Kaiden nodded and placed his empty glass on the table, pointing to the bottle. Laurie chuckled and poured him another glass. Pity he didn't seem to be having any himself. This stuff was great.

"I think I get it, but why am I here, then? Weren't the others getting their set-up downstairs?" he asked.

"Normally, yes. The gear we use is a simple set-up, devices that not only activate the EI but transmit neural waves through the skin in fragments as a user learns. However, a couple of years ago we—or, I should say, *I*—discovered something interesting." He sighed as he continued to tap his chin. "The one downside of coming to create at this institution is that no one bathes in my greatness as regularly as they should. It's a damned shame."

"What was it you discovered?" Kaiden queried as he took small sips from his glass.

"There were people with a certain genetic trait—we call it the Gemini factor—who can gain enhanced compatibility with these waves. Through it, they and their EI can actually be on a similar plane or wavelength with one another. Through this, they gain knowledge much quicker and can use it practically at a much faster rate than we normally see."

Kaiden started to fit the pieces together. "So I'm here because—"

"From what we have discovered, you *have* this trait," Laurie finished with a smile. "We don't get many of you here. Most are discovered early and taken in by other science divisions or programs. I've only had the opportunity to work with a few, and what I've seen them do is extraordinary... Well, more so than the already incredible highs I'm accustomed too."

"So, do I get special treatment or something?" he asked. "If it means more of this liquor, I promise I won't complain."

"Well, that depends on you," Laurie said. "Personally, I would have already had you in the operating theater, but the board tends to frown when those kinds of things are forced, and many look dreadful without the frown as it is." He swiped on the surface of his table, and a holographic projection of a device floated above.

Kaiden looked it over. It was a ring with four long protrusions behind and one in the center that looked like an antenna. "That looks like a torture device."

"Not the most aesthetically pleasing design, I concur." Laurie frowned. "However, that is the implant device that was created for those who had this trait. It took a few trials to craft. The circular design works as the base and assists in powering the device, and the energy is perpetual. The prongs are designed to reach the appropriate parts of the brain and the—"

"You want to put that in my head?" Kaiden shouted in shock. Good God, how many people there were gonna toss these horrific things at him like they were normal requests?

He felt a chill as he reached the conclusion that they

might *be* normal requests to those people. Then he realized that if he didn't have this special factor, he would be downstairs with the others getting the normal gear and probably on his way by now.

Being special was starting to sound like it fuckin' *bit*.

"Well, yes, but as I said, it is up to you," Laurie admitted. Kaiden picked up a downtrodden tone in the last few words. "You can use the normal gear as all the other initiates. It is what we are known for and what all your peers will use, after all."

Laurie then reached across the table and clasped Kaiden's drinking hand. The half-empty glass shook with the sudden pressure. He looked into the former gang member's eyes, almost pleading, his composed swagger falling away slightly.

"You must understand, Kaiden. You could be the future of this technology, and of this academy," he declared. "It is through the information we gain from using theories and devices like these that we advance our potential, and you could give up a chance to reach heights you probably can't even comprehend until they become commonplace for you."

Kaiden looked casually at the pleading genius. He leaned forward and tilted their clasped hands to finish his drink. He recalled the memory from his meeting with Mya.

Jake's demand to never settle.

He laughed. Of all the things Jake had beaten into him, it was probably this mantra that would eventually get him killed.

"I don't gotta pay anything extra, right? I'm already looking at around five million credits here."

"Oh no, I'll take on any excess fees. I'll do the procedure myself, in fact," Laurie proclaimed, his good mood returning. "Or, rather, the robots I created and programmed will."

"Well, I can always use a leg-up. I'll…dammit…alright. I'll do this. Just don't leave any scarring or I swear I'm goin—"

"Of course not. It is a simple and painless procedure. You won't feel a thing, and you will begin integration as soon as you wake-up," Laurie insisted. He had fully recovered his previous aplomb.

He retrieved a tablet from his desk drawer and handed it to Kaiden, who put his glass down and took it. A form of some kind displayed on the screen.

"It just states that you understand what the procedure is and give your consent," Laurie explained.

Kaiden nodded and scrolled down. It was pretty basic, but he supposed it wasn't used often enough to warrant some sort of massive contract. He added his signature and placed his thumb against a scanner on the screen. It beeped in confirmation, and Laurie retrieved it and placed it on a stand.

"This is fantastic. I promise you, this is where your true ascent begins, Initiate Jericho," the genius exclaimed, filling another glass halfway and handing it to Kaiden.

He raised it in salute and downed it. "Lookin' forward to it. Do we schedule a date or something? The semester starts pretty soon, right. Gotta be ready beforehand."

"Oh, we start immediately. Just as soon as the medication takes effect."

Kaiden nodded. "All right, sooner the better. Give it here."

"You've been drinking it," Laurie admitted, pointing to the glass in Kaiden's hand.

He looked at the man and then at his empty glass, "Oh... Well then." He realized that the calm sensation he had previously felt had gradually increased. It washed over him now, suddenly irresistible as the professor became blurry. "That's... That's kinda fucked up, Prof..."

"Wasting time is a sin. Besides, you *did* say yes."

He placed his finger on a panel on the desk. Kaiden could vaguely hear Laurie shouting, "Prepare the theater." It seemed to issue from a long tunnel rather than from the man across the desk.

As the final lights of consciousness faded, Kaiden slumped into the chair, and a thought came to him.

Semantics are a bitch.

CHAPTER FIVE

Kaiden woke in a darkened room. He looked around for the professor but saw no one. In fact, he realized with a vague feeling of alarm, he saw nothing at all. He sat up and peered into the darkness across the room. What little light there was only shone a few feet in front of him.

"Hey, Professor, where ya hidin'?" he called. Then he heard a shrill buzz that doubled him over with an accompanying white-hot shard of pain. He clasped his hands over his ears to try to muffle the sound, but he could still hear it clearly.

"What in the hell is going on?" He gasped, and the sound stopped abruptly. Slowly, he stood and looked around. No one and nothing occupied the dark space.

He was now growing concerned.

"Kaaai-den." He heard a new sound, raspy and muffled, like talking to someone over a bad connection. His head pivoted left, then right, looking for speakers, but he found nothing. Then, as he looked up, he realized he couldn't even see a light illuminating him from overhead.

Now *this* was getting *bizarre*.

"Kaiden? Initiate Jericho, can you hear me?" It was Laurie's voice, coming from everywhere all at once.

"Yeah…yeah, I hear you. Where the hell are you and where the hell am I? Answer the last question first. Am I in hell?"

A shimmering figure appeared beside him. He jumped back and raised his fists into a boxing position. The thing was composed of numerous tiny lights that began to swirl in place. Kaiden took two steps back as he watched the lights start to align, taking human shape.

His eyes narrowed. At first, it was nothing more than a solid form, but as he watched, some lights disappeared, and others rearranged, giving the being more detail. Hair, facial structure, and body shape came into view. Kaiden began to recognize the form.

"Wait a moment, trying to sync the connection here," Laurie's voice called. This time, it came from the lights rather than as an echo. Finally, with a vivid flash, the lights formed into a silhouette of Professor Laurie, his body perfectly molded in white light with certain features such as his eyes and mouth formed by the negative space around him.

"Good God, Prof, what's going on with you? You look like something out of an old black-and-white comic," Kaiden asked, bewildered by the surreal apparition before him.

The professor smiled. "A simple avatar I created to interact with the system. I wish I could have crafted something a little more elaborate, but I didn't want to potentially cause any burnout in the systems, not with you inside, anyway."

"The system?" Kaiden inquired. "And burnout? What might burn?" His eyes opened in alarm, his voice shooting up an octave in mounting panic. "Did you *fuck up?*"

"Calm yourself, Initiate. No one likes such a frenzied tone," Laurie's avatar stated with a negligent wave of the hand. "You certainly have no decorum, do you? I recommend a class or ten after this is all done."

"What exactly is being done?" Kaiden didn't give a rat's ass about decorum right then. Without thinking, he lunged to grab the man, but his hands and body passed right through the professor. He stumbled and dropped to the floor, feeling no real impact but landing on his hands and knees.

"I would recommend you grow used to this, dear Kaiden," Laurie admonished, placing a hand on his shoulder.

Kaiden couldn't feel any weight from the gesture, and it didn't really look like it was actually interacting with him—more like a projection hovering just above his body.

"We are currently within the pride and joy of Nexus Academy, The Anima System," Laurie explained, standing at attention with his hands clasped behind him, his eyes roaming around. "This is a simple simulation I loaded to help you get your bearings and make your EI integration easier. The Anima System is an advanced virtual reality technology that the academy uses to train their students, faculty, and the occasional soldier or freelancer who can pay for the services."

Kaiden looked around, struggling to tamp down definite feelings of something that might be hysteria. There still wasn't much to see, but nothing seemed off to him. He had used VR devices before, mostly for gaming or to meet with friends or fellow Dead-Eyes in discrete hangouts that could be blocked off to prying eyes. However, in those instances, the artificiality was obvious. Digitized replicas of himself and others wandered about, or modified skins of pop culture characters or in-game personas.

This, however bizarre, looked real.

"I'll give you a few moments to compose yourself. Also, I'll take your eloquent silence as a compliment to myself," the professor said, his grin widening. "I actually provided the latest upgrade myself, and all subsequent updates were designed by me and a team of top developers, doctors, and technicians."

He whisked himself around, his translucent, digitized white eyes staring into Kaiden's. Without warning, he reached out an arm, and another mass of light formed in his palm. It quickly took shape, molding into a square with a protruding handle. It was a hand-mirror, this one black with a reflective surface. More importantly, it looked real, unlike the professor's current features.

"Take a look. I made sure to replicate everything in the finest detail. It may be a little uncanny at first, but you should grow used to it in no time," he promised, presenting the mirror to Kaiden with a dramatic flourish.

Kaiden took a look at himself and was both impressed and a little shaken. Laurie was right; it did look freakishly uncanny.

His hair was combed and long in its usual pompadour, coal-black with the sides of his head buzzed down to almost nothing. His blue eyes stared back at him in their naturally pointed, piercing way, contrasting with his tanned skin tone. The bridge of his nose even had the slight crook to it from a fight three years ago when it was broken then set improperly.

"Not bad. Must have taken a good while to replicate something as nice as me," Kaiden commented with a smirk. He tried to hand the mirror back to Laurie, but it simply disappeared in a flash of light.

The professor scoffed. "Hardly. My system's scanning abilities can't be compared to any other corporation's or supposed genius designer's. Honestly, I felt some improvements could have been made to some of your…shall we say, less-than-pleasant features while the operation was underway." He ended the statement by tracing the bridge of his own nose.

"Appreciate the thought." Kaiden rolled his eyes to add emphasis to his sarcasm. "How did it go? Did ya get that claw-looking thing in there?"

"My reputation apparently needs some restructuring. You should know better than to insinuate that I could fail at such a task."

"You said you don't get to do this often, so call it giving you a handicap," Kaiden said, folding his arms. "Besides, you could show a little more appreciation. Not everyone would be such a good sport about letting a stranger mess with their brain for shits and giggles."

The professor leaned toward him again. Kaiden could see his desire to retort, but he sighed and nodded. "Fair enough, Initiate. I do confess I may be a little rusty at the moment. The surgery went smoothly, but the setup of the nerve gear device and linking it to the Anima did take me longer than anticipated. I went over my self-allotted time of three hours by eleven minutes, and who knows when I'll get another chance to best myself?" Laurie admitted his shortcomings with a sigh. "Life can be so dull when you have no true competition. You must create your own challenges at times."

Kaiden nodded, keeping his face neutral but unconsciously tapping his fingers on his arm. "So it's in there, and I'm in this Anima System thing. What else we got? 'Cause I'm feeling peckish."

The professor tilted his head. "Well then, how about you introduce yourself to your EI?" he asked.

Laurie stepped back a few paces, motioning Kaiden to do the same.

"Begin EI integration," he declared into the void.

At first, nothing happened. Then a large orb appeared between them, similar to the one he had seen in Mya's office, but this one had no unique color. It emitted the same white light as everything else.

"Initializing, beginning start-up and user integration," a disembodied voice intoned. It was entirely mechanical, similar to the artificial voices Kaiden heard at information kiosks or cheap advert displays.

"Why does it sound so basic?" he asked.

"All EIs are loaded clean. The user chooses their EI's customization settings, like their appearance and personality," the professor explained, walking around the orb.

The EI's light faded in and out, glowing rhythmically as it loaded its initial functions. Then the monotone voice spoke again. *"Initial components loaded, ready to begin integration with Nexus Academy Initiate Kaiden Jericho."*

Kaiden looked toward the glowing balls and saw a smaller, brighter circle that seemed to track him as he shifted in place. He forced himself to stay still, rather uncomfortable with this unexpected development. "Ready whenever you are, uh, chief."

"EI does not recognize chief as a function or executable. Is this a designation?" the voice asked.

"What, like a name? Yeah, sure, go for it." Kaiden shrugged. He'd grown a little impatient and really didn't feel like playing five hundred questions with the device. It was much more interesting to see what the EI was capable of.

"I would be a little more cautious, dear Kaiden." Laurie stressed the word "cautious" as he crossed over to his side. "EI's are a pain to reset in even their commercial forms. I don't think being haphazard with yours is so wise, especially since it will essentially be bonded with you from here on out."

Kaiden had forgotten about that. He supposed it wasn't like he could merely pop open the back of his head and replace the thing. He mulled it over and gave another shrug. "Chief ain't such a bad name. I'll be sure to comb over the rest carefu—"

"EI, designated Chief, shall begin start-up sequence requesting user preferences. Expected time for set-up approximately five to six hours."

He shook his head. "Oh, to hell with that. You got an express install?"

"Express installation is available; this option will load this

unit with all basic Nexus Academy features and necessary programs. The user will then decide on this unit's cosmetic settings and personality profile to finish set-up. Expected time to install ten minutes."

"Kaiden, I really believe that you should take the time to —" Laurie began before Kaiden cut him off.

"No, I'm good, Prof, but it's probably already night time, and I got other tasks I've got to get to before the weekend is over and the Academy starts. I'm okay with not specifying if I want it to have a fuzzy dice accessory and what my preferred coffee temp is, all right?"

The professor still had the you-are-making-a-mistake look in his eyes, but he lifted his hands in faux-surrender and backed away.

"Go ahead," Kaiden instructed the EI.

"Beginning installation, downloading drivers and basic programs..." The EI droned on for a few minutes.

The light went back to flickering in and out as it installed. Finally, Kaiden saw it return to normal. The orb was no longer a simple blob of light but had gained a more intricate design all around, like gas swirling through a clear bubble. Its little eye once again looked at Kaiden. *"Installation complete, basic design loaded as a temporary template. Please designate model, colors, and personal preferences."*

Kaiden looked it over. It actually looked fine as it was. Besides, he wasn't looking to make a mascot. "You look fine, Chief. Maybe do somethin' about the color. It's a little plain, but beyond that, you're good."

"Recommendation, mood coloration palette. This model's primary coloring will change depending on the different situations and feelings of that conversation."

"You have feelings?" Kaiden asked, looking at Laurie, whose smile deepened while his eyes flicked up and down a few times.

"This model's programming is loaded with functions and algorithms that allow for the simulation of displaying human emotions. It is not a chemical construct and therefore cannot feel in that capacity. This was a cosmetic option made available by this model's designer Alexander Laurie."

Kaiden's gaze lowered, and he shook his head. "How is this an advancement, exactly?"

"It's practical. In the heat of battle or during times of stress, a person may not think clearly. The EI monitors their user's blood pressure, heart rate, and other states of excitement or mood and adjusts its algorithm to better comply with its user and offer advice that the user is more likely to understand or require during those situations. The differing colors merely added a touch of flair," the professor explained. "I would actually recommend it. If you're going to leave it with its basic template, you might as well let the poor thing add a touch of color."

"Yeah, sure, go ahead," Kaiden ordered, not bothering to hide his apathy. "What's next?"

"Personality Profile."

"What are the options?"

"There is a list of over one thousand basic personalities installed on this unit. However, it would appear that we have access to the databanks of the academy and can synthesize one using psychological evaluations and descriptions stored within."

"Is that basic?" Kaiden inquired looking to Laurie once again.

Laurie coughed into his hand. "Not entirely. I

performed the operation in my personal theater and therefore set up your access into the Anima through my personal network which has a bit more clearance than most." He began pacing around the EI. "That option is normally used to create EI's to mimic the personalities of persons of interest when the authorities may have a use for it or in the creation of war games to create different scenarios for the students to run, not usually for personal entertainment."

"Well, I don't see a point to it myself. Ain't got anyone in mind," Kaiden said as he tapped his chin thoughtfully. "Can't really say I got a preference, honestly."

"Your lack of imagination is disturbing, Kaiden my boy." Laurie huffed, clasped his hands behind his head, and leaned back. "This EI will be your partner for the rest of your stay here, and on top of that, will be following you into battle. Are there *no* dulcet tones you wish to hear in your times of relaxation, no brave words you wish to hear when charging through hell? Perhaps I could offer some suggestions?"

"Hell no, thanks." Kaiden grimaced. He didn't want to make too many assumptions, but with Laurie choosing his new little mind-mate, he might have to deal with his EI doing a cheerleading chant in the middle of a battle zone just so he could play with his new toy at Kaiden's expense.

"Well then, is there truly no one you can think of that you would like to accompany you?" Laurie inquired.

"I can't say off-hand. The only person I ever worked with or took orders from was Jake," Kaiden said thoughtlessly.

Laurie raised an eyebrow as Kaiden grasped the bridge

of his nose in annoyance. He probably shouldn't have let that slip.

"Who might that be? A friend? A sibling? You could start there and find something similar."

"Jake Havik? Also, hell no. Jake was…he was a mentor, I guess, but he was a pain in the ass. I mean, I guess…he was a good guy, but damn if he wasn't a grumpy bastard too." Kaiden growled his irritation and cracked his knuckles. "Would always boss me around, put me through all sorts of damned torture while training me. He was a constant smartass…"

Kaiden trailed off. He could feel a coldness coursing through his stomach as he recalled the last couple of weeks and his constant reminiscing. For all the anger he had toward Jake, maybe he didn't feel so indifferent. He should, but…

He sighed as he crossed his arms again. "I mean, he was a bastard, but he did look out for me and the others, I suppose. Wasn't so rotten. Could have a smaller stick up his ass, though. To be honest, I would like to have him around again."

"Understood, forming personality around profile Jacob Thomas Havik from the database."

"Oh, dear God, no," Kaiden whispered as he could feel his pulse quicken and a cold sweat break out.

"Well, that worked out wonderfully. You see, it wasn't so—"

"Turn it off. Make it stop," Kaiden said, running over to Laurie. "Ain't no way I'm gonna have that idiot in my head 24/7. He was bad enough when I saw him irregularly."

Laurie's avatar put up his hands. "Don't be so theatrical.

The EI isn't a séance. It is only constructing a personality using descriptions and historical files from a government profile. You're being melodramatic." The professor looked thoughtful. "Besides, it isn't like you had a plan B, and I thought you were ready to go."

"I thought you said that this was against the rules."

"I said it wasn't normally what that function was used for, but I'm always interested in something different," Laurie answered with a sparkle in his eye. "Besides, you would probably be in more trouble than I would. I'm the head designer, but you're merely an initiate who was playing around with things you shouldn't have been."

"That you gave me access too." Kaiden countered.

Kaiden could see the professor's avatar start to fade. "I'm going to finish up and prepare for your return. Get to know your EI a little more and tell him to deactivate the link in a few minutes." This last instruction hung in the silence, the final accompaniment to the only part of him left—his devious smile.

"I hate you! You dandy bastard!" he screamed at the disappearing avatar.

"You signed the form," the professor reminded him.

Goddamn semantics. With that, the avatar completely disappeared, and Kaiden turned back to the EI.

"Complete," it said, still in that monotone voice.

"Ya don't sound any different. Guess it didn't work?" he asked, relief returning to him. slowly

"You didn't give me time to sync, jackass," Chief retorted. Its voice now had a noticeable drawl like Kaiden's with a synthetic veneer on top of it.

"Oh…fuck me." Kaiden sighed. He hadn't made it

through one sentence before he wanted the basic tone and personality back.

"How do you think I feel? Couldn't even be bothered to set me up right. You gotta fuckin' slumber party to get to, or did I interrupt your nap? Come on man, you had one job."

Kaiden's fists clenched. "I didn't give you the go-ahead to choose this personality. You just decided to go solo and made that stupid decision without me. Change it."

"No can do, jackass. Because of the safety measures, I would have to be wiped clean and start from scratch, so now I'm stuck like this and with you until professor Frakenposh out there can do something about it." It punctuated that sentiment with something that sounded like a growl.

EIs could growl?

Kaiden eyed the construct. "Sounds like that sucks for you more than me. You're stuck with that half-assed accent. Did you load it up from some two-bit western world amusement park?"

"Nah, I just listened to you and looked up southern dipshit, and this is what came up." Kaiden could see the little orb that he called its eye actually furrow like it was trying to stare daggers at him.

"Oh, I'm going to waste your beachball-looking ass the second I got a chance," Kaiden threatened.

"Yeah, sure, do that. I'm in your head now, buddy. Even if you wanna try taking a screwdriver to the dome yourself, you're gonna do more damage to yourself than me. Well, maybe you might miss your brain. There's so much room in your skull that it might actually be quite comfy in here."

"Ya know what, the sweet silence of death may actually

be preferable to having to continue listening to a Christmas ornament's snappy comebacks."

"*Damn, man, you have problems,*" Chief grunted, its eye widening again.

"Everything is prepared, Initiate Jericho. Have you and your new EI become fast friends?" Laurie asked, his voice now echoing in Kaiden's mind again.

"Again, *hell* no! Are you sure I can't smoke this thing?" he pleaded.

"Not currently. The installation is too fresh, and this is your first time using an EI of this capability so there could be a good chance of brain damage and the potential that it could corrupt future use of the synapse function," the professor stated flatly. *There goes my last hope.*

"*Sucks to be you, KJ,*" Chief added with amusement.

"In addition, considering the EI is loaded into the neural gear itself, the trauma that it could possibly endure if removed so suddenly without proper precaution could fry the chip and therefore delete the EI."

"*Dammit all,*" Chief snapped. "*What the hell did you use to make me? Recycled toothpicks and aluminum wrap?*"

"Seriously, Prof, ain't this supposed to be the next stage of technological advancement or something? I thought this was supposed to be hot shit?"

"*It seems I might literally be.*"

"It's experimental. I explained that it's new and not thoroughly tested, but it does work as intended despite that. The fact that someone might want to remove it due to idiocy and negligence was not a consideration," Laurie chastised in a kind of I-told-you-so tone that pushed all Kaiden's irritation buttons. "Now, if you would come back to reality, we can have one final inspection, and you can be on your way."

"Sweet Jesus...he said deactivate the link, puffball," Kaiden chided when the EI made no response.

"Didn't wanna have to listen to ya babble on anymore anyway."

"You're in my head now, smartass."

"And I bet this basic bitch doesn't even have cable," it remarked, getting one last jab before disappearing.

Kaiden's vision began to blur, and he could see his body fading. Despite the growing inferno in his chest at the realization that he was now stuck with this thing for the foreseeable future, he couldn't help but smile regardless.

"Little bastard is almost like Jake." He chuckled into the descending darkness.

CHAPTER SIX

Kaiden gasped for air, his eyes snapping open though it took a moment or two to focus fully. He sat up and looked down at his hands, pressing them against each other and then to his chest, checking to see that his body had come back in one piece.

"Don't be so silly, Kaiden my boy," the familiar sing-song tone of Laurie admonished. "Your physical body wasn't in the system. It's perfectly fine."

"Just wanted to make sure you didn't make any improvements while I was under." Kaiden grunted his annoyance.

"Wasn't in the contract."

He turned to see Laurie descending a staircase on the far side of the room. He looked around to see that they were in a domed suite, the walls a solid gray that seemed cold and sterile, a sharp contrast to the emotions roiling within him.

He lifted a hand to the back of his head and could feel

minute lines around the base of his skull. "Do ya got a mirror?"

The professor moved to his side, reached over him, and brought down an overhead screen. "Take a look."

The monitor showed Kaiden the surgical work clearly. After a quick study, he had to admit, he was impressed. He could barely make out the incision lines detailing the professor's work. Two crossed lines formed a neat 'X.' Give his hair enough time to grow out a little, and one probably wouldn't be able to see it before too long.

"Nice stitchwork, Prof.," he said, probably giving the professor his first real compliment since their acquaintance.

"Much obliged, but it is not really stitchwork. Cooling lasers were used to bond the skin back together." The professor motioned upward with his arms, and two long robotic devices descended from the ceiling. "Although these two were the ones who did all the real work—precision surgical droids. I call them Nightingale and Blackwell."

"Uh, nice to meet ya," Kaiden said with a curt nod. The droids seemed to nod back before ascending back into their compartments. "Lasers, huh? I gotta say, whatever you did, I don't really feel any pain. You work cleaner than I would have thought."

The professor smiled at this and revealed a small vial of cloudy liquid. "It's a personal favorite blend of mine—not particularly legal, but if you can keep a secret, I can too."

"Just keep the good stuff flowin' and you got my word," Kaiden proposed as he hopped off the operating table.

"Before you go, activate your EI. We need to make sure that the integration was a success."

"Oh, good, there go my few moments of peace." Kaiden sighed. "Hey, Chief, you online?"

"Yeah, making room and decorating in here," it said in a sarcastic tone.

"It's fine," Kaiden grumbled. "Can't see it but I can hear it."

"Ah, on that note…" Laurie reached under the table and brought a case out. "Have a look, dear boy."

Kaiden opened the case to see a pair of shades. They were circular and with clear lenses and a translucent frame. He put them on cautiously, not entirely sure what he expected but almost certain he wouldn't like it, whatever it was. When he saw nothing different, he looked at the doctor with a puzzled expression.

"Normally, an EI is inserted directly into their frame or gear, but since your EI is connected to a neural link, I found a neat little workaround to this particular complication," Laurie explained. He walked over to Kaiden and placed his hand on his shoulder. "Chief, I believe it was, please be a friend and cast into the oculars Initiate Jericho is wearing."

Kaiden saw a light flicker in his lenses, then he could see Chief pop up in the corner of his right lens.

"Howdy, ya bastard," it said, its shell assuming a muted blue color.

"Your EI can be cast to any device that can be loaded with an EI and which has an open link," Laurie stated. "But the further away you are, the more the capabilities and power it has are reduced. It needs a strong connection with the neural gear to function at its peak."

"Uh, interesting…" Kaiden said, trailing off. "Sorry, I was just kind of shocked at how it obeyed a command without fuss."

"Don't let the personality confuse you. An EI is programmed to listen to its user. It wouldn't do much good in intense situations to argue constantly with it, now would it?" Laurie noted with a definite edge of humor in his tone.

"Doesn't mean I can't remind you when you mess up, and since you and I are all buddy-buddy now, let's keep that to a minimum, huh?" Chief's color changed to a hot red when it nagged.

"You got a mute function?"

"That would interrupt our potential bonding," it snarked in response. *"But alright, you'll be back."*

Kaiden took the lenses off and folded them up. He removed a smaller container from the case and placed them inside, then slid it into his pocket. "Well, thanks, Prof. Do I have to come back for check-ups or will I just be seeing you around?"

"Oh, I will be checking up on you," the professor assured him. "For now, however, simply follow orders and be sure to make the most of this new opportunity. I'm excited to see how it all goes."

"That's nice and foreboding." Kaiden looked around. "You got my jacket?"

"Of course." Laurie pointed to a chair where the jacket was folded up neatly. "I took the liberty of finishing all other particulars required, so the rest of the night is yours.

Be sure to get some sleep. Tomorrow will be your job evaluation."

"Appreciate it." Kaiden thanked him with a wave of the hand, but as he turned to exit the theater, he called back, "Before I come back looking like a fool, how do I get out of here?"

"Out the doors and to the left, there is an elevator. Take it down to the ground floor, and there will be a map to the exit. You will find the temporary dorms for SCs on the map as well, and Kaiden—"

He looked back as he stepped out the doors. The professor smiled, and the droids, once again in view, seemed to be waving at him. "Remember, only *you* can decide whether your time here is spent in vain or in joy. Keep being you, dear boy, and I think you'll find it a delight."

Kaiden gave him a hesitant nod as the doors closed behind him. He doubted that he would make any personal requests of him in the near future.

He traced the lines on the back of his head with his forefinger as he headed for the elevator. Damn shame he had this epiphany hours too late.

Kaiden walked across the moonlit grounds of the academy, taking in the sights of the buildings around him. They were an impressive sight from a distance, but up close, they really made the whole experience feel real.

He stopped at a crossing and looked over to the center of the island. The main Academy building towered in the distance, alight against the darkness of the night with the spire swirling with white, blue, and purple stripes.

A little awed, he took a moment to take it all in and

perhaps let everything that had happened in the last twenty-four hours really set in. He had gone from no plan to a potential bouncer job, then to beating up some rich punks—his personal favorite—and a chance to attend this prestigious academy. He'd taken a chance, met aliens, and signed a contract that would put him millions of credits in debt.

Then, in some bizarre twist he still couldn't quite wrap his head around, he'd found out he had some special mutation that allowed him to have some swanky crackerjack stuck in his brain. Now, he gazed over the island he would call home for the next few years, still half-questioning whether he hadn't somehow dreamt it all.

He shook his head and smiled, wondering how the others back in Fresno were getting on. There weren't many left, but he did pray that they had found some kind of solace. He'd started to feel a bit more at peace himself, even among all the crazies he had met so far.

Still, he had to admit they were his kind of crazy, at least.

He continued walking in the direction of his lodging for the evening. As he crossed the courtyard, he could hear several agitated voices coming from near a fountain on his left. He looked over to see five figures gathered around, with four of them seemingly ganging up on the fifth, their voices raised as if in accusation.

Kaiden recalled the fight at the bar and began to wonder if he would need to make a repeat performance.

He began to walk over, removing his hands from his pockets and cracking his knuckles.

"That it? Got nothing to say? I don't want to start nothing. I just think it's suspicious," one of them said. Kaiden noted the speaker, a guy with blond crew-cut hair talking to the fifth figure.

"If you didn't want to start anything, you should have kept your thoughts to yourself, Initiate Finnigan," the apparent victim said, her voice calm but with an undercurrent of anger simmering below her control. "I will repeat myself this once. I have nothing to say to you, and your accusations either stem from paranoia or envy or perhaps a mixture of both."

Kaiden moved to the edge of the group, his arms folded as he tried to keep himself somewhat hidden as he scanned them. Two men and two women, all wearing the academy uniform with blue rings on the jackets, stood in a circle.

The fifth was a girl with long black hair and pale skin, curved eyes, and lips now pursed together in annoyance. Her arms were crossed in front of her, and if she was at all worried about the others possibly abusing her, she certainly didn't show it.

"Maybe you don't realize..." The man trailed off as his gaze darted over to Kaiden. "Who are you?"

"Someone looking for some nightly entertainment," Kaiden responded in a lowered voice. "You seem to be looking to release some energy yourself. I could oblige."

"If so, could you please do it somewhere else? I have to get back to my dorm," the girl interjected.

"Look at you, keeping such a...nice person like her out so late. Why are you trying to start trouble?" Kaiden inquired as he slid his gaze around the group, bravado overtaking him.

"They aren't trying to start trouble," she said, looking at

Kaiden. "Because they are rule-abiding students of this academy who understand the repercussions that inevitably occur should they cause problems on campus, particularly to a sponsor's daughter."

This caused the man and his friends to stiffen visibly. Their jaws clenched and fists balled, but finally, the apparent leader exhaled and shook his head.

"Fine, whatever, Chiyo. We'll leave." He grunted his displeasure as they started backing away. "You can't act like this is normal, though. Others will be after you too, so you better start figuring out your explanation by then."

With that, they departed, leaving Kaiden and Chiyo standing by the fountain.

"Ya mind me asking what the hell that was about?" Kaiden asked, earning a suspicious glare from her.

He raised his arms and backed up a step. "Look, I thought we were all supposed to be friendly with each other and such. If I've actually walked into a *Lord of the Flies* thing, I would like a heads up."

She shook her head and sighed. "No, nothing like that. It was a…disagreement."

"I thought those were more civil."

"He passionately disagreed." She finished this noncommittal statement with a nonchalant wave of her hand.

"Well, whatever it was, glad it turned out alright for ya." Kaiden reached out his hand. "Kind of an odd moment, but it would be impolite to not introduce myself. Kaiden Jericho."

She looked down at his hand and then back up at him, raising an eyebrow. After a moment, she shook his hand quickly before turning away. "Chiyo Kana. I see you're not in uniform."

"Nah, haven't been fitted," Kaiden chirped, sliding his hands back into his jacket pockets.

"You're an SC then?"

"Special case was what a lot of people called me, even before I got here."

"Humph, you don't seem capable of giving straight answers."

"I can. I just have the willpower not too," he quipped.

She stepped closer to him. Kaiden could see a familiar shimmer in her eyes—EI contacts. She tilted her head, and Kaiden saw her eyes looking toward him but not at him. She was reading something.

"Well, it seems you have been truthful. I wonder if you would have told me about your past affiliations had we continued."

Kaiden was briefly taken aback before composing himself quickly. The teachers knowing about his past was one thing. Now this random girl, too? He started to get a little homesick. At least in Texas, your private life was pretty easy to keep private.

"Tell me, what are you here for?" she asked.

"The world-renowned pole dancing classes. I was told I got talent." Kaiden smirked.

She sighed, looking back up at him but this time, clearly looked right at him. "What are you here for?"

Kaiden leaned back a bit, a little annoyed by her attitude. "Why does it matter to you? I thought I was gonna help someone not get their head caved in, and now I'm playing twenty questions with you."

"So, you don't know then?" she questioned.

"Look here, darlin', you're starting to act like one of those imps from folktales that steal a person's soul for not answering their riddle properly. So please, back away to a safe non-soul-sucking distance or at least get out of my personal space."

Chiyo closed her eyes and sighed as she turned and walked away without looking back.

Kaiden took the hint and decided to leave as well when he heard her say, "So, you don't have a path then?"

"What are ya on about?" he snapped, looking back.

"If you have no path, then you have no future here," she said, the words a definite challenge though she made no effort to look at him. While he searched for a response, she shrugged and added, "You seem interesting. You should find a path for yourself and stay awhile." With that, she walked away.

Kaiden watched her disappear behind the buildings. His wit had failed him for once. He considered her words as he continued his own walk to the SC dorms. Distracted by her statement, he thought back to all the people he had met recently. They had all talked about the future in one way or another.

The idea of a future had not been something Kaiden paid much attention to at any point in his life. Maybe *living* to see the future, he could concede that much, but he'd never really considered some predetermined course. Should he? Would he lose out if he continued in his old patterns of behavior? On some level, he resented the idea that some unknown future could impose strictures on his natural inclination to live in the moment—no matter where that took him. Then again, that impulsiveness seemed to have brought him to a place where he was forced to consider at least the possibility that a defined future was important.

His destination materialized in the semi-darkness up ahead, maybe two hundred yards away, pulling him from his musings. Kaiden stopped once again and looked up into the night sky. He could see stars, which should have been impossible with all the lights around the building obscuring the sky. It was probably a projection from the dome, he decided.

He chuckled at the irony. Natural beauty was obscured by artificial lighting, so someone simply replicated that natural beauty artificially—a wonderful little circle. He did admire the thought behind it, however. Sure, things *should* have been one way, but they weren't and so what, they simply made it seem like it was supposed to be the way it was.

Yeah, maybe that girl was right. He didn't have a path, maybe he didn't have a real future set for himself. But he did think he had it all planned out at one time, and those plans went to hell incredibly fast. Yet somehow, he made it through that and he was there now, still breathing, still moving, and soon, improving.

As he finally went to check-in, a thought occurred to him. He might not have had a set path, but he made it to the same destination as those who had. Not too bad for wingin' it.

Those who questioned his path—or, rather, the lack thereof—should wait to see what happened when he applied himself.

CHAPTER SEVEN

A cacophony of electronic noises dragged Kaiden from sleep. He groaned as he twisted on his bed, glow strips around him bathing him in blue light.

"Good morning, Initiate Jericho. It is 5:30 a.m.," a monotone voice declared. "Your tasks for the day include completing your career evaluation test, then visiting the Academy Supply Depot, after which, the rest of the day is yours."

"Yeah, yeah, got it," he muttered groggily. "Open the capsule."

"Understood. I recommend beginning the day with a hearty breakfast at the cafeteria. Carpe diem." The computerized voiced seemed infuriatingly cheerful in a bored kind of way. Kaiden heard a ping and felt a whoosh of air as the door to his sleeping capsule opened. He slid out and stood in his quarters, stretching as he looked around the room.

A few dozen other SC initiates shared the hall with him, all of whom were either climbing or falling out of the capsules in various states of undress. Kaiden chuckled slightly at the scene in the dim artificial light. It almost looked like the living dead had invaded the Academy. Apparently, he wasn't the only who still had to adapt to this new routine.

One initiate yawned as he rummaged around in a backpack for something. He finally pulled out a black box and then a tablet from within. "Jeeves, please bring up a map of the Academy. I forgot where the cafeteria is."

Kaiden scowled as he remembered his new partner. Chief had been quiet so far, but he knew he would have to deal with him again sooner or later. As he stretched to bring life to his arms, he recalled Laurie's words about the EI's personality not interfering with its functions. The thing might give him lip, but it was still under his command…supposedly.

He sighed as he decided to bite the bullet and reactivate the snarky bastard. He would have to get used to him eventually or his time here would probably be pointless. Then he paused, realizing that overnight, the EI had somehow gone from being an it to a him. For one short moment, he felt as if a line had been crossed. A device remained a device, didn't it? Devoid of personality and therefore undeserving of a real pronoun. Then he remembered their previous brief conversations and shrugged. Chief was in his head—to some extent at least—so making it a him felt somewhat more comforting than a simple electronic presence he had no relationship with. Wait, relationship? With an EI? Was that even a thing? He scowled. There was only one way to find out.

Time for some bonding.

"Hey, Chief, you there?"

"Good morning, you wonderful bastard," the synthetic southern voice chirped in his head.

"It's Kaiden."

"Cockbite," he replied with something close to demented glee.

Kaiden let out a low growl as he leaned against the wall of his sleeping capsule. "Look here, you glow-in-the-dark floating testicle, I need directions. You can do that much, can't you?"

He almost swore he could hear the EI snort. *"Yes, of course, I can, but it would probably help you if you put on the optics unless you want me to try etching a map onto the back of your skull,"* Chief advised. *"Also, it will make you not look like an insane person to the rest of your bunkmates."*

Kaiden's raised an eyebrow as he looked slowly over to see a trio of other initiates looking his way. They were in the middle of getting dressed, and while they all had optics of their own on, Kaiden could feel their suspicious gazes.

He tried to remain unperturbed as he looked away and raised his hand to his opposite ear—as if he were using a com-link—in an effort to play it off with a reasonable explanation. It seemed to work as they lost interest. He walked around to his capsule and opened a compartment in the side, revealing his clothes from yesterday along with a fresh uniform of Academy track pants and a long-sleeved shirt.

He dug around in the pockets of his jacket to find the case containing his optics. The display lit-up almost instantly when he put them on.

"There's that lovely mug. Can I get a smile?" Chief asked as the orb bounced onscreen, turning a pinkish hue.

"You certainly seem a bit more chipper than yesterday." Kaiden snorted as he pulled on the Academy-issued clothing.

"Eh, what can I say? I'd just woken up and was a bit cranky. More importantly, I saw your little stunt last night at the fountain. It gave me a new perspective on you."

"How so?"

"Since I pretty much know your brain inside and out, I won't get into the specifics too much. It would be wasted on you, no hard feelings," Chief stated nonchalantly, earning another annoyed grunt from Kaiden. *"But like the dandy professor said, our algorithms help us determine the best way to assist our hosts, both on and off the field. One of the ways we improve the algorithm is simply by observing the nature and personality of our hosts, gaining new insight along the way."*

"All right, but don't you already have my personality profile installed? Also, you keep saying host. I prefer commander or master."

"I prefer being hosted by someone who isn't an impatient asshat and actually took the time to install me properly, but we all gotta live with the crappy cards life deals us sometimes, huh?" Chief growled, creating a rumbling buzz in Kaiden's ears which elicited a wince. *"Which, by the way, was one of the reasons I was so grumpy yesterday. As for the profile? Ha! That didn't exactly give me a lot of hope."*

"Counselor Mya said I had great potential," Kaiden retorted as he tied the laces on his boots.

"Counselor Mya is a counselor; her job is to make people feel

good about themselves, nitwit. You think they'd keep her around if she couldn't sell anyone on this?"

Kaiden stopped tying his boots for a moment, his eyes shifting left and right as he contemplated his response. "Doesn't make her wrong, though."

"As tempting as it is to keep grinding down that ego, I'll give you this—from what was available to me, I figured you would at least make for a good raider or bounty hunter, so it wasn't a complete waste. Sure, I would be stuck with nothing better than a gun jockey, but there are certainly worse options.

"So, what made you come around?"

"I haven't made a one-eighty here, but watching you confront those haughty brats last night showed me that you are willing to take action, at the very least. Then you didn't immediately plow into a potential four-on-one brawl, which means you do consider your actions...or, perhaps, aren't a hothead."

Kaiden recalled the fight back at the bar that led him to the Academy in the first place. He decided to not bring that up.

"So yeah, you earned a bit more of my respect, but you still got some ways to go. You have successfully earned the slight promotion from dumbass to meathead. Congrats."

"Much obliged," Kaiden muttered. The concession didn't seem like much, but if it meant a little less headbutting, he'd take it.

He locked his fingers together and stretched his arms to the ceiling. Looking around, he saw most of the others leaving the room.

"You got that map for me, Chief?"

"Onscreen."

Kaiden saw a small overhead map appear on the lens. It zoomed in to reveal the immediate area around him.

"Give me the directions to the cafeteria, would you?"

"Can I get a please?"

"Can I get a cooperative EI?"

"Ohhh, what a skillful retort. If only you showed such cleverness yesterday, we would probably both be better off."

An arrow appeared onscreen, pointing toward the door.

"That'll lead you to the cafeteria. Sorry I can't hold your hand on the way."

"That's all right, buddy, I got another way you can be helpful." Kaiden chuckled.

"How's that?"

"Audio off," Kaiden commanded.

"You sorry sack of—" Chief began before the sound cut out. Kaiden grinned as the orb's pink hue became a blazing red. The little bastard might not call him Commander, but he was definitely in control.

Kaiden walked out onto the pavilion outside the cafeteria with a tray in hand. He'd piled it with a fruit bowl, oatmeal, pancakes, breakfast sausage, boiled eggs, orange juice, and tea. He had to admit, the Academy fed them pretty damn well.

The sun had begun to peek over the horizon, and Kaiden winced when the rays of light seemed to spear right into his eyes.

"Chief, turn on the shades," Kaiden ordered, watching

the orb turn to the side, its eye looking up into the corner, acting as if it didn't hear him.

"Come on now. If you're a good boy, I'll get you a treat." He chuckled and the eye rolled around, but Kaiden could see his view darken. It continued the process until his vision was completely obscured."

"Ha ha, jackass."

Chief once again returned to its delighted pink hue. The lenses brightened a little until he could see again, but sufficient filter remained to dampen the sunlight.

"Thanks."

Kaiden walked around, looking for a place to sit and enjoy his breakfast. As he passed a patch of trees and grass, he spotted a familiar figure sitting at a picnic table beneath the shade of a tree. It was the girl from the night before. Chiyo Kana.

He wondered for a moment whether he should go and talk to her again. She seemed nice enough when she didn't go into that cryptic speech that made her sound like someone trying to invite him into their new-age religion.

He considered his options, but he could feel his stomach rumbling. More to the point, he could do with a bit more info on what was going on. He sighed as he decided to walk over, admitting to himself, at least, that he could always use more friends.

It could also piss her off, which seemed more likely, but he'd roll the dice and see what happened.

"Mind if I join you?" he asked politely.

She turned to look at him, seemingly disinterested until he noticed a brief flash of recognition in her eyes. Her EI contacts shimmered, which made him a little uncomfortable.

"Well, hello again," she said, waving a hand in front of her. Kaiden took this as permission to sit, and he placed his tray on the table and sat across from her.

"Howdy." He opened a pack of utensils and began to dig in. "Gotta admit up front that I ain't one for pleasantries and small talk. I was wondering if you could answer a few questions for me."

She crossed her arms on the table and leaned in. "A nice change of pace. What do you want to know?"

"Look, without going back into the whole 'what is your future thing,' I gotta be honest. I don't really work that way. I'm more of a wing-it-and-we'll-see sort of guy, myself," he admitted as he began cutting into his pancakes. If she noticed the slightly defensive edge to his confession—even a little defiant—she didn't comment. "I was actually recommended to come here only two days ago."

She raised an eyebrow curiously, then chuckled. "I see. Continue."

"Well, I still don't have an answer to your little riddle, but I suppose I could ask what you think of everything. I guess you've got a future you're planning?"

"Of a sort…" she began, her voice lowering slightly. "I must admit that how we came to be here isn't too different, technically."

"You beat up some slummers in a bar?"

She looked at him incredulously, blinking a couple times. "I…no, I meant that neither of us originally had the intention of coming here."

"Ah, so a bit more tangential, then."

"Moving past that, my point is that if you're asking what I recommend you do, it all begins with what you want to accomplish."

"Yeah, yeah, I figured that, but isn't that the whole point of this place?" He pointed around the area with his fork. "They're supposed to lead you down some path or something, find out what you're good at."

"You don't seem like the type of person to be led around on a leash," she remarked.

"Depends on how kinky I'm feelin' and the amount of alcohol in me, honestly."

The blank look returned to her eyes. Kaiden shrugged internally and sipped his tea slowly.

"Yes, the Academy can put you on a path depending on the criteria you fit and the skills you have. However, I would see that as a waste. You can decide your fate here and beyond."

Kaiden finished his tea and flipped the cup over on his tray. "A few people have told me that, but it seems kinda pointless since we're all gonna be contracted to the highest bidder at the end of it all. Why shouldn't I just do what I do best?"

"If that's the case, why bother being here at all? Shouldn't you already be on the streets making money 'doing what you do best?'"

Kaiden cocked his head to the side in thought. He noticed Chief bouncing up and down in his lens and scowled. Was he *laughing*?

"I was offered a chance to come here because I kicked ass. I thought I would have more chances to do that. Why shouldn't I simply gun for being a badass?"

"Because everyone here is."

"You're telling me you're also going to be a soldier?"

"Not like that." She huffed, twisted the top off a bottle of water, and took a few sips. "Everyone in the Academy, whether by schooling, trials, or invitation, is here because they have proven viability in a field or discipline. They don't merely take in any nobody off the street because they can make a fist or solve simple division. No matter what they come in for, they will leave as some of the best in their professions as long as they stick to their training. So, if you continue down your road, you will certainly be a badass, but a faceless one among many."

Kaiden nodded, the picture becoming a little clearer. "Well, I'm a little out of my depth in the whole planning department…"

"That's become quite clear," she responded between sips.

"Good to know you're following along," he muttered, pausing to think while he polished off his fruit. "I ain't exactly the type to ask for handouts, but if you have any advice…well, I'll hear it."

She froze for a moment, swishing her water bottle around in her hand. "The only other time you saw me I was getting yelled at by my classmates. That doesn't strike you as an odd person to get advice from?"

"Who gives a damn about them?" Kaiden scoffed. "I ain't the greatest when it comes to readin' people, but they seemed to have a stick up their ass. You seemed to know about my…affiliation when you looked me over last night, and that didn't bother you, so you seem all right. By the way, how did you do that?"

"It's one of the reasons I'm here. Secrets of my trade," she responded unhelpfully. "Although, since we're on the subject, I wanted to thank you."

Kaiden finished his meal and wiped his mouth with a napkin. "What, for last night? It's all good. That's what I do."

"It may seem inconsequential, but it does show a good side to your character, and it spared me from having to deal with them for a longer period."

"My natural charisma is another good show of character, yeah?"

"Perhaps, but it is dulled by your conversational skills."

Kaiden grimaced as he saw Chief light up again in delight. He made a mental note to look for an EI skin that was invisible.

"You have yet to complete your job evaluation test, correct?" she asked.

"On my way there after this."

"My only advice, for now, is that you answer the questions truthfully. Most of the people I have talked to always provided skewed responses, answering how they felt they should as opposed to how they wanted to. Don't make that mistake."

She stood up from the table and picked up her tray. "Don't know when I'll see you again, but good luck. If you have any more questions, next time, feel free to ask me. As long as I am not in the middle of something, I enjoy the distraction." With that, she left, dumping her trash in a bin and before walking into the crowd.

Kaiden leaned back, contemplating the conversation.

She was a bit dry, but she didn't act like he was an idiot. That made her nice enough.

Chief bounced up and down on his lens, trying to get his attention. He sighed.

"Audio on."

"Nice job not looking like gutter trash, but seriously, you sounded like a moron. Also, 'doing what you do best?' Were you turning tricks in an alley before you came here?"

"Audio off."

"You can silence me, but you'll never silence the tru…" Chief's voice faded out.

"Smartass," he muttered.

CHAPTER EIGHT

"So, what did you get?"

"Mechanic."

"Just like your mom, huh? I got Medic."

"Oh, cool. I mean, you *have* been training for that up till now."

"It was an obvious choice. What about you, Lisa?"

"Finances."

"That was an option?"

"Probably going to take a firearms secondary course, make sure I'm just as useful with a trigger as I am a spreadsheet."

Kaiden listened to the group of initiates discussing their evaluation verdicts as they walked past. He had sat in the waiting room for the last hour, twiddling his thumbs and overhearing the dozens of different designations that the others had received. Some, he had expected. Others seemed rather unfortunate.

It seemed a damn shame to come to a fancy institution

like Nexus only to be stuck as a pastry chef.

He had overheard options like bounty hunter, soldier, and bodyguard, all of which seemed more up his alley. He kept thinking back to Chiyo's last words to him to answer truthfully rather than how he felt he should. Kaiden mulled it over a little while he waited. He had been told that you weren't necessarily compelled to follow the test designation, but you wouldn't know it listening to the others.

They made it sound like it was the secret eleventh commandment; don't steal, don't kill, don't back-talk the eval test.

He wondered if he would actually be all right with something like medic or engineer. The chance of that outcome for him seemed like a long shot. It was pointless giving a job to someone when it wouldn't benefit them or they didn't already have the skills to benefit from further training. Besides, they had his profile and history. They wouldn't give a former gang member something so humdrum, right?

Then again, considering his last twenty-four hours there, maybe they simply like screwing with him.

"Initiate Kaiden Jericho, please enter bay thirty," a calm, synthesized voice directed over the intercom.

He stood and walked to the testing hall entrance, following a sign that pointed in the direction of bay thirty. He noted that all other directions seemingly held multiple bays but didn't pay it too much mind. A little twinge of what might be anxiety nagged at him as he followed the signs until he found himself at the end of a long hallway, the only room left being the one marked with a stylized '30' on the door.

Now, he began to feel a little uneasy, recalling that the last time he was shuffled away from the rest, he ended up in Professor Laurie's overzealous clutches. As long as that wasn't a recurring pattern, he might give this the benefit of the doubt.

As he entered, he noticed the room was surprisingly sparse. A couple of computers were set up on either side of the room, and in the middle was a large tube. Long wires connected it to both computers, and there was no window to see what was inside.

"Well, hello again, my dear boy."

Oh, sweet Jesus, no.

Kaiden turned around to see none other than the immaculately dressed Alexander Laurie, a beaming smile on his face and, no doubt, various tests and hypothesis running through his mind. None of those were likely to really consider his wellbeing, or if they did, it was possibly secondary.

As he was about to release a dramatic sigh, he noticed another figure walk up behind Laurie, this one also familiar. It took him a moment, but he recognized the unique oculus device wrapped around his head and the formal way he carried himself.

It was Commander Sasha, the man who had offered him the chance to be there in the first place.

"Howdy, what are the two of you doing here?" Kaiden asked as he stood a little straighter "The Academy must be really low on manpower if they gotta send the higher-ups to run one test."

"Yes, well, about that…" Laurie began, tapping the side of his chin in a gesture that became more irritating each time Kaiden saw it. "You see, Kaiden, when I spoke with the Board about our little arrangement, I ran into a bit more pointless protest than I expected."

"Initiate Jericho, what my...colleague here is trying to say is that the operation you agreed to and underwent might have some ramifications that were insufficiently considered by the professor and so might entail some problems with your training here at the academy."

"What are you talkin' about?" Kaiden challenged. "That dandy bastard said it was fine, made me sign a form and everything—said this was supposed to be the next step in technological, or human, or techno-human advancement or some shit."

"I believe my response was more sophisticated," Laurie commented with his usual urbane tone.

"I should probably clarify," Sasha acknowledged. "I by no means wish to make it seem like you are in danger of being expelled from Nexus, or that what you agreed to was necessarily wrong. Professor Laurie was within his authority to offer the operation, albeit with the knowledge that he should inform the Board."

"I did—eventually. In such circumstances, time wasted is a sin."

"Is that your catchphrase or something?" Kaiden huffed, still a long way from mollified by the assurances.

"As it stands, the problem is not that directly, but the potential...difficulties that might arise," Sasha explained.

Kaiden leered at Laurie. "I thought this was supposed to help me."

"And it will. Just in a bit more...uh, *roundabout* way," Laurie said defensively. He moved past Kaiden over to one of the stations and began typing something into it. The tube lit up.

"What's he doing?" Kaiden asked.

Sasha walked up beside him, looking on as Laurie moved over to the other station. "The professor explained the Animus System to you, correct?"

"Sort of...it's a virtual reality system that we use to train, right?"

"Correct. The pod you see before you is what you and the other students will use to access the system during your time here. It scans your physical body to create an avatar and then integrates with your EI to link you into the system. Metaphorically, it separates you from your body and immerses you into the simulation."

"Okay," Kaiden acknowledged with a hesitant tone and slow nod. "So, if this is so normal, what makes this difficult for me?"

"Almost all the normal pods in the Academy grounds are calibrated specifically for the usual EI systems that the other students use—their oculus devices, neural links, and other traditional devices. That is to say"—Sasha turned to look directly at Kaiden—"everything that isn't *your* device."

"Wait, what? I thought mine was basically a neural link. He *burrowed* it into my skull."

"Again, you truly bastardize the grandeur of my work," Laurie shouted from across the room. "Your device is beyond the basic passive abilities of a simple neural link. It does not require activation. It is a part of you and you of it."

"Yeah, you mentioned that the first time. But I still don't see how this doesn't make me a cyborg," Kaiden shot back.

"Technically speaking, it is an enhancement. It does not replace anything in your body, as cybernetics would," Sasha explained, and Kaiden shot him a glare.

"All right, I'll drop it. So what's the deal if mine is supposed to be superior."

"Probably nothing. Merely some of the Board being paranoid sycophants," Laurie chimed in, his fingers pressing keys with a rapidity that was a little disconcerting.

"It could also mean brain damage," Sasha added.

"Explain. You're starting to seem like the reasonable one," Kaiden stated, although he should also dock points for technically putting him in this mess.

"Oh, he's being melodramatic. The Board asked me to write up a small list of possible complications of using the present software in the pods to integrate you into the Animus using your current system. That possibility has an improbably small chance of happening."

"The list was not small. There were over two-hundred items listed," Sasha corrected quietly.

"I noticed he said 'improbably,' not 'impossibly,' too," Kaiden added, his tone clipped with displeasure.

"Don't listen to him, my dear Kaiden. I was beginning to feel that one day, I could grow to see you as my personal ward." Laurie sighed as he went over to activate a console on the tube.

"Do you think he knows the difference between a ward and a project?" Kaiden asked Sasha in a hushed voice.

"I have seen nothing to suggest it, really. I have heard him call some of his robots pets," Sasha replied, and Kaiden groaned.

He mulled over his options. Right now, he was honestly

beginning to feel like a test subject to be thrown around and prodded as they pleased. Attention was nice, sure, but he hadn't even been offered dinner before they inserted things into him.

Should he simply have the implant removed and go with the traditional system? His so-called improvement seemed more of a headache, both literal and metaphorical. He might not have the benefits it offered, but learning things slower seemed a small price to pay for being able to keep his brain function normal.

It was quite funny if he took a moment to think about it objectively. He had never really taken too much pride in his basic motor function up until the moment where it could possibly be zapped out of him.

"Never settle."

Goddammit.

"What are you doing, exactly, Laurie?" Kaiden asked as he walked up to the professor.

"What I was trying to explain to the Board. I can configure the current software to read and integrate with your implant by having it register as a neural link. It will probably slow down your synapse-connection to basic levels for now until I can make a proper update," he explained, once again moving back to one of the stations and inputting more commands.

"All right, but everything else will be fine?" Kaiden asked.

"Indeed, your implant will still be fully functioning outside the Animus. Then, when I update the system, it will work as intended, and I will show them and the world that we have merely scratched the surface of what we are capable of," Laurie declared with gusto. "I won't let this opportunity for technological advancement be halted because the Board feels squeamish. Oh, your safety is also paramount in all this."

"Glad to know you care, Prof." Kaiden sighed with a roll of his eyes.

He looked back to Sasha "You sure there's no alternatives?"

"Well, obviously you could have the implant removed and go the traditional route. I'm assuming you've already contemplated this."

"Yeah. I'd rather not if we can make this work."

"There's that drive that I admired during our initial meeting," Laurie exclaimed proudly.

"You could possibly work with the professor exclusively until he makes the proper upgrades to the rest of the pods. He has one of the few systems that would have no issues running your implant," Sasha suggested.

Kaiden recalled the operating table with the robotic surgeons he initially awoke on, deep in the bowels of Laurie's private domain.

"I'll chance the pod that might make me incontinent, thanks."

"And again, you wound me," Laurie whined, his expression an exaggerated sulk.

Sasha nodded as he walked over to the pod. "I'm here as an ambassador of the Board to oversee the test. I'll also act as your proctor for the evaluation once you're linked," he explained. "Are you almost ready, Professor?"

"Just about, taking one last scan through the changes."

"Feel free to take a couple more, just to be safe," Kaiden

offered, his arms crossed across his chest to emphasize his displeasure.

"I'll need your help for the last of it, Kaiden," Laurie stated, turning to him. "Remember how I said you could cast your EI into any system with an open link and proper power source? Well, why don't you give it a try?"

He pointed to the pod. Kaiden cocked an eyebrow, puzzled.

"What do I do?" he asked, flicking his fingers at the pod as if he were splashing water.

"Just tell your EI to connect itself to the pod's system." Laurie shook his head, clearly irritated. "Please stop, you look like a wizard from a pulp fantasy."

Kaiden rubbed the back of his head sheepishly, then coughed into a closed fist. "Uh, all right. Chief, connect to the pod."

Kaiden heard a low sound like the hum of a computer powering on, but it had hardly started when it went silent almost immediately. Then he saw Chief's glowing blue orb appear on the console screen on the pod that Laurie used.

"Chief, is it? I need you to tell me if the new commands and changes to the code are all properly in place and synced," Laurie asked.

Silence.

Sasha and Laurie looked over to Kaiden, who rapped his fingers on his arm. For a moment, he wondered if something had gone wrong before the obvious occurred to him.

"Right, right. Audio on."

"Everything is fine, Professor, although I was kinda hoping

you would put him in for a dry trial run for kicks." Chief chortled.

"A rather odd choice for an EI personality, Initiate," Sasha observed, looking at the illuminated eye on the screen.

"It wasn't really…mistakes were made," Kaiden admitted.

"Regardless, it is an interesting ability to have, being able to have your EI gain control of any open system. It would have more use to a hacker or technical specialist, I would imagine."

"Give me a few more years, old fellow, and I expect all our future recruits will have the ability to do so," Laurie avowed. "Kaiden, those oculars I gave you, put them on."

He obliged, and when the display activated, he could see a new screen that presented options he originally hadn't seen before, along with a graph showing levels of various markers such as power and connection.

"What is all this?" he asked.

"When your EI is in a new system, it allows you to control that system remotely, as long as there is nothing blocking the connection or trying to boot you out of it," Laurie explained. "Now start simple. Tell your EI to start up the pod."

"Fire it up, Chief," Kaiden ordered.

"Finally, we get to do something," Chief quipped, and with that, the pod lit up and Kaiden could hear the surging bellow of generators and electric feedback.

"Now, on your screen, look at the field labeled 'activation.' It should give you a prompt to open the door," Laurie instructed.

Kaiden did so, looking at the activation tab and staring for a moment as the field highlighted and opened, revealing several options including 'open door.' He watched as it highlighted briefly before confirming, and Kaiden looked over to see a segment of the pod unlock with a hiss and slide open to reveal a metallic interior.

"Well done. I would have you play around a bit more to get used to the different functions, but we have things to do. In this case, we should figure out your potential future."

"Step into the pod, Initiate, and close the door. The professor will take it from here. The link only takes a few moments to establish, and we will begin the evaluation once that is complete." Sasha inclined his head toward the pod.

Kaiden nodded, walked over to it, and stepped inside. It was an odd sensation to know that he voluntarily stepped into a device that would essentially digitize him in a few minutes.

"Chief, close the door," he instructed.

"See ya after the jump. Hope you don't have any fillings."

With that, the door closed, and a dim white light shone beneath him. He saw pools of blue circle around him, scanning him, and he felt a heaviness in his mind. It surprised him that it resembled the same feeling of descending as he did when he finally succumbed to sleep.

For a moment, his eyes closed, then he snapped them open. His mouth fell agape, and he trembled slightly. He looked around and couldn't help but smile slightly at the surrealness of it all.

He certainly wasn't in the Nexus anymore.

CHAPTER NINE

The sky was the first thing to catch Kaiden's attention. It was an unnatural hue of ethereal blue, visually beautiful if rather uncanny. He looked down to see a valley. The land was gray but not sickly, as if the color was never there to begin with.

To his left and right were titanic mountains, towering into the sky, which followed the monochrome color of the land with patches of black and white accenting the gray earthly bodies.

Was earthly correct in this instance? He wasn't exactly sure. The odd flickering of the sky and the rustling of the grass beneath him, moving to no wind, didn't really help him make a decision on it.

"Can you hear me, Initiate Jericho?" Sasha's voice erupted in his head. Kaiden startled at first, but with his previous experience after his surgery with Laurie, he was better prepared for the whole disembodied voice talking to him.

At least enough not to question his sanity.

"Yeah, I read ya," Kaiden answered, taking a few steps forward and peering down the hill he stood on. "This is… different. Does the Academy not usually spring the extra money for color? Is that DLC?"

"Professor Laurie booted up a basic map for your initial link. Considering the circumstances, we wanted to make sure that there weren't any unnecessary items loaded or processes to hurdle, just in case."

"Well, I appreciate the thought, I guess." Kaiden scratched behind his ear. "However, I'm pretty sure that this is what ghosts see in limbo. Mind if we get a little fancier? I'd even be happy with the sky not having the color of a broken LCD screen."

"Don't worry yourself, Kaiden my boy," Laurie chirped, his cheery voice sounding almost sing-song in his head, "This was merely a test. Everything seems to be in working order, and I don't see any problems with integration back here. We'll get you on a proper testing field in but a few moments."

"Well, to be fair, it is better than the endless void you loaded me into the first time around," Kaiden admitted.

"Of course. This time, you will see the *true* capabilities of my system," Laurie bragged. "First things first, though. Make sure your EI is with you."

"Chief, get out here, we got stuff to do," Kaiden yelled.

"Oh, good. Something to do. That is better than what we've been doing." The EI would have deadpanned if it had a face, Kaiden decided. Its floating form appeared in front of him in full glory.

"Well, look at you all out and about. What took ya so

long? I've been here a full two or three minutes, man. Get your life together," Kaiden complained sarcastically.

"Yeah, yeah, you're right. Next time, you do this, I'll be sure to half-ass the link-up process. It'll be quicker." Chief huffed his exasperation. *"I'm sure nothin' bad will happen. You may have a couple extra appendages or somethin' when you load in, but hey, easier to hit the ground runnin' with five legs. Or maybe losin' a few billion brain cells will just mean less processing."*

"Aren't you precious?" Kaiden retorted. "I'm pretty sure if something fries my brain, you'll be in *just* as much trouble."

"Considering what I'm working with now? I'd probably not notice a huge difference." It glowed brightly for a moment before disappearing.

"Cheeky bastard," Kaiden scoffed.

"I'm starting to love these pet names," Chief jested, now appearing in the top left of Kaiden's view.

"Guess there's no need for optics in here, huh?" Kaiden inquired of his omnipresent teachers.

"Correct. Your EI can act in both a heads-up display and a simulated physical manner, for lack of a better word," Sasha replied. "With that, I believe we are prepared to load you into the proper evaluation map. Are you ready, Initiate?"

"Sure. I guess I gotta log out and then back in or something?"

"Certainly not, although I would recommend standing quite still," Laurie advised, "Nothing should happen, really, but some seem to get...disoriented the first time they switch between maps."

Kaiden crossed his arms, tightening his muscles in

preparation. It wasn't like there was anything to hang onto, so self-control was his only failsafe.

"Beginning transfer in three…two…one…" Sasha faded out.

Kaiden saw the valley begin to warp, some parts twisting into themselves and others vanishing. His eyes widened, and he could feel himself hugging his chest tighter as he watched the world seemingly implode in front of him.

He always liked to consider himself someone who was always ready for anything. He still did, just not this —*never* this.

Then, flickers of light and color appeared and came together, and the vistas he'd seen twisting and collapsing began to reform and stretch out. He saw random items—barrels, tables, and chairs, among other things, appeared from nothing and moved into place by themselves. The sky disappeared, and a metal ceiling now loomed above him—very high above him, in fact. That fact seemed oddly unexpected and out of place. The ground morphed into linoleum flooring, and walls rushed by and stretched beyond his visual range.

He closed his eyes for a moment as a brief respite from the chaos, but when he opened them slowly, everything was calm. He looked around cautiously. He was in a hanger and could see a shooting range on one end and what seemed like an obstacle course on another. Gun cabinets and lockers were easily identified, and he could see other rooms behind doors and windows and various vehicles parked randomly in the enormous space. His surroundings were now full color though limited to somewhat drab military colors such as brown, grey, white, green, and blue.

This all seemed a bit more official, though a part of him also felt it was a bit anticlimactic after the whole rearranging the world process he just went through.

"So how was it, Initiate? Quite the thrill, yes?" Sasha asked.

Before he could answer, Chief piped up. *"I took the liberty of monitoring his vitals while it was going down. My initial readings come out as 'scared shitless' but perhaps 'petrified stupid' would be more accurate, after further study."*

"I'm fine." Kaiden grimaced. "Just... It was a bit of a shock, I'll admit."

"Oh, it is always a fascinating experience the first time around," Laurie gushed. "Don't worry, though. We don't generally transfer maps in the middle of a test or exercise. There's no need to. However, I recommend getting used to it for personal training. It allows you to get more done."

"Noted," Kaiden acknowledged as he walked around the bay. "So, where do I start?"

"Usually with the basic personality test, but we'll save that for last considering the circumstances," Sasha explained. "My guess is that you'd probably like to get a little energy out of your system."

"I wouldn't say no." Kaiden chuckled as he walked over to what seemed to be the shooting area. He stood in front of a dividing wall that separated him from a line of featureless target dummies.

"Loading the firearms test," Laurie stated. Kaiden saw all the lights dim around him except for those above the shooting range. The target dummies disappeared, and a gun cabinet on the wall vanished before reappearing beside him.

Kaiden examined it cautiously. He looked at the door and saw no lock on the handle, so reached down and tugged at it, and it simply snapped open. He exhaled in relief. Something was easy going, for once.

The locker was completely empty. "You know, not to try to one-up the teachers or anything, but a firearm is usually needed in the firearms test, I would think," he called, turning to look at the ceiling where he assumed the professors were observing him from. "Maybe I'm naïve, but it's pretty traditional."

"You are naïve, Initiate. Just not about this," Sasha assured him. "Take another look."

Kaiden obliged and saw five lights form into different shapes. Then, in a brief flash, he saw the five lights become five different pistols—ones he had never really seen before.

He ran his hand briefly over all of them. They felt real—the coarse grips, the dense weight, the thermal lining, and exhaust nozzles on the plasma models. He picked one up and looked it over, studying the silver body and black notches on the tip of the barrel. His gaze paused on a glowing circle on the back of the chamber. He frowned and focused until he found a latch on either side of the muzzle. Tentatively, he pressed them down and drew them back. The top sprung open, and he saw arc-jumpers and a feeder. This was an electromagnetic-model. It delivered a hell of a punch in firing speed and rate, along with a kick that could send the gun rocketing back into your face if you weren't careful.

Of course, they were also technically fake, being digital and all.

He closed the compartment and looked the weapon over again. It looked like a Fulgora model, made by Tera Sovereign Arms, a damn expensive piece on the black market. Anyone who had one certainly made a statement.

If you missed, you would probably be shot dead before you lined up another shot considering how long it took to prime, but those were your dice to roll.

However, when he examined it more closely, he noticed that there were small differences between this gun and the one he was familiar with. The color scheme, extra exhaust ports, and the arc-jumpers seemed to be more streamlined, and looking at the glowing circle on the back, it seemed you could choose how much power you had behind the shot. That certainly wasn't an option with the Fulgora.

"What is this?" Kaiden asked, expecting a reply from his professors, but he saw a stream of white cover the gun and then a box pop up on his display. It seemed to be a summary of the pistol's make and model, a Thunderbird-M3 created by Nexus Security Development Division.

Kaiden snorted. Security was probably right. Making sure that whoever was on the receiving end would be plowed into the wall was a safe bet for defense.

"These are the five sidearms we offer at the Academy. They were created in-house by some of our best and brightest, along with some help from contracted sources. All initiates train with a variety of weapons and arms, but these pistols will be your most consistent companions during your training in the Animus," Sasha noted.

"Just in the Animus?" Kaiden said with a slight twinge

of sadness. "Seems a waste, honestly. This place is cool and all, but how can you truly experience the feeling and power of a gun in VR?"

He heard a low chuckle. Surprisingly, it sounded like it came from Laurie. "Try it out, Kaiden," he suggested.

Kaiden saw one of the target dummies reappear down the firing range. He snapped his arm toward the target, centering his view on its chest with his arm relaxed but grip tight.

He exhaled evenly as he pulled the trigger. The pistol vibrated, and the circle filled slowly with a bright blue light in a counter-clockwise fashion.

As it drew closer to filling up, he felt the gun shake and feel heavier. He placed his other hand slowly over the one on the gun and braced himself. When it reached the pinnacle, he released the trigger and saw a flash along with a crack like lightning. He moved his head slightly to the left as the gun and his arms snapped back and over his shoulder. His feet slipped back before he balanced himself and looked ahead at the dummy.

It had flown at least ten feet, colliding with a wall at the end of the range. Its chest looked like it had evaporated. Everything from its left pectoral to its shoulder and upper arm had disappeared, and what remained of the arm lay a few feet in front of the dummy, a sizzling mess.

"Sweet and sour Satan! What the hell was that?"

"That would be the real feeling of firing a Thunderbird at full power." Laurie chuckled.

"It is a heavy pistol, created in part by improving on the initial build of the Fulgora model by Tera Sovereign Arms. We acquired some of their schematics in exchange for some contracts with recently graduated soldiers and engineers…along with a considerable fee," Sasha added casually.

"Yeah, I thought it might have been a modded version." Kaiden groaned as he placed the gun back into the cabinet and rubbed his forearms.

"Much more so, but we can talk shop later," Sasha stated. "Please take a look at the supplied weapons. Professor Laurie will load in some more targets if you wish to practice or get a feel for the individual characteristics of each pistol, but you will choose one of the five and take the test with the chosen gun."

"I gotcha." Kaiden grunted, looking at the other pistols. "Chief, scan the rest would ya?"

"On it. Don't just go for the shiniest one," Chief cautioned sarcastically.

Kaiden shook his head as he saw each gun light up briefly before four other boxes of information popped open in his display.

He perused them, picking each pistol up to take a look as the other boxes shrank and the corresponding box enlarged and pointed out each feature of the selected gun.

The first one, a black-and-grey hand cannon, was bigger than even the Thunderbird yet slightly lighter. The model name read Black Dog. It was meant for close quarters and fired metal shrapnel in wide bursts with a large magazine that allowed for up to eight shots before needing to reload.

Kaiden placed it back in the cabinet. He wasn't a fan of close quarters combat if he could help it and firing this thing from a considerable distance would probably be more useless than simply chucking jars of bees at his opponent.

Next up was the Yokai, a slim model in pure black aluminum and polymer. Kaiden guessed by the name and style that it would be based on a Japanese model. It was incredibly light and had a narrow line of sight. He pointed the gun toward the firing range, and another dummy materialized. Unhurried, he squeezed the trigger and let go, and he barely heard a thing before he saw a small hole appear on the dummy. From this distance, it didn't seem to be very deep.

He pressed the trigger again, aiming at the head. This time, he heard a very quiet whir and felt as if something in the gun was spinning. Another hole appeared right where the dummy's mouth would have been. He'd heard little more than a slight whoosh as the bullet left the barrel.

He examined the weapon critically. A magnetic model meant for stealth, it was interesting but also not his thing. The charge up and impact was not something he wanted to bother with in the middle of a firefight.

The Phoenix was more of a submachine gun, light with a white-and-red color scheme. He pointed toward the range again, and another dummy popped up. His action calm and measured, he pulled the trigger and saw holes pepper the dummy in rapid succession. He paused, then looked at the gun. His display now highlighted a switch just above the trigger.

He flipped it before shooting the dummy again, and bullets flew as if they had tracers on them. When he saw the dummy burst into flame, he gave an approving whistle.

However, he could feel the gun heating up way faster

than it should, and when he examined it again, he noticed the thermal lining on the body. He looked over the info and saw that it used ignition clips instead of energy or bullets. He growled in annoyance. Ignition clips were somehow the best and worst of two worlds. You could fire more ammo than a gun that used bullets and energy-based weapons had more punch, but they also had the nasty habit of overheating, either becoming temporarily useless while they cooled down, or they simply exploded.

Can't reload a hand, can you?

He sighed as he placed it back in the cabinet. *Why are all the cool guns such a pain in the ass?*

The final gun, a Siren, was energy-based. It looked to be more of a stun gun, better used against robotics and tech than human mercs or the like—maybe good against aliens? He didn't feel much like taking a biology course.

"These are all specialist weapons," Kaiden called. "I mean, they look good, feel good, got some nifty abilities and all, but don't you have somethin' a little more…I don't know, classic?"

"Well, we do train specialists here at Nexus," Sasha reminded him. "However, I see your point. We may have something."

Kaiden saw the guns in the cabinet disappear to be replaced by a single pistol—black and copper with a long barrel and a curved grip and trigger. He picked it up and examined it.

"Debonair." He smiled. The name was certainly better. It looked like a rapid single-shooter. Aim, then pull the trigger. It was all up to you how many you killed and whether you were still standing.

"It was one of our options for a few years, but it quickly grew obsolete in the eyes of our students and development teams. It's energy-based with a strong piercing shot but only fires as fast as you can pull the trigger and doesn't have a lot of stopping power or shielding damage. Unless you can hit the same target multiple times, of course."

Kaiden smiled. It worked for him.

"Give me a few targets," Kaiden requested. The bullet-riddled dummies disappeared and were replaced by five new ones in a V formation.

He pointed to the one furthest to the left, exhaled, then pulled the trigger.

It felt as if he'd hardly touched it when it fired, sending a streak of heat from the barrel into the chest of the dummy, dead center.

Oh, *hell* yes.

He shot quickly down the line; one to the head, then the chest and appendages, adjusting to the firing speed and recoil. The gun was brisk, accurate, and left a hole. The guys who wrote this thing off must have been spoiled as hell.

"I'll take it," Kaiden exclaimed, pointing the gun to the ground as he looked over to see the bullet-riddled dummies disappear.

"Well, congratulations. I'll add it to your academy profile for future use," Laurie confirmed. "Now then, before we begin the test proper, I need to try something first. Hold still, would you."

"I thought you said we weren't doing any more of that map swapping stuff." Kaiden sighed, his belligerence returning now that the gunplay was over for the moment.

"We're not. I merely need to test the damage output. It's more difficult to hit a moving target, obviously," Laurie explained.

"I see… Wait, am I the—" Before he finished his question, Kaiden felt a searing pain in his chest as he was knocked to the ground, coughing and sputtering as he rolled behind the cabinet and scrambled to his knees.

"Asshole!" He growled his fury.

"That seems sufficient, although I suppose I should ask…" Laurie mused. "Is it real enough for you, Kaiden?"

"Yeah, no, it's great," he snapped back.

"Very well, let us begin," Sasha instructed.

Kaiden looked out from behind the cabinet and saw a number of faceless, humanoid beings materialize in the bay. They were all different colors—white, black, red, blue, and yellow. Some held guns while others had melee weapons, and some held nothing at all.

"The test will begin in thirty seconds. Each target is worth a certain number of points depending upon weapon, shots required to destroy them, and ability. Your final score will depend on your points earned, and for every hit you take, you will have points deducted." Sasha's voice droned the instructions without apparent emotion.

Kaiden saw a red number '30' appear overhead in the ceiling and begin to count down.

"I hope you're ready," Sasha cautioned.

Kaiden's smile returned as he faced down his targets, raising Debonair with a measured movement. "Damn straight."

CHAPTER TEN

Kaiden dove behind a low wall, barely dodging a blast of electricity fired at him from above. Flying bots, yet another thing he was not prepared for.

Still, that only made two things out of a potentially infinite number of possibilities to be prepared for.

Still looking good.

He peered briefly around the wall, sighting on two bots which climbed a stack of boxes to try to reach higher ground. They stood right out in the open.

He ducked out, aimed, and pulled the trigger twice. With one hit in the head and the other through the neck, both disappeared. *If you wanna be that dumb, I'll be happy to take the free points.*

Of course, he realized he was trash-talking artificial opponents that probably couldn't register insults at all.

"Die, you pale meat-sack." Kaiden heard another bot yell at him in a stilted voice, and he looked over to see one aiming a rifle barrel at his head from a few feet away.

Instinct took over. He leaped down and back, firing a shot that pierced its knee. It fell as he placed two more shots into its chest, then it vanished.

"Pale? I'm not pale!" Kaiden huffed.

"That's what you're focusing on?" Chief jeered.

Kaiden looked around. "Makes me sound like I'm sickly or something."

"He also called you a meat-sack."

"Eh, I've seen Sci-Fi. That's kinda basic for droids and the like, right?" Kaiden asked, drawing the top of his gun back to reveal a larger exhaust vent. He let it go, and it snapped back into place after it cooled a bit.

"Still disgraceful, though. On your left, up high," Chief warned, his tone suddenly brisk.

Kaiden looked back to see the three smaller flying creatures from before. He took off in the direction of a pillar. Security walls and reinforced barriers popped up throughout the bay, but they also seemed to disappear or deactivate every so often while the pillars had remained so far. They were the safer bet.

Even among all the chaos and gunfire, he could hear the static discharge as the flying bots' guns charged up. He looked back to see if he could take a quick shot. The flying group broke out of formation, seemingly anticipating the possibility, but he saw his chance. Kaiden reached back and aimed a bit further to the left of one of the disengaging flyers. He squeezed the trigger, and the bullet intercepted the flyer as it tried to bank out.

Yes. He smiled as he leaped out of the way of the blasts from the other two and behind the pillar. He slumped down as they flew by and prepared to fire as they circled around.

"Hey, watching you get shot at is fun and all, but mind if I get in on the action here?"

"Sure. What are you going to do? Blink furiously at them?"

"Tell me what you think of this, smartass." With that, Kaiden saw Chief's avatar disappear.

"Did...did he just bail on me?" he asked, perplexed.

So much for a faithful companion.

The hum of the flyer's electric gun snapped him back. Dammit, he'd let himself get distracted. However, as he went to realign his shot, he saw the flyer on the right slam itself into the other, knocking it out of the way as it fired, missing Kaiden. Then it turned its own gun and blasted itself into oblivion.

"What?"

"Pretty bitchin' right?" Chief asked gleefully, his avatar reappearing on display with a new tab of functions.

"Where'd you go? What's onscreen?"

"Look to your left."

Kaiden did, seeing the flyer hovering right next to him. He jumped up quickly before realizing it wasn't following him or charging its gun.

"The dandy professor loaded these things up as drones, which means they have a connection I can jump into," Chief proclaimed proudly. *"All simulated, of course."*

"Huh...that actually is pretty cool," Kaiden admitted. "I would have thought he would have blocked that."

"No need to, typically, remember? Not just anyone can do what I can," the EI bragged.

"Technically, it's because of the special device in my skull, not just you," Kaiden reminded him.

"Not that you remembered, you trigger-happy dunce."

"Dammit." He sighed. "Okay, I'll give you that." Kaiden took refuge behind the pillar again.

"So, what do ya got for me?"

Kaiden looked back. He didn't see any more flyers, but the soldiers were loaded in at a much more rapid pace and quickly made their way over to him. He looked at the board—he still had more than three minutes to go.

Plenty of time for extra points.

"You could be bait."

"Sorry, forgot a wig."

"Then you go get 'em, buddy," Kaiden suggested dryly.

"Semper fi, motherfuckers!" Chief bellowed as he flew off, blasts of electricity following in his wake.

Kaiden moved out from his hiding spot and dashed across the room, firing shots along the way. The soldiers were now a massed rainbow-colored group. They seemed to have stronger weapons than him, but they now had a distraction to deal with.

He continued to fire as he saw a barrier appear about twenty yards away. Two minutes and fifty seconds left on the clock. Three shots were immediately followed by three dead grunts. Good to see he hadn't gotten rusty.

"Chief, how ya doin'?" Kaiden asked and received a cacophony of curses, yells, and excited exclamations in response. "Double back. They're all making a beeline this way."

"Gotcha. Like shooting anthropomorphic skittles over here!" Chief hooted. Kaiden then heard a loud bang and another

zap. *"Son of a bitch. Flyers are back. They are upgraded and very pissed."*

"Can't you just cast yourself into one of them?" Kaiden questioned, watching as Chief flew back into range with a trio of V-shaped flyers speeding after him like frenzied sharks chasing a maimed barracuda.

"Nah, they're firewalled this time. I guess the professor patched that. I don't suppose you know how to hack, do ya?"

"Trigger-happy moron, remember?"

"Oh, then that gives us a new option. Shoot *them, you* moron," Chief roared, his orb glowing red in Kaiden's display.

"Say please sometimes. It's like you don't care about my feelings anymore," he replied sarcastically.

Kaiden whipped around and fired at the flying bots. He was able to graze a couple, but they weaved between his shots. Chief was right. These were an upgrade. He saw the barrier that was protecting him begin to vanish and grunted in annoyance.

"Chief, fly past me and keep steady. I'll get them from behind."

"Gotcha," the EI acknowledged. He cut hard to the left and began to serpentine to avoid more shots from the other flyers.

Kaiden ran off, rolling and dodging between shots from the now distracted ground bots. Another wall loomed a few feet ahead and he rolled behind it but felt a shot make contact with his calf. He hissed in pain. Simulated or not, it felt like fire just tore through his leg.

He saw Chief and his pursuers fly past, rolled onto his back, and steadied his aim.

"Drop out of the air on my mark, then retreat," Kaiden ordered. He exhaled as he lined up his targets.

"Mark!" he yelled. Chief's flying bot deactivated briefly and dropped out of the air like a brick before reactivating and speeding in the opposite direction of the enemy flyers. Kaiden pressed rapidly down on the trigger, landing multiple shots on the flyers. Two evaporated, and the remaining one banked left.

It circled around and gunned for him. It streamed smoke but remained airborne. Kaiden cursed and tried to fire, only to hear the buzzing error alert from his pistol. It had overheated. With a loud expletive, he opened the exhaust vent, but he knew there wasn't enough time. He was gonna take some shots before the gun cooled.

"Oh, I got this bastard," Chief exclaimed. An electric surge crashed into the remaining flyer as Chief flew past. The bot stalled and then crashed into the ground and evaporated.

"Damn. Nice shootin', Chief," Kaiden called.

"Heh, I just showed that son of a—" Kaiden heard a loud bang, and Chief's avatar bounced around on the screen. *"Biiittttccchh!"* it cried as Kaiden heard the sound of metal crashing into the ground in the distance and a small explosion.

Kaiden saw Chief flash between a rage-fueled red, a disgusted green, and a somber gray.

"You flew straight into the mob, didn't ya?"

"I'm flying with one eye. My depth perception is shit," Chief retorted.

Kaiden couldn't help but chuckle. He looked over and saw that there were only four seconds left. "It's all good,

Chief. You were pretty badass there for about three seconds."

A loud buzzer went off. Kaiden closed the exhaust vent on his gun as the remaining bots dissipated. He walked out into the center of the bay, limping slightly, though he was certainly healing faster than he would in reality.

It still stung like a sonofabitch.

"Nice job, Kaiden my boy," Laurie remarked cheerfully. "An excellent use of your EI's capabilities, I must say."

"It was actually Chief's idea. I hadn't considered it," Kaiden admitted.

"It is a wonderful thing, the partnership between an initiate and their EI," Laurie mused poetically.

"Not exactly intended, however," Sasha noted. "This was supposed to be a test of your firing and survival skills in their natural state."

"I showed plenty." Kaiden huffed his only slightly defensive disapproval. "Besides, we're supposed to use our EIs here. I thought that was the point."

"You are, but this evaluation test was supposed to create a baseline of your normal abilities," Sasha explained.

"Oh, come off it, Commander." Laurie sighed. "Like you said, this was a test of survival as well as weapon skills. The initiate simply used all tools at his disposal to create the best scenario in his favor. There's nothing negative about that."

"I'm not in disagreement, but considering the circumstances, I have to reconfigure his final score considering the tools used," Sasha announced.

"Do what you have to." Kaiden yawned. "Chief just

made this a bit more fun. I think my skills speak for themselves."

"As long as you understand, please proceed to the designated room for the profession exam," Sasha said.

Kaiden heard the 'click' of a door unlocking and turned to see lights turning on behind a window pane and a green light glow over the entrance to the room. He walked over to it casually after rubbing his leg briefly, stretching his arms along the way.

"Surprised you didn't pipe in there," he said in a hushed voice.

"Eh, didn't feel like bickering. If they didn't want to give me my due, screw 'em. But I gotta give my props—gotta crack shot as my partner. That'll be handy,"

"So, I'm a partner now? I'm not a host anymore?"

"Well, it ain't that pretty in here and the food bites, so you don't exactly make a great one, anyway."

"I only break out the good stuff for the classy people," Kaiden jested.

"So what, you want to get a bowtie or somethin'?"

He laughed. "Kinda hard to see you as a badass with a bowtie."

"Ah, to hell with ya. I'd rock that," Chief gloated, his hue changing to an amused pink.

Kaiden's smile widened, and he released a relaxed sigh as he drew closer to the room. "Guess there's nothing you can tell me about the exam, huh?"

"About a profession exam? Nah, it's not like a test of skills or something. It's like a questionnaire and a few simulations to see how you would handle different situations. Even if there was a real exam, they would probably tune me out anyway, considering

how commander/professor buzzkill just got all uppity," Chief surmised, shaking his body back and forth onscreen in a weary manner.

"I getcha." Kaiden nodded. "Guess I'll just have to see what happens. It's not like I have anything else to worry about. I was probably just gonna end up a grunt anyway. The best damn grunt on the planet, *sure*, but still a grunt."

"What about that thing that girl said?" Chief asked. *"Chiyo? She said that people answer how they feel they should, not how they want to or something like that? Maybe think outside the micro-brain on this, and you might get something better than spare blood for a career,"* Chief suggested. *"Just don't go on autopilot like you did when you installed me, and you'll be fine."*

"You ever gonna let that go?" Kaiden asked.

"Hell no." Chief chuckled. *"But hey, I'll admit, it ain't startin' to feel like too much of a slog now."*

"Well, glad to see ya come around."

"Keep this up, and I might even invite you to my next barbeque."

"What the hell are you doing in my head?"

"Oh, look, you're here. Best of luck and all that," Chief gibed before fading out.

"I can still see you in my HUD," Kaiden said before the avatar disappeared. "Cheeky bastard." He shook his head as he opened the door to the room.

A lone chair stood on a circular pad in the middle of the room. Kaiden walked over to it. "I'm here, what's next?"

"A moment, Kaiden. Sasha is finishing up tallying your score from the firearms test," Laurie said.

"Got it, but do I just twiddle my thumbs or what?"

"You can go ahead and take a seat. I'm sure he's almost ready."

Kaiden obliged, sat down in the chair, and leaned back. He pondered Chiyo's words. Should he answer like he wanted to? He tried to make sense of the words. Why shouldn't he simply go with his experience? He was good at shooting, fighting, and general violence, sure, and he had some other basic skills, but the combination probably wouldn't turn heads or anything, even outside this place.

He wasn't a hacker. Most of his engineering knowledge was mechanical rather than technological, but maybe that could be something? He thought back to the Tsuna he had met at the train station, Geno. He wondered if he cared what others thought he was supposed to do, or if something like that was even a factor to them. Maybe stressing about something like this was a completely foreign idea to them, or maybe they were like ants or something and had a job right out of the womb.

Then he began to wonder if that was how the Tsuna were born in the first place and realized he was getting off track.

"Initiate Jericho." Sasha's voice intruded, pulling Kaiden from his daze.

"Howdy, Commander Sasha."

"It is Professor here."

"The only other professor I know so far is Laurie. It's giving me mental whiplash to think of you both that way."

"I…hmm, I suppose it is not technically inaccurate. I would prefer to differentiate myself from him in this case."

"You know I can hear the both of you," Laurie muttered.

"Nothing against you, Prof, just a difference in character and esteem," Kaiden pointed out reasonably.

"Ah, but of course. The, ahem, *commander* is a good man, but he is leagues apart from myself in terms of wit and glamour."

"Yeah, of course." Kaiden resisted the urge to snicker at the unabashed vanity.

"We are prepared to begin the professional evaluation part of the exam. You will answer an assortment of questions with regard to your personality, preferences, and skillset, along with a number of opinion-based questions that you are to answer in line with your own views and values. The exam will end with a handful of different scenarios that will be created according to potential professions garnered from the previous answers you gave, so make sure to consider all options carefully," Sasha explained.

"Yeah, I gotcha," Kaiden acknowledged.

"Also, the EI will not be allowed to help you in any manner during this exam...not that the EI should tell you what to do."

"If the EI did try to manipulate him, that would be rather a concern," Laurie admitted.

"How's that?" Kaiden asked

"Are you ready, Initiate?"

He sat back and folded his arms. "Gotcha, let's do it."

CHAPTER ELEVEN

"Does *emotional music have a significant effect on you?*" a robotic female voice asked, yet another of the seemingly hundreds of questions Kaiden had answered thus far.

Dear God, this was dull.

"Why yes, *Ode to Joy* always gets my lions a-shakin'," he responded, a definite sneer in his tone.

"Understood. Registering answer as 'yes.' Other response is unnecessary."

"My ass."

"Please await next question."

Kaiden groaned as he slumped back into the chair. It seemed like he had been answering these questions for ages. More than an hour, at least, though it could've been ten, or even a couple of days or weeks. He couldn't see a clock.

"Do you enjoy activities of your own choosing?"

Were they just fucking with him at this point?

"I only obey the commands of great penguin gods of the

frozen north. Enjoyment is unnecessary," he jeered, his voice lowering to a dull monotone.

"Please answer in the positive or negative."

"Please answer my prayers and kill me," Kaiden droned.

"Initiate Kaiden, please take this seriously. I told you at the beginning that answering all questions truthfully will help in deciding not only the final scenarios of the exam, but potential paths to consider for the rest of your tenure here," Sasha ordered, his tone crisp and no-nonsense.

"What does this have to do with anything? The first handful seemed to make sense. Now, I just feel like I'm on some quack's big chair."

"You are in the psychiatric portion of the test. This is simply to obtain a more solid reading of your personality for your profile."

"Are you telling me everybody has to go through this?"

"No, others didn't tamper with their prior permanent record."

"This is starting to feel like discrimination."

"Perhaps. Maybe counselor Mya had the incorrect information. I can call up the police divisions in Texas. Perhaps they wouldn't mind taking a look to see if everything is accurate."

"I often partake in activities I find enjoyable, yes."

"Understood, loading next question." The computer acknowledged his capitulation with not even a slight hesitation.

"Very good. You are just past half complete, so keep it up," Sasha said.

Kaiden fumed and began to wonder if it was possible to somehow knock himself out in virtual reality.

"Questionnaire finished. Loading mission scenarios."

Kaiden almost felt like doing a twirl. He was finally done with all the hum-drum questions. He could see the light at the end of the tunnel.

Assuming, of course, that whatever those scenarios were didn't take an eternity, either.

"Well done, Initiate." Sasha congratulated him with brisk approval. "The system will load three predetermined scenarios. You have only your wits and personal knowledge at your disposal to find a solution to the problem set out before you. There are multiple options and no single right answer."

"I gotcha… Wait, predetermined? I thought you said that the questions helped decide the final scenarios or whatever?"

"To some extent, sure, but for SCs, what they are brought in for typically determines the grouping they fall into. The questionnaire narrows the field down slightly."

"What the hell? Why did I have to go through all that?"

"I told you before, we had to make corrections to your profile. Mya found most of what could be found of your real history, but other things were unaccounted for, so we simply decided this would be the easiest option," Sasha explained.

Kaiden could swear he could feel the onset of an aneurysm. "So what, I'm here to get a handle on my statistics?"

"No, that's what we're here for. You're here to see what profession and skills you may wish to pursue, along with calibrating the Animus for your unique situation, of course."

"You couldn't just ask me?"

"This would provide more accurate measures," Sasha confided. "Plus, would you have taken it seriously if we didn't do it under the guise of it being criteria for enrollment?"

"Under the… Wait, I don't need to be here?" Kaiden's mind began to fizzle, and he ground his teeth.

"All special cases need to come here, my boy. Other initiates come through to get a better understanding of their potential career paths and what skills they should practice or consider during their stay. I mean, did you really think someone coming here as a mechanic or broker would also need to be a skilled marksman?" Laurie trilled a short laugh. "Could you imagine? Training all your life to be an EI technician, and suddenly, someone thrusts a rifle in your hands?"

"Wait, you haven't learned how to shoot a gun? Even after being here for like a decade?" Kaiden asked incredulously.

"I have robots for dirty work. Besides, I helped design that barrier around the school for good reason."

Kaiden could feel his eye twitch. He recalled his conversation with Chiyo. She never mentioned having to do this. Instead, it had sounded like she came there knowing what she was going to do… Then that meant—

"So was I getting shot at for kicks?"

"No, for practice and combat readings. I wouldn't put too fine a point on it. You will be fired at plenty as your time goes on," Sasha stated.

"Don't be so fidgety, Kaiden. You'll pop a blood vessel. Besides, most who come here do so to work in combat fields anyway, just in varying capacities."

"I...I just... I thought you people were supposed to be professional."

"Oh, we are. Very professional," Sasha responded, each word drilling into Kaiden's head. "One thing you will learn, along with every student here, is that professionalism is about getting the job done, not worrying about how you look while doing it. Or even the methods, for that matter."

Kaiden wanted to snap back a sharp retort, but as the last of Sasha's words sank in, he decided to keep it to himself.

"How did I get myself into this?" he wondered aloud.

"That would be me if you recall." Sasha sounded amused.

"Ah...right, yeah, thanks for that."

"You say that sarcastically now, but I was not trying to fool you during our first meeting, Initiate Kaiden. Not everyone gets this opportunity. I would make a wager that by the end of this year, you will see the fruits of your labor and thank me sincerely."

Kaiden snorted. "What makes you so confident?"

"The same thing that made you stay when you were told the debt you would accrue, the same thing that gave you the confidence to allow Professor Laurie put that implant in your skull just to get an edge, and the same thing that stops you from demanding we terminate the exam you now seem to believe is pointless." Sasha paused for a moment, letting the words hang briefly in the air. "The thing that drives you in your life that tells you there is something to be gained here. What your life could be entices you more than simply going back to how things were."

Kaiden pondered this for a moment, looking at the blank screen in front of him as he brushed against the tattoo on his arm underneath his shirt. He recalled his time back in the Dead-Eyes. He'd had purpose there. That was why he gave it his all, why he learned and adapted and became the best shot and fighter he could be.

He had a real purpose back when he could hear the cheerful voices of his friends after a successful job, the camaraderie whenever they mourned a loss together, and the confidence of going into the fray with the baddest bastards in Texas.

He didn't have that now.

Sasha continued, "This academy must seem like no more than a business to you, Kaiden. I will admit that certain evils must exist to keep the world turning, as it were. However, I would not be here if it were so clinical. Professor Laurie would not be here if there were no opportunities to advance his work and see it blossom almost immediately."

Kaiden gripped his arm, tapping his finger on the taut muscle.

"If it means anything, I did not simply offer you admission because I could see you knew how to make a fist. You took on a group of thugs to help a person you did not know, and you beat them with focus and ease, not simply to fight."

"I was trying to get a job as a bouncer. It seemed like a good show," Kaiden admitted half-heartedly.

"Yet you still chose this over a guaranteed job."

"Yeah, well, that guy gave me his chip, hyped it up, you needed bodies, and it seemed like it could be interesting. Besides, it's starting to seem like I'm nothing more than another cog in y'all's machine."

"For what it's worth, I would have offered you my recommendation without Initiate Hargrove handing you his chip," Sasha said. "We may not know each other all that well, but if you give me any credit at all, make it that I am not a person of blind charity."

Kaiden stopped tapping his finger and exhaled, rocking his head left and right until he heard a few pops. "This got real rather quick."

"It always has been. You're simply catching up."

Kaiden smirked. "I guess, from a certain point of view, you're right. If nothing else, I'd say you're pretty good with words."

"I'm a commander, I have to be."

"Ah, dammit. I guess I'll just have to get used to things being a little nutty around here. Start the scenarios."

"Right away," Laurie shouted.

Though Kaiden couldn't see him, he heard a rustle and an affirmative grunt, which sounded like Sasha had given his approval. "Your first two scenarios have no time limit, but the longer you go on, the more it will affect your final score."

"This for real or another score for giggles?"

"Always real, Initiate. If you're asking whether there's

some sort of consequence, I can ask the chefs in the cafeteria to give you an extra cookie if you do well."

"Ha-ha, smartass."

"Respect the rank, Initiate," Sasha reminded him. "Your final question will have a five-minute time limit, so be prepared. Starting in three…two…one…"

The board in front of Kaiden flashed to life again. He saw a holographic alleyway appear, revealing a wire-framed figure holding another in front of it with a gun to its head.

"Scenario: An assailant that you have tracked down has taken a hostage. Your gun is drawn, but it threatens to kill the hostage unless you back away. What do you do?"

Kaiden thought for a moment. "Do I gotta bring him in alive?"

"Unnecessary."

Kaiden studied the image. "It's easy then. Move the gun down as if you're gonna put it away, then angle the shot just above the hostage's shoulder and fire. It will clip them but won't be too severe, and it'll hit the shooter dead center in the head, a relatively clean kill.

"Possible faults: Reaction time of shooter, precision of shot, performing this action in quick succession. Demonstration needed."

The image grew and expanded until it filled the room, Kaiden was now ten yards away from the image of the shooter. His gun, Debonair, appeared in his right hand.

"New fault: Position of shooter and assailant. Assailant's head is over hostage's right shoulder, shooter is left-handed."

"Now I'm starting to see why you guys need better info," Kaiden mused. The figures began to move, indicating the beginning of the demonstration. He made as if to move his gun down and quickly flicked his wrist, shifting the gun to his left hand. In one motion, he aimed and fired. The shot sliced into the hostage's shoulder then pierced the assailant's head. The figure went limp and the hostage moved away, holding its shoulder.

"I'm ambidextrous," Kaiden said with a confident smirk, Debonair evaporating in his hand.

"Demonstration complete, answer proven. Adding new info into data banks. Loading next scenario."

The map shrank again, this time changing to what seemed to be the floor of an office building. The wire-frames turned red and separated into four figures in a group. Then two yellow-colored wire-frames appeared across the hall, barricaded in a room. A final blue-colored wire-frame was just outside the room, pressed against the wall.

"Scenario: A terrorist group has infiltrated a server farm. Two are in heavy armor with heavy weapons. You are represented by the blue figure; the yellow figures are civilians. How do you eliminate the terrorists while saving the civilians?"

"I gotta keep the civilians safe? That's inconvenient."

"To clarify, the primary objective is to eliminate the terrorists. The civilians are expendable."

"Well, that's way more convenient," Kaiden chirped. "But I'm guessing I would be docked points if they die?"

"Correct."

"Then they're lucky I'm competitive…" Kaiden studied the map. He could probably take out the two without armor easily. There wasn't a lot of room to maneuver, so if the two heavy terrorists had explosives or miniguns, he was screwed—or the civilians would be, at least, if they started shooting wildly.

He looked a little more closely at the room, focusing his attention on the details. The terrorists were in the server bay, while the civilians seemed to be in an adjacent area—maybe another hallway that was barricaded due to lockdown?

He recalled talking to one of the techies in the Dead-Eyes. They were preparing to infiltrate a server farm themselves, trying to get access to the offshore accounts of a conglomerate head for some easy cash. He remembered that the techie was insistent that they only use archaic weapons with real bullets because of something to do with the fire system.

It clicked "Do I got my gun on me? Debonair?"

"For this scenario, yes."

"Then I would go into the room with the civilians, firing at the ceiling before I closed and locked the door. The fire safety system would activate and drain all the air out of the room, suffocating the terrorists."

"Understood. Solution plausible and accepted. Beginning final scenario."

Kaiden cracked his knuckles. He was enjoying this.

The map changed again. This time, a long hallway stretched before him with two paths cutting across it. On one side stood six red figures, and on the other, four blue figures with one slumped over.

"Final Scenario: You and a team of three other soldiers are dealing with an opposing force. One of your team is injured. They will not survive without medical assistance, but they are too weak to administer it themselves. They require the help of one

of the other team members. The primary objective is the elimination of the opposing force."

Kaiden fists balled tightly. This was…uncomfortably real.

"You have five minutes to give your answer, beginning now."

He looked over the scene quickly, searching for insight. There didn't seem to be any shafts for them to climb through. The injured teammate was in the opposite corridor to the others, meaning that if one wanted to help, they would be in the opponent's line of sight, even if only for a second or two.

He looked at the opposing side. They were all focused down the one hallway. To flank them using the opposite hallway was the easiest and obvious option, but if they all followed that route, the enemy would probably catch on quickly and simply gun them down when they moved around the corner, not to mention the other teammate dying.

One of them could lay covering fire so another could help the wounded teammate…then perhaps two could try to get down the second hallway? That would leave the wounded teammate and whoever helped them vulnerable, plus the enemy could still catch on.

So, one helps the wounded, one goes around, and the other faces them down the main path…he wouldn't wanna be that guy.

"You weren't that guy," he muttered, then caught himself. He hadn't even realized he was talking. His breath hitched as he opened and closed his fist. "Make the map bigger. I'm going to do another demonstration."

"Confirmed. One minute and twenty-two seconds left."

The map encompassed the room again. The hallway was a little smaller than it seemed to look from an isometric view. Kaiden took the place of one of the figures against the wall, Debonair reappearing in his hand.

"Please explain the plan to commence the demonstration."

"I will lay covering fire so the teammate right behind me can go and help the wounded one. They will move them away, and the last teammate will circle around, using the empty hallway, and finish off the remaining opponents while I keep their attention."

"Confirmed. Reenacting."

Kaiden hissed his instinctive alarm as simulated gunfire zipped past him. Holding his breath, he fired blindly around the corner, then leaned out slightly to fire quick shots down the hall. He made two solid hits and seemed to graze another. They weren't down, but it stalled the firing for the moment. He motioned for the teammate to hurry over. They rolled past him and began helping the wounded one.

The last teammate turned the corner into the empty hall. Kaiden vented his gun for a moment and turned the corner, firing rapidly at the enemy. He had to keep their attention if this was going to work—he couldn't simply hole up around the corner.

Just a few moments, that was all that was needed. But a lot could happen in only a few moments.

He continued to fire, saw two fall dead, and another collapsed but reached for a pistol on its belt. With another shot to the throat, it slumped over. In the same instant, he felt an impact in his right shoulder and cursed. He hadn't paid attention and now saw a rifle peek out from behind the corner. The bullet had hit him in his shooting arm.

Kaiden dropped down and rolled to the side, switching the gun to his left hand at the same time. He fired and knocked down the rifleman, but not before it got off another shot, and he cursed again as he felt a searing pain in his leg. Angry now, he looked up to see the remaining two now moving in for the kill.

He reached up and fired two shots. The first grazed the head of one and hit the arm of the other, but Kaiden couldn't focus. He tried for another shot but heard the error noise of his gun overheating. Frantic, he willed himself to move his arm to open the exhaust vent. *Dammit.* The final gunman loomed over him, the weapon raised as it prepared to shoot. Kaiden saw the opponent behind it collapse and saw the blue frame of his teammate turn and prepare to fire as the final opponent began to pull down on the trigger.

Then his vision went white.

CHAPTER TWELVE

Kaiden awoke with a gasp, seeing only darkness for a few moments before the familiar low-light of glow strips illuminated his surroundings.

"Welcome back." It took a few moments to register, but the sing-song tone was already unmistakable.

"Hey, Prof." Kaiden groaned. "What happened...where am I?"

"A moment," the professor answered. Kaiden heard a hiss and the clank of metal, and a rectangular shape of light formed in front of him. It peeled off to the side, exposing more light. He winced and shielded his eyes as they adjusted and focused on the silhouette of the professor before him.

"It always takes a moment for one to adjust when coming out of the Animus—a bit like waking from a dream," Laurie reassured him. "You're back to reality. Take a moment to refocus yourself, then step out of the pod."

"Don't I get room service or something?" Kaiden

groaned again as he reached out and grabbed the side of the exit door and hoisted himself out.

"No, but I'll talk to the chefs about that cookie Sasha promised," Laurie said with a chuckle.

"That mean I did all right?" Kaiden asked, his last few moments coming back to his mind. "What happened at the end?"

"You ran out of your allotted time," Sasha stated coming over to them., Laurie helped Kaiden out of the pod. "Interesting choices you made during the exam. That last scenario was a particularly innovative gambit."

"Did I lose or what?"

"Technically, no."

"What do you mean, technically?" Kaiden asked, annoyance creeping back into his voice.

"Since the scenario did not run until it's final completion, the last few moments were calculated by the system. The final opponent would have completed his shot, and you would have died," Sasha admitted nonchalantly.

"That sounds pretty definitive."

"Well, that was not the mission, was it?" the commander hinted

"Sorry?"

"The mission was to defeat all opponents with the extra objective of saving your dying teammate. The teammate was saved, and the final opponent was taken out by your own teammate who had flanked him."

"Wouldn't make it back for celebratory drinks and strippers, though," Kaiden noted with a false grin.

"Perhaps not, but it was an interesting development for me."

"Glad I could be your entertainment for the evening...it is evening, right?"

"Just past seven p.m., or 19:00 or however they say it," Laurie added.

"Your final score was impressive, but we look at more than mere numbers. Statistics help us understand and compartmentalize a student's abilities, talents, and knowledge. However, things like character and ingenuity are a little trickier to narrow down into a few words or put onto graphs," Sasha explained.

"I'm hoping this is leading somewhere. If you're asking me to share my feelings...well, that last psych who tried ended up quitting and becoming a drug dealer," Kaiden said bluntly.

"Noted, but no. I was referring to how you handled the different objectives and saw something I did not expect." The commander paced back and forth, holding the tablet behind him. "In the first scenario, you deftly handled the situation quickly with little damage to the hostage and quick elimination of the target. You didn't think to negotiate, to try to separate the hostage from the assailant, or even take the easier shot of simply shooting through the hostage to get at the target."

"I honestly thought that would have been frowned upon."

"Like I said, multiple options should always be considered. In your favor, however, it would have made you appear careless, or perhaps more careless. You did not ask for more information on the target, nor whether the hostage was a valuable asset or person of interest."

Kaiden opened his mouth to retort that he didn't know

he could or should do that, but then again, he had no problems asking the computer for info when it came to killing targets. He decided to let it lie.

"Even if you decided on your actions because you thought it would go against your final score, you showed quick action and at least a small willingness to consider repercussion, points in your favor."

"Neat, so I do get that cookie?"

"Moving on to the second scenario."

"You're killing me, Commander."

"A rather ingenious answer to the problem you faced. There could have been problems with the enemies that had heavy arms blasting through the doors you and the civilians hid behind, but again, quick action and, in a lockdown situation, probably one of the better options to try to eliminate the targets while keeping the civilians safe and not risking yourself foolhardily."

"That was actually the primary concern there, for me anyway."

"Really now?" Sasha questioned as he turned to look directly at Kaiden. "Because the final scenario would say otherwise."

Kaiden leaned against the pod and crossed his arms. "And what does the final scenario say?"

Sasha stood straight, his face perfectly still and his dark oculars hiding any emotion he might have shown in his eyes. "There were a number of options that did not put you at risk. You could have stormed the hall with the others in front of you. You could have been the one to flank the enemy through the other hallway, taking another teammate with you while another provided distraction. The wounded teammate was a liability in this scenario—in fact, all your teammates were simply artificial beings, yet you acted as if they were real."

Kaiden glanced to the side, away from the scrutiny he sensed behind the ocular shield. "Eh, I didn't know how the computer would run the bots. Better to take the hard part myself. As for the wounded guy…well, it was extra points, right?"

"So, you just wanted to win?" Sasha inquired, a wealth of other questions behind that simple query.

"I suppose…" Kaiden murmured. "It worked, yeah? Plus, I knew it was a simulation. It wasn't like I was actually going to die—hurt like hell, though."

"True, you wouldn't have died, but you still knew the pain that would be inflicted on you. Yet you still choose that route. It was an interesting development."

"Glad ya think so," Kaiden said, brushing it off. "So, where does that leave me? I'm guessing soldier or something?"

"Soldier, yes, but that was never in question. Soldier is simply the division you are designated to, not your class."

"Division?"

"Yes, your field of expertise. You have seen other students with different colored armbands, correct?"

Kaiden thought back to the train ride over to the station, remembering the various colored bands the other non-SC students wore.

"I have. I thought those were like merit badges or something."

"Not quite. Initiates are separated by division—their designation."

"The fields are Soldier, Technician, Mechanic, Logistics, and Medical," Laurie explained. "Each field has multiple classes within it to account for different areas of knowledge or craft and various opportunities available to them." He whirled his hand dramatically in the air before placing it on his chest. "For example, I would be in the Technician field, but my class would be Robotics as my skills focus on technology development and enhancement."

"I see. So you would be a Soldier, too, then?" Kaiden asked, looking back at Sasha.

The commander nodded. "When I came through, I was a Soldier, starting in Marksman."

"Starting? You switched?"

"Yes, after a couple years, a mentor of mine recommended a different field, one where my already developed skills were still of use but were not so apparent at the time and could be better realized. It is not very common, but it does happen."

"I think I follow. So where does that place me?"

"You have a few options, actually," Sasha said, bringing the tablet back out and tapping on the screen a few times. "I could go down the line, but I would make a recommendation."

"Oh? Let's hear it," Kaiden said, a little bemused as he tried to wrap his head around all this new information and its implications.

"I would recommend the Ace Class," Sasha stated, holding the tablet to his chest.

A pause hung in the air. Kaiden waited for the two to burst into laughter, having set up this joke while he was in the Animus. However, as the stilted pause began to hang in the air, he realized that Sasha did not strike him as the joking type. Ace? What kind of title was that? He certainly liked it, and he certainly didn't mind it as a nickname—it had a nice ring to it, sounded flashy, even—but it also sounded like a title you would give to somebody who…had a sense of discipline?

"What does that mean exactly?" he asked when the silence seemed almost excruciating.

"The Ace Class is for those who show extraordinary ability in the principles of a soldier. In your case, your skills with guns and combat are certainly ahead of the curve, both among our prep-students and even a number of our Nexus-trained ones as well. There are other things you can work on. You could study up on the functions and abilities of your EI, for one, and learning the benefits of stealth and strategy would also be a great benefit. Also, discipline."

Called that one. Kaiden kept the thought to himself.

"However, along with your gunplay, you're physically impressive. You have a knack for on-your-feet tactical thinking and a keen sense of survival."

"Being a good shot really helps with that last one too," Kaiden agreed.

"You may not be at the top of the class, to begin with, but I feel it would offer the greatest benefit to you in the long run." Sasha walked a few steps closer to Kaiden. "It would put you on the path to being possibly one of the most well-rounded soldiers you could be, along with other opportunities you may not have considered if you simply go in as a marine or bounty hunter."

"I see…well, I suppose I could always change it, but as

long as I still get in the dirt and pull triggers, it's all good by me. It wasn't like I had a real game plan beyond that."

"Such a wonderful show of conviction," Sasha murmured dryly.

"Well, ya got anything else?"

"Just a quick EI check, make sure it synced back properly," Laurie requested.

"All right." Kaiden nodded, reached in his pockets for his oculars, and put them on. "Hey, Chief, come on back."

"Howdy, how'd ya do?" Chief asked, his orb rolling around in the display.

"You weren't watching?"

"Nah. Figured I'd let it be a surprise and played solitaire in the meanwhile."

"You know, I keep thinking you're fucking with me, but the more you comment, the less I'm sure."

"One of the great questions in life, partner. Now, how bad did ya screw up?"

"Sorry to disappoint you, but the commander here says I'm an Ace."

"Like that your worth is one point?"

"I have just finished loading your designation into your profile, Initiate. You and your EI can see for yourself," Sasha commented.

"Bringing it onscreen."

Kaiden saw a box with his picture in the corner pop up onscreen. His name, birthday, and all the basics were there. Then he could see a marker labeled Field/Class and beneath it, Soldier/Ace (SC).

"Well, that's a twist," Chief muttered, surprise evident in its voice.

"I'd give you flak, but I'll be honest, didn't think I'd walk out of here with something so fancy."

"*No kiddin'. Maybe when I see other EIs, I can actually look them in the face instead of hanging my head in shame.*"

"You know, it's those kinda compliments that gave me the confidence to get here."

"*Careful, your head gets too big, and it makes for a helluva easy target,*" the EI chided.

Kaiden smiled and shrugged, then looked back to the commander. "Anything else? I seem good to go."

Sasha nodded. "You are done here. I would recommend heading to the supplier to get the rest of your requisitions and materials. You will also be issued your Nexus academy jacket with your Soldiers' band, as well. You can also request a bunk in the Soldier's dorm if you wish."

"I'll pass for now. Seems less stuffy in the SC dorm," Kaiden quipped. He nodded to the professors before heading to the door. "See y'all around. Maybe we can go for drinks or something if y'all get the time."

"I have quite the selection back in my office," Laurie offered.

"As long as it doesn't knock me out again, I might take you up on that. Later," Kaiden called over his shoulder as he left the room.

Laurie watched him go, walking beside Sasha to the exit. "I'm glad that went so well. I'll update the system when I return to the Center." He held a small drive in his hand. "Although I must say, getting a recommendation for the Ace Class is quite an achievement. I wouldn't have thought he would have been offered that considering he is an SC. I thought only the preps had a chance to make it in."

"The system didn't make the recommendation," Sasha said, handing the tablet to Laurie. "*I* did."

Laurie looked down to see the assorted options Kaiden was selected for: Marksman, Security, Marine, and Bounty Hunter, among other basic classes, were highlighted. Then he swiped over to Ace and saw that it was faded out. A glowing Nexus symbol hovered over it, indicating that it had been bypassed and registered by authority.

"Well, I must say, Sasha, you must really have taken an interest in our young friend," Laurie commented, handing the tablet back. "I wonder what the Board will think about this."

"I am part of the Board, Laurie. Besides, it is not so unusual for a staff member to help guide the students. It's why we're here in the first place."

"Yes, I do believe I've heard of a few instances before—like that girl who came back a fighter pilot thanks to some nudging by a teacher, or that field surgeon who originally merely wanted to work in medicine development."

Laurie walked off casually, tapping his finger against his chin once more. "I also heard about a boy a couple of decades ago who was pretty good with guns. He came to train up and depart for the war front but changed his class a couple of years later on a recommendation."

Laurie spun around, a jester-like smile on his face. "Ended up in the Leader Class, I do believe. Not many did, back in the day, or even today. They actually changed the name because they thought students were too frightened or unsure to take on that responsibility. What did they change it to?"

"You certainly seem to be enjoying yourself," Sasha

muttered. He walked over to one of the computer stations and placed the tablet on it. With steady fingers, he unlocked the grip on his oculars and removed them from his head.

"It's coming to me...ah, that's right." Laurie strolled right up behind Sasha. "It became Ace, correct?"

Sasha straightened and turned to look at the professor. Laurie smiled as the silver eyes gazed at him, seemingly weary, but there still seemed to be a good deal of grit in them.

"You would be correct; do you want a prize too?" Sasha scoffed.

"Oh, I'm fine, and more than amused right now. I guess I can't call nepotism since he isn't your son, but I'm guessing you see a bit of yourself in dear Kaiden?"

"I see someone with tremendous skill who can possibly achieve something he hadn't considered. Similar to me." Sasha nodded, taking a seat. "The difference was I was prepared to shoulder the responsibility and make the most of it."

"You seem to be saying you don't think he can," Laurie noted. "Why put him in that class if you think he'll squander the opportunity. The Academy isn't exactly fond of failure."

"No, I do not believe he will fail." Sasha leaned back in the chair. "He comes across as too fixated on what he is rather than what he could be, but he got this far on his tenacity and self-developed skills. He'll need more polishing than I did, so better to start him early."

"You seem pretty sure about all this, but you're basing

all this on what? A psyche profile and two days of familiarity?"

"Just trust me on this, Laurie," Sasha answered. "I'll go over a few things on my tablet then leave in a bit. Go update the systems and we can meet for dinner if you want some company."

"Fine by me." Laurie acquiesced with a shrug. "I'll see you then. Try not to get so absorbed in your work. It makes you a bit grumpy." With that, he turned and left the room with a brisk stride.

Sasha looked down at his tablet, picked it up again, and flipped through Kaiden's scores.

Kaiden Jericho
Targets Eliminated: 55
Accuracy: 92%
Damage Taken: 1 Shot
Final Score: 13,441 points (Top 1% of current year / top 10% all time)

He looked over his survey answers. They indicated a hothead, reckless but efficient—a good attack dog was what most people would see. But it was the more personal answers that interested him—something that hinted, if only slightly, at someone who probably had cared about something at some point and perhaps had the ability to do so again.

Sasha ran his hand along the collar of his shirt and pulled it down, and in the slight reflection of the tablet screen, he could see the fading tattoo of a skull with Peacemaker gun barrels for horns and a lone star in the right eye.

CHAPTER THIRTEEN

Baioh Wulfson looked out over the Nexus Academy docking bay with a steely glare.

He had waited on a shipment for nearly two hours, and the unlucky and unconscious man lying on the floor at his feet had just informed him that it had been delayed until tomorrow evening. The string of his patience had sizzled down toward an explosive temper for some time now.

Some relaxing violence was past due.

He was a tall man, standing nearly seven feet, with long, dirty-blond locks tied into several lengths behind him and the top of his head hidden under a black bandanna. He wore a black muscle-shirt, grey cargo pants, and black boots, with an administrator's badge pinned haphazardly near his left shoulder.

A long, greying beard that fell to just above his chest swayed in the ocean breeze which did little to calm his temperament.

The only reason he had to not really lash out was the

willpower he had learned due to years of training and involuntary therapy. Also, the fact that no one had bothered to even get within thirty yards of him was probably for the best.

"Why, if it isn't Wulfson the Hellhound—fancy meeting you here. Why so glum?" a serene voice called, seemingly ignorant of the seething temper of the man it called to. Wulfson the Hellhound was a nickname that was bestowed upon him for reasons that would be quite unpleasant to most. Again, this person was either playing the fool or was tragically ignorant.

Baioh looked over to see the jovial smile and wagging fingers of Professor Alexander Laurie. He scoffed and then turned to look out at the bay once again.

"Why are you here, narhat?" he asked, his voice deep and guttural even though he spoke quietly.

"I won't bother getting that translated and simply assume it was a friendly greeting," Laurie said in a dry tone.

"It wasn't, but keep living in your fantasy." Baioh brushed it off with a shrug. "As long as you keep making your flashy little knick-knacks, you still have a use."

"You're too kind. Keep speaking to me that way, and I'll make sure to leave my defense drones on the next time you wish to use my lab as a gunsmith."

"Go ahead. I need the workout. Haven't shot anything that fires back in a few years." He huffed his irritation. "Maybe the next time the Board is kissing your ass, you can persuade them to reactivate the firing function of the bots at the range."

"I may, if only because you asked so very nicely." Laurie

all but purred the response. "However, it may not turn out as well as you think. My relationship with the board has soured slightly over the last few months. I'm not exactly the prodigy son I used to be."

"What a damn shame. Does that mean they aren't giving you your weekly basket of wine and cheeses? The budget only allows for fruit baskets?" Wulfson snickered.

"More along the lines of my projects getting a little too fanciful and microscale for their tastes. I've been here so long, and I've yet to get them to understand the need for personal projects from time to time. I suppose I have to find a way to deal with Neanderthals." He sniffed. "No offense to your family line."

Laurie soon found himself in the air, snatched by the security officer in one swift motion. "Cute little joke, fool. If you wanna cheer my spirits up so badly, then try not to thrash around for a few minutes," the angry giant threatened.

"I certainly do. That diet of beer and frothy saliva must leave you so empty inside, certainly in the head." Laurie smirked in jest, a hand moving to the side of his belt. "But come now, you know how this dance between us goes."

A vivid flash of light followed a loud hum, and Baioh's hand was forced open. He stumbled back a few steps, recovered, and looked up to see the professor dusting himself off. He pointed down to his belt to show a device on the buckle that now lit up and hummed with energy.

"And you know that I like to lead," he finished, his expression smug.

"You and your damn gadgets." The mountain of flesh

growled as he straightened. "Feels more like I'm fighting a robot than a man."

"I would prefer we didn't fight, Wulfson, but I would be lying if I said that it didn't amuse me."

"I swear, one of these days, I'm going to smother you in your sleep," Baioh threatened.

"Just be sure the pillow is hypoallergenic. I wouldn't want to die sneezing—I'd look awful at the funeral," Laurie mocked, flicking the last of the invisible dust off his jacket. "Now, since I have your attention, I have something that may prove interesting to you."

Baioh folded his arms against his chest. "Really now? Unless it's a new gun you want me to try or some killer robot you want me to put through its paces, I'm doubtful."

"I actually did have said killer robot at one time, almost complete too. Then the Board halted the development indefinitely, said there could be unforeseen consequences and that it wasn't a proper technology for study in the Academy."

"Pah, Kronidiots," Wulfson sneered.

Laurie nodded. "Right? Although I did forget that I was able to make a copy for experimentation in the Animus System. Never got around to it—oh well, thoughts for later. I wanted to bring to your attention an initiate I have come across."

"What about him?"

"Well, you see, he is a rather interesting case. Professor —although I suppose I should say Commander—Sasha found him a couple days ago, taking out a few thugs in a bar."

Baioh raised an eyebrow. "What? Did Sasha give this kid a ride simply because he could throw a punch?"

Laurie shook his head. "Not entirely. He seems quite taken by the young chap. I wasn't aware of him myself until his file came across my desk. Turns out he had the Gemini gene, a wonderful little surprise for me," Laurie explained, his enthusiasm plain to see.

"Yeah, yeah," Baioh muttered, spinning his finger in a circular pattern to tell the professor to hurry up.

"Long story short, I placed an experimental cerebral EI system in his head—I had consent, don't worry."

The giant grunted. "I wasn't."

"The Board took issue with it, as they are wont to do. So, I got Sasha to vouch for me and did some technical work that I won't waste time explaining to you. It's looking good as far as my ass being covered, but considering all the hullabaloo, I want to make sure that my metaphorical golden goose sets a shining example and the Board allows me further time and finances to continue study and potentially develop this technology for further use."

By this point, Baioh was staring into the middle distance, a disinterested look glazing his eyes. "Good for you, I'm sure. What makes me care?"

Laurie's brow furrowed. "Well, besides allowing me to improve my cerebral EI system and allowing it to become the premiere system among all Academy faculty—and using it to potentially fix that damaged brain of yours..."

Baioh's eyes glared at Laurie, whose hand went back to the trigger on his belt. He held up his other hand in caution. "I would be willing to bargain with you if you would...*assist* this initiate in his studies for a while."

Wulfson leaned back a little, cocking his head. "And why do you want my help? Sasha brought the kid in by the sounds of it, and if he's so interested in him, shouldn't he want to train him?"

"Sasha is a member of the Board. He has other tasks to worry about. If he did help the boy, he could potentially jeopardize his position and, more importantly, *my* safety net. Plus, you know how Sasha is. He's a bit too standoffish; doesn't really show that he cares all that often."

The security officer let out a low, deep rumbling laugh and pointed to himself. "And you think I will?"

"Your training tends to be a bit more hands-on—a little too much so, if you recall."

He huffed once again and rolled his shoulders. "Eh, if they wanna coddle the few kids in the foundations class, let them. They'll wish I was still there when the real blood starts flying."

"Too true, which is why I think you would be perfect to develop this student for the future. I personally have little doubt that he will be exceptional with the right amount of time and training, but if we could speed it along and show some true promise quite quickly, I would get my grant that much sooner."

"What would I get out of this? Besides being some pet project's nanny?"

Laurie pursed his lips. "Well, besides actually getting to teach again, you would get your precious training hall back to the way it was. Since you would actually have visitors other than yourself, the Board would have to give you your stipend back for the upkeep and stock. Once others begin to see how much he improves, I'm sure many more will start coming to improve their skills outside of the Animus as well."

Baioh stroked his beard, contemplating the potential of Laurie's words. "Perhaps...but that will take time, even to get the commission approved. What about some sort of advance?"

"You have always been a hard man to please." Laurie sighed. "I was prepared for that, however. I will grant you access to a personal workshop of mine to do whatever you please with. You will also have a fifty thousand credit limit monthly for supplies and materials for up to a year, even if he does not train with you for the whole year."

This got the battle-hungry man's head nodding. "I see... not too bad an offer, Laurie. But before I go potentially wasting my time, how are you even sure I can make anything out of this kid? Clay that is too wet or rotten will not take even the simplest shape."

Laurie lifted his hand off his belt and moved it into a pocket on the inside of his jacket. "I have some wonderful little statistics to show you, actually. Sasha and I just finished running some tests on him, and I was able to discreetly transfer the scores over to my personal files."

"Do you ever wonder why people around you treat you with suspicion?" Baioh asked mockingly.

"Take it from someone raised with proper manners, Wulfson, they are simply used to hide all the dark secrets of the real person," Laurie admonished. He removed a short stick that he pinched on both sides and pulled apart, revealing a holoscreen that he tapped on a few times. "Have a look for yourself."

Baioh took the tablet from the professor and read the

screen. His eyebrows lifted slightly, and he stroked his beard again.

"Interesting. There might certainly be some greater potential in him…just have to carve it out with a little appliance of force."

"So, then, do we have a deal?"

He tossed the tablet back to him, crossing his arms again. "I want the robot."

"Beg your pardon?"

"That killer robot you said you were working on, I want it."

"I told you, the Board nixed it. They have it in some military base outside the Academy."

"Hmm." Baioh's forehead creased in thought. "You said you uploaded a copy to the Animus, right?"

"I did." Laurie nodded

"Give me access to that. I'll find a use for it."

"Very well. It was collecting dust, anyway," Laurie said with a shrug. "Now, do we have a deal?" he asked, offering his hand.

"We most certainly do," Baioh agreed, squeezing down on his hand with glee.

The professor recoiled after pulling away from the giant man's grip. "Well, good. Finally happy to see eye-to-eye on something."

"Finally happy to see you offer something that makes sense," Baioh countered. "Now, where is this initiate? I would like to get started right away."

"It's almost dinner."

"He should start preparing for spontaneous training, just like in battle."

"I... Well, I suppose I'll leave the convincing to you. I'm sure you can be suave." Laurie sighed. "If he's not at the Cafeteria, Sasha sent him to the supply center."

"Are you kidding me? I have to fill out a request form in triplicate for a training gun with rubber bullets?" Kaiden growled his frustration. "I'm from Texas. They provide guns at the shooting range and the first hour is free."

"Well, this is Nexus Academy, and if you want to shoot things so bad, then just go in the Animus," the supply clerk responded, barely looking away from her console.

"We can just use those?" Kaiden wondered.

"First years can't, but classes start in, like, thirty hours. Simply make sure to sign up for plenty of firing and soldier courses, and you can get your fill until next year where you can enroll to be considered for Animus passes."

"That's my point. If I can't get into the Animus on my own time, then I'll need a little extra on the side if I wanna catch up to some of the preps. I'm showing some initiative here. Give me a break, bob-cut."

"Stellar cut down, cock-bite," Chief jeered.

The clerk simply frowned. "Just fill out the damn forms if it's so important to you. Then I can process them while you apply for access to the firing range and a permit to carry, and you should have everything ready to go in about a month."

"Good God with the rules—isn't this a military academy?"

She glanced at him, a tiny smirk on her face. "Only

mostly."

Kaiden seethed, heated breath escaping through clenched teeth, "You people will give me an ulcer."

"If you keep up the melodramatics, I'll have to call Reggie," she warned.

Kaiden shook his head, "Who the hell is Reggie?"

"The supply division's personal…defense droid. At least, that's what they call him. I'm not sure what you call a repaired and rewired kill-bot."

"You're bluffing." He tried to stare her down.

She rolled her eyes and turned to her left, looking over her shoulder to throw her voice. "Hey, Reg! Got someone who doesn't wanna follow the rules."

Though he couldn't see him, he heard the loud boom of an engine powering on, followed by the whir of gears and parts shifting into place. Then Kaiden saw two red lights in the darkness of the supply room behind the clerk.

"Reggie online, give kill orders and level of pain," a clickity, robotic voice requested.

Kaiden paled. "So where can I find these forms, exactly?"

She smiled and looked up, pointing behind him. Then her eyes widened as she noticed something and quickly scooted back from her station on her rolling chair.

Kaiden turned and stared at long strands of hair on black cloth. He looked up slightly to see it was attached to a Goliath of a man with dirty-blond and greying hair. He looked Kaiden up and down as if sizing him up.

For once, he was a little hesitant to ask if he wanted someone to fight.

"You Kaiden Jericho?" the man-beast asked in a deep,

heavy voice.

Kaiden remained silent as he contemplated fight or flight.

"Hey, I know I usually like to give you shit and mock your pain, but uh...remember, if you die, I technically die too."

"Noted," Kaiden whispered. He really wished he had a weapon right now—hell, he would take a prison shank or even a jagged spork.

"This is Initiate Jericho, yes, sir," the clerk answered and disappeared rapidly into the supply room.

Kaiden whipped around, wide-eyed before his eyes narrowed at her and he muttered, "Evil bitch."

"Good, I found you." The giant grabbed Kaiden's collar and began to drag him away. He called over his shoulder, "Hey, clerk! Send *all* his supplies to his dorm pod. On my authority."

"Yes, sir, Officer Wulfson," she called.

"Officer Wulfson? At least we know the name of your murderer," Chief noted, actually somber for once. His caution wasn't encouraging. *"Honestly, you should hope all he wants to do is kill you, though there's not much you could probably do if he had other plans."*

Kaiden tried to wrest himself out of the man's grasp but to no avail. He'd even grabbed onto the sides of the doorframe as they left the room, but with one seemingly effortless tug, he was ripped away and was surprised he didn't take chunks of wall with him.

He never really considered himself a religious person, but he found himself making deals with every god he had ever heard of as he was pulled out of the building and into the night.

CHAPTER FOURTEEN

Chiyo Kana sat alone in the academy library.
It was a large space with wide windows, several staircases, multiple information stations and computers, and clinical-white flooring and walls.

She sat alone on a table in the center of the building. Her foot tapped silently on the wood. The place was quiet, and the main lights had been cut off some time ago. Only glow strips now dimly illuminated her surroundings, along with orbs of light that hovered silently around the building.

Chiyo looked over a tablet filled with information on a tactical hacking application and proper procedure in the field. She wondered if she should reconsider her plan for the Academy's Technician Class test. It seemed solid enough considering the other technicians she had observed in her dorm and the files she had cracked and gained access to.

She knew there was a rule that those files were technically not for initiates' eyes and that breaking into said files could be punishable by expulsion, perhaps even jail time.

But she also knew that there was an unspoken rule that if you were a hacker at this academy and got caught doing something so basic, you probably shouldn't be there to begin with. Besides, considering how almost insultingly easy it was, she wondered if it wasn't some sort of test in the first place.

It's fine.

But as she looked over the rosters and many of the other class's skills and talents, she noticed most of them did have some sort of training in field support or the like, something she did not.

She wasn't aware of the specifics of the inauguration field test. Chiyo could probably find out more by poking around further in the Academy's data banks, but she couldn't help but wonder if that would truly help her in this case.

Of course, it would—practically speaking, anyway—but the test was supposed to help determine the individual skill of each initiate, and how would she know where she stood if she gave herself an advantage?

Then again, going back to that unspoken rule, it seemed to be a part of some underlying test for those with her class and particular set of skills. Preparation was fundamental to the proper execution of a job, test or not, and her specialty was infiltration of networks and systems and immobilizing or corrupting them.

She was simply doing her job, what she came here to do.

It's fine.

She placed the tablet down and interlaced her fingers, leaning her chin in them as she contemplated her next move. Her father would probably tell her that she was letting personal morals or tradition get in the way of her drive. She wasn't raised with many rules to follow, but that was one of the few things equal to sin in the eyes of her parents.

She sighed, thinking back to the days of her childhood. All that training and study, merely to end up there. She was supposed to be an heiress or perhaps her father's right hand. Yet all those conniving bastards who hid in his shadow had cracked the foundations of that path.

Perhaps, if it was something she truly wanted, she would have fought harder.

"Pardon me, could I request some assistance?" a muffled voice asked behind her, sounding as if it spoke through a gas mask.

She turned around, and her eyes narrowed. The being had a violet-hued skin tone and black orbs for eyes with tattoo-like markings around them.

It was dressed in a blue and black one-piece with a grey academy coat over it and an orange armband, indicating an engineer. A circular plate around its neck seemed to be filled with a liquid of some kind, a square mouthpiece uniting the sides in front of his head.

It was a Tsuna, she realized. She was somewhat familiar with them, her father's Zaibatsu—conglomerate—having had a few dealings with their representatives and had attended conferences with them present, though she'd never come face to face with one before.

"My apologies for disturbing you, but I was looking for

an index to gain more familiarity with your planet's machinery and armaments. I cannot seem to find the librarian or any scribes."

Chiyo turned slightly, resting an arm on the table, a small smile crossing her face. "I believe the head librarian is out for the evening. As for any scribes, it would probably be helpful to know that they haven't been a part of our normal society for quite a few centuries."

He looked around before directing his stare back at her. "I wondered why they were so scarce. Glad I did not spend any more than an hour looking for them here. They didn't seem to have too many places to hide," the alien noted as it stretched its arms downward and clasped its hands together.

"Well, I'm happy to have spared you some time." Chiyo chuckled, placing her cheek against the palm of her hand.

"I most certainly appreciate it. My assigned name is Geno Aronnax. I am a Tsuna, here to study in the engineering field."

"Chiyo Kana, Technician…a pleasure." She offered a hand, which caused Geno to cock his head slightly to the side before he nodded in acknowledgment. He unclasped his hands and took Chiyo's in both.

"I must say, it is nice when I meet friendlier humans. The more…*aggressive* ones have become a nuisance." He let go of Chiyo's hand after a speedy shake.

"Have you had a lot of trouble with others?" Chiyo asked.

"No, not trouble, merely nuisance. The time it takes me to physically beat them into unconsciousness when they accost me is time that I could better spend on research or practice." His reply was delivered without rancor or emotion, merely a statement of fact.

Chiyo's eyes fluttered wide for a moment before she snickered. "I see. I can appreciate someone who understands the importance of study."

"Oh, most certainly," Geno exclaimed, placing one hand on his chest and another pointing in the air, two fingers extended. "To gain knowledge is to gain the currency of life itself."

Chiyo gave him a quizzical, albeit entertained, look.

"It is a rough translation of one of our...I suppose you would consider them proverbs," he explained, lowering his hands. "Many believe them to be teachings left by ancestors long before us. We do not have complete translations, but most clans abide by individual lines of these teachings, depending upon their clan job, though all can take some guidance from each." He now pressed both hands against his chest. "My clan, for example, have had the honor of progressing our society in the ways of machines and alchemy for a few thousand of your years. We are, admittedly, the newest of the clans to be granted this honor, but we have made great strides in our peoples' advancement and have earned our keep."

She leaned a bit toward him. "Did you say *alchemy*?"

"Yes, I—" He stopped speaking for a moment. "Oh, dear, did I use an antiqued term again?"

"Probably the translator's fault," Chiyo said with a wave of her free hand. "My guess is that the developers responsible for them are still working the bugs out. I would assume it would be something similar to our chemists?"

Geno moved the lower part of his coat out of the way,

revealing a large compartment wrapped around his leg. He undid a latch and pulled out an EI console. "Saren, would you please look up the definition of the word—"

"No need. It was merely a curious observation. We should probably get back to the original question."

Geno blinked, and Chiyo noticed that he had two sets of eyelids—a horizontal interior set and a vertical outer layer. He shook his head apologetically and pressed the tablet against his chest. "My apologies, was I explaining too methodically? I have been growing accustomed to human language, but the amount of words and time it takes to exchange information has been of particular difficulty."

"Actually, the distraction has been nice, but as you said, it is time that could be spent studying, right?" Chiyo reminded him.

"Of course," he exclaimed. Speaking through the mask made it sound like excited bubbling. He pointed two fingers in the air again and pressed the other hand tighter to his chest, but before he said anything, he looked sheepishly off to the side. "Um… Perhaps now is not the time to be quoting the teachings. Teaching myself would be wise, though." He moved his hands behind his back, the gesture suggestive of a chastened response.

"Certainly. You said you were looking for information pertaining to Earth machinery and weapons?"

"Yes. Earth, in this case, meaning the planet, not the element."

"I understand." Chiyo smiled "You can find almost any information pertaining to your field at the designated station." She pointed to a fixture in the distance. Illuminated orange rings circled around several pillars that each had dozens of ports attached to them. "They are marked in your field's color. Simply connect your EI or a tablet to a port on the station and it will bring up a directory that will let you download notes, entries, and the like on a subject of your choosing. But make sure to delete the information after a period, or you may find yourself running low on free space after a while."

"I see. And for more general information?" he asked.

"Second floor." Chiyo pointed up for emphasis. "Each floor is specific. Second floor is encyclopedia, guides, and dictionaries, third is non-fiction works, and fourth is fiction. The stations are all marked and labeled with what they provide. If you have trouble, I'm sure you can simply scan the lettering with your console."

"I am actually able to speak the English language," Geno said pressing a webbed finger to his temple. "They actually loaded a synapse language point into us before we descended onto earth."

"Really?" Chiyo asked, a little shocked. "With no training and gradual leveling? That seems a little dangerous."

"We had to go through a boot camp of sorts, actually. Getting the Animus system to sync properly with our minds is a little different—and difficult—for us or any of the other non-human species. So, when we are accepted into the Academy, we have to go through a few months of preparation and take a few classes to make Earth life easier as well as set us up for the Animus training. By the end, we get one synapse point to spend in the social tree." He moved his finger down from his temple and to the side of his right eye. "I chose reading comprehension since we have translators and the like. It seemed pointless to get an EI app for writing translation. Having to point my EI console at everything to translate it seemed silly."

"Why not use oculars?" Chiyo asked.

Geno laughed—or gave what seemed like a laugh— as if he were saying, "Hmm." Quickly and in a high-pitched voice, he added, "No, no, no, they don't exactly have them in my size." His mirth continued. "We have some prototype goggles that another clan developed. They work well enough, but a group of them have reported sickness, the equivalent of your headaches and nausea, which are quite terrible for us even when we aren't getting used to a new atmosphere."

Chiyo acknowledged the logic of this. "Smart decision."

"I take pride in them, and also the safety of my eyesight," Geno affirmed with a nod. "Thank you for your help, Chiyo. I do hope I see you again. You make the second initiate that I have had a nice experience with."

Chiyo smiled and nodded. "I'm glad to make the list. I hope I'm in good company."

"I do not keep a list, but yours and that man's were both positive conversations that I enjoyed." Geno stepped away, though he still faced her as he talked. "Although you did not use as many funny words as he did."

"Funny words?" she asked.

"Yes, words that my translator did not understand— things like yonder and howdy, but they seem nice," he explained, raising a hand and waving it awkwardly. "Have a good evening of study." With that, he turned and went up the staircase.

"Yonder and howdy?" Chiyo muttered. The words originated in what was the American South...could it mean that man she met the previous night? Kaiden had a southern accent, although she doubted he was the only initiate there from the South.

Her thoughts led her back to their conversation at breakfast. He seemed a different breed from either herself or many of the other first-years she had met—or many of the people she was used to being around at home.

He was skillful enough to be there, apparently, but a bit brutish and not very forward-thinking. Yet they both now called this place home despite their different ways of obtaining membership.

Beating down thugs in a bar...she wondered who would consider that criteria for Nexus potential.

Still, he seemed at least willing to use all the amenities available to him, even willing to go through the tedium of class evaluation. He might not have known what he wanted to do, but he was certainly willing to do whatever it turned out to be. Yet she still pondered on her place here, even though she was completely aware of why and for what.

She looked down at the tablet again and read the title out loud. "The Basics of a Support Technician." She scowled. Just looking at the title made her feel a sense of loss.

Chiyo had never been a leader, and she worked well alone, using her own skills and plans to accomplish the jobs of people with thrice her experience. More important, she had never failed. There wasn't a system she couldn't get into when she set her mind to it, and now she was here, looking at a different career altogether?

What would that accomplish for her?

"Kaitō." She spoke aloud, and the image of a fox in white wire-frame appeared in the corner of her eye.

"Yes, madame?" he asked in an ethereal voice, sitting patiently on his hind legs. Chiyo brought out a console from her bookbag, turning it on with one hand as she reached behind her and detached a dongle from a device clipped to her waist.

She placed the dongle into a port on the console, and the EI disappeared from her eye and appeared on the screen. "Prepare Infiltration Suite, then when I get access to the security networks in this building, set the cameras to loop in a four-second span."

"Understood, madame. Please be aware that you will have only six hours to do whatever task you are attempting to accomplish before the sun rises and the video looks suspect."

"I'm well aware. It should only take me a couple hours, we'll be fine."

"Of course." The fox avatar nodded. Chiyo began the process of circumventing the comparatively light security of the library's interior security system. A glance at the operations of the library's network defense told a different story. That one looked like it was developed by someone who cared.

She again thought back to her hypothesis that a number of these defenses were made more inviting to let those initiates like herself truly test their abilities on and off the field. Or maybe she was simply that much better than her peers.

Chiyo was happy with either.

If they wanted them to show some initiative, she would

happily do so. Then, when she came out in the top tier of the Technician's Class test, it would grant her the silence of the paranoid idiots who felt she shouldn't be there. It would be a demonstration of her gifts and expertise, making her place among them no longer in doubt.

Then, perhaps, her own path would be that much clearer.

CHAPTER FIFTEEN

Kaiden was tossed, quite literally, through the air. After he recovered, he scrambled swiftly to his feet and took in his surroundings.

He stood in a domed building, smaller than any of the others he had been in thus far. A sharp click echoed in the space, and lights snapped on. He winced for a moment as he adjusted to the sudden brightness. Curious now, he studied the area more closely. Various training and workout equipment filled much of the space—weights, dummies, straps, presses, and weapons.

Weapons? Kaiden looked over to see a rack of what appeared to be rifles. He glanced at the giant who had dragged him there—Officer Wulfson, he recalled the clerk saying—who now fiddled with the door. Suddenly alert, he took the opportunity to dash for the guns, closing the distance quickly as Wulfson looked casually at him.

"My advice is that you shouldn't mess with those," he warned.

Like he was going to listen to the guy who literally dragged him here against his will.

Kaiden was only a few steps away and reached out to grab a rifle before his hand crashed into something. He felt a shock run through him and yelped as he was thrown back to bounce off the floor mats before landing hard on the padded ground.

"Mösstock." Wulfson sighed, walked over to Kaiden's collapsed form, and crouched over him. "You really think I would leave guns out in the open and unprotected? I blocked them off with a repulsion barrier." He chuckled, shaking his head slowly "You aren't the first student to try to shoot me."

"That's a hell of a way to make a first introduction." Kaiden groaned, leaning over to one side. "Also the kidnapping."

"Pah, I call it administrative detaining. Either way, it won't be a bother," he scoffed. "Now, get your ass up. We got work to do."

Kaiden sat up, resting on his elbows. "*We* don't gotta do a damn thing. What *I* wanna know is who the hell you are."

Wulfson stood up and rolled his shoulders. "Ask your EI. If it's worth a damn, it'll have my file. I have to prepare for the bout." He turned and walked away, heading to a console at the back of the room.

"Chief, who the hell is this guy?" Kaiden asked, standing on shaking legs.

"Baio Wulfson, head of security for Nexus Academy," Chief informed him in a hushed voice.

"Why are you whispering? Only I can hear you when

you're not in another device." Kaiden shuffled around in his pockets for his oculars.

"I ain't gonna take the chance that the shaved yeti can't hear me," Chief confessed, continuing to whisper. *"Don't know how he feels about you, but I'm pretty damn sure he doesn't care about me."*

"Safe bet," Kaiden acknowledged with a nod. He finally located his oculars in his jacket pocket and donned them, then looked around again. Most of the floor and walls were padded, and most of the machinery and items in the room were…rather archaic.

There didn't seem to be too many pieces of modern tech in the place besides the console where Wulfson worked. All the weights were metal bars with circular weights of varying size and mass, and sandbags, large tires, and ropes tied to large rocks or chunks of metal made up the balance.

He took a look back at the weapon rack he'd attempted to get to before. "Chief, scan those rifles over there, would you?"

"Gotcha…" A white line glided across his display, a small group of infoboxes popping in after a few seconds. *"Damn, these are old. They're all replicas, too…gotta admit, it's kinda funny that these guns are thirty-year-old copies of guns that are even older."*

"They're all mag-models too. Use live ammo rounds," Kaiden noted. "You got anything more on Mr. Happy Hands?"

"Comes from Sweden. Former army captain of the Unified Earth Military who headed up his own division. Apparently, he's a master in hand-to-hand combat, grappling, firearms, and likes

to modify guns and machines in his spare time... a lotta his personnel file is blanked out or locked. I'm grabbing what I can from the Academy directory."

"Does it mention a criminal record?" Kaiden whispered, really hoping there wouldn't be an answer in the affirmative.

"No, but you should recall that the Academy seems to not have a problem clearing those."

Kaiden rolled his eyes. "Shit, good point."

"A recommendation for the good of us both." Chief's avatar turned a pulsing yellow. *"But I would say it's time to man up and try to figure out what this guy wants."*

"Doesn't strike me as the small-talk type. I might find myself eating a fist."

"Better you bite a bullet than eat a bullet," Chief countered. *"Besides, you're an ace now and should probably get used to situations like this."*

"This sort of thing common?"

"You mean you don't... Whatever. I'll fill you in once we get the hell out of here. For now, go make nice with the bridge troll."

Kaiden sighed. The little bastard gadget had a point. He collected himself and walked over to Wulfson.

"Stay in the arena," the officer barked, and Kaiden froze instinctively.

"Arena? This is an arena?" Kaiden questioned before shaking his head "Look here, you...forget it. Whataya want from me?"

"A fight," he answered, continuing to type something into the console.

"Pardon me?"

"Not a chance," Wulfson stated, his tone almost disinterested. He pressed a button on the monitor and the lights in the room dimmed. Kaiden saw glowing patches appear beneath different spots on the mat.

He walked over to one that glowed red, knelt down, and reached out to hover his hand over it. The immense heat emanating from it made him jerk his hand away and spring into the air.

"What is that?" he yelped, clenching his hand to his chest.

"*A holotrap—a barrier modification,*" Chief stated.

"Modified for what?"

"*A good modifier can take a barrier panel or the like and either jailbreak the settings or get a chip that will do it for them. Then they can modify the energy output, activation settings, or whatever they wish. Holotraps are a pretty typical barrier mod and basically do damage to anything in the area when triggered. A fun switcheroo from what a barrier is supposed to do. What the trap is or does depends on what the modder set or the bypass chip that was used.*" Chief paused for a moment. Kaiden saw numbers flash across the screen. "*I count eight in total—two shock traps, two burn traps, and four snares.*"

"You couldn't have mentioned this before I put my hand over the burn one?" Kaiden grumbled as he flicked his hand back and forth, trying to cool it off.

"*Should I also remind you not to stick your dick in a light socket?*" Chief huffed his evident annoyance. "*Besides, how could you not have come across these things? I'm pretty sure you would have seen at least a few back in your glory days.*"

Kaiden placed his hand against his chin, looking off to the side. "I mean…maybe? Most of the traps we had to deal with were a bit cruder. Also, sharper and more explosive."

"Well, I suppose you should feel lucky I am not trying to have a dead initiate on my hands," Wulfson called. Kaiden looked back to see him standing at the edge of the arena.

"Could you give me some answers, dammit?" Kaiden demanded. "You said you wanted a fight. Fine, I'll give you one, but why did you want me?"

The officer crossed his arms. "Tell you what, you win, and I'll not only let you go on your merry little way, I'll even answer any question you have, boy." He then extended a thumb and pressed it against his chest. "If I win, you train with me until you're worth a damn."

"I would like to take a moment to remind you that getting your skull caved in will definitely damage my system," Chief warned. *"It's a miracle it's working on what little brain power you do have. Let's not try to tempt fate here."*

"All your bellyachin' ain't helping me think." Kaiden hissed his frustration. He looked Wulfson straight in the eye. "How exactly are you going to enforce that? I'm not gonna sign anything until you tell me what's going on. I'm cranky enough as it is dealing with the parade of crazies I've come across so far. Adding you into the mix is starting to get me real pissed."

"Then this should be a good opportunity to blow off some steam," Wulfson jeered. "As for enforcing our little wager, I'm good with a verbal agreement between men of honor." He returned Kaiden's stare with ferocity.

"My, my, isn't that amicable of you," Kaiden commented sarcastically. "Still don't see why I gotta stay. I saw you messing with the doors, but I could probably bust through a window, or maybe get my EI to give HR a call."

"*Don't get me into this.*" Chief sighed.

"You're already involved, you glorified ping-pong," Kaiden admonished him sharply.

"*I'm starting to feel more of a bystander than an accomplice,*" the EI retorted.

"Is that how you're going to be?" Wulfson sneered. He removed a remote from his pocket. "Very well then, go on and get out of here." He pressed a button on the remote and Kaiden heard a click and the door open in the distance.

"*Interesting strategy...I guess?*" Chief sounded thoughtful. "*I say get out while the gettin' is good.*"

"What's with the sudden change of heart?" Kaiden asked.

"*Who cares?*" Chief exclaimed.

"I was promised a chance to have a go at someone who might be a challenge," Wulfson bellowed. "But I do not have the time to waste sitting here and squawking with a coward."

"What the hell did you just call me?"

"Coward! Are you deaf as well, boy? Might explain why I keep having to spell things out for you like you were a babe."

"*He's baiting you,*" Chief pointed out.

"So, I'm a coward because I don't wanna wrestle with some old bastard who looks and acts like an ape? Did you club all your dates over the head too? Or were those nights of passion out of pity for whatever physical disorder gave you that ugly stick-beaten face?"

"*Bringing up a list of funeral homes in the area. Take your pick for the aftermath.*"

Kaiden tore off his oculars and placed them back in his jacket pocket. "Keep quiet, Chief."

"Normally, I would be delighted to, but you need to learn to keep your cool. Besides, if we really are gonna fight this guy, then I should probably load up—"

"Audio off."

"Hold up a sec, you impa—" Chief tried to protest before he was silenced.

"I see you're all riled up now." Wulfson chuckled, even the fragments of his laughter coming out like booming bass notes. "If you aren't a coward, then accept my proposal. I'll even sweeten the deal and will answer your questions regardless of whether you win or lose. What is it going to be?"

Kaiden continued to stare Wulfson down as he made his way to the door. The Officer's eyes narrowed in malice. He reached the door and grabbed the handle, slamming it shut before making his way back to the arena.

"How are we going to settle this?" Kaiden demanded, standing back in the center of the floor.

"One-on-one combat, obviously. Anything goes in terms of fighting styles," Wulfson explained, finally standing on the mat. "No time limit, no ten count, no points, and no ring out. The winner is whoever is left standing."

Kaiden could feel the trepidation creep back into him. He was already in serious trouble before, but now, he had no way of getting a technical win over this guy. Even if he could fight as well as his opponent—a doubtful prospect considering he'd had years of training in an army and was the head of the academy's security and probably spent at least a little time in the Animus training even further—this man-beast had longer reach and at least a hundred pounds on him. Though probably, he thought gloomily, closer to a hundred and fifty.

He clenched his teeth as he took off his jacket and tossed it to the side. It was a bit too late to consider the repercussions, considering how mouthy he had been. But if this guy wanted a fight, Kaiden was angry enough to oblige and determined to make a hole in Wulfson's stalwart bravado.

"Fine by me. Hope you're ready," he challenged, moving a few steps closer to the hulk.

"Pah. Of course, I am," Wulfson chided. "You aren't going to use your EI?"

"What for? This is just a regular fighting match. What can it do for me here?" Kaiden asked.

Wulfson smiled slightly, stroking his beard. "You're quite green, aren't you, boy? You need to learn all the advantages you have when going into battle. Even the slightest edge could mean the difference between victory and death."

"Death? Is that an option I should be worried about?"

"Not if you can back up your bark," Wulfson challenged. "Now then, shall we get to it?"

Kaiden struggled with mixed feelings. On the one hand, he was tired, it was already quite late, and he had now been roped into a second scenario where he had to fight for the amusement or interest of another person, seemingly for kicks. On the other hand, he was able to actually look that person in the eye and punch him in his stupid bearded face.

On the *other* other hand, for all the insults that he could hurl at this guy, most of them centered on the fact that he was really fucking big and really fucking scary. When the worst thing you could say about a person was that they could probably kick your ass, confidence was a little harder to come by.

Then again, the giant had a point, even if Kaiden didn't care to accept it. He had trained all his life to be the best fighter he could. Was he simply going to run away now? He had fought others who were bigger than him and probably even had more experience, but he was still standing while most of them were six feet deep.

He also had weapons in those instances.

"I don't have all night, boy. Fight me or flee. Those are the only two options you have and the only ones that matter," Wulfson declared, his mocking grin dragging him back into the present.

Kaiden cracked his knuckles and raised his fists. He had already turned down the option to flee, so he was left with fight. He was far better at one than the other.

He shifted around for a moment before taking in a deep breath and stilling himself, his arms placed close to his chest and fists at the ready. "All right, let's go."

CHAPTER SIXTEEN

Kaiden had barely said the word and Wulfson was on him. He leaped to the side to dodge a wide swing from the heavyweight, landing with arms stretched forward and using his momentum to gain more distance.

"Pretty good moves, boy, but if you hadn't dodged an attack that obvious, I'd have been disappointed." Wulfson cocked a mocking eyebrow. "And you'd have been concussed."

Kaiden tried to keep himself aware of his surroundings, specifically the traps on the floor. He realized those were probably his best bet to do any real damage to this big bastard. He could probably get a good few hits in himself, but if he merely swung wildly, he was more likely to hurt his own hand than his opponent.

Wulfson charged again. This time, his punches were direct, sending one fist flying forward for Kaiden to dodge or block. He pulled it back while the other fist rocketed forward, continuing to advance all the while.

Kaiden kept pace, waiting for the right moment. He was leading Wulfson to one of the shock traps. The opportune moment to dodge would be when they were both right on top of it. A few more punches came his way with relentless ferocity. Kaiden weaved between them, drawing his opponent a few steps closer, then he saw his chance.

His back was to a shock trap. One misplaced step and he'd be caught, but he wouldn't be the one going in. He waited for Wulfson's punch. This time, he would side-step it and then move around him, kicking his legs down and then pushing him in. It probably wouldn't stop him, but hopefully, it would wear him down enough to make the fight a little more even.

"What are you thinking about?" Wulfson asked, a smile creeping onto his face. "That's a nice trap there behind you."

Kaiden's heartbeat sped up. He was really relying on the whole big, dumb meathead stereotype for this.

Wulfson huddled down, his fists unclenching into open claws. "I'm sure you really put your brain through the wringer to think of this. Pity to let it go to waste."

Kaiden contemplated moving to the side and rethinking his strategy, but he didn't have the time.

"Don't worry, I won't let it, but how about—" Wulfson ran directly at Kaiden, who tried to get away but was caught in the wide arc of Wulfson's grasp. They now both fell toward the trap. "You join me!"

They landed on the mat, Kaiden's head bobbing up as he collided with the floor. No sooner did he get his bearings than he could feel the pain of electricity coursing through him. The crazy bastard had thrown them both on the trap, reckless son of a bitch.

Kaiden gritted his teeth and tried to push Wulfson's arm off him. He didn't exactly have the greatest control of his extremities at the moment, but neither did the giant. As he slowly pried his heavy arm away, he tried to shuffle along the floor and out of the trap's area. Kaiden felt the demanding tug on his shirt and looked back to see Wulfson trying to keep him in the field.

"Get...the hell...off...me," Kaiden demanded through pained gasps. He mustered enough control to turn his body and raise his boot, kicking Wulfson in his face. The giant's grip fell away, letting Kaiden roll out of the field. He continued to roll for a few more paces before he lay motionless on his back, dragging in large gulps of air, his body still twitching slightly.

"Are you...done already, boy?" Wulfson growled a challenge.

Kaiden looked over to see him already getting to his feet, blood streaming from his nose onto his beard and chest. He grimaced. What the hell was this guy made of?

"This is...new territory...for me," Kaiden grumbled, getting slowly to his feet. "Don't think I've fought... someone this stupid before. Do you even feel pain?"

"Of course I do. Doesn't mean I'm going to let it stop me," Wulfson bellowed, wiping the blood from his face with the back of his hand. "What you need to learn is advantage." He now walked around the trap and crept toward Kaiden. "It was obvious what you were doing, trying to trip me into the trap if I took another swing. However, if I'd backed up, you could've simply strolled away and repositioned yourself. So I took a little dive to make sure you learned better and how costly foolish mistakes are in battle."

"Oh! How very," Kaiden grunted as he stood up straight, his muscles contracting and aching as he rolled his shoulders, "kind of you. Do you like to consider yourself a teacher or something?"

"I was a teacher at one time, but too many students coddled by modern tech and prep life took issue with my training methods. My class was shut down, and I was moved to security."

"A modern tragedy," Kaiden jeered, raising his fists in a boxing position and taking a few quick jumps to loosen himself up. "So you're trying to make new friends now? I ain't exactly a social butterfly, but I could give you some pointers."

"Save your breath. You'll want to have as much as you can on hand when I get a solid hit on you," Wulfson warned, now only a few yards away. "Besides, why are you complaining, boy? We've only talked for about twenty-five minutes, and I can tell this is much more your speed."

"It might be a pleasant change of pace, sure," Kaiden acknowledged, backing up as Wulfson came closer. "I thought the whole point of this place was the Animus System training. I already got fighting skills."

"Not worth a damn." Wulfson chuckled, crouched down, and raised his fists. "You're tenacious, I'll give you that, but this isn't the slums anymore. When you go on missions, you're gonna be facing some true devils who have a real talent for murder and maybe more blood on them than in them."

"You're preaching to the choir, old man. Also, how the hell does everyone know about me?"

"I can promise you that you haven't faced the worst out there. Hell, *I* may have never faced the worst. Who knows what's really out there in that eternal abyss." He looked up for a brief moment. "But all of that is null and void if you can't even handle what we got for you. You can train all you want in the Animus, but unless you commit, you'll only be as good as everybody else."

"So I should spend my free time getting kicked in the balls by you?" Kaiden snarled, throwing a punch that Wulfson sidestepped.

"Training with me, though, this might happen"—Wulfson kicked low and Kaiden reacted quickly, jumped over the attack, and leaped backward on landing—"if you don't keep your guard up."

"Yeah, yeah." Kaiden scoffed. "So what are you offering me, exactly—a big ass sparring buddy?"

"A mentor," Wulfson stated, making a few quick jabs that Kaiden blocked. "Someone who will put you through the wringer, get you some grit and scars to go along with all the fancy tech this place is giving you."

"You think I can't train myself?" he asked. Wulfson snorted before he suddenly sent a fast, powerful kick to Kaiden's chin. Kaiden brought his arms together and intercepted the kick but was knocked a good five feet back before stumbling and falling to the floor.

"I'm sure you could run some laps and do basic drills with the rest of the soldiers. Maybe you'll grow smart enough to take a class in foundations, but that won't get you much further than you are now," Wulfson chided, standing straight and crossing his arms.

Kaiden wiped his brow as he pushed himself off the floor, leaning forward with his hands on his knees for a moment. "Am I supposed to guess that all this caring advice comes from the giant's heart of gold? Trust me, I've only met a few people here, and I know it doesn't work that way."

Wulfson's grin returned. "Of course not. I am certainly getting something out of this myself, whether you agree or not. But I was a teacher before, and not because taking maggots and turning them into warriors was a do-nothing sweet gig."

"So it's principle?" Kaiden asked.

"It's dedication, wanting to know that I had a hand in making the heroes of tomorrow."

"Then you wanna tell me why you're here instead of being a general or something?"

Wulfson's grin disappeared. "Another time, perhaps. Now, are you going to continue?"

"Obviously." Kaiden stood upright again and raised his fists. "At this point, my only dedication is kicking your ass."

"Pah. Then it's something you still need to work on," Wulfson sneered, also moving into a fighting stance.

Kaiden decided to take the initiative this time, dashing forward and striking Wulfson's gut. His opponent grunted but barely flinched. Kaiden dipped back to avoid retaliation before closing in again for another hit to the ribs. He kept this dance up—a quick hit or two before ducking out—but it began to feel like he was trying to take him down with bug bites.

His fists throbbed and he tried to keep focus, but his quick strikes weren't allowing him to position himself all that well, and his hands and arms were taking the strain.

He needed a way to get a real opening, something that would allow him to really let loose and attack him with all his might—or whatever was left of it.

His expression carefully deadpan, he moved back and looked around, seeing a shimmering grey pool a few feet away. A snare trap. That could definitely help, but he couldn't simply bait him into it. The ploy hadn't exactly worked well the last time.

Wulfson began striking back, massive swings and quick jabs, along with the occasional sweeping kick to try to catch him off guard. Kaiden parried and blocked, looking for a way to try to knock him into the trap without being too obvious.

Right now, they were fighting between two traps—the snare and a heat trap—something Wulfson used to his own advantage as well. He made wider arcs with his attacks and attempted to grab Kaiden as his options for dodging became a little more limited.

He was currently allowing the officer to lead him around, but right now was the perfect place to get him into the trap. Somehow, he needed to swing this around.

Then Kaiden thought of something. As Wulfson went to grab him again, clutching a small edge of his shirt, Kaiden yanked his shirt off quickly and wrapped it around his hand, tugging at it to pull Wulfson toward him. The officer grabbed a full handful of the fabric with his other hand and pulled, trying to yank Kaiden into his grasp.

He obliged, using the momentum of Wulfson's pull to

sail right by him and over the snare trap. When he landed, he spun quickly and grabbed the shirt with both hands and heaved, catching Wulfson by surprise before he let go and stumbled onto the trap.

A whoosh sounded as a hexagonal pattern of lights enveloped Wulfson from his chest down. It looked like a defensive barrier had been flipped inside-out. Wulfson cursed and struggled against the snare, the patterns moving slightly but holding taut.

Kaiden wasn't going to waste the opportunity. He ran up and began hitting the officer with everything he had. While he had to leap into the air to actually strike his face, he used everything at his disposal—his fists, elbows, and head, even getting a few kicks in.

Wulfson's face was bloody and bruised, and his eyes were closed. Kaiden couldn't even tell if he was conscious or not.

"So, do you give?" Kaiden asked, panting as he once again leaned forward and braced against his knees, sweat dripping off him. It had been a while since he had a good fight. The one at the bar was almost a joke. This one he had to work for.

"Is that the best you can do?" Wulfson asked, spitting out some blood.

"Are you kidding me? What can you do now? How are you even talking?" Kaiden demanded.

"A neat little trick—worked better than the first time, at least." Wulfson still sounded infuriatingly arrogant. "But I told you before, I'm going to put you through the wringer…" The barrier around him began to buckle as Wulfson pressed against it. Stretching his arms out, he roared as he forced his arms apart, shattering the trap.

Kaiden backed up as Wulfson stepped forward, taking deep breaths as he balled his fists. "Congratulations, you really pissed me off."

"How is that a—" Kaiden began, but Wulfson charged him, closing the distance incredibly fast despite his injuries. "Oh, shit—"

Kaiden was too worn out to dodge quickly enough. Wulfson barreled down on him, knocking him to the floor before he was picked up. The giant had his arm in a vice grip before he turned and threw him down like a rag doll. Kaiden grunted at the hard impact, feeling like he just slammed into a brick wall even with the mat on the floor.

He tried to roll back and recover, but when he opened his eyes, he saw Wulfson's boot coming right for him. He lifted his arms to deaden the blow, but the force behind the kick was much harder than any strike Wulfson had dealt before. He felt a stinging pain as the boot connected with his arms, and he was knocked back. Helpless, he rolled off the mat and collided with a wall.

Wulfson had been holding back this entire fight. The sudden insight brought an alarming clarity—the stark truth was not good for Kaiden.

He planted a hand on the floor and struggled to push himself up. Finally, he was able to sit up and lean against the wall, dragging in ragged breaths. He saw Wulfson begin to march over to him. Kaiden shook his head and used the wall to help himself stand, damned if he would get his ass beat while sitting on the ground.

After he managed to stand up all the way, he opened

one eye to see Wulfson right in front of him, his eyes like stone and blood running down his face. "So, do you give?" he asked. His low, threatening tone made it hard to tell if he was mocking him or dead serious.

"Is…is that the best you got?" Kaiden retorted, certainly mocking though even he wondered whether it was real gumption or simply stupidity. He folded and bent over, his vision blurred.

Wulfson leaned back, and Kaiden heard a low chuckle come from deep in the giant's belly. "You are probably one of the biggest dumboms I have ever met, but you do put up a good fight. I'll give you that, Initiate."

Oh, good, he'd graduated from boy. It only took a liter of blood and what was assuredly at least a broken nose and a couple ribs.

As his vision darkened, Kaiden looked back to see Wulfson cock an arm back. He grabbed Kaiden by his left shoulder to steady him. "I would simply declare the match in my favor, but if you aren't going to throw in the towel… Well, it was the first one down, and rules are rules."

Kaiden nodded, not really self-aware anymore, though, as Wulfson's grip tightened and he reached his arm further back. Kaiden did have one last thought.

"This is probably going to hurt like a bitch."

Then darkness enveloped him, and he felt nothing.

CHAPTER SEVENTEEN

Streaks of laser fire zipped past, missing him narrowly, and dust kicked up around his feet as live ammo studded the ground. Kaiden dashed quickly across the alley, catching sight of slumped bodies and melted flesh in his periphery.

He wondered where they came from and how they were able to get through their turf without alerting anyone. The alarm had already sounded. Reinforcements should have been there by now. A chill surged through him. How many did they take out before getting there?

An instinct for survival pressed him up against a wall, and he tried to catch the attention of Rocco, one of their enforcers. He couldn't hear him, not over all the shouting and chaos of battle. Once again, he tried his communicator. Nothing. The signal was still dead, so it must have been jammed or blocked. He looked around for signs of Selena or Devin. They were the last two techies he remembered seeing before the first shots. Somehow, they had to get the comms back up.

He saw a small orb fly past him, bounce off the wall, and roll back. It was a metal ball, and a red light on top began to blink rapidly.

Shit, a thermal grenade.

Kaiden rushed to try to toss it back, but he couldn't close the distance. He felt as if he wasn't moving at all. Then he saw Rocco throw himself on it. Two other Dead-Eyes came up behind Kaiden and began pulling him back, while Rocco looked up and screamed at him to get the hell away.

As his eyes widened and he called to the enforcer, he heard one last shout of, "Get back!" before the explosive went off, knocking him and the other Dead-Eyes off their feet. His head collided with concrete as he drew in a sharp gasp of air.

Kaiden sat up in shock before feeling a dense pain across his chest that forced him back down. His head rested on a rather comfortable pillow. He groaned as he ran his hand across his chest, pressing down lightly on different spots to check the damage. It felt as if his ribs had been struck by a battering ram. Then, as his memories started to come back, he realized he wasn't all that far off.

"Hello again, Initiate Jericho." A calm voice greeted him.

Kaiden turned his head slowly to see a somewhat familiar sight. He was in the med bay, being treated by none other than the doctor who did his initial exam.

"Howdy, Doc," he mumbled, words tumbling out of him in pained grunts.

"I must admit, I hadn't expected to see you so soon—less than two days, that's quite the record considering training hasn't officially begun yet."

"Yeah, well, perhaps not for most people. I like to think of myself as a go-getter." He chuckled, stopping himself quickly and wincing. It hurt to laugh.

"Perhaps not a particularly wise one," the doctor noted dryly. She held something up. It looked like a small stick or tube of rubber, and she placed it over his mouth. "Bite down on this, please."

Before he did as she instructed, he cocked an eyebrow and asked, "What for?"

She twisted around and took something from a tray next to her. It was a syringe which held some sort of blue liquid and had a rather thick needle.

"Hold steady. You should feel a tingling sensation in a moment." She placed the needle on his chest in the area over his heart. Before he could bark out for her to wait, she pierced through his skin and injected the liquid into him.

The only noise he could make was a surprised squeak.

After a few moments of feeling nothing but surprise, anger, and confusion, Kaiden started to feel rather elated. The pain seeped away, and soothing warmth stole over him.

"Oh, that's good stuff," he said, a smile coming over his face as the rubber thing rolled onto the floor.

"It's a personal blend I developed a few years ago. It'll take a while, but once you rest a few more hours, you'll be back in working order."

"Ya make me sound like I'm some sort of robot, Doc."

"You are dense enough," she stated, her tone mildly disapproving. Kaiden could feel his smartass nature kicking up, but he felt too fuzzy inside to really be bothered to retort. Whatever this stuff was, he wanted a couple of vials for the weekend.

"Maybe, but what makes you say that?" he asked finally after a moment of shifting around the bed to get comfortable.

"Well, considering the reason you are here is that you decided to have yourself a brawl with Officer Wulfson, I can make an educated guess that self-preservation may not be a high priority to you."

"It was a matter of honor…and I really wanted to punch him in his rock-like face, too." Kaiden admitted. He'd started to feel rather chatty. "How did I get here, by the way?"

"Officer Wulfson brought you here, of course," the doctor explained. "You can thank him yourself. He should be coming back over here after Nurse Yates finishes patching him up."

This got Kaiden to snap out of his delighted haze for a moment. "Please don't leave me alone with him. He might eat me this time."

"Don't be silly. Besides, I have to finish stitching you up and apply mending gel to your wounded areas, so I'll be close by."

"You got security turrets in here or something? You know, to be on the safe side?" Kaiden asked, looking up at the ceiling as he tried to locate hidden compartments—a task that grew steadily harder as his mystery-liquid-induced high return.

"We do, but I doubt that will be necessary." She slid off the medical bed. "Besides, I don't see why you are fretting so much. He said that you were the one who requested to train with him in the first place."

He could feel himself wanting to call bullshit, but all that came out now was a satisfied sigh.

"I have to go and get the gel and utensils. I would say wait here, but I don't think I need to worry about that."

"Yeah, no, I'm doin' pretty good now," Kaiden assured her, giving a quick thumbs-up.

"That's good. I'll be back soon. Oh…well, looks like you'll have some company while I'm gone," she said, waving to someone outside Kaiden's vision. "Hello, Officer Wulfson."

"Evening, Doctor Soni, you get my ward back on his feet yet?" he asked, his massive frame coming into view. Kaiden looked him over and felt a small sense of annoyance. His face was all better. He wanted to feel like he'd left some sort of mark on the bastard.

"Not yet. I gave him an injection of rejuvenation serum that will take some time to relax and restore his muscles, then I have to apply mending gel to surface injuries and do some stitching on deeper wounds." She crossed her arms. "I would like to request that you do not make a habit of sending any student who is willing to train with you immediately to the medical bay. We will have to file a report if it becomes too common."

"Just letting the skitstövel understand what he's in for. Kid's got guts. I'm sure he'll do better," Wulfson said, but as he turned to look at Kaiden, he began scratching at the back of his head. "However…maybe I can admit I went a little overboard." He actually looked a little sheepish.

"It would be a good place to start." Soni sighed. "I'll be back soon. You can talk to him if you like, but I'll need you to depart once I return."

"Understood, Doctor." Wulfson nodded. Soni returned the nod and left, calling for a nurse.

Wulfson took a moment to watch her go before turning to Kaiden. He was silent as he walked over to the side of the bed, grabbed a rolling stool from the neighboring bed, and slid it over to him. Without a word, he sat down as he continued his one-sided staring contest.

Kaiden, for his part, tried to return the glare, but he was far to goofed out to wipe the smile he could feel plastered across his face. "So, how are ya feeling?"

"I'm guessing better than you." Wulfson chuckled, placing an arm on his own knee and holding up his chin with the other.

"Oh, I doubt that, unless you also got some of that blue stuff. It is quite good."

"So, I've heard. Never touch the stuff myself."

"You're missing out."

"I prefer to work through the pain. Speaking of which, I do have to give you your due, boy—"

"Oh, I'm back to boy again. Neat," Kaiden mumbled, though the blue goo effectively robbed it of any belligerence.

"You certainly did a number on me—pretty good at thinking on your feet and got some real strength behind those fists," the officer complimented him. "But you're rash, your defense is spotty, and damned if you aren't a mouthy little bastard." Wulfson then tapped a finger to his temple. "Plus, you don't make use of your full arsenal. Why didn't you use your EI?"

"What are you talking about? We were fighting each other, not shooting each other…though I wouldn't have minded that now that it's all said and done."

"Pah, kronidiot. Your EI is more than just an aim-assist tool or scanner. You don't know about its Battle Suite?"

"Do what? Chief, you there?"

Silence.

"Oh right, I keep forgetting that—audio on."

"Well, how do you do, moron?" Chief grumbled.

"What's this about a battle suite?"

"It's what I was trying to mention before you shut me off. Thanks for that, by the way, ya dick."

"Hey, man, mistakes happen."

"I'm starting to feel like they're just your normal decisions." The EI snarled disdain. *"Anyway, the Battle Suite is a specialized set of apps and functions used by those in the Soldier Division. Each division has their own unique suite to aid them in their field. You would have learned about them on day one training, but considering the circumstances, I was going to give you a crash course to hopefully give us a leg-up on old knuckle-beard over here."*

"You think it would have helped?" Kaiden asked, trying to sit up a little on his bed and not fall back into a daze.

"Probably. You would have at least known that the snare trap could be broken, and it might have saved you a smackdown. Would have helped you find weak points and given you warning and predictions where he would attack, among other useful tips

and tricks that would have spared you an ass-kicking. Or at least one that maybe wasn't so humiliating."

"Well, I— Huh, that actually does sound useful."

"Like I said, I tried to tell ya, cock-bite," Chief admonished. *"I only keep insulting you to build character. You won't learn otherwise."*

"You and I are having words after I get back to the dorm," Kaiden warned. "As for you"—He looked over to Wulfson—"where do we stand?"

He stroked his beard in contemplation. "Well, you lost, but a deal is a deal. I said if you fought me I would answer a few questions for you. You got any?"

Kaiden sat up successfully, rolling his head around to face the giant. "Just the one. Why did you want to fight me in the first place?"

"Simple. I was told that you could be a potential trainee for me. I've been looking for a good few soldiers to take under my wing. I used to be the headmaster of foundations training but got booted for being too harsh—that would be the Board's words, not mine."

"All right, who told you about me? Or should I assume my reputation precedes me?"

Wulfson let out a loud laugh. "You don't have no reputation around here, boy, but keep it up and you might have one at some point. No, that mad idiot Professor Laurie pointed me in your direction."

Even as the chemicals in his system continued his feelings of euphoria, Kaiden felt the heat of rage building in his veins. "Oh, did he?"

"Yeah, filled me in about your little EI and all. I'll admit, it is an interesting idea, but it won't mean a damned thing if you can't muster up the backbone to put in the work to use it right."

"What are you talking about? The whole idea is that I get a little boost in points or something while training in the Animus and get a few extra synapse points over time," Kaiden explained. "But because of Laurie's crappy foresight, I don't even get that right away. He's gotta update all the systems or something before I can do that. Otherwise, my brain might fry."

"Well then, it's a good thing he came to me. Because after our little match, I had an epiphany while I was dragging your ass over here."

"Which was what, exactly?"

"Training in the Animus is only one component of actually getting synapse points. The other two big ones are comprehension and technique. I can help you with both of those."

Kaiden gave Wulfson a look of incredulity. "You don't strike me as the kind of guy to know all about the ins and outs of a mind-melding, virtual reality interface." He raised a weak hand in mock surrender. "Not wanting to make assumptions here, but your little dojo back there seemed more like a junkyard than a gym."

"It is a proving ground in my eyes, and my in-depth knowledge of the Animus isn't the point. What I'm offering is to help you train outside of the Animus. You only do as well in there as you can out here, at least until the synapse starts kicking in. You'll not only get a leg-up on your competition, but you'll be able to get points faster the better you are. That's simply a fact."

Kaiden mulled this over. While he wasn't exactly

thrilled at the beat-down he received, he did have to admit it was nice to get back in the fight. His little trial run showed him the potential and power of the Animus, but he did have to admit the uncanniness of it made it feel a little hollow, no matter how real it seemed.

"I'm back," Doctor Soni announced. "I hope you apologized to the young man, Wulfson."

"Not entirely. After all, it was a mutually agreed upon fight."

"Yeah, and Stockholm Syndrome is another way to make friends," Chief muttered.

The doctor sighed her disapproval. "Well, I won't force it. Wouldn't do any good, probably." She looked at a tablet in her hand while walking back to Kaiden. "Either way, you need to leave now. Once I'm finished with the patient, he'll need to rest for him to recover in time for the start of the semester."

"Aye, no worries. I'll get out of your hair," Wulfson agreed as he stood and walked away, "Get some rest, boy, but think about my offer. Originally, I didn't care if you joined me or not, but now?" He chuckled as he looked back at Kaiden, a wide smile on his face. "You might just make yourself a worthy warrior—if you got the dedication for it."

Kaiden watched him walk away, sinking back into his bed, deep in thought.

"Well, whatever this is about, I would recommend not making a habit of visiting here too often." She added, "Otherwise I might think you were getting beaten only for the drugs."

"I won't lie, that has been the upside of this," Kaiden joked.

"Might wanna be careful. This stuff has some really nasty effects after a while."

"Wait, nasty effects? Like what?"

"I'll let you think about the possibilities for a bit. Consider it my way of making sure you learn a lesson this time around."

"Your version of caring is terrible."

"You do realize she can't hear me?" Chief reminded him.

Kaiden looked over to see Doctor Soni's annoyed glare and frown. He apologized quickly and tried to explain that he wasn't talking to her but the EI that flew around in his head.

She knew about it, of course—she was the one who forwarded the info to Laurie, after all. Still, it was fun to watch him squirm for a bit.

CHAPTER EIGHTEEN

"So I told him to piss off. If he wants a yes-man, I'm sure there are plenty of kiss-ups looking for a promotion among the tech administration, though they wouldn't be able to match my skills." Laurie regaled them with the story between quick sips of wine. "Or, perhaps, take two hundred credits to a red-light district, though they wouldn't be able to match my skills either," he added with a laugh.

"Alexander, if you keep that up, you might find yourself employed there." Mya snickered.

"I certainly have the wiles for it," he concurred with mirth.

The two Nexus Academy administrators were dining at the restaurant, Belle by the Bay, the silver carpeting and dark walls awash in soft blue and white lighting. The room had a circular design with large windows in the south of the room, looking out at the bay. The waitstaff were in all-black dresses or suits, moving quickly from kitchen to bar to table as the night went on.

As the professor and the counselor continued trading stories, Laurie saw a familiar man dressed in all white with a black tie approach their table, accompanied by a woman with hazel eyes, dark skin, and curly hair. She wore a gold dress and matching earrings.

"My apologies for being late," Sasha stated, drawing back a chair across the table from the other two and offering it to his companion before seating himself

"Wonderful of you to finally join us, Sasha. I see you brought Ms. Faraji as well."

"You can call me Akello, Alex. We shouldn't be so formal," the lady in question retorted, a playful smile spreading on her face.

"First name basis is so banal for someone as regal as yourself," Laurie returned suavely.

"You don't seem so reluctant to address me by my first name," Mya jested, elbowing him lightly in the ribs.

Laurie feigned suffering, doubling over in mock agony. "Not if you keep up displays such as this. They are why I feel the need to carry a personal barrier field."

"Usually, you say it is to give you breathing room from all of your admirers," Akello reminded him.

"A device can have multiple uses." Laurie finished off his glass and raised it slightly in the air, signaling a waiter for a refill. "These fancier restaurants really need to have automated bars."

"Perhaps you need to order a bottle instead of one glass at a time. By this point, I would imagine you know that whatever limits you put on yourself are pointless," Sasha mocked him with a wry smile.

"He complains, but he likes being pampered." Mya grinned, taking the sting out of the words.

"Well, but of course. After what I accomplish on a daily basis, is it not justified?" Laurie asked, a hand moving in a circular motion before he placed it upon his chest.

"Considering most of your physical labor is done by robots?" Akello questioned.

"That I designed," he retorted.

"Then program them to give you a pat on the back in the future," Sasha said, a light chuckle escaping him.

"You are all so devilish." Laurie sounded exacerbated, but he enjoyed the verbal sparring.

They continued joking and trading compliments until a waiter came to refill Laurie's glass, taking their orders along with Sasha's order of two bottles of red wine. For the sake of the staff, was his reasoning.

"It is a wonderful night. Pity it might be some time before we get together again like this," Akello remarked wistfully, looking out one of the windows at the bay shimmering in the moonlight.

"Perhaps, but we do have a promising new crop this year —at least the ones I admitted," Mya noted, taking a sip from her own glass. "A lot of different fields and class potential."

"You mostly had special cases this year, correct, Mya?" Sasha inquired.

"Yep, got to process a few Tsuna this morning as well, the last of the initial batch."

"Should certainly shake things up. This is the largest

group of alien initiates we've ever had." Akello's tone carried a note of anticipation.

Sasha nodded. "This is the first year we've allowed full integration like this. We've only had initial integration in administrative positions or in special cases, never as a full unit of initiates."

"Well, the Tsuna were the only ones that could actually integrate with the Animus, and even then, it took a bit of tweaking," Laurie explained. "Surprising, really. I would have thought the Mirus would have been more receptive, considering their psychoactive status."

"I thought you and your team were working with the Mirus to integrate them with the system?" Mya asked.

"Oh, we did, but didn't exactly have the outcome we were hoping for," he confessed. "When we thought we found a proper wave pattern to use to establish a link, we tried to integrate a Mirus volunteer."

"How did that go?" Akello asked.

"Not well." Laurie took a slow sip of wine. "A lot of shaking and what I assume were convulsions. Its eyes went from black to a faded gray color, then he exploded."

By this time, the other three table guests were giving him looks between incredulity and horror.

Laurie continued, "I told their—I believe their term for a scientific officer is the equivalent of 'maestro,' as they deem science closer to art in the culture—how envious I am. Anyway, I apologized, and he was actually quite practical. He said that this was a possibility and that it was acceptable in the name of further study. The World Council put the project on hiatus for now. They said that despite the indifferent reaction, they didn't want to risk possibly angering our new friends. I must admit I gained a new-found admiration for those people over the course of the study."

After blinking rapidly for a moment, Mya piped up, "You know, Alexander, I keep forgetting that as fun as you are, your version of practicality is quite horrifying."

"Professor Laurie hasn't gotten this far by letting morals stop him," Sasha said sarcastically.

"Why, thank you, Sasha. Nice to know that you acknowledge my accomplishments." Laurie somehow managed to make sarcasm sound cheerful.

"He is so easily placated," Akello whispered to Mya.

"Now, what about you, sweet Akello?" Laurie asked, looking at her, causing her to plaster a smile on her face and sit a little straighter. "You will probably have it the hardest of the four of us for the next few weeks. The first year Animus trials are always hard on the instructors. Not to mention you're an advisor now."

"You got promoted, Akey? Congrats!" Mya leaned over to clink glasses with her.

"Thanks, Mya, it was only a week ago. Adviser Zhang is now head monitor. I got his position."

"What happened to Sadira?"

"She was offered a position at the World Council—speaking of that, I don't know where exactly, but she'll be a liaison of some sort."

"Former HM De Silva will actually take over the role of liaison between the Council and the Academy. It appears the Council would like more frequent updates and figured having a former administrator will offer better insight," Sasha explained dryly.

"You know, all this bureaucracy is really beginning to give me the perception that we are not trusted by our superiors." Laurie huffed his indignation.

"Careful, one of those superiors is sitting right across from you," Mya teased.

"I am actually inclined to agree with Laurie in this instance," Sasha admitted.

"Well now, that's both exciting and terrifying." Akello's eyes went wide with feigned horror.

"The WC has always had a hand in the Academy, along with the other four ark schools in the world. But their increasing micromanaging and inquiries are giving myself and many members of the Board the feeling that something is brewing."

"Any ideas on what that might be exactly?" Laurie asked.

"Nothing good. They have no fiscal hand in the Academy, and we have neither offered nor demonstrated any reason that we are in dire straits or are doing anything malicious. So, if they aren't trying to take a more active role due to internal problems, then there must be something they aren't telling us or a suspicion they have that may have enough truth to it for them to start acting as they are."

"They are the Earth's government. Paranoia is rather common for them, isn't it?" Akello pointed out.

"Perhaps, but considering that the last four years have seen an increase in almost all fields—admittance, technological, and medical advancement—even the scores of our graduated and training students are steadily increasing.

Nothing would indicate that we should be a priority in their eyes."

"You think we are doing too well for them?" Laurie chuckled.

"Honestly? Perhaps," Sasha stated. "You remember why the Nexus Academy got started in the first place?"

"Of course, it was purposed just before the first contact with the E.T.T.," Laurie reminded them.

"The what?" Akello asked.

"The Extra-Terrestrial Trinity. It was a nickname given to the first three races humanity made contact with—the Tsuna, Mirus, and Sauren," Mya explained. "It was before our time."

"Hmph, thanks for making me feel old, Mya," Laurie chided. "Yet another reason I don't address you by your last name."

Mya rolled her eyes. "You want to continue, Sasha?"

"Of course. Back when Nexus Academy was first being built, it was not to be an ark academy like it is today. It was to be a military training acceleration program to help in creating advanced military weapons and training soldiers quickly with the aid of chemicals and EI integration tools."

"So, super soldiers?" Akello summarized.

Sasha nodded. "To put it plainly, however, aside from some initial skirmishes with the Sauren on the moon and Station Zappa, no full-scale war was waged. However, the foundations of the program were already laid and money spent."

"And considering that the Council decided peace was a better option than interstellar war, maybe it wasn't the greatest image to be building a factory to mass produce super soldiers and weapons that could potentially destroy cruisers—and also, to create possible alien plagues."

"Did you have anything to do with it, Alex?" Akello asked, giving the professor a suspicious glance.

He frowned. "Darling, I'm forty-seven. I would have been ten years old when this was happening. Granted, I was a prodigy, but the government would possibly be a little wary of giving a child high-level clearance, I would guess." He finished another glass of wine and wiped his mouth with a napkin. "My father, however, very much was. To this day, I have never seen him so enthralled with his work as he was then. For a few years, my mother and I seemed more like people he would visit between jobs than family."

"Oh, good, Daddy issues. I can help you with that," Mya offered cheerfully, causing Akello to giggle.

"I can assure you, my relations with my father are fine. Though getting chances to talk are scarce, since he's working on the designs for Station Icarus."

"They are naming a space station after a fable character who fell from the sky?" Sasha asked.

"He has actually suggested a name change on the grounds that it might contribute to hesitation from potential backers."

"Before we get off track, I would like to know why you brought this up to begin with, Sasha," Akello interjected.

"Well, ever since the Council decided to restructure Nexus into an ark academy, there have always been a militant few who believed the initial plan should not have been aborted, simply restructured and moved elsewhere—somewhere our new allies couldn't have observed too easily."

"They wanted us to keep making weapons for the specific purpose of alien annihilation?" Mya questioned.

"They would classify it as preparation, and while I disagree with the overall method, I can understand the concern."

Akello raised an eyebrow. "How so?"

"Well, think about it, my dear," Laurie began. "We happened to be quite lucky if you consider our first encounters with the beings in the great unknown, but do you believe that they are the only ones out there?"

"Wouldn't they tell us if they had fought or come in contact with hostile races?"

"The Tsuna have, but they weren't spacefaring and merely observed. The Sauren make a sport of hunting down dangerous creatures from other planets, but the few logs of conversations I have found or documents that have come across my desk indicate they haven't found any other intelligent races other than the Tsuna. There was a war between them, reportedly, but they were able to declare a truce after some sort of ritualistic combat that took over a month to come to a conclusion."

"Blood-hungry yet honorable, a fun mix," Laurie noted.

"Wait, why didn't we have to do that?" Mya asked, causing all eyes to stare at her in befuddlement. "I mean, I don't want a fight to the death, but if that's how it goes…"

"The short answer is we had bigger guns," Sasha explained. "However, a more involved explanation would be that during the battle on Zappa, a condensed version actually did happen. One of the Sauren warlords went into battle against a sergeant from the United Earth Army. They battled each other for the equivalent of three Earth days before a recovery unit was able to come in and retrieve him. It was apparently enough to earn the respect of that warlord, and it gave us an olive branch that we were able to use in creating a truce."

"Who was the sergeant?"

"A Swedish man by the name of Wulfson. He works as head of security at the Academy, as a matter of fact."

"I actually ran into him on the way to my office. Had a nice little chat," Laurie chimed in.

"Really now? Doesn't he usually detest you?" Sasha inquired.

"I had a couple tricks up my sleeve, so no worries." Laurie smiled broadly.

"Well then, what about the Mirus?" Akello asked, looking at Laurie.

"We did trade some history during my time with them, as a matter of fact. Besides ourselves and the other known races, the maestro said they came across two other races that could have the potential to be spacefaring. One ended up causing a nuclear apocalypse and eradicating the entire race, and the other has been hindered by a planet-wide civil war."

"You know, it's starting to seem like we were simply moved to the front of the line rather than truly being interesting enough to bring into the great galactic family," she remarked dryly.

"If it makes you feel better, we are the only race to house delegates from all three races, along with developing technology with them as well," Laurie pointed out, his expression a little smug.

"You know, it actually does," Akello said with confidence.

"It could simply be because they all want to keep an eye on us," Sasha suggested.

"Don't spoil the mood, Sasha," Mya chided with pretended affront.

"Wait, dammit, we went off tangent again." Akello huffed her irritation.

"It's fine, Advisor Faraji. It is simply speculation at this point. If it is something that we should look into further, I'll let you know." Sasha's tone was calm and reassuring.

"And right on cue too, food is here!" Laurie exclaimed as two waiters came up to them with trays of food.

After the plates were passed around and the academy teachers began eating, the mood lifted, jokes and tales were exchanged, and ideas were offered by some as solutions to the problems of others.

As the night went on, the four friends enjoyed their time together. Soon, the year would truly begin, and they could all feel the anticipation of the unknown along with the excitement.

CHAPTER NINETEEN

Kaiden awoke in his pod and yawned. He didn't quite recall how he got here, and he was already missing that blue stuff.

"What time is it?" he asked aloud, trying to stretch out as much as he could in the enclosed space.

"0500 Monday morning, the 10th of September," the synthesized voice of the capsule's monitor announced.

Kaiden jerked up in shock, knocking his head against the ceiling. "Gah, sonofa— What did you say? It's Monday? How did I miss a whole day?"

"The nurse who brought you back from the bay put some relaxation oil in the diffuser of your capsule. Knocked you right the hell out," Chief explained.

"What the hell for?"

"Well, 'To get some rest and prepare for the start of the year' was her official response, but if I had to take a personal guess, it was because you kept hitting on her and she really wasn't into it."

"Good God, man... Shit, my classes start in like an hour. What are my classes even?"

"It's a damn good thing you've got me around, ain't it?" Chief chuckled. *"The first day is all about the Animus set-up. You can sign up for finger painting and exotic dance later."*

Kaiden pressed the button to open the capsule, slid out, and stretched once he was on his feet. He was the only one out at the moment, but he could see other capsules lighting up and figures moving around.

"Open locker." He turned as he heard the whir and click of the drawer under his pod snap open and slide out. All the supplies he had requested were present, some wrapped and others bagged. He found a complete set of clothes—a black shirt with a small Nexus Academy logo in blue, black pants, socks, and boots.

He remembered personally requesting black as his primary colors and the supply clerk trying to explain to him that it had to be a mix of standard colors. But seeing as all his clothes were indeed black, maybe Wulfson had put enough of the fear of God into the clerk for him to get his way.

At least all the abuse was good for something.

Then, as he sifted through the new items, he found his jacket—silver in color with white trim and blue accents and a royal-blue band wrapped around the arm, the official designation of his status in the Soldier Division. He also saw a logo, a black triangle with a star on the inside, in white.

"Hey, Chief, you know what this logo on the armband means?"

"It's your class, year, and status. The Star logo means Ace,

the white coloring means first-year, and the black triangle indicates that you're a special-case registrant. You're official now, buddy."

Kaiden chuckled. He had to admit, he was feeling it. For all the crazy experiences he had gone through over the last few days, this did make him feel quite sentimental. No going back now. He was there to stay.

He put the jacket on and zipped it up. A few other initiates now climbed out of their beds or got dressed. The SC dorm was certainly less crowded, so most of the others must have gone to their designated division dorms. He guessed he would be prodded along to do the same eventually. For now, he would enjoy the quiet.

He grabbed his oculars and left to get a head start on breakfast. He could feel his stomach growling and had to make up for a couple of lost meals.

Kaiden took a seat at the same table he had previously chatted with Chiyo at. The sun was barely coming up, but he knew that he would want the shade when it finally came through.

He looked down at his tray—omelet, waffles, bacon, breakfast potatoes, oatmeal, apple, coffee, orange juice, water, and a chocolate chip cookie that the cafeteria personnel insisted he have.

Guess Sasha kept his word. Even his jokes were serious.

As he began scarfing down his food, he wondered what was in store for him. "Hey, Chief, you got any idea what I should be looking forward to?"

"Yeah, a few things, but do you really wanna spoil the surprise?"

"Haven't I had enough of those?" he lamented.

"Not when they are so much fun for me to watch."

"Just give me the bas—"

"Mind if I join you? Or are you enjoying the conversation you are having with yourself?" a familiar voice asked.

Kaiden looked over to see Chiyo, tray in hand, a darkness under her eyes indicating she hadn't slept too well.

He pointed casually across the table, offering her the seat opposite him. "Sure, feel free. I ain't talking to myself. I'm talking with my EI."

Chiyo sat down and began opening her pack of utensils. "How is that? I don't see a tablet or the oculars you wore before."

"It's a voice inside my head," Kaiden stated without thought. Chiyo momentarily stopped pulling at the packet of cutlery and stared at him.

"Most people can't do that. We're special, remember? Now explain it to her before she thinks we're the wrong kind of special," Chief demanded.

"Oh, yeah, forgot. You're the first person I've talked to who doesn't know."

"About what, exactly—the voices in your head?" Chiyo deadpanned, fishing out a fork and knife from the now opened packet and cutting into her pancake.

Kaiden quickly summarized the events that led to him getting Chief— his meeting with Laurie, the Gemini factor, and the EI implant in his head, along with bragging about some of its capabilities.

Chiyo maintained eye contact and nodded along.

When he finished telling his story, she pursed her lips and tapped a finger against them in thought. "That is...quite interesting. You say you got to meet Professor Alexander Laurie?"

"Yes, an experience that I'm hoping eventually pays off. I don't want to be adding therapy bills to my Academy debt," Kaiden grumbled.

"I would love to have a chance to meet him. His work on the Animus system alone seems fascinating."

"Well, I would say I would put in a good word for you, but I would be afraid that I would then have to tell the police the last time I saw you alive."

Chiyo rolled her eyes and sighed, pushing a lone grape around on her plate for a moment before looking back at him. "I should also say that I'm honestly shocked that your Gemini factor was discovered so late in life."

"Well, the Dead-Eyes didn't require annual physicals, you know?" Kaiden chuckled.

"Still, it is an incredibly rare trait. The implications for humanity the more we augment our bodies with EI and bionic implants are quite valuable."

"Are you saying that if I had played my cards right, I could be living the dream life as an exhibit in some science department?" he joked.

"Potentially, but I've heard more stories of corporate slavery, illegal testing, and cadavers with the trait being sold on the black market, earning high prices for recent and clean kills."

Kaiden waited for her to smile or shake her head, indicating a joke, but it didn't happen.

"I don't want to be special anymore."

"It's not all bad, obviously. Truly, I would kill for the casting function you spoke of."

"I really need to get that gun from supplies," Kaiden muttered under his breath.

"The interface capability has great potential, and I would guess the raw power of the EI implant itself means that it can process much faster than even the Academy's premier models."

"You and Laurie sound like you would have a great old time talking about me." Kaiden huffed his annoyance. In the cold light of day, his so-called special gene seemed more of an irritation than a real benefit. "I'm more than merely my implant, you know."

"Maybe, but it is the most interesting thing about you so far."

"I like this girl," Chief exclaimed.

Kaiden gripped the bridge of his nose in annoyance. "People skills seem to be lacking in general at this place."

"I'll be sure to consider it when I use my synapse points," Chiyo noted dryly.

"It would be appreciated," Kaiden concurred before shaking his head as a small smile formed on his lips "I kid…somewhat. It has been nice to have a couple of conversations with someone who is more my speed, or at least doesn't seem to think of me as an experiment first and foremost."

Chiyo finished eating a piece of toast, pausing for a moment to swallow. "Well, for all the talk of the implant, you do seem interesting for who you are. It makes for pleasant company."

"What do you mean?" he asked.

"Most of the other initiates here—myself included, to be fair—all came here with a plan in mind. For some, it's simply a goal to strive for, while for others, it's almost an obsession. It's been nice to talk to someone who isn't preoccupied with all that."

Kaiden leaned back slightly, looking off into the sky. "To be honest, I wasn't even aware of this place before I got the invite. All my life, I've simply gone with the flow. I had a family of sorts, and everything seemed pretty good. Guess I'm just looking for a place again."

He looked back down to see Chiyo staring at him and gave her a quizzical look. "What? Too mushy?"

"No, it's quite…I can understand," she admitted.

"You know, we've only talked about three times, right?"

"Correct."

"Somehow, I've always been the topic of conversation. I can't say I know too much about you, but you seem to know all about me with just a glance."

"I simply modified the normal scanning function in my lenses. It gives me the target's personnel files rather than only their Academy I.D."

"I thought you had to be staff or something to have access to that?" he asked, and she shrugged.

"Take a look at her armband," Chief hinted.

Kaiden did. It was silver with a golden triangle outer logo and a white insignia that looked like the numerals 101.

"Silver band means she's in the Technician Division. The IOI insignia means she's Infiltration Class. She's a hacker."

"What does the golden triangle mean?" Kaiden whispered.

"Merit-based admission, a different version of SC. It means that while you got a lucky break getting here, they wanted *her to come here. Since she's a hacker, it means don't fuck with her unless you want the oxygen chamber in your capsule to mysteriously malfunction or your permanent record to suddenly have 'known serial killer and has a llama fixation' suddenly appear one day."*

Kaiden nodded, now understanding how she knew his background the first time they met. It was actually something of a relief. At least it hadn't been passed around.

"So then, what are you looking for here?" he asked.

"In what way?"

"Well, going back to our other talks, you mentioned a path and all that. You said that you share most of the other initiate's goals. You're in Infiltration, but what do you hope to get out of it?"

Chiyo looked off to the side for a moment, then took a deep breath. "I'm not too clear on that, honestly. I had no reason to come here until about a year ago. While our stories differ slightly—or perhaps strongly—we were both brought here by chance."

"Well, it is nice to see that we share something similar."

She looked back at him with half-open eyes. "I recall that you said you got here by getting in a fight?"

"I *won* a fight. Against four guys at once," he retorted.

"They were just slummers. Don't make it sound like you took on a group of battle-hardened mercs, you ego-tripping bastard," Chief jeered.

Kaiden clenched his jaw to keep from responding to the EI.

"Either way, I was scouted by the academy for my talents. They are a bit...subtler than yours are."

"Hey, everyone's got their use. Gotta be some impressive skills if a place like this takes notice of you," Kaiden said.

"Well, I wou— Thank you. I try not to dwell on things, but I have been working on my abilities since I was a child."

"Hacking is a rather interesting hobby to pick up in elementary. What brought that on?"

She looked away again, watching the sun climb slowly over the mountain range. "I wanted to be of... I had a knack for it, felt it was a skill set that could take me somewhere in life."

"Rather clinical of you," Kaiden commented.

She looked back at him, this time with a flash of annoyance in her eyes. "What do you mean?"

Kaiden shrugged. "I mean, call me a meathead if you want, but I got into fighting, guns, and all that stuff because I liked it. I eventually got better and started to treat it seriously with time, sure, but it all started with that."

"You were how old when you started shooting guns?"

"Eh, about eight or nine, maybe? I fired my first shot when I was a baby. My grandpa helped me hold it."

She blinked, not saying a word.

"Look, I ain't a guidance counselor or trying to sell you a self-help pamphlet or something. However, if I can offer a piece of advice for all the advice you've given me until now, you gotta have some fun with what you're doing or at least take some pride in it. Otherwise, what's gonna keep the drive going? I'm sure you're damn good at whatever ya do. But you gotta know that they'll eventually slap a grade on you, and you'll grow comfortable with it. There won't be much left for ya."

She continued to blink, her mouth opening for a moment before shutting tight. She then took in a deep breath and said, "That may be the most eloquent and well-thought-out thing you have said to me so far."

Kaiden chuckled. "It's only a personal philosophy. You can't control everything in life. You can trust me on that. Fate is more than happy to bitch-slap you when you get too smug. It's in how you deal with fate's bullshit that you gain a sense of direction."

She nodded slowly, apparently genuinely impressed.

"Well, look at that—two whole paragraphs of something clever. Makes me so proud," Chief chirped. *"Maybe Wulfson's fist made some cracks in that thick skull of yours."*

Kaiden rolled his eyes and chuckled. "Well, I hope to see you around again. Looks like breakfast talks might be our thing. I gotta get going to the Animus center unless you care to join me?"

She tilted her head slightly. "You still have initiation and loadout, correct?"

Kaiden cocked his head and considered this, realizing he was unsure of the answer.

"The answer is yes," Chief told him in an irked tone.

"Yeah."

She shook her head "Then no, thank you. I have already completed mine. Most of the SCs and late attendees are the only ones left to go through it. I don't have to report to the Center for another two hours. I'll be headed to the library."

"I gotcha," Kaiden acknowledged, standing up with his empty tray. "See you soon, hopefully."

As he left to dump his trash, Chiyo noticed the Ace insignia on his armband. As she stood up to leave herself, she thought about it. Before their conversation, she would probably have been more surprised to see that, but now?

She could admit to herself it made a little sense.

CHAPTER TWENTY

Kaiden took in the sight of the Animus Center. It was a large, circular building, at least eight stories tall. Reflective glass wrapped around it, mostly clean of aesthetic touches with the exception of a large Nexus Academy symbol in metal framing hanging over stylized lettering announcing Animus Center above the six pairs of doors at the entrance.

He watched a stream of initiates enter, nearly getting knocked over as others rushed passed him. This wasn't even all the students, and the flow of bodies moved in like a raging river.

Briskly, Kaiden walked to the entrance, squeezing himself into the crowd as he moved into the building.

"Chief, I could use a map if you got one," Kaiden requested, taking out his oculars and putting them on, pushing them a little farther up the bridge of his nose in hopes that they wouldn't fall off as his body was shoved forward.

"Good idea. Onscreen," Chief acknowledged. A map of the building's interior materialized in the display, a translucent blue arrow pointing northwest.

"I marked your Animus Hall on the map. Also, tell me what you think of this."

Kaiden felt the back of his frames lengthen, wrapping around the back of his head and what felt like prongs dig in. The lenses pressed against his eyes, but the screen jutted out slightly, giving him the feeling that he wore goggles.

"What's this?" he asked.

"A neat little function the optics have. It's called hazard mode, and it straps the oculars to you when you're moving quickly or are on rocky ground so they don't fall off. Plus, the display keeps any debris from reaching the eyes."

Kaiden adjusted the fit slightly. "Not bad. Guess Laurie does have some cool trinkets."

"I ain't gonna take offense to that since I'm not technically his creation, but watch yourself, smartass."

Kaiden entered the main part of the building. Each floor was sectioned off and encircled the rotunda every twenty feet all the way to the top. The walls were a dark-oak color, and the floors were black tile. He followed the arrow on the map to a bank of elevators, leaning against a wall as he waited for one to free up.

"So, what did you get?" he heard one of the initiates ask another.

"Marksman. What about you?"

"I got into Engineering, Goliath Class. Get to work on heavy arms, power suits, tanks, and the like."

"Damn, that sounds intense," another initiate stated. "I

got field surgeon. Guess it's a good thing you know me, right?"

Kaiden continued to listen to the excited chatter. He had to admit it would have been nice to chat with someone about what was about to go down. He wasn't completely sure himself, but hey, two minds with half a thought gotta equal a whole one, right?

"Excuse me, but I remember you."

Kaiden looked over to see a Tsuna. He shifted in surprise for a moment but quickly found his bearings. It wasn't so surprising the second time around.

"Howdy... Wait, are you the one I met back at the train station?" he asked, pushing himself off the wall and turning to look at him face to face. "It was…Geno, right?"

"Correct." The alien nodded, placing a webbed hand on his chest and two fingers in the air in a salute. "Geno Aronnax, Engineering Division, Mechanist Class." He ended his salute before extending a hand. "It is good to see you again, Initiate Kaiden Jericho."

"Likewise," Kaiden concurred with a grin, shaking the alien's hand. "Mechanist, huh? Seems kinda like an oxymoron. Don't all the engineers mess with machines?"

"Well, yes, but a mechanist excels with all kinds and is not a specialist of any particular group or type of machine."

"Jack of all trades, then?"

"This would be an appropriate term, yes." Geno nodded. "We are more likely to have direct action in the field. I must admit it is both troubling and exciting for me."

"How so?"

Geno tapped his fingers together, his head bobbing from side to side. "I'll do my best to explain without going into trivial details. You see, my people are separated into groups. Every group has a specified task, and they don't usually mingle outside of free time. To be able to work on machines and weaponry while also going into battle… these jobs would not usually be intertwined where I come from. If a vehicle or device needed repair while out in the field, we would send a drone to do it while controlling it remotely. That way, the warriors would not have to concern themselves with casualties."

"I think I follow. So are you saying you don't have any combat experience at all? How did you get saddled with that?"

"No, you misunderstand, or I didn't explain properly. All Tsuna are taught the basics of combat among other skills, but when the time comes for us to begin our profession, the continued training in skills that are not a part of the profession is frowned upon. It is seen as time wasted."

Kaiden crossed his arms and leaned back against the wall. "All right…but I mean, if it makes you so skittish, why not ask for a different class or explain the situation to one of the counselors? I'm sure they don't wanna piss off any of your… I don't know, is it elders?"

"I do not have a problem with my designated class…not personally. It is merely the potential ramifications with my clan, though I am not completely certain how they will react. Possibly just bewildered."

"Still, I gotta say it's still kind of shocking you got a class that sees field work with only basic combat skills."

"That would be where most of my hesitation stems from. You see, my clan used to be warriors many of your years ago. We were designated scientists after three of my ancestors, brothers from the same clan matriarch, created a device that had permanent luminescence," Geno explained, placing a closed fist onto his chest. "It is funny to think about—in these modern times, their device is considered little more than a bauble—but at the time, it was a controversy. A Tsuna going against their designation could be traumatic for our society. Everyone had their place of importance, and we have a saying: 'The pillars of our kingdom are not built of stone, but people.' And they went against that."

Kaiden nodded along, wondering if this was leading to something. "I getcha, but why is this leading to your little crisis of faith?"

"The original clan was divided, with some continuing as warriors, and the brothers became the head of a new clan that was designated scientists. They struggled for many years to shake off the stigma of our ancestor. We are the only clan to have had our designation changed, but we persevered, and now, we are held in high esteem. However, when I learned more of our past, I grew curious. I would spend my free time learning the ways of the warrior to feel closer to my clan's roots."

"So that's why you got mechanist? You can repair a droid just as easily as destroy one?"

"I find the destruction of one to be less time consuming," Geno said, a little of his previous melancholy leaving his eyes.

"Well, I can't say I can relate with the whole clan thing, but I would say don't let it bother you." Kaiden smiled. "If you're so interested in your ancestors, think of yourself as a new version of those brothers in the past—a trailblazer.

Besides, it's like you're combining the best of both worlds."

Geno stood up a little straighter, cocking his head to the side. "That is an interesting way to think about it, but I still worry how my clan will be seen by society."

"Hey, man, I don't know exactly what went on when the treaty was signed and they sent you guys down here, but this had to come up. Look at it like this…you're on your own now. Whatever happens when you get back, tell them you were showing the humans what your people can do."

Kaiden heard a ding from an elevator reaching the floor. In the time they had been chatting, the hallway had cleared. He looked back at Geno who was staring off at nothing, obviously contemplating his words. "I'm gonna head over to my hall. You wanna come with?"

Geno snapped back to reality. "Ah, no…thank you, I am waiting on some of the others to arrive. Also, I would not be going to the same hall as you. Tsuna are currently assigned our own hall until some of the Animus specifications become universal."

Kaiden nodded as he approached the open elevator. "Good talkin' with you, Geno. Don't sweat the small stuff. You'll do fine."

"We do not sweat as you do, but— Ah, that was an idiom. My thanks and best wishes to you, friend," Geno said, waving farewell.

Kaiden waved back as the doors closed. He was friends with an alien now. How about that?

INITIATE

Kaiden entered hall seven and saw rows and rows of tubes, similar to the one he had been put into during his exam with Laurie and Sasha but which seemed more streamlined. These were on the ground at an angle, rather than standing vertical, with cords and wires strewn about.

He joined a group of students, hearing from the chatter that no one was really sure if they should get in the pods, when a voice called.

"Good morning, initiates. Welcome to the Animus Center." Everyone turned to see Akello holding a tablet and dressed in a long white-and-silver staff jacket with black pants and silver boots. "I would recommend getting used to this place. You'll be spending a hell of a lot of time here."

"Are you the guide?" an initiate asked.

"I am Advisor Faraji, but I used to be a guide, yes," she explained. "I will be overseeing all of you until a new guide is appointed. Don't worry, I won't send any nasty beasts after you in the Animus...unless you annoy me."

"How magnanimous of her." Kaiden chuckled under his breath.

"Hey, she is the one with all the control over the pods in this section. She could send in a lot worse," Chief cautioned.

"I can imagine. I won't open my mouth too much."

"Damn straight."

Akello punched something into her tablet. "Please choose a pod. Walk slowly and carefully, and when you choose one, stand by for attendance scan."

All the initiates followed her instruction, walking around the hall and looking at the different pods.

"Oh, get that one. 7-G5," Chief exclaimed.

"They all look the same to me," Kaiden noted.

"That one looks better in the light."

"Before anyone tries to find the one pod with racing stripes, these won't be your assigned pods," Akello called. "We will only use these to set up your profile and loadout for now. You will be assigned a personal pod for the year after the Division test."

"What's that, now?" Kaiden asked.

Akello gave him a quick look "I'll explain once you're inside."

"Yay, ominous foreshadowing," Kaiden mumbled.

"Don't worry about it for now, but I would recommend you pay careful attention to your loadout once we get in there."

Kaiden walked over to the pod Chief had pointed out, if for no other reason than he didn't particularly care which one he got.

"There is a scanner next to each pod. Please place your hand on the screen so it registers you and I can count heads," Akello ordered.

Kaiden walked up to the scanner and complied. A white light moved up and down for a moment before the panel flashed a couple times and he saw a green light. He removed his hand and saw his academy I.D. appear on the screen.

Akello looked at her tablet as she walked across the room. Kaiden saw her stop and look in his direction, and a sense of unease began to swirl within him.

If nothing else, he was at least more confident that he could take her on rather than Wulfson.

She walked over to him, placing the tablet against her chest. "Kaiden Jericho, correct?"

"Yes, ma'am," he answered, wondering what it was about *this* time.

He got a pleasant surprise when she smiled and offered him a hand. "Nice to meet you. Professor Laurie told me a bit about you."

"Did he now?" Kaiden asked, taking her hand in a firm shake. "I can't say I'm confident that he said nice things about me."

She laughed. "Laurie is sweet—a little strange, but sweet."

"I will at least agree with you on the strange part."

She withdrew her hand. "He wanted me to tell you he updated the system. You don't have to worry about any problems during the sync."

He nodded. "Appreciate it. Not having my brains leakin' out of my ears is a plus."

"I will be on the lookout if it makes it easier for you, and of course, I will make sure that nothing happens. This is merely basic stuff."

"Nah, I ain't too worried. If nothing else, I'm pretty sure Laurie wouldn't let his experiment die on him."

"We certainly agree on that." She gave him one last smile before walking away.

He saw her walk over to a large console in the back of the room, place her tablet in a slot, and turn back. "Everybody is here and accounted for. We are about to begin. I hope you are all ready."

Kaiden could hear the excited chatter begin again. He turned to see a white light blinking at the head of the pod. The door to the chamber opened, and Kaiden saw that the interior was padded.

"At least I'll be comfortable as my mind is ripped away from me this time."

"Quit your gripin' and get in the casket," Chief ordered.

Kaiden placed one boot in first before bringing the other up and turning around, facing out and watching the other initiates enter the pods.

"Now everybody, relax. I know this is the first time for some of you, but I promise that everything will be all right. I'll be here to walk everyone through it," Akello assured them.

Kaiden saw the blinking white lights from the other pods turn a solid blue as the doors closed. He was in darkness for a moment before the familiar dim light of glow strips illuminated his pod. Curious now, he sat back and prepared for the sync.

Akello's voice surrounded him in the chamber. "Pods are ready across the board. Is everyone ready to go into the Animus?"

Kaiden saw a screen pop-up in front of him. It read, "Enter Animus?" with a green and red box underneath. He pressed the green box, and the screen disappeared. He saw the light pulse around him, and another light began to scan his body. He felt the same heavy feeling as before and closed his eyes.

Off he went, back to the virtual wonderland.

CHAPTER TWENTY-ONE

They were in the clouds, no ground beneath them and no stars above. Kaiden could see the dozens of other initiates getting their bearings—or at least as much as they could while standing on air.

"Don't look down," Chief chirped, his orb form popping in and hovering next to Kaiden.

"Fortunately, this isn't my first rodeo," Kaiden said dismissively. "Can't say the same for some of them."

While the majority of the other students seemed to be fine, jumping up and down or walking over to one another, he noticed a handful who were waving frantically about or crouching down in the fetal position.

"Eh, they'll get used to it. Builds character."

"They better get used to it quick. Gonna have a traumatic time otherwise."

"Sync complete. Welcome to the Animus initiates," Akello's voice called from the sky.

"Where is the *ground*?" a panicked initiate cried "This is *bullshit*—are you *insane*?"

"Now what did I say about annoying me?" Akello asked.

The screaming boy suddenly dropped out of the air, falling away from the others who remained in place. He released another loud scream. Kaiden watched him disappear, and his voice faded away, but only for a few moments. He could hear the yelling slowly grow louder, sounding as if it was coming from the sky.

All the initiates looked up to see the crybaby now coming down from above. As he began to fall past them all, his descent slowed rapidly before he was dumped unceremoniously back into his original spot.

"While at the main console of this hall, I am in complete control of the Animus. The normal laws of reality don't have to apply here—like needing to stand on ground."

"I think he figured that out," Kaiden mused with a laugh.

"Good thing those pants are virtual too."

"Now then, let's get into a more relaxed mood, what do you say?" Akello suggested.

The sky around them went from a clear blue sky to a violet, twilight hue. Kaiden looked behind him to see the sun fading into the distance.

"Now, let us begin by going over synapse."

A large screen appeared before Kaiden, showing him a screen of statistics—his statistics, he noticed. However, before he got a good look, the screen opened into a new tab and showed him a purple-colored bar lying horizontally on the screen. The inside of the bar was only slightly filled, and he saw an indicator registering five percent underneath.

"What you are all looking at is a synapse experience bar. It measures the amount of experience you gain during training, and when it is full, you gain a synapse point."

"How do I have five percent already?" Kaiden wondered.

"Probably got it during that exam with Sasha."

"I only got five percent doing all of that?"

"Don't worry. You'll get more and get it faster as time goes on. You gotta wait for your mind to get used to all this."

"I thought that was why I had you."

"Heh, think about what I got to work with here."

Kaiden rolled his eyes, "I think you're not pulling your weight."

"Technically, I don't have weight. But if you wanna feel what it's like to be in the Animus without a buffer, be my guest."

"Nah, I'll pass."

"Then tell me you're sorry."

"Sure, just give me a moment to choke down the vomit."

"Sassy bastard."

"Everyone got that?" Akello asked.

"Oh, probably should have been paying attention to that."

"Eh, just wing it."

"When you get a synapse point—or SP for short—you can use it to gain a talent."

The screen changed again, showing a panel with multiple tabs— General, Soldier, Ace, Fitness, and EI.

"The tabs before you represent the trees you currently have access to for now. You can potentially gain new ones if you take the proper courses. For now, you have a tree for your division and your class, along with three universal tabs that all initiates have access to. Go ahead and look around. You can hover over an icon to read what the various talents offer."

Kaiden opened the Soldier tab, revealing dozens of boxes with small logos in each. He moved his hand over one of the boxes at the top showing a pistol being fired.

Crack Shot: Improves the steadiness and accuracy of the user with small arms.

Status: 0/2

"Zero out of two for Crack Shot? Why is it zero?! Shooting is my thing!" Kaiden asked aloud.

"That would probably be why it's so low. For most people, Crack Shot is zero out of four or five," Akello responded.

"Wait, so it's different for everyone?" another initiate asked.

Akello nodded. "The potential of the synapse is limitless. Our scientists, developers, and technicians are always working to improve the system. Perhaps one day, certain areas could be expanded to push your abilities even further. But as it stands now, the Animus downloads your personal information and skill assessments from your EI. It then bases your potential upgrades on your currently cultivated skills and how much it can improve them without things getting…messy. It would be dangerous to increase it beyond the current ability. You should use your points on talents that are underdeveloped or new."

Kaiden continued to look around the Soldier tree, highlighting another box that had a picture of what appeared to be some sort of automaton with a hole in the chest.

Robotic Termination: Grants user the skill and knowledge to understand the anatomy, weaknesses, and damage points in most robotic units.

Status: 0/3

He moved his hand to the box next to it. This was darker than the other boxes, showing a logo of some four-armed being with a hole in the chest.

Mutant Termination: Grants user the skill and knowledge to understand the anatomy, weaknesses, and damage points in known mutant species.

Status: Undetermined (Locked)

"You know what this is about, Chief?"

"The Animus and Academy staff only know so much about an initiate. So, until you take a course in a particular field, some talents are gonna be locked until they can get a baseline on your abilities in a certain area."

"Like killing mutants?"

"You ever fought a mutant?"

Kaiden shook his head. "Haven't had the pleasure, no."

"Then you don't know jack shit about them. Maybe you're an idiot savant and can kill a battalion with a butter knife, but we don't know, and therefore, it would be better that you don't simply start jamming info and skills into yourself."

"How would having new skills be a bad thing?"

"The same reason you don't keep pumping air into a balloon. It explodes. Without a proper understanding of an initiate's abilities, a proper path can't be created. What you are asking to do is take something that requires surgical precision and saying, 'screw it' while trying to force everything down with a plunger."

"So if I were to start choosing random abilities…"

"Depending on what they are, it's the difference between a badass and a bloody mess."

"I think I'll skip that for now."

"Yeah, good idea."

"All right, initiates, let's move on. The trees are now loaded into your EI systems so you can go over them at your leisure. If you have any more questions, you can consult your EI or ask me after we're done."

The screens disappeared. Kaiden saw translucent boxes appear around each initiate, darkening after a moment. A box engulfed him, blocking his vision of the others.

"Now comes the fun part—your personal loadout."

On the darkened wall in front of him, Kaiden saw his reflection. Next to it, a number of options popped onto the screen.

"This is possibly one of the most important options in the early days of your tutelage. What you choose right now is what will be your basic loadout for your training, practice missions, and tests. You will choose your armor, primary weapon, a sidearm, two gadgets, and a melee weapon. Take all the time you need. When you are done, simply confirm your choices, and you will be taken to a testing field. After you're done there, you can work with your loadout some more or finish up, get debriefed, and de-sync from the Animus for today."

Kaiden pressed the options for armor, getting choices for a complete set of options to look at each individual piece.

"You have an opinion here, Chief?"

"Not much of a shopper?"

"Didn't usually have this many options. Actually, I usually didn't have armor in a fight."

"Well, in that case, let's not be stupid with it." Chief's avatar disappeared from Kaiden's side and appeared on the wall. He acted like a mouse cursor hovering over different options.

"You'll definitely want some, just to be safe, but if you've survived this long, that means you gotta be pretty quick. You don't wanna sacrifice that too much."

He opened the tab for chest piece and selected a slim model, black-and-grey. Kaiden saw it appear on his chest and could see the fit in his reflection. It felt sturdy but flexible. While it probably couldn't take heavy damage, it could take a few good hits before busting. It wasn't that heavy, and he could feel padding on the interior.

Chief quickly whisked through the other options, adding gloves, bracers, shin guards, shoulder pads that also protected the top of his arms, and a belt and back strap to hold his weapons and items.

"How do you feel about a helmet?" Chief asked.

Kaiden mulled it over. It was preferable to a shot to the head, but he didn't want his vision obscured or anything too heavy. "You got any alternatives?"

"Let's give this a shot."

A mask materialized and covered his face from his chin to the top of his brow in a metallic-looking plate. The visor was clean and wide, a long strip that circled his face and gave him a wide range of vision. It looked like it was made of the same material they used in a two-way mirror. He could see his reflection, but he couldn't see his eyes.

"It's got a rebreather to recycle air when you're in situations

where your oxygen is obstructed. The visor not only blocks debris but actually wipes away anything that obstructs your vision. The metal plating will help defend against head strikes and small arms fire. The top of your dome is still exposed, but I'll leave it up to you to not get shot."

"Doesn't look too bad, Chief," Kaiden said appreciatively. "Nice work. Let me have a quick look around before we move on."

Kaiden flipped quickly through the screens. He found a long black jacket that added extra protection from blades and light ammo and placed it over his armor, completing the look.

"If nothing else, you'll die looking good."

"That's obvious even without the armor. I could wear a sack into battle, and it wouldn't make a difference," Kaiden jeered, popping his coat open and stretching. "Guess we'll have to see when we get into the training field, but I feel pretty good about this."

"On to weapons then?"

Kaiden nodded, hitting the confirmation button on the armor setting and moving on to the weapons loadout.

"See if you can find that gun I used in the exam—Debonair."

"On it," Chief confirmed, scanning quickly through the options in the primary tag before moving onto side arms. He stopped as he hovered over a picture of the pistol. *"Got it right here."*

It appeared in Kaiden's hand, and he looked it over and smiled. If nothing else, he knew he could have more fun with this. "I certainly want this, but I can't say I have much of an opinion on the other slots...maybe a shotgun or rifle for my primary."

"You sure you don't want a machine gun? Makes things a little easier if you run into a hoard."

"Nah, Debonair's fire rate is fast enough. Maybe if they let us mod them later, I can fix the overheating problem. See what you can find in shotguns."

Chief obliged, opening the tab and sifting through the choices. *"Looking for anything specific?"*

"Quick-fire rate, longer distance...don't make the grouping too wide."

"It sounds like you want a shotgun that is a rifle."

"Well, kind of, I guess. The most experience I had with a gun that wasn't a pistol or SMG, was the X7-Eviscerator, a Tera Sovereign model. It wasn't as powerful as some of the other shotgun models, but its accuracy was second to none, and it packed a punch even at greater distances. It walked the line between the two, so to speak."

"I follow. Don't think the Academy has that model on file, but if I had to take a guess, the technicians have probably whipped up something similar." Chief looked around for a few moments before sailing down the screen and hovering next to a picture of a shotgun somewhat rectangular in shape with a long barrel and stock in a gray color.

"Check this out. Just as I suspected. The boys at the Nexus R&D made this puppy. It's called the Raptor—lever-action, small spread, it's primarily plasma-based but has a second chamber for ballistic ammo, and it has a pretty damn long range for a shotgun."

Kaiden held out his hand as the gun materialized. It was

remarkably light and had a solid grip. He pressed the stock to his shoulder and moved around, then nodded his approval when he moved remarkably fast, even when looking down the sights. He wanted to fire to see the kick, but he figured that was best saved for when he wasn't in an enclosed space.

"Looks good to me. I'll keep it. Let's hurry and wrap this up, I wanna put these guns through their paces."

"I'm with ya there. For the gadgets, I recommend a portable barrier in case you get caught with your pants down and thermal grenade to give you a little something to deal with groups or heavily armored opponents."

"Good suggestions. I'll take them. As for the melee weapon, I think a knife is always good."

"All right, but what kinda knife?" Chief asked, bringing up the page for knives. *"You're looking at different blade designs, different types, and different styles. Got anything to narrow it down?"*

"I'll probably use it to either cut into a device or cut through hardened material more than as a weapon, but combat should always remain an option. Give me a curved blade with either a plasma or igneous blade."

Chief quickly found an igneous model. The metallic blade was crescent-shaped with a device on the back of the blade near the grip—an ignition trigger, a device that would instantly heat the blade to scalding levels that would allow it to cut through many dense materials.

"I'll take it," Kaiden said with confidence.

"That wraps everything up." Chief disappeared from the screen, reappearing in Kaiden's vision. *"Just confirm everything and we'll get to try it all out. Cut loose a bit, blow things up, make a day of it."*

"I'm ready." Kaiden pressed the confirmation button at the top of the screen. The reflection and loadout options disappeared as a countdown began onscreen, starting from five.

When it reached zero, Kaiden saw the world around him fall away, same as before. Just before the darkness surrounded him, he saw pieces of light shoot past him, a new facade forming before him. He could see a battlefield created out of a desolate city and heard various types of gunfire going off and explosions erupting in the distance.

"They started without us," Kaiden noted in mock disdain, taking the Raptor in his hands and snapping the lever.

"We'll just say we're fashionably late."

CHAPTER TWENTY-TWO

Kaiden fired his shotgun into a group of advancing enemies, a mixture of droids and mercenaries. His shot tore through the shoulder of one of the mercs and knocked down a droid behind him.

"I am loving this!" He cheered, quickly cycling the lever and firing again. This shot took out two droids at once, a few plasma shots barely missing his head.

"You ain't gonna love it when you get evaporated in laser fire. Keep moving." Chief huffed his disapproval.

"Right," Kaiden acknowledged, firing off two more rounds and sprinting along the wall he was barricaded behind, heading into the dilapidated city.

He continued running deep into the center of the buildings, seeing other initiates battling as he ran by. Goliaths ran around with plasma or Tesla cannons, and panzerjocks rode their fusion rigs into the thick of the fight. Marksmen sniped opponents, and bounty hunters tested out different gadgets and snares. He even saw a few field surgeons and battle angels mending the wounded.

Kaiden eventually came to a stop, looking around and figuring he was probably in what was supposed to be the downtown district of the city. He holstered his Raptor on his back and began walking down the street.

"What are ya doing?"

Kaiden looked at the buildings, noticing the details in the rough surfaces and unique touches such as graffiti and scattered bits of trash. "Just taking a look around. I'm not in a rush."

"I guess, but don't you at least wanna keep blasting away? Come on, man, we just started," Chief whined.

"I think I'll have plenty to shoot, so just wanted to see the sights. This is way bigger and more detailed than any of the maps I've been in so far," Kaiden said, looking over a mostly destroyed building to see a freeway in the distance beyond the destroyed streets. Close by, the walls were cracked and worn. "It's impressive. Kinda spooky too."

Kaiden saw a white scanning line trail over the scene. *"It's based on an actual field of battle. This is supposed to be Melbourne, Australia, back in 2113, during the Garett Gaol Riots. A local gang, The Hanging Tree Dukes, tried busting some of their boys out of the Garrett Gaol Prison Facility. It worked a little too well. Over eighty percent of the inmate population got out. During the chaos, a terrorist organization called The Blake Lake swooped in and only made the situation worse. Took three weeks for the World Council to get everything under control."*

Kaiden scanned the horizon, trying to imagine the fighting. "I vaguely remember one of the guys telling me about that. His dad lived there when he was a kid and watched it all go down. The WC was only just put in place a couple years prior."

"Not exactly the greatest way to start planetary unity. It's what launched the United Earth Military proposition."

"Kinda funny when you think about it. The WC got blamed for not reacting fast enough, yet they somehow got more power by uniting all the countries military forces under their banner."

"I guess you gotta figure..." Chief's voice went silent, Kaiden could see his avatar glitch momentarily.

"Chief, you all right?" he asked worriedly.

"Y-y...Yea-ye... Yeah, I'm good. Don't know what that was about." Chief's voice sounded somewhat hazy.

"Well, run a diagnostic or something. You sound like you're trying to cough up a furball."

"Yeah, I'll get right— Oh, shit, enemy incoming."

Kaiden turned and saw another droid in the distance, staring him down. This one was far bigger than any he had seen in his life—at least fifteen feet tall—and stood on four pointed legs. It had a cone-shaped head with one arm with a three-pronged claw and the other some sort of cannon.

As it pointed the cannon in his direction, Kaiden could see sparks swirling in the barrel. It was a Tesla cannon. That was not good.

He whipped out his barrier quickly, activating it just before the droid fired. He didn't have time to set it, instead holding it up like a shield as the blast came his way. Lightning slammed into the barrier, and Kaiden was tossed back as the barrier disintegrated. He was knocked down the hill he'd stood on, tumbling to the bottom.

Out of breath, he sat up and coughed from the force of

the impact. His visor wiped away the dirt with some sort of light. He stood up and took out the Raptor, snapping the lever as he backed away from the base of the hill.

He could hear the droid charging from atop the hill. Kaiden looked around quickly for refuge. Seeing a half-destroyed multi-level parking lot, he dashed toward it, vaulting over the wall to kneel behind it.

"Good God, this got intense fast."

"No kidding. Why the hell do they have an Asiton Reaver here?"

"Is that a bad thing?" Kaiden asked, peering carefully over the relative safety of the wall.

"It's not great," Chief retorted. *"Think for a minute—Asiton? As in Asiton Crisis of 2094? They were the droid models that went haywire and laid waste to a shitload of eastern Europe and China."*

"I'm learning so much today," Kaiden noted dryly. He saw the killer robot appear at the edge of the hill, it's spider-like legs bending before it leaped into the air, landing roughly a hundred yards away from him.

"Got any bright ideas?"

"We don't gotta stay here. This is just practice, remember? Supposed to test out the doodads and skedaddle?"

"What happened to all that enthusiasm?" Kaiden jeered.

"Look, you may not be able to die in here, but pain is still a thing. Plus, I don't like that little glitch that happened a moment ago. Let's not forget that."

"Good point." Kaiden looked down at his belt and counted three thermal grenades. "Hate to say it, but I'm probably gonna have to give Laurie a house call—after this, that is."

"You really wanna take this thing on?"

"Like you said, let's make a day of this," Kaiden quipped. He fished out a clip of ballistic ammo from his belt, sliding it into the secondary chamber of his gun. "Also, if we make enough smoke, maybe a goliath or panzerjock will come by and lend a hand."

"*If we're really gonna do this, let me go ahead and activate the Battle Suite,*" Chief offered.

"You do you, Chief."

Kaiden saw the words "Battle Suite Engaged" flash across his display as his vision changed. He seemed to perceive everything more clearly, time felt like it dilated, and all other boxes and info disappeared from his visor, including Chief's avatar.

"This is the Battle Suite? What does it do?" Kaiden asked, bewildered.

"*It's a unique system for Nexus EIs and their users. They give the EI complete control of all functions in the EI system in order to help their user perform at their peak ability for a short time.*"

"There's a time limit?"

"*It takes a lot of juice. Also, it's not good for the user to do it for too long—bad reactions. What I'm doing with your eyes would take too long to explain, but in short, it's something akin to an illusion to give you better perception in battle. I'll show you weak points for the enemy, give strategic advice, monitor physical status, the works. I'll also give subliminal commands to help you dodge and fire.*"

"What do you mean, subliminal commands? That sounds suspect."

"*I ain't gonna do anything to you, idiot. I'm in here too, remember?*" Chief sounded belligerent for a moment. "*I'll explain when we kill the big metal bastard. Right now, you just gotta go and shoot shit."*

Kaiden nodded, placing his gun across his chest. "How much time do we got?"

"Let's keep it under five minutes for now. You got four left."

"Do you got a recommendation on how we should start?"

"Let's take out the cannon. Toss a thermal into it as it's charging up. If you need to buy yourself some time, shoot the head with some ballistic rounds. That should rattle its sensors."

"Good plan." Kaiden peeked over the wall once again, seeing the droid patrolling the area. "Give me a mark."

"4...3...2...Mark!"

Kaiden leaped from his defensive position, tearing down the field. The Reaver was on him instantly, raising its claw to attack. He flipped a switch on his gun, changing to the ballistic rounds, and fired two quick shots at its head. The explosive force was enough to rattle it, causing its claw to freeze and the robot to stagger back.

The thing was relentless. The moment it recovered, it began chasing him down, swiping at him in wide arcs that either barely missed him or he was able to dodge. He took out one of his three thermals and activated it, tossing it at the Reaver to try to deal some damage. It snatched it in its claw, right out of the air. He heard it go off, but the blast was contained. What the hell was this thing made off?

Kaiden tried to gain some distance in an effort to force it to use its cannon. Every time it composed itself, he fired another round, causing another delay and giving him more time to strafe around it. On his display, he saw a red light glow from the robot's head, a warning signal popping up in the corner.

"Activating sound dampeners," Chief called. Kaiden could feel the area around his ears tighten and the mask clamp down, muffling the outside noise. Even with that, he could hear a piercing shriek from the Reaver.

"Why is the robot screaming?" Kaiden yelped, covering his already protected ears with his hands.

"A high-pitched sound wave to paralyze targets. Give it another couple shots to stop it."

Kaiden was happy to do so, quickly taking aim at the robot's head and sending two more blasts. The Reaver's head rattled, and the screaming ceased.

"Disengaging sound dampeners," Chief reported. *"Hurry up and get back."*

"Chief, it's not firing the cannon, and I only got a few ballistic shots left. Will the plasma shots do it?"

"Won't do us any good. It's got a barrier. The ballistics and grenades are solid and move right through it, but plasma won't do much good unless you can wear down the barrier."

Kaiden hid inside a dilapidated toll booth, huddling down behind the wall. "How many shots will that take?"

"Way too damn many. Gotta end this quick—two minutes and ten seconds left on the Battle Suite."

Kaiden cursed under his breath. He looked back at the droid as it drew closer, then looked under the legs, noticing that they weren't very well defended. "Chief is there a way to hobble it? For it to use its gun?"

"You can try shooting the legs out with your last ballistic rounds. Gotta aim for the central point, and the legs themselves could probably take a couple hits before collapsing."

"I'll need those to finish it off, won't I?" Kaiden asked

"Well, yeah, but if you take out the legs and cannon, that just leaves the claw. You could probably finish it with bug bites from your plasma rounds."

"There's no other way?" Kaiden saw rocks on the floor start to rumble from the weight of the Reaver closing in.

"I mean unless you wanna run underneath it and cut out the compression lines— Oh, dear God, don't do—"

Kaiden holstered his raptor on his back and dashed out of the booth, getting his blade out as he closed in on the droid that was still barreling down on him.

"You crazy bastard!"

"Just tell me what lines to cut," Kaiden called. The Reaver raised its claw, thrusting it down toward him. Kaiden almost felt like he was in slow motion. He saw the angle of the strike and was able to guess how long before it hit. Just as it neared him, he slid onto the ground, kicking up dust and avoiding the jagged metal. The claw came down behind him, sinking into the dirt.

"*Chief*," Kaiden yelled.

"*The yellow ones, just behind the top of the legs—onscreen.*"

Kaiden hit the ignition trigger on the hilt of the blade. He could feel the rush of heat encompassing the steel as he stopped himself from sliding further. He saw the wires highlighted in his display and struck at the ones on the back two legs, cutting into the metal at the bottom of the droid for good measure.

He rolled out as the Reaver stumbled and collapsed, trying to balance itself on its two front legs for a moment before crashing into the dirt. Kaiden leapt back as he took a thermal from his belt. The top half of the droid spun in place, aiming the cannon at him.

Kaiden pressed down on the top of the grenade, activating it. He flung it at the center of the cannon's barrel, and another warning flashed on the screen.

"It's going to screech again. Activating sound dampeners. Get out of the way."

As the cannon charged, Kaiden took out his Raptor again, taking a shot at the robot's head. The impact knocked the Reaver back, pointing the cannon into the air. He retreated as quickly as he could, hearing the cannon go off and the muffled explosion as a wave of force knocked him off his feet.

He hit the ground and tumbled before he managed to stop. Adrenalin still racing through him, he stood and looked back at the Reaver. The entire left side of it was destroyed, and the remains of its legs lay strewn about the dusty field. There were still lights active in its head, though, and he saw the claw twitch.

"Go ahead and deactivate the Battle Suite, Chief."

"With twenty-four seconds to spare. Not bad."

Kaiden's vision returned to normal. His readouts appeared onscreen again, and Chief popped up in the corner *"How do you feel?"*

Kaiden could feel nausea settling in and a headache developing. "Like I have vertigo."

"That's normal. Probably went on a little too long, so we'll try sticking to four minutes next time."

"Sounds good." Kaiden groaned. He straightened before walking over to what remained of the Reaver. It looked at him for a moment, trying to raise what was left of its claw to strike.

Kaiden chuckled. "I'll give it points for being a tough son of a bitch."

"I should give you the same. Also, I should mock you for your stupid little stunt, but since it worked out so favorably, I'll let it pass. Just don't try doing it in real life, all right?"

"No promises." Kaiden chortled, taking another thermal from his belt.

"Figured."

"Can you go ahead and confirm my choices and get me out of here?" he asked.

"Gotcha."

Kaiden activated the grenade and rolled it at the Reaver, then turned and walked away. He saw the buildings and sky begin to fade away and heard the last beeps of the grenade as he was taken back to reality.

CHAPTER TWENTY-THREE

Kaiden exited his pod wearily, shaking his head and adjusting his oculars.

"You make it back in one-piece, Chief?" he asked. Chief's bulbous form appeared in the display, glowing a serene blue.

"Feelin' better than you're looking. Your first experience with the suite must have been a trip, huh?"

"A head trip, maybe."

"Don't do puns. Not a good look for you," Chief admonished.

"Yeah, yeah, you can go ahead and disable the hazard mode or whatever. It's digging into my head too much." After a moment, Kaiden felt the frame unlock behind his head and shrink back to behind his ears, the lenses returning to the circular shape and moving back down the bridge of his nose.

"Appreciate ya." Kaiden yawned. He turned to see Akello at the console, a small group of initiates surrounding her. As he walked over, the group dispersed and left the hall.

"Did I miss the debriefing?" he asked, scratching the back of his head.

"This one, but I can give you a quick rundown," she said, smiling "I have to say, I'm impressed that you took down that Asiton Reaver all by yourself. I was kind of surprised to see it there."

Kaiden looked at her, confusion evident on his face. "You didn't put it in there? I thought you said you controlled everything."

"I am in control, but I'm more of an overseer. I merely chose a training ground from a preapproved list. The particulars are decided on by an Animus design group headed by one of Professor Laurie's proteges."

"And the electric engine of nightmares isn't the norm?" Kaiden inquired,

Akello crossed her legs as she swiped through her tablet. "Not normally, no. The training ground for the loadout practice is usually only cannon fodder and simple enemies, one step above target dummies." She put the tablet down and leaned against her desk. "Guess they wanted to have a couple of surprises for the new crop."

"Never enjoyed those, personally," Kaiden grumbled. "So, what's the debrief?"

"Nothing too much." Akello shrugged. "I wanted to make sure you didn't have any further questions about the Animus, synapse, anything like that."

"Nah, I'm pretty good there. But I remember you saying something about a Division test?"

"Right." She nodded. "At the end of the first week, after

letting all the first years get a chance to grow accustomed to the Animus and find their feet at the Academy, each division has a unique test that all members must complete."

"What do I gotta do?"

"It's slightly different every year, but for soldiers, it's essentially an obstacle course. You have to make it from point A to point B in a limited amount of time. There is no set path, so it's up to you to get to the finish line however you like. There are enemies and traps along the way as well as collectibles and helpful equipment."

"Doesn't sound too bad. Might be fun."

"Well, you'll also compete with other soldiers, in groups of fifty. You gain points for defeating enemies, finding collectibles, and disarming traps along with a bonus for the first twenty-five initiates to make it to the end. You have three lives, and you get docked points for however many you lose. Lose them all, and you fail."

"You also fail if you don't make it in time?"

"Obviously."

"All right, I follow. What happens if you win and what happens if you fail?"

"Well, failure leads to a number of things, depending on your final score. Anything from mandatory overtime in the Animus, extra classes, and possible Class or even Division reassignment. We've had a few people over the years simply withdraw. They had to return their EIs and pay off any debt they accrued, even during their short stay."

"So not simply a swat on the ass then?" Kaiden chuckled.

"If the swat is a bat and the ass is a head, it would be closer." Akello laughed.

"Well, I got the spooks now. But do I get anything shiny for winning?"

"There are prizes for the top few, but they change every year. I don't know what they are this year, but previously, it's been things like passes to the Animus Arcade, gourmet meal tickets, unique skins for your armor or weapons in the Animus, or unique avatars for your EI."

I want that. The sleek design the Reaver had makes me feel fat.

"So novel knick-knacks and the like?" Kaiden asked.

"Well, for seven out of the top ten. The top three get things like Academy credit and rank-ups."

"What are those?"

"Academy credit is essentially money you can use around the Academy for things like extra food, custom clothes, and the like without jacking up your debt. A rank-up is what it says on the tin. You gain a higher rank."

She lifted three fingers in the air. "For each year, there are three ranks along with rank zero. You gain your first rank as long as you finish within the top twenty-five of the Division test. Then it's merit-based, or you can take a ranking test as long as you get the approval of at least two Nexus Academy staff."

"So, I could have the chance to go directly to rank two by the end of this?"

"Correct."

"What does that get me?"

"Since you're a first-year, not too much, but you get a few perks like being able to take advanced classes and training courses, better sleeping quarters, you don't have to fill out forms and wait for filing for mid-level supply requests—"

"What was that?" Kaiden asked. "Out of curiosity, do training guns count as mid-level supplies?"

"Yep."

Kaiden felt his blood start pumping with a surge of excitement. He bounced lightly on his feet, renewed optimism providing impetus for the celebratory response. "Well, I just found my motivation."

"I'm glad. Keep it up, and you'll go far, kid," Akello said encouragingly.

"It's a bit past two. Did you still wanna swing by Laurie?"

Kaiden stopped bouncing "Oh, right." He looked back to Akello "You've mentioned Laurie a couple times. You know him?"

"I used to intern for him back at his old company. We eventually became pretty good friends. It was actually because of his recommendation that I got my start here."

"So, he *does* have a heart?" Kaiden asked mockingly.

Akello chuckled. "I said it before: he's strange, but he means well. He might give you the impression that you are nothing more than an experiment, but he is on the lookout for you."

"Warm fuzzies all around," Kaiden droned. "Still, I do need to see him. You happen to know if he's in?"

"You really think you can simply walk in and talk to Laurie? You might be one of his pet projects, but good luck getting past his army of technicians and advisors."

"I doubt I have to worry about him wanting to see me, especially considering it has to do with said pet project. Chief was glitchin' while I was in the training course."

"Your EI?" Akello picked her tablet back up and scanned through it. "I can't find anything on the readout. An EI glitch is quite serious especially in the Animus—are you sure?"

"Positive. We were talking when he suddenly went silent—his voice shorted out, and his avatar went hazy. I haven't seen him do that at all and considering that his EI system is in my head, I would rather not take chances."

Akello tapped her cheek a few times. "Might be nothing more than an A/V corruption, or it could be a link issue… I guess you're right, don't wanna take any chances." She began typing on the pad. "I'll send him a notice and tell him you're on your way. He'll make sure someone meets you and brings you to his office."

"Thank you, ma'am." Kaiden gave her a brief nod. "If that's it, I'll head out."

"That's all I got. You should get your class schedule by the end of the day. It'll be sent to your EI. If you have any questions about the Animus, just talk to me. I'll be in charge here until they get a new guide to take my place."

"I'll see ya tomorrow, then." And with that, Kaiden left the Animus center.

"Kaiden my boy!" Laurie greeted him, his arms out wide in invitation.

He gave him a wave as he approached the Professor's desk. "Howdy, Prof, got some problems with my EI." He settled easily into a chair, a little more relaxed this time around.

"So I read. It sounds like it could be nothing more than simply an A/V problem, but something so trivial shouldn't even be possible with the implant."

"You did tell me it was experimental," Kaiden reminded him, placing one arm over the back of the chair and leaning back.

"Experimental doesn't mean that it should experience such basic problems. Tell me the details."

Kaiden quickly summarized his first few minutes in the training grounds—taking out a few targets, running through the city admiring the sights, then the sudden short-out.

"That all?"

"All that matters. I didn't even take a hit or anything."

"That wouldn't matter in the Animus. It certainly shouldn't affect your hardware."

"My oculars were in hazard mode when I went in if that means anything."

"Again, not a problem. Unless your hardware is damaged or corrupted, it shouldn't interfere with your integration. Are you sure you didn't leave out even a little detail?"

"Not really. Chief and I were talking about the map, how it was based on the Garret Gaol Riots, the trouble they had in containing it, and making a few snarky comments about the WC."

Laurie folded his hands and leaned forward. "Like what exactly?"

Kaiden eyed him cautiously. "What? Can't take a few jabs at the Council? I know they're the overlords of this place, but it's not like we were planning a bombing."

"No, no, nothing like that. I'm merely curious. Then what happened?"

"Then Chief blinked out for a moment and came back almost as quickly. Good thing too, as he warned me about the Reaver coming for me." Kaiden rotated his free arm, feigning that he worked the stiffness out. "Go ahead and thank whatever smartass put that thing in there. It gave me a hell of a time."

Laurie raised an eyebrow. "A Reaver? Asiton model?"

"The very same," Kaiden said nonchalantly, checking his nails "Chief and I took it out ourselves. Pity I couldn't get any bonus SP for it. Speaking of that, how is the upgrade coming along?"

"I'm working on it, but are you saying that an Asiton Reaver was in the training grounds?"

"Yeah. Advisor Faraji said one of your flunkies probably put it in there as a surprise or something. Tell them to keep it to themselves next time." Kaiden put his hand down and smiled. "Not that it stopped me."

"I see. I'll be sure to do that." Laurie's voice was oddly quiet. "So, you and your EI were in the training grounds, you were talking about the Council when he had a momentary glitch, then the Reaver appeared?"

"That about sums it up, with the exception of Chief and I taking it down."

"Interesting…" Laurie whispered.

"So, can you help?" Kaiden asked.

"What's that? Oh, yes, just a moment." Laurie opened a drawer and pulled out an EI pad, switching it on. "Cast your EI into the pad, if you please."

"You heard the man, Chief." Kaiden saw Chief's avatar disappear and reappear on the pad.

"I'm going to run a quick diagnostic, maybe fix a thing or two under the metaphorical hood. It shouldn't take but a few moments.,"

"Well, last time we talked you said we should have a drink. I'm open."

Laurie revealed a bottle of cognac and poured them each a drink. They chatted briefly while Laurie worked, and after a half-hour, Chief was back in Kaiden's oculars.

"That should do it."

"You feelin' any better, Chief?"

"Didn't really know what was wrong in the first place, but I ain't glitching, so it's a start."

"What did you find?" Kaiden asked, finishing off his drink.

"Nothing concrete, but I deleted some unnecessary files and adjusted some of the settings. You shouldn't notice a significant difference, but it is better to err on the safe side for now."

Kaiden shrugged. "If that's all we can do for now, so be it." Kaiden pushed up from his chair. "This was actually quite pleasant, Laurie. Keep it up, and I may have a more pleasant picture of you."

"Even more than now?" the professor inquired.

"Certainly," Kaiden promised. "I'm going to head out and get some lunch, then I gotta pay someone a visit."

"All right. Well, you take care dear boy, and of course, if you notice anything else suspicious, let me know. Although next time, we may have to go back into the operating theater."

"I'll do my best to avoid that if it's all the same to you. We're just starting to build a real rapport." Kaiden gave the professor a wave and left.

Laurie watched the soldier leave and then glanced back at his monitor. He had found something quite interesting in the EI—not something he should bother the boy with yet, but Sasha would probably be interested.

It would appear the Council might have more liaisons than they were aware of, and they had been playing with Laurie's toys.

Kaiden walked across the plaza of the academy, hearing the birds chirp and the excited chatter of other initiates.

"So, where are we off to now?"

"Like I said, cafeteria, then I gotta go have a talk with someone."

"Brain cell for your thoughts."

"My brain cells are currency to you?"

"Just spill it."

Kaiden folded his hands behind his head, looking up into the mid-afternoon sky. "I was thinking about the Division test and the prizes."

"I wouldn't mind a spiffy new look. You owe me for giving me this disco ball looking outfit," the EI mumbled.

"I'll be sure to ask for one as a secondary prize, but I want that rank-up."

"It's not a guarantee that you'll get it, even if you take the top spot."

"Still wouldn't want to miss out on the chance to get it. Besides, I'm competitive."

"What do you want it for, anyway?"

"Having a gun again would be nice. I left my old one with Julio back in Seattle, figured it wouldn't be such a pain to get one here."

"So you merely want your baby blanket?" Chief questioned wryly.

"The floating melon is going to criticize my choice of accessories?" Kaiden retorted.

"Again, not my choice."

Kaiden sighed and continued his walk. "Besides, it's more than the gun. If I got an opportunity to be better, I'm going to take it." He felt the wind pick up as he approached the cafeteria. "In any case, I'll need a leg-up if I wanna chance at getting to the top."

He walked to the cafeteria's entrance, the doors sliding open as he approached. "And I'll need fuel before I get there."

Wulfson was practicing his strikes on a target dummy when he heard the door open and paused. He turned around and grinned as Kaiden took his jacket off.

He looked calmly at the officer. "You still willing to train me?"

Wulfson cocked his head, standing straight and still as he studied him. "Do you want to train?"

"I want to win," he replied.

The giant smirked, walking up to Kaiden as he placed

his jacket on a bench. "It's a goal to start with," he said, offering a hand.

Kaiden gave it a firm shake, then Wulfson picked him up and threw him on the mat.

"And we start now."

CHAPTER TWENTY-FOUR

The rest of the week went by in a blur. Kaiden's mornings started with breakfast, then training in the Animus until noon, followed by lunch before training with Wulfson—somehow the officer was able to make it count as a foundations class, though he never bothered to ask how he managed that. Thereafter, he returned to the Animus for classes and did extra training of a couple hours. Finally, he had dinner and another session with Wulfson before crashing into his capsule at the end of the night.

He had kept this up for the whole week in preparation for today. The Division test.

His alarm was set to wake him at five o'clock sharp. He'd hoped to get an early lead on the other students, but as it turned out, he was far from the only one with this idea. A large group had already dressed and were leaving by the time he slid out of his capsule. He cursed as he dragged his clothes on and ran out the door.

He stopped by the cafeteria to grab a couple of nutrition bars and a bottle of orange juice and water, downing all of it as he continued his march to the Center. As he headed down the path of the plaza, he noticed a large group of other students heading to another building in the distance.

"Where are all of them going?" he heard an initiate ask.

He heard another reply, "Those are the second- and third-years. Since the AC is packed because of the test, they take the day off. Most of them are going to the observation theater to watch the tests as they happen."

"Some of them place bets on the first-years, and others go to cheer them on," a third voice added.

Kaiden ignored them and quickened his pace, pushing past many of the other students. He really didn't want to sit and wait all day for his turn.

Waiting in the lobby of the Animus Center, it occurred to Kaiden that there were a hell of a lot of students in the first year.

He sighed, reached into his jacket to fish his oculars out of its inner pocket, put them on, and activated them.

"How long do I have to wait, Chief?" he asked groggily.

He saw a schedule appear on the display, showing his position in the queue. *"Not much longer now. Maybe a little more than an hour, tops."*

Kaiden groaned, leaned back, and staring at the ceiling. He was ready—even excited. The anticipation for the test had been building throughout the week.

And all that excitement had been reduced to him twiddling his thumbs because he forgot to take a number.

"Hello, Kaiden."

He looked up. "Chiyo?" he asked, a little surprised to see her standing before him. "Hey! How have you been?"

She leaned against the wall across from him. "Very well. Getting accustomed to the Academy over the first week was quite easy, certainly more so than I expected."

"That's good to hear." He offered her his chair, but she waved him off. He ran his fingers sheepishly through his hair. "Sorry I haven't stopped by during breakfast like I thought I would. My days got a bit more hectic." As he looked off to the side, he noticed a few people down the hall staring at her and whispering to each other. "Those guys from the first night we met haven't given you a problem, have they?"

"Obviously, it's not only them," Chiyo said, brushing some of her long hair behind her ear as she nodded at the gossipers down the hall. "But that was always expected. Don't fret. Hot air is about all they can muster. They wouldn't dare try anything more."

Kaiden huffed, straightening in his chair. "Good to know, I guess." He tilted his head, fixing her with a curious look. "You take your test yet?"

She shook her head. "Not yet, how about you?"

"I wouldn't be here people-watching otherwise," he grumbled. "Been waiting over two hours now. How long do these things take?"

"It depends on the test, but I believe a soldier's test can be completed in an hour. The time limit is three."

"Damn, really?" Puzzled, Kaiden scratched his chin as

he considered this. "Guess it's an endurance test along with everything else."

"Of a sort, although if you believe three hours is a long time in the field, you may be in for a rude awakening."

"I can handle it," he said, knocking on the wooden armrest of his chair. "I've got plenty of stamina. Plus, I doubt there's anything they could throw at me that I can't handle." He couldn't resist the impulse to brag.

"I see." Chiyo looked at his armband for a moment. "Tell me, what have you learned about being in the Ace Class?"

Kaiden gazed at his armband and shrugged. "That I am apparently supposed to be a Swiss Army knife on legs." He sighed. "They've drilled every little survival tip, medical chart, weapon schematic, and all sorts of other things into our heads. If it wasn't for the soldier's classes and getting some practice in the Animus, I'm pretty sure I wouldn't have been able to fire a gun after the loadout."

"Do you know why they have you do that?" she asked.

"Well, they want me to have a wide array of abilities, be more than just a gunman."

"Correct, but do you—"

He raised a hand to stop her. "If you're asking if I figured out that aces are supposed to be leaders in battle, I've come to that conclusion already," Kaiden stated, shifting his right leg over his left.

"Oh… You are all right with this?"

He shrugged again. "To be honest, I haven't really thought much about it," he admitted. "I took the class on a recommendation. I figure I'll stick with it for now, see where it goes. If nothing else, I can always go into bounty hunter or assassin, something a little more my speed."

"Are you thinking like this because you don't feel you fit in?" she asked, her voice lowering as she maintained eye contact.

Kaiden scoffed. "Please, darling, if there's any class in this Academy that gives me a title that I live up to, it's Ace."

"Then does it bore you?"

"It's not exactly my idea of a good time, but I can see the value. I've learned more about mutant anatomy and poisonous flowers in a week than I cared to my entire life. But I still get my time in the Animus and have some outside training to boot, so it's not so bad."

"Then why are you contemplating moving on?"

Kaiden moved his oculars down his face to give her a confused look. "Do you ask me these things because you're bored?"

She pushed herself off the wall, taking a few steps down the hall before turning to address him. "Of course not, but the last time we talked, you said something that I found…inspired."

This got his attention. "Really now, I don't think I've ever been paid that compliment." A smile crept onto his lips. "I could always do with a little praise. What exactly did I say that was so inspired?"

"About how you deal with what life throws at you is how you truly take hold of your fate."

Kaiden's eyes narrowed in annoyance. "Am I supposed to note the irony?"

She crossed her arms. "I know you haven't made a decision regarding changing your class, but if I may offer a guess as to why you are contemplating a change, it is because the idea of responsibility does not appeal to you."

"Can't say that it does," Kaiden confessed. "I can barely take orders, much less give them, so might as well take a class that I already have a talent for. I would get more out of it."

"It would also be easier for you."

Kaiden rolled his eyes. "I enjoy it when our conversations become a fun, sporting round of interrogation," he jeered.

"Am I wrong?"

"Not really, but to play devil's advocate, aren't you doing the same thing? You get here with your hacking skills, and you're a hacker. Sometimes, you just have a calling, right?"

Chiyo glared at him. Kaiden felt the mood shift and a chill course through him for a moment.

She took a deep breath, exhaling before she spoke. "My goal in life was not to be a hacker. I had another hope, but it was…complicated by the feelings and actions of others. So I decided to find a new path."

"You gave up?" he asked.

She glared at him again, and he held up his hands. "I don't mean to knock you, but you've struck me as someone with a plan. You had it all figured out and whatnot. I'm just surprised to hear you decided not to go after whatever this goal of yours was."

She looked away, lowering her eyes. "Like I said, it was…for the better in the long run. The more I've thought about it, the more I realize that perhaps I've never truly known what I wanted." She looked back at him, a renewed determination in her eyes. "That is the difference between us, Kaiden. I am trying to make a new path using the abilities I have acquired. I wanted you to know that I feel you should do the same. There are many ways to be a leader, and I think you have the potential to be a great one."

Kaiden now sat up in his chair, his mouth slightly agape. He was silent for a moment before his smile returned and he pushed his glasses back over his eyes. "Well, the mood certainly changed quickly." He leaned back against the chair, forcing himself to relax. "I keep hearing people talk about my potential. It's a new concept for me. Growing up in the life I had, you either *did,* or you *died.* Thinking about what you could be…that kinda had the same meaning as an imaginary friend."

Chiyo looked up to the ceiling, watching all the students on the upper floors of the Center with a faraway look.

"Maybe an imaginary friend is silly to other people… but I'm sure it meant a lot to the person who dreamt them up."

Kaiden laughed. "Well, look who's being all inspirational now."

She gazed at him, a small smile on her face.

"Hello, friends," a muffled voice called.

The two turned to Geno who walked down the hall toward them, greeting them with an exuberant wave.

"Good morning, Geno," Chiyo responded.

"You know him too?" Kaiden asked.

"We met at the library one evening and have seen each other there almost every night since."

Geno stopped just short of the two and looked at Kaiden. "Yes, Chiyo and I have exchanged many fascinating notes and articles on various subjects. She has also helped me add more words and slang to my translator." He placed a hand across his chest. "I now know what a 'howdy' is."

"Oh, good, progress." Kaiden chuckled.

"Have you taken the Engineer's test yet, Geno?" she asked.

"Not yet. I am next in the queue." He rubbed his webbed hands together. "How exciting. I have yet to test my skills since I arrived on your planet."

"You still got the blues over your class?" Kaiden inquired.

"I am more a pale purple color than blue," Geno noted with a slight frown.

Kaiden exchanged a quick glance with Chiyo, who shrugged. "He's learning slowly, but keep the idioms and hyperbole to a minimum."

He looked back at the alien and tapped his armband. "Are you still conflicted about your class?"

Geno shook his head. "Not as much, not since our discussion. I do wonder what sort of hysteria will greet me upon my return home, but I also agree that it is a unique opportunity for me. I am interested in seeing where it leads."

Chiyo flashed Kaiden a look full of meaning. "I believe he understands the potential in something new."

He twirled his finger around in the air. "Hooray for metaphors."

"Will you be taking a test with a mixed group or only Tsuna?" Chiyo asked.

"There aren't enough Tsuna in the Engineering Division for a proper test, so it will be mixed." He looked around the room, his expression an amusing mix of curiosity and excitement. "I am interested to see the results. I have met some nice humans in Engineering during the last few days, but I still look forward to beating them."

"Nothing wrong with a bit of healthy competition. Besides, that's half of what this is about if you think about it," Kaiden commented.

Geno nodded. "Yes, it is as you said before. I do wish to show others what my people can do—what I can do."

"Well then, when you get out there, show— Hey, man, your…uh, pants are shaking."

Geno looked down and unlocked the compartment on his pant leg, taking out a tablet and swiping along the screen. "It seems my test will begin shortly. I must head to my hall. I wish you both well in your tests."

"Good luck, Geno," Chiyo said with a wave.

"Break a— Do your best," Kaiden caught himself in time to avoid confusion.

"I shall. Farewell."

The two of them watched the alien depart, Kaiden chuckling with something that might have been affection. "That guy is just too precious. He's gonna get eaten alive."

"Don't count him out so easily. There was a reason he was selected to be a part of the first group of alien students."

"Oh, you don't need to tell me that. I got to hear quite a bit of family history last time we talked."

Chiyo giggled, a light appearing in her ocular lens. "Looks like it's my time to go as well."

Kaiden stood up, extending a hand. "Best of luck to you."

She shook his hand briskly. "Luck has never been good to me. Fortunately, I have the skills to compensate for that."

"Damn straight. Go do whatever voodoo you do."

She gave him a small bow before walking to the elevators, leaving Kaiden alone once more.

"I'm all warm and fuzzy now you've got friends," Chief chirped, his avatar changing to a delighted pink.

"I guess I do. Never considered myself much of a people person," he admitted with a low chuckle.

"I always had you pegged as a softy."

"Catch me in the right mood, and I can be downright amicable."

"So, how do you feel about the test now?"

Kaiden sat back down. "I ain't too worried."

"You never really scoped out the competition beforehand," Chief noted. *"Could be some other badasses hidden around here."*

"Maybe," Kaiden agreed with a shrug. "Don't got a partner like mine, though."

Chief shifted to some sort of odd purple color, his avatar turning away on the screen. *"Hey now, I'm only here for the food."*

"You don't eat, smartass."

"I ain't going to admit you're a good guy just yet. Still some stupid we need to fix."

"I'm sure we'll get there eventually." He leaned back into the chair to relax, reaching up to take off his oculars.

Kaiden heard a light beeping. *"Hey, don't get too comfortable. Looks like we got bumped up in the queue,"* Chief informed him.

"We did?" Kaiden asked, sliding the oculars back on. He

saw a message on his display, telling him to go to hall seven. "How did that happen?"

"Looks like a big batch got taken out all at once. Ain't that a damn shame."

"Sure is for them." Kaiden chuckled, stretched as he got up, and headed for the elevators.

"You want me to do a little cheerleader jig to psyche you up?"

"I'm gonna request that you not. I'll be fine getting my head in the game."

He reached the elevator hallway and slid into a cramped carriage. He pressed the button for level four and stood back.

"Here we go, ladies and gentlemen."

CHAPTER TWENTY-FIVE

Kaiden opened his eyes, greeted only by Chief's avatar floating beside him in the darkness. He was in the Animus.

Either that or dark space. That would be troubling and confusing, he decided.

"Guess we're waiting on everyone to load in?" Kaiden inquired.

"If I had to hazard a guess, they are probably prepping the loadout screen," Chief said, floating around the vast emptiness.

"Thought we didn't get to mess with that much before a mission?" Kaiden asked, looking down and checking his equipment. "Everything I chose last week is here, except my guns and accessories."

"Isn't it great that a grenade is considered an accessory?" Chief chirped. *"And you're right. Usually, you don't get to swap out armor and the like before a mission. You gotta buy it and*

equip it well beforehand, but you can mod your weapons and swap out gadgets—the small stuff."

"Got any recommendations?"

"Nah, keep what we got. They play to your strengths, and we don't wanna get too crazy since we don't exactly know what we're up against."

"Good point," Kaiden agreed, then he saw wisps of light swirl around him.

They moved up his body, spinning faster and faster as they encircled him. Then, as they continued to climb higher, the lights expanded a few feet all around him. Color and texture began to settle into place, and a chair with a safety bar appeared behind Kaiden. He took a seat quickly. If this chair had safety bars, he would probably need them.

His surroundings finished forming—padded walls all around and the outline of a door in front of him with a monitor off to the side. There wasn't a lot of light outside of some glow strips on the ceiling. For a moment, he was confused. It looked like he was back in the tube, but after a moment, he could hear the loud roar of rushing wind outside.

"Chief… Are we in a—"

"Ejection Pod. Better snap that harness into place, buddy. Gonna be a bumpy ride, I'm guessing."

Kaiden did so quickly, pulling the harness down around his shoulders and gripping the handles tightly. The monitor turned on, revealing a man with greying hair in a formal military cut, brown eyes, and Asian features on the screen.

"Good afternoon, initiates," He stated, his voice smooth

but commanding. "I am Head Monitor Zhang, the overseer of the Animus center. I would like to welcome you to your Soldier Division test."

"Kind of odd to be welcomed into a war zone," Chief noted.

"This test was designed by a team consisting of members of the Animus Center—including myself and Advisors Palaye, Faraji, and Wilhelm, teachers and officers from the Soldier's Workshop, along with guidance and design by Nexus' Technician department and R&D sector."

"With a special thanks to Mr. Mittens, my house cat, and a special foreword by my children's nanny…" Kaiden grumbled. "Let's get on with this."

"You will enter the test zone in ten minutes. In that time, you are allowed to change the accents section of your loadout, including gadgets and colors, and apply modifications to weapons and armor if you have any."

A separate screen opened to Kaiden's left, showing him his loadout.

"While this is a test of each individual initiate's skills and actions in the field, it will also be treated as a practice mission. In accordance with this, familiarize yourself with this map of the test zone and an index of potential hostiles and traps you may encounter."

Kaiden saw a new tab appear on the loadout screen. He clicked on it and saw a bird's-eye view of the area. A spot highlighted in yellow was titled "starting point," while on the opposite end of the map was another area highlighted in green and titled "end point."

"You will not have access to this map in the field. You are to rely on your personal acuity and the abilities of your EI to help you reach your destination. It does not matter what it takes to get there but reaching the endpoint is the bare minimum to meet victory conditions and pass this test. The first twenty-five initiates to succeed will receive extra points toward their final score, with first place being allotted ten thousand points."

The screen changed again, showing the index of hostiles and cycling through them.

"Of course, we are here to test your mettle along with your mental capabilities. There are numerous enemies along all paths. They vary in difficulty and in abundance, and each of them grants points upon take-down. Their values depend on difficulty rating, so it is up to you whether the risk is worth the reward."

Kaiden pressed the option for the glossary to appear in sections. He scrolled down the page, seeing the usual suspects—some random merc grunts, a few heavies, some robotic enemies of various types, and even a couple of mutants.

"Guess we'll get to see if you're a natural-born mutant slayer."

"Yeah, maybe…" Kaiden whispered, his focus on the index. When he reached the bottom, he saw the silhouette of an enemy with the statistics and descriptions left blank. "Hey, Chief, what do you figure this is?" he asked, pointing to the unknown being.

Chief hovered closer, scanning the picture. *"I got nothin'. No info appears in my databanks."*

"Can you take a guess from the silhouette?" Kaiden quizzed him.

"Already thought to try, but still nothing. Whatever it is…I mean, maybe we probably shouldn't mess with it."

"I'm sensing that there is a reason we should?"

"Well, the only field that is filled in is the points it's worth. Take a look."

Kaiden did, letting out a sharp whistle. "One hundred thousand. You think that would put us safely out on top?"

"Oh, hell yeah. If we did somehow take this thing down alone, we would have to either die or not make it within the time limit to fail."

"...should you not make it to the endpoint in the allotted time." Kaiden snapped back to reality with Zhang's warning.

"Damn. Probably should have been paying attention for the last couple minutes," Chief mumbled sheepishly.

"You will begin to lose one hundred points per minute, and you get five-thousand for getting to the end point, which again, is the bare minimum needed to pass. If you have less than five-thousand by the time you arrive, or you lose all three of your allotted lives, you will fail and be subjected to any number of punishments and/or corrections decided by the leaders of your division along with a talk to your assigned counselor."

Kaiden shuddered. Considering that Mya had pointed turret barrels at him as a joke, he was slightly concerned at what she might do if he actually fucked up.

"This is the end of the test introduction. Once it signs out, your ten minutes of preparation shall begin. At the prep time's conclusion, you may jettison your pod at your discretion within a certain time limit. If you do not, you will be considered forfeit and fail the test."

Kaiden tabbed back to the map, zooming in at the starting point. He saw a number of paths, fields and mountainsides, each with potential pros and cons such as being near enemy bases or on higher ground.

"With that, I shall sign off. Good luck, initiates. Show us what our future soldiers are made of," Zhang commanded, the screen going black as he finished.

Kaiden looked over the map again. "Chief, got any suggestions on what we're looking at?"

Chief disappeared to reappear on the screen and hover over the starting zone. *"Most of the map is jungle. The starting zone and the edges of the map are beaches, random hills, and ridges, and a couple of mountains that we probably won't have to worry about... Though I would bet my color-shifting skin that there's probably some aerial hostiles coming from there we gotta worry about."*

"No doubt," Kaiden concurred, looking back at the index and seeing a few flying drones and some sort of mutated bird-of-prey. The name read Devil Bird, and it had deep-red flesh with only a smattering of feathers, a long lance-like beak, and talons like scimitar blades. He would be happy to not have to bother with it.

Chief moved down into view, getting Kaiden's attention. *"Let's make a game plan. You trying to get that finishing bonus?"*

Kaiden shook his head. "I ain't a sprinter. I was gonna shoot my way to a win if it's all the same to you."

"Figured that. Smarter move. Some of the preppies probably got cross-country medals."

"Speaking of them, do we gotta worry about them turning on us?"

"I wouldn't sweat it. Most will probably be too worried about staying alive and getting to the finish to go commando on

everyone else. Plus, you don't get any extra points for taking out other initiates."

Kaiden sighed. "Well, there goes that backup plan."

Chief's avatar turned a slight red. *"Wait, you were planning on doing that?"*

"If it was an option...and depending on the point value."

The EI cooled back to its natural blue. *"You know, I was gonna say somethin', but at least you're showing initiative."*

"Don't make a pun."

"Tempting, but no. Besides, if it was an option, that would mean most of the class would be kicked out in the first five minutes in a clusterfuck of gunfire. Not good for the Academy's bottom line."

"Good point...what about working together?"

"Not a bad option. There would be chances of survival, and around twenty percent of initiates do go in groups during the test, but there are some problems. Two particularly important ones."

"Such as?"

"Well, the first issue is you, in that you would have to actually have to find at least one other person who wants to work with you. To get in a party, you have to have someone accept an invite you sent or have someone send an invite to you."

Kaiden scoffed. "What? You think I can't make more new friends?"

"Not quickly. Besides, with the all-black get-up and the mask you got on, you look like a cyborg grim reaper."

Kaiden opened his collar with a dramatic snap. "I happen to think it looks good."

"Maybe not too bad for striking fear into your enemies or

impressing the other non-conformists at the Academy, but it doesn't make a great impression for small talk."

He scowled. "Do I gotta remind you that you helped me pick this out?"

"You're the one who hit the 'okay' button," Chief said with a roll of his eye. *"Wasn't my place to judge."*

Kaiden tapped a finger against his head in annoyance. "We'll circle back to that, maybe. What was the other problem?"

"Well, when you are in a party, points are shared. Which means we probably won't end up in the money unless we genocide the island."

Kaiden nodded, crossing his arms and tapping a foot. "That's definitely an issue."

"Figured you didn't want to share." Chief chuckled

"That's not the problem," Kaiden stated, shaking his head. "It's that there probably isn't enough time to comb the island and kill off every last point piñata."

"You know, it's a good thing that we're talking about virtual people and things right now. Otherwise I might have to report that to a psych evaluation."

"Hey, remember what Sasha said? We do whatever we need to do to complete our jobs, and we are very good at what we do," Kaiden reminded him with a smirk. "Could we just shadow a group?"

"Nice idea, but no, you'd be automatically linked if you are too close to another initiate or party for too long."

Kaiden leaned back, his fingers tapping a tattoo on his arm. "Can't you game the system? Get far enough away before you're linked?"

"Might work if we weren't being monitored, dumbass."

"Oh…that's right." He grunted, crossing his legs. "Clever bastards."

"Less clever and more we've been doing this for more than a day."

"Think that's called wisdom, Chief."

"Which you lack, you unwise ass."

"Worth a shot." Kaiden shrugged. He looked back at the screen—four and a half minutes left till ejection. "So we'll go solo. Where should we start?"

"How do you wanna get to the end?"

"Why not simply go through the middle?" he asked, looking at the map. "I don't see any dead-ends or hazardous terrain—a few enemy camps and possible patrols, but as long as we stay just off center, we'll be off the open road and won't make for easy targets."

"Guess I can't fault that logic, but it seems a little too obvious. Probably lots of traps that way. Plus, I'm sure at least some of the others are thinking that way too."

"Maybe, but all it means is that we got some meat shields around just in case."

"Your sense of empathy is staggering," Chief stated sarcastically. *"But, if that's how you wanna roll, I'm good with it. I'll keep more of a lookout for traps, and you focus on moving and taking out…point piñatas."*

"Sounds good. So where should we hop out?"

"Right here," Chief announced, moving the map back to the starting zone and marking an area at the northern end of the zone. *"I'll give you a mark, but we'll jump right before the countdown ends. It'll land us on a high ridge that we can use to sneak into the canopy. There's a small camp we can take out for some points, and we'll go on from there."*

"Gotcha." Kaiden nodded. "Now that we got a better understanding of the field, you sure we shouldn't pack anything different?"

Chief opened the loadout tab *"We should probably change the armor colors, give you a bit of camo,"* he suggested, changing his individual pieces, from his mask to his boots, to a jungle camo pattern and the suit underneath to dark-green. *"As for the weapons, don't got any mods yet, but I doubt anyone else has either so no big loss there. The barrier and the thermals...perhaps change the thermals to shock or smoke grenades and the barrier to a chameleon generator for a stealthy approach?"*

"Most of my points are gonna come from kills, Chief, so probably better to prepare for a big fight than try to keep everything on the low."

"Good point. Subtlety ain't really our style, anyway."

As Kaiden looked over the choices, he noticed a new box at the bottom of the screen. "What's that new field, Chief?"

The EI moved down and hovered over the box. *"Supply pouch. Can't change it. There are items you can collect on the field—health packs, different ammo types, grenades, stems, that sort of thing. An extra pouch is standard in the field."*

"Good to know."

The lights went red. Kaiden looked up to see that the timer had hit zero. The map changed, showing a triangle moving across the screen, heading toward the starting zone.

"Right on cue. Get ready to eject in twenty-five seconds."

Kaiden saw Debonair appear in its holster on his left hip, along with his other gadgets and clip of ballistic ammo for his Raptor materializing on his belt. Said Raptor appeared on a rack next to the door of the pod. He felt the security bar press against him slightly, locking into place. Kaiden steadied his breath, the timer reaching its mark.

"Pull the red lever on your right in ten."

Kaiden looked up to see the red-and-white patterned handle, taking it in his grasp.

"Five...four...three..."

He felt his heart beating against his chest. Even with all he had been through, this was a rush.

"Eject," Chief shouted.

Kaiden pulled the lever down. The whole pod shook as he felt it rocket to the surface, he looked at the screen again. One minute until landfall.

He loosened up, preparing for deceleration and impact. Kaiden could feel the adrenaline surging and knew he was ready. The pod slowed as they passed the halfway point, reverse-thrust activating to slow the descent. It struck the earth, and he shifted around in his seat for a moment. Sounds of impact echoed all around him as other pods landed.

He forced the security bar off, and the pod door began to release with a hiss of air as the seal broke. In a single swift motion, he grabbed the Raptor off the rack as the door opened to reveal a cloudy sky and the view of the beach that led to the damp floor of the jungle beyond.

Kaiden grabbed the sides of the door and flung himself out of the pod. He tore across the sand of the beach and headed to the jungle. Other initiates raced off in different directions, all headed to the same destination.

Caught up in the rush, preparing to take on whatever came his way, he heard Chief yell.

"Kaiden! Watch out for the—"

He briefly felt his foot connect with something, then he heard a loud beep before being engulfed in an explosion.

In the excitement, he had forgotten mines were probably something to look out for.

CHAPTER TWENTY-SIX

In one blink, Kaiden saw fire and smoke. In another, he was back in the escape pod. He sucked in air and pressed his hands against his head.

"What the hell happened?" he shouted.

"Tripped over a pulse mine. I should probably take some of the blame for that. I did say I would look out for traps," Chief mumbled. *"Granted, you could have been a little less gung-ho than to race into a literal island of death, but we'll say that we were both wrong and move right along."*

Kaiden growled as he stood up from the pod's chair, grabbing the Raptor from the rack once again. "So I'm already down a life?"

"Yep, but consider yourself lucky this is merely a simulation. Mines have the habit of exploding all your bits, not merely sending them back to the starting point."

Kaiden hopped out of the pod, sliding the Raptor into the holster on his back. "So if I die again, I'm coming all the way back here?"

"There are probably a couple checkpoints along the paths, but they would be deep in the jungle. If you want my advice? Play it safe and don't die again. It's not like you can punch in a cheat code and get a bonus life in reality."

"I figured the reaper wouldn't accept credits." Kaiden huffed his annoyance, once again heading to the canopy. Now, he moved at a brisk jog instead of a sprint with his eyes scanning the ground and surroundings much more carefully.

"Treat it like you would one of your old jobs—be on your toes and trigger-ready. You may not be able to die, but pain is still a thing. Speaking of which, how do you feel?"

"Well, I've got a hell of a headache," he stated, finally making it off the sandy beach and heading into the dampness of the jungle.

"Be sure to chew some pain meds when we get out. That'll probably carry over."

"Oh, goodie," Kaiden muttered sarcastically. His pace slowed slightly as the incline began to steepen and the wet ground became noticeably slick. "You still keeping a watch?"

"Yeah. Not picking up anything around here. Probably some smartasses in the Technician department having a laugh, seeing if anyone would fall for a trap right at the beginning."

"Well, I'll probably end up in a compilation video of Initiate Fails for the year." He sighed and began to hear the sounds of gunfire—the echoing cracks of bullets and dissonant noise of plasma fire, and even the occasional zap of electricity. Tension coiling at the base of his gut, he quickened his pace. "Looks like that was enough for us to fall behind."

"It'll even out," Chief assured him. *"I don't think all those fighting will get out without a scratch. Some may get kicked back to the beginning themselves."*

"Still, those are enemies we could be getting—extra points," Kaiden countered. After a few more steps, he came to a split in the road. New tracks branched off in different directions, none of them continuing straight forward. He looked down each path for a moment. None of them provided any clues as to what laid beyond. "Hey, Chief, I know that we didn't get a copy of the map, but you had to have analyzed it, right?"

"Obviously." The EI chuckled.

"Care to help me out here? Which way should I go?"

"That's not so easy."

"What do you mean?"

"Well, again, this isn't these guys' first rodeo. They probably expected everyone to make a copy of the map themselves, but it was really basic. It didn't show individual pathways and all that."

"So no good here, then?" Kaiden asked, folding his arms.

"Well, we already know that there are no dead-ends if we keep moving forward."

"There's no path down the middle," he observed, pointing into the thicket.

"I can see that, idiot, but we already agreed that we would probably have to stay off the main path anyway to reduce that chances of being caught off-guard in plain sight. Guess that will happen now rather than later."

Kaiden removed his igneous blade. "Guess I better keep this one on me."

"Another piece of advice, buddy. Be careful with that ignition trigger. The blade burns so hot it's certain to start a blaze, even though most of the greenery is wet. You'll make yourself and the entire jungle go up in flames."

"I'm keeping it prepared to cut through shrubbery and potential sneak attacks. Didn't plan on a barbeque." Kaiden chuckled, heading down the unpaved path of vines, moss, and overgrowth.

"Yeah, yeah, keep that attitude..." Chief muttered with a roll of his eye. *"What's the worst that could happen?"*

Commander Sasha was in a private room on one of the top floors of the observatory. He scanned through over a dozen screens, each one with a different view and angle of the action going on in the Soldier's test.

He watched as some initiates triumphed; enemies that fell to their blasts, the circumvention of traps, claiming hidden items for bonus points…all good. Then he would move over a screen or two and see other initiates failing. Hard. They would die in hails of gunfire or spike pits, or random beasts throughout the jungle would leap out of the darkness and slay them. Sometimes, they would simply fall to their own idiocy. Sasha saw one initiate somehow entangle himself in a vine. He went to cut himself down without realizing there was one wrapped around his neck, and when he cut the vine trapping him, he fell to the ground, the other vine holding and snapping his neck.

Then there was what happened to Initiate Kaiden… He

made a note to save it and have a copy on his pad the next time the ace wanted to give him lip about his abilities.

"Well, hello there, Sasha."

He turned to see Laurie enter the room with a giddy smile and waggling fingers.

"As I recall, I set the lock on the door to private. How did you get in?" Sasha grumbled.

The professor scoffed. "Please, you really think something so basic could stop me?" He held up a silver card with a black line on it. "Plus, I have a universal access card."

Sasha sighed as he turned to look back at the monitors. He reached down to a panel in front of him and began pressing different keys. The views on the monitor changed accordingly, showing different views of the field or switching to follow certain students.

"Aren't you supposed to be overseeing the Animus operations?" Sasha asked.

"That's technician Arvin's job now. What's the point in me training other people if I still have to do all the drone work?" he asked, making his way to a miniature bar at the side of the room and pouring himself a drink. "Since I'm feeling so bold, I think I'll retort by pointing out that you are usually the one designated by the Board to be the adjudicator for these sorts of tests."

"A rather fancy way to say umpire," Sasha gibed. "And I have been for the last ten years. They sent in a replacement. The board wanted me to have a break this year."

Laurie walked up beside him, swirling the glass in his hand. "I see...I feel we need to have a talk about your comprehensive skills, Sasha," he said and took a sip of his drink. "Either that or an intervention for your addiction to work."

"How many robots have you tinkered with in your free time? Or new devices you came up with while daydreaming?" Sasha inquired.

Laurie took another sip. "Oh, somewhere in the range of shut the hell up, smartass."

This caused a genuine grin to appear on Sasha's face. "By-the-by, I am not watching the tests due to workaholism. I am observing the various students due to personal curiosity—plus preparation, of course."

Laurie gave him a confused look. "Preparation? Oh, yes, the League. I always seem to forget about that every year."

"Am I to assume that means you won't be taking part?"

"Perhaps not. I always seem to delegate a subordinate to watch over my rosters for me anyhow," the professor noted. "Plus, I would probably say that it is safe to assume that both you and I would be trying to get a hold of at least one student."

Sasha left the console, walking over to a group of four chairs in the middle of the room surrounding a table with a large monitor in front of each seat. He sat down and took out his tablet. "If you are referring to Initiate Jericho, he is a potential on my list, but it takes more than one student to create a winning team."

"Well, that sounds surprisingly dismissive, coming from you," Laure stated. Sasha connected his tablet to the monitor and obtained an isometric view of the island the Soldier's test was held on. Laurie took the chair across from him, turning his monitor to the same feed. "After all the little nudges and special treatment, I would have thought Kaiden was an obvious choice for you."

"Preference doesn't always lead to better outcomes, Laurie. I see potential in the boy, but I like to win. However, as of right now, he is still my top pick, but we'll see after this test."

"I suppose you do have a title to keep," Laurie said with a hint of mirth. He paused as he was about to take another sip. "How's he doing so far?"

"Well, he began the test by exploding."

Laurie froze, his expression startled. "Exploding what?"

"Himself. He tripped a mine."

Laurie placed his glass on the table and leaned back in his chair. "That's not good for either him or me."

"I suppose the higher-ups will wonder why you gave such expensive and advanced equipment to someone who appears foolish to the point of suicide, but that's just a guess." Sasha chuckled.

"He can make up for it before the end," Laurie avowed, running a finger along his jaw in thought. "Though I wonder if his EI warned him. Its defensive systems should be running properly. I made sure to restart them after the diagnostic."

Sasha looked at Laurie from across the table, surprise evident even though his eyes were obscured by his dark optics. "You had to repair his EI already?"

Laurie waved him off. "Not repair, but he had a glitch during training, and I looked it over—which is a nice way to circle around and tell you why I came here in the first place. You see—"

Sasha held up a hand. "Quiet for a moment. It appears Kaiden is coming up to his first Merc group."

Laurie looked at his own screen and saw Kaiden ducked down behind the large base of a tree, his shotgun in his hands. A patrol of mercenaries—four basic and two heavies—came through the deep jungle, seemingly unaware of his presence. "Well, let's see if he's kept up with his studies."

"You gonna engage?" Chief asked.

Kaiden pressed the Raptor against his chest. "Obviously." He kept his voice to a low whisper. "Need the points to make up for that loss of a life earlier." He crawled carefully around the tree as the merc patrol moved closer. "Besides, it was the game plan, anyway."

"Sure enough," the EI agreed. Kaiden saw the white scan line move briefly over the six opponents. *"Four in the front got light armor and pulse rifles, two in the back got heavy armor and ballistic launchers."*

"Gotta take them down first. Don't wanna draw this out or use my barrier just yet. Waste the power," Kaiden stated.

"You gotta plan?"

Kaiden took another peek at the group as they began walking past. He noticed two large boxes hooked to the belts of the heavies. "Chief, what are those?"

"The one on the left is an ammo crate filled with explosive rounds. The other is a larger clip for holding grenades and probably fits around six to eight."

"Frags?"

"Thermals, more likely."

Kaiden took a moment to think. He reached over to his own belt and took one ballistic bullet from the clip. He slotted it into the secondary chamber on the Raptor. Calm now, he flipped the switch to change over to the auxiliary barrel and snapped the lever. "Yeah, I got a plan. Do me a favor and put on the sound dampeners."

"Gotcha," Chief acknowledged. Kaiden felt the sides of his mask expand and his hearing muffle.

He took aim at the pouch of thermals and snapped the lever. A couple of the grunts stopped and turned back to look for the source of the noise. He fired the explosive round.

This close, he both saw and felt the force of the eruption, and the group of mercenaries was flung to the ground.

"Chief, quick—give me a reading."

"Three dead…two grunts, one heavy. The other heavy is unconscious, and the remaining two are hurt but awake."

"Not for too long," Kaiden said, taking aim through the smoke at a figure that tried to stand.

"At least we don't have to bother with subtlety," Chief noted.

"Right?" Kaiden chuckled, taking the shot and seeing the spread of plasma energy hit the grunt's shoulder guard and exposed neck. The merc crumpled to the floor. He saw the other conscious merc struggle quickly to his feet, scrambling for his rifle and helmet that had been knocked away in the blast.

Kaiden holstered his shotgun as he took out Debonair. The merc found his rifle and turned to fire, but Kaiden's trigger finger was much quicker, sending a white-hot streak of laser right through his head.

"*That was fun and helpful,*" Chief chirped.

"Extremely," Kaiden agreed, looking over to the unconscious heavy. "I get any points for him?"

"*Since it's a K.O., yeah, but he'll probably go warn others if he wakes up.*"

"Like the explosion wasn't a tip-off?" Kaiden said with a roll of his eyes. He fired three quick shots to the chest from Debonair, the first one melting the exterior of the hard armor, the second drilling partially through it, and the final shot tearing right through and scorching through the merc's organs. "Better to be safe. I guess. Time to get going, either way."

"*You wanna make sure you don't want nothing from the bodies?*"

"Like what?" he asked, opening the vent on Debonair.

"*Armor, guns, ammo, that sort of thing. Just take a quick look and make sure there isn't something valuable or helpful for later. You get a few points for it, too, so that's a plus.*"

Kaiden took a look at the grunts. Two of them were charred, and the remaining two only had their armor and rifles, a downgrade compared to his loadout. He moved over to the heavy and sorted through the items, noticing a lockbox attached to his waist, dented from the explosion and impact but intact. The explosion even broke the lock, or perhaps the crash did.

He opened it up to find a tube of thermal grenades, a small clip of ballistic rounds, and a small syringe with a medical symbol on it.

"That's a coincidence," Kaiden said, sliding the tube of

grenades on his belt followed by the extra clip and placing the syringe into his pouch. "I can use all this stuff."

"Virtual world. You have a good drop rate."

"Guess so… Wait, there's something else." A small black box nestled within the lockbox. He removed it and opened it up, revealing a thin silver square with a red circle in the middle. "A mod?"

"Looks like it. Increases the damage of laser weapons—at the cost of increasing the overheat rate, though."

"That would work for Debonair…" Kaiden muttered thoughtfully, closing the vent. "But it's overheating problem is bad enough."

"Well, keep it anyway. When you finish, it will be added to your loadout inventory. I'm sure we can find a use for it eventually."

Kaiden nodded, placing it in the supply pouch. He slid Debonair back into its holster and began to run deeper into the jungle.

"Keep to the plan?" Chief asked.

He nodded "We still got some mileage to make up…" He looked back at the defeated group of grunts with a smirk. "But I'm having fun so far."

CHAPTER TWENTY-SEVEN

Sasha and Laurie watched the ace leave the scene, observing what was left of the patrol he had just ambushed. The smoking remains of the three guards killed in the explosion vanished almost immediately after he left, but the others lingered for a minute before doing the same.

"That was rather violent." Laurie chuckled. "A smart solution to taking out a group on your own, though it doesn't really say much for stealth."

"I believe that was probably never an option for him," Sasha surmised, switching the screen to track Kaiden once again. "Should probably consider telling him he needs to take a workshop on that."

"To be fair, he does have the cover of ninety-nine other soldiers running around causing chaos," Laurie commented, getting up from his seat to pour another drink. "Personally, I think it makes for a much more enjoyable watch. Care for a drink, Sasha?" he asked, turning to the commander from the bar with a shaker in hand.

Sasha shook his head, flipping through the points-of-view of various soldiers on the field before tapping on the scoreboard tab on the top of the screen. "That got him some points, but he's currently in the middle of the pack. He'll have to hurry if he wants the bonus for being in the top twenty-five."

"He can make up the distance with the right path," Laurie stated, pouring a few different liquors and a couple of spices into the shaker. "As long as he makes it into the top ten, I would consider it a success. Most special cases don't get higher than the twentieth position on a good year."

Sasha nodded slowly, hardly listening to the professor at this point as he saw a trio of soldiers disappear off the map, ported back to a checkpoint approximately two miles back. It would appear they ran into something particularly nasty or were caught off-guard. The commander selected one of the three students, accessing their POV camera, then he rewound it to the point of their death.

His eyebrows raised for a moment, observing the creature that had killed the students. He leaned back in his chair and thought for a moment, looking at the position of the creature on the map and Kaiden's current trajectory.

The ace had finished off a four-man team of grunts while he was looking at the other students, but as he continued to make his way across the map, Sasha could see that he would run far beyond the position of the creature.

He felt a little disappointed. In all honesty, he wanted to see Kaiden take it on. He had no statistics on how the soldier would deal with such a problem. Then he saw the creature's dot on the screen begin to move rapidly across the map—heading in Kaiden's direction, he realized. At its current speed, it was highly probable that it would intercept him.

"Laurie, you may want to hurry with that drink," Sasha informed the professor as he switched back to Kaiden's POV. "We could be in for something quite exciting."

Kaiden lobbed a thermal in the direction of a pack of armed droids, their lightly armored chassis little help as they were ripped apart in the blast. He scanned their remains quickly, Raptor at the ready, and got the all clear from the scan. Both were sufficiently deactivated.

"Ah, those sweet, delicious points," Chief murmured happily. *"Don't have the point totals for every student here, but you'll get that at the end."*

"How do you think we're faring so far?" Kaiden asked as he looked over the broken droids for salvage.

"Could always be better. Our current score is eleven thousand, but besides those heavies in the first group of mercs, we haven't had any real big hitters."

"Point piñatas," Kaiden corrected with a grin.

"You trying to make that a thing? Probably not gonna happen."

Kaiden shrugged as he continued his run through the jungle. "How far in are we? Or do you even know?"

"Not without an overview of the real map. According to your steps, we've gone over five miles, but considering the fighting and slight change of paths, we're probably a little under that.

"So no time to rest then?"

"Depends on how fast you can run and how many more points you wanna rack up. The finish line is a little over twenty miles from the starting point."

"Really? That ain't too bad. I can run twenty miles in an hour."

"I'm guessing on flat ground? Without a pack of weapons, gadgets, and armor?"

"Good point," Kaiden conceded begrudgingly. "Probably won't be one of the first ten to get there."

"Probably not, but on the upside, those who do are probably skipping out on kills and collectibles."

"I wish there was something that could really give us a boost. Speaking of others, haven't seen too many other initiates along the path."

"It's a big jungle. Plus, we lost some distance with the mine fiasco."

"Pretty sure at least a few have died in the time that we've…actually, how long have we been out here?"

"Thirty-two minutes and fifty-three seconds."

"See? Not too bad."

Kaiden heard a crack come from somewhere ahead. He stopped mid-stride, drew Debonair, and slid behind a tree. "Chief, scan for enemies," he commanded, peeking from behind the protection of the tree.

"On it," Chief acknowledged, the white line moving through his vision. "Nothing onscreen obviously...but I got some venting exhaust coming from behind the tree fifty feet ahead...and a Prisma glitch."

"Meaning?"

"The exhaust is from a weapon. From the venting, I deduce the model isn't something the mercs or droids have used. The

Prisma glitch means that I'm registering a body but no vital signs or physical details. Looks like someone's got a stealth generator."

Kaiden lowered his weapon slightly. He sucked in a breath—time to take a chance. Carefully, he leaned out from his cover and shouted, "I'm Kaiden Jericho, Ace in the Soldier Division. If you're another Soldier, I recommend coming out now. Otherwise, you'll probably lose a life in the next thirty seconds."

"Awfully cocky, aren't we?" a voice with a notable Australian accent called back. Kaiden saw a body suddenly appear in the middle of the thicket, dressed in camo light armor like himself with a hood over his mask. Two eyes stared out from behind circular lenses. "Especially considering I had my sights on you before you ducked behind the tree," he added, holding up a black-and-silver sniper rifle. Kaiden could tell from the design it was a magnetic model. It looked like a sniper version of the Yokai pistol he'd toyed with during his tests with Sasha.

"If you wanted to do any real damage, you would've had to charge up the shot. Considering you were right in front of me, my EI would have seen the magnetism activating in your sniper rifle and warned me before you got the shot off."

"And what? You would have ducked behind the tree? This is a Revenant model, mate. It would have pierced right through the tree at full charge."

"That would also depend on you being a good shot."

The sniper lowered his weapon and tilted his head. "Cheeky bastard, aren't ya?"

"Might as well be a second language," Kaiden admitted.

The man chuckled, then looked back. "Marlo, Amber, you guys can come out."

Kaiden saw two figures emerge from behind the trees. One was a rather large man with a cannon-like weapon, decked out in heavy red armor. The other was a woman with camo light armor and a full helmet with a large visor that covered her entire face.

"The big one is Marlo, demolitions, and the other is Amber, a battle medic," he said as he turned and placed a hand on his chest. "Name's Flynn—marksman, obviously."

"Nice to get acquainted," Kaiden said with a nod. "I was just wondering about the fact that I hadn't run into anyone yet."

"Yeah, we broke from the group about five minutes in. Most of them ran into a camp on the western edge of the starting zone for some easy points. Good call on our part. The majority ended up getting caught in a detonated explosion and lost a life."

"Wow, that makes me feel a little better."

"No kiddin'," Kaiden whispered.

"What was that?" Flynn asked.

"Talking to my EI," Kaiden answered with a wave of his hand. "So, how you guys doing so far?"

"Can't complain." Amber walked up and crossed her arms. "The big man here has taken most of the damage for us."

Marlo chuckled. "The blood-red armor gives them a nice and easy target, but it's so thick that I barely get hurt. Flynn takes them down from afar, and Amber patches up any boo-boos I happen to get from their pea shooters."

"You're lucky we haven't run across a group of heavies. You need to be more careful," she warned.

"Sure thing, Mom. I'll be sure to play nice with the other nice boys with Tesla cannons," he scoffed.

"You've been on your own, I'm guessing?" Flynn asked.

"Yeah, being a team player is a little…let's just go with the truth that collateral damage is a thing when I fight."

"Might wanna work on that if you're an ace," Amber stated.

"So I keep hearing, but that's what the training and workshops are for, right?"

"Only if you're willing to learn, but it seems to be working for you for now. That's an impressive point score you got," Flynn admitted.

"You can see my points?" Kaiden asked.

"Yeah. When your EI sees another initiate in a war game like this, they can read their basic stats," Marlo explained.

"Huh. Chief give me a readout." Kaiden commanded.

"Your EI's name is Chief?" Flynn asked.

"Better than yours." Amber snickered. "Seriously, Jeeves? You miss the butler back at your posh abode?"

"He was like a father to me," Flynn declared.

"Still think you should have gone with Dingo," Marlo muttered.

"That's a stereotype, Marlo, as I've told you at least a dozen times now."

As the trio made small talk, Chief got their stats, giving him their names, classes, divisions, weapons, armor, and gadget readout, point score—each of them had sixty-five hundred points—enemies killed—fourteen between them

—and zero collectibles earned, along with a picture of them without armor. Kaiden also noticed a small blue circle with the number three within it.

"Guessing that little circle means they're in a party?" Kaiden whispered.

"Yep. Could use it to our advantage. Wouldn't be a bad idea to stick with them."

"Wouldn't work out with our plan. Like you said, the points split when you're in a party. They've killed more than we have but they have fewer points."

"Also sound like they haven't really run into anything worth much, but you're right."

Kaiden nodded as he looked back at the trio. "Well, nice to meet you, but I got more ground to cover."

Flynn looked back. "Same here, but it was nice to run into someone friendly. Hope to see you at the finish line."

"You could stay with us," Amber offered.

"I appreciate it, but like I said, collateral damage," Kaiden reminded her, and when he looked past them, he saw the foliage begin to sway and the wind kicked up slightly.

"You don't need to worry about that. I'd be the one in front," Marlo declared, placing his cannon on the ground and flexing an arm. "And I can deal with anything."

Just then, Kaiden saw talons dig into Marlo's armor, and in a single moment, he was gone. The others jumped back as they heard a loud yell in the air. Kaiden drew his Raptor.

"What the hell was that?" he growled, scanning the air.

"Where's Marlo?" Amber yelled, pulling a sub-machine gun from her hip holster.

Then, in the distance, they heard him scream. *"Sssshhhh-hiiiiitttt!"* It faded away after a few seconds.

"Dammit, Marlo's dead." Flynn cursed vociferously. "He lost a life and got ported back to the checkpoint."

"That's almost a mile back," Amber yelled, backing up against a tree.

"Well, depending on what this is, we may be joining him soon," Flynn muttered.

Kaiden continued to scan the skyline, reaching for his ballistic shots to load into his gun.

"I should remind you we haven't gotten a checkpoint so—"

"If I die, it's back to the start."

"Helpful tip: don't die," the EI warned.

"Wasn't planning to— Oh, shit! Hostile inbound," Kaiden cried out.

A flying red creature with a long wingspan, pointed tail, and massive, scythe-like talons dive-bombed from the sky. They fired simultaneously—plasma shots from Kaiden, metallic spikes from Flynn, and rapid-fire lasers from Amber. The beast maneuvered around the shots, barely grazed at best as it tore through the sky.

"Devil Bird," Amber yelled. "We have to run."

"Like hell." Kaiden roared his fury, switched to auxiliary fire, and began blasting ballistic shots into the air. The monster halted its decent and swung away to avoid the explosive projectiles.

"We can't take that thing without a heavy weapon. It'll tear us to shreds," Flynn cautioned.

"Then get the hell out of here and get your big gun," Kaiden called back, continuing to fire. "You said he was less than a mile away, right? Can't you track him? He should be on his way."

Flynn charged up another shot. "Yeah, but he's in heavy armor, remember? He can't exactly sprint." He fired at the Devil Bird as it came back into view.

"Cover me. Need to reload ballistic rounds," Kaiden ordered, quickly ejecting the empty clip from the secondary port and inserting a new one. Amber ran out of the cover of the tree and fired into the sky.

Kaiden closed the port and aimed upward, firing at the giant bird as it ascended. "Get back to him. I'm either gonna take this thing down and get the points or I'll die trying, and you should be back by then and have better luck."

"You're insane, mate. It usually takes a team of hunters to bring this thing down," Flynn explained.

"My plan was probably insane to begin with, anyway, considering everything on this paradise island they loaded us on. Your ID said you got smokes—mind popping one before you go?"

Flynn took out a large black sphere. He pressed a button on the side and tossed it out onto the field before activating his stealth generator and disappearing. "You got brass balls, Kaiden. See you at the finish. Amber, retreat, and let's go get Marlo."

"Acknowledged," the battle medic shouted, stopping her assault and venting her weapon. "Best of luck to you."

"It's been shit overall, but good in spurts." Kaiden chuckled as he used the cover of the smoke to find a hiding spot, waiting for the Devil Bird to hit the ground.

The other two disappeared into the forest. Kaiden

prepared to fire in case the monster went after them, but after a minute in which it circled the area, it landed. He waited, taking a good look at the crimson predator as he heard it growl while scanning the tree line.

"Since when do birds growl?" he whispered.

"Since when do they come in that terrifying flavor? It's a mutant, dumbass. It's not exactly playing by mother nature's rules."

Kaiden pressed up against the tree as the Devil Bird looked in his direction, black eyes with red irises leering his way for a moment before it shifted to look the opposite way.

"Got any helpful tips for taking it down?"

"A shitload of bullets usually does the trick, but we would probably get eaten before you caused any real damage."

"Does it have any weak spots?"

"Top of the head is pretty malleable, but you'd have to climb a tree or something to get a clear shot. Even then, it would probably notice you before you got up top."

Kaiden pondered this for a moment as he studied the curve of the creature's back. The beast was big, at least seventeen feet. That gave him a new idea.

An idea he would soon come to regret—or at least Chief would as Kaiden holstered his rifle and took out his knife.

"Oh, sweet deviled eggs and Christ child, don't do this..." Chief moaned.

"Too late." Kaiden raced toward the Devil Bird, leaping into the air just as it turned its head to see him. He ignited the blade and dug the knife into the creature's back. It shrieked in anger and pain, thrashing about.

"You're not using my helpful tip," Chief yelled angrily.

"If I can stab it in the head, maybe the heat of the blade will let me burrow into the skull and stab its brain. That should do it, right?" Kaiden asked, holding onto the pterodactyl-like bird for dear life.

"Yeah. If it doesn't kill you first. And if it doesn't…" Chief's voice faded out as the Devil Bird expanded its wings, and with one hard thrust, took to the skies.

"Take off."

CHAPTER TWENTY-EIGHT

Flynn slid down the small hill, waving to Marlo. "Good to see you're all together, mate."

"What the hell happened?" he demanded, shouldering his cannon. "One moment we were chatting it up with that ace, then next, I am skewered through my shoulders and rag-dolled through the air."

"The fall killed you?" Flynn asked.

"I fell over two hundred feet. My armor was compromised, anyway."

"Yeah, that would about do it. Guess you aren't that tough of a walnut to crack."

"I guess I better hope I don't run into any mercs with trampoline launchers, or I'm screwed," Marlo jeered, rolling his eyes.

"Good to see you, Marlo, but we have to double back," Amber shouted from atop the hill.

"Why, what's going on?" he called back.

"What took you out was a Devil Bird. Kaiden—that Ace

we were talking to—stayed behind to try to take it out," Flynn explained.

"With those little guns of his?" Marlo asked, astonished. "Dumb bastard will probably get killed before he makes a dent."

"That's where we figured you'd help out. If we move fast enough, we can probably help him take it out before it eats him."

"And we've wasted enough time talking. Let's get moving," Amber commanded.

Marlo primed his cannon. "Right. Which way?"

Just then, the trio heard the roar of the Devil Bird, the wind howling as it tore through the sky overhead. They also heard a man screaming.

"Fuuucccckkkkk!"

"Is that…" Marlo's voice trailed off.

"Looks like that way," Flynn declared, arming himself. "Let's roll!"

"We aren't gonna catch up to a Devil Bird at full speed," Amber exclaimed as she slid down the hill.

"Probably not," Flynn admitted. "But I would like to see the aftermath."

"Is that the last of them, Izzy?" Silas, a Marine Class Soldier, asked the scout.

"Looks like it. Nothing else on the radar," she stated, looking up from the group of merc and droid bodies.

"We certainly fell for that ambush," he muttered, placing his rifle back into its holster.

"Sorry about that. Should have set the scan for motion instead of heat."

He waved it off. "Not on you. It's not like you were the only scout here."

"Speaking of that, how many do you think died?"

"Of the initiates? I think there were around twenty-four of us running through here. We seem to be the only ones still alive."

The scout wiped the brow of her helmet dramatically. "Man, are we lucky."

"Or I'm that good." He chuckled.

"I'm here too, you know," she pointed out, crossing her arms.

"I'm sure you got a couple." He shrugged, "But, yeah, good work."

She sighed before looking at the ridge. "Where should we go now?"

Silas walked over to the clearing, looking down over the mountainside into the vast expanse of jungle and beach that made up the rest of the island. "Looks like there's some sort of lab or something up a couple miles after we get off the mountain. It's pretty close to the end zone so we might score a few more points before we get there."

"Sounds like a—" The scout's voice was drowned out by a rush of air. The two turned to see a Devil Bird flying toward them. They both pulled their weapons as the mutant avian banked left and flew away, a man clinging to the side of the bird.

"*Soooon of a Biiiiiitch!*" They heard him scream as the monster flew away.

"What the…who the…" Silas muttered, confused and bewildered.

"Doesn't seem like he's having a good time," Izzy mused, turning around. "Come on, let's see if we can catch up to that bird."

"Bonus points?" Silas asked.

"Obviously."

"Hey, Raul, how much longer we gotta walk through this mess?" Cameron asked.

"I'm a tracker, not a scout," Raul grumbled. "Besides, you're a bounty hunter. Shouldn't you have a doodad or something that could help us out?"

"It's not like I could shoot a tracer at the end zone from my escape pod on the way down," Cameron grumbled.

"Quiet down, you two," Jaxon, the ace and leader of their party, demanded, looking back at the group. "We still have a pretty good lead on the others if I had to take a guess. I don't wanna risk it by getting into a large firefight because your bickering brought a battalion down on us."

Cameron sighed. "Understood, Jax."

"Yeah, yeah, I hear you." Raul sighed and looked over his shoulder. "Luke, you keeping up?"

"Don't worry about me." The titan chuckled, a large hammer on his back and a hand cannon at the ready. "I certainly ain't lagging. Besides, if something does attack us, you really want me to be far behind?"

"If you aren't taking bullets then you aren't exactly useful," Cameron stated.

"Nice to know you care, Cam," Luke muttered.

Jaxon stopped and held a hand up for them to wait. "You feel that?"

The trio behind him looked around, Raul shaking his head and Cameron shrugging.

"Don't feel too much in all this armor," Luke said

"All you heavies have the same one-liners." Raul huffed, clearly irritated.

They looked at a group of trees, their branches and long leaves blowing in the wind. "The wind is changing. It's getting stronger."

In the distance, they heard a loud, raging screech. The four quickly readied their weapons. Raul took out a rifle, Cameron a shotgun, Jaxon a machine gun, and Luke held up his hand cannon to the sky.

"What do you think it is?" Luke asked.

"Devil Bird, no doubt. My EI has a screech on record that matches that one, and it was in the glossary they showed us before the test," Raul explained.

"Oh, goodie. At least you can't blame us for this, Jax," Cameron noted.

"Just don't blame me if it rips your head off," the ace retorted.

With another cry and a rush of wind, the Devil Bird streaked past the four. They weren't able to get a shot off with the high velocity of the wind almost knocking them down.

As they recovered, they heard a cry as the monster flew away, *"Mmooottthherffuuckker!"*

"Is that also the normal cry of a Devil Bird?" Luke asked, looking at Raul.

"Not unless they're adapting to our swearing for some reason," he said, a hand clutching the side of his helmet as if trying to hold it in place.

"There was someone on the back of it," Jaxon stated, putting his gun away.

"How the hell did they manage that?" Cameron asked.

Jaxon shrugged. "Beats me, but if they survive this, we definitely won't have the lead anymore."

"No kidding." Luke still stared into the now empty sky.

Jaxon looked over to the tracker. "You got something, Raul?"

He nodded. "Got the heat signature. We can follow it up to three miles in any direction."

"Is it still flying away?" Cameron asked

"It is, but it's slowing down. Looks like it's getting ready to land."

Jaxon looked forward, rolling his shoulders, and beginning to sprint. "All right, double time, boys. Let's catch up."

"We gonna take that thing on?" Luke asked, putting his hand cannon away and charging forward with the others.

"Might be worth it for points if whoever is on that beast doesn't take it down first," Raul stated.

"Please, like one guy can take down a Devil Bird." Cameron laughed.

"Well, this has certainly gotten exciting." Laurie's eyes remained fixed on the screen. Kaiden thrashed about as the Devil Bird circled the sky. "Don't suppose this was a master plan of his?"

"Doubtful," Sasha noted dryly. "It would be quite something if he makes it out of this."

"Well, it certainly looks like he has backup on the way," Laurie chirped, looking at the map to see a couple dozen dots converging on his position. "If he wants the points to himself, he had better hurry."

The doors to the room opened, and both men looked over to see the head of security, Wulfson, step into view.

"What the hell are the two of you doing here?" he asked, his arms at his side.

"A good afternoon to you too, Wulfson." Laurie sneered. "Commander Sasha here was watching the tests from this room. I decided to keep him company."

"That's what I mean. I usually watch the tests from here. Who do you think stocks the bar?" He eyed the drink in Laurie's hand and looked over to the bar to see a few drained bottles. "Something I see you've taken to quite enthusiastically."

"Bill me later," Laurie said dismissively.

"I thought you had one of those fancy rooms for Board members to watch the tests, Sasha?" Wulfson asked, grabbing a bottle of scotch before sitting down at one of the screens at the table.

"I am not one of the overseers this year, so I decided to watch from the observatory. My apologies for taking your space, Wulfson."

"Eh, no trouble, I suppose. Glad to have someone to chit-chat with for a while. Care to make a wager?" the giant man suggested.

"If we do, my guess is the commander already has his

pick." Laurie took a swift drink. "He's had his eye on a particular student even before he got here."

"Oh? And who might that be?"

"Initiate Kaiden Jericho," Laurie confessed.

Wulfson paused, looking from the professor to the commander. "Well now, ain't that interesting."

Sasha looked up. "How so?"

"Your pal here had me take your little protégé under my wing. It took a little tough love, but I've been training him this past week."

Sasha raised an eyebrow, looking at the professor who continued to casually finish his second drink. "Laurie, that night at the restaurant, you said you ran into Wulfson."

"Some dealings may have occurred." Laurie shrugged. "But I have a vested interest in our boy as well, Sasha. Wulfson seemed to have the right…personality to be more of a hands-on guide for our little initiate."

Sasha looked back to Wulfson. "And how has that been going?"

"Pretty well, actually," he boasted, popping the top off the bottle and taking a large gulp "The boy can really work when he puts his mind to it. Took a few rough blows, but med bay does good work. Though I should probably watch out and make sure he doesn't get addicted to that blend Doctor Soni made. He really likes that stuff."

"Please do." Sasha pressed a button on his tablet and Wulfson's screen turned on. "Currently, Kaiden has found himself in quite a predicament."

Wulfson looked at the screen for a moment before beaming and beginning to laugh. "Ha! Riding on the back of a Devil Bird—that boy has got guts."

"Let's hope he can keep them all inside. It looks like they are going to land." They watched the action unfold and saw Kaiden begin to climb up the mutant bird's back. "Although…it seems Kaiden is getting rather impatient."

"Son of a…mutant…featherless…*whore*," Kaiden growled, stabbing his blade into the Devil Bird as he climbed his way to the head. The monster screeched and howled, thrashing about in pain as Kaiden reached the apex.

"Deep breaths, partner. You fall now, and I'm pretty sure this thing will disembowel you."

"You think it wasn't going to before?" Kaiden yelled, gripping the predator's large neck as it tried to throw him off.

"Might have let you off with a beheading, but I'm pretty sure you hurt its feelings and pissed it off."

"I'm going to do a hell of a lot more than that," Kaiden declared, reaching the head and holding his knife up in the air, readying it to bring down on the crown.

"You sure you don't wanna wait for it to land?" Chief exclaimed.

"Fuck that." Kaiden drove the knife into the skull of the beast, which roared in pain and shook its head wildly. He could feel the knife burrowing down but not far enough. Knowing he had little time, he yanked it out and began thrusting indiscriminately, sometimes stabbing, sometimes slicing, trying to get to the brain.

"Let's upgrade that to pissed off and furious," Chief yelled.

Kaiden could feel the blade cooling. He couldn't trigger

it again so soon or he'd risk breaking it entirely, but it was enough. He had made a hole in the dome of the Bird, and as he pushed the knife into its sheath, he grabbed a thermal from his belt.

"How the hell *did I get stuck with your* crazy ass?"

Kaiden ignored him as he activated the thermal and slotted it in the hole.

"Bail!"

Kaiden threw himself from the Bird. He turned in mid-air to see it staring straight at him, then the explosive went off, taking the beast's head as its body tumbled from the sky.

Right toward him.

"Shit! Barrier—now!"

Kaiden dragged the barrier out and activated it to create half of a sphere in front of him. The Devil Bird's carcass bounced off it and knocked Kaiden back, rocketing him even faster to earth.

"Face the ground with the barrier. It's our only hope to not splatter."

Kaiden did so, turning to the jungle below as a mass of trees came into view. He collided with them, bouncing as the barrier absorbed most of the impact, but damn, his chest felt ready to burst.

The device deactivated as he slammed into a branch, and he tumbled for a few more seconds before stopping. As he looked up, pain shot through him and his mind thumped in agony he looked over to a clearing. The Devil Bird's headless corpse sprawled on the ground.

He stood up wearily and walked over to it. Placing a

hand on the body, he scowled a mixture of satisfaction and discomfort. "Gotcha, you big bastard."

The corpse lingered for a moment, then disappeared, morphing into a wire-frame before vanishing completely. Behind it, Kaiden saw a large group of soldiers in full view.

He moved a shaky hand to the holster. "God, I hope they're friendly."

The crowd was silent for a moment before excited yelling and claps erupted. It was somewhat surreal as the cheering crowd was all decked out in armor and weapons, their faces hidden behind various styles of masks and helmets, but it certainly felt nice.

"Well, I'll be… I think this is the first time I've ever had so many people excited about me killing something." Kaiden chuckled.

"Just take it all in and don't say anything stupid to spoil the moment," Chief ordered.

"I'm a bit too tired to do even that much." He sighed.

"Bloody phenomenal, Kaiden."

Kaiden turned to see Flynn and his partners run up. "You really took that thing down all by yourself? I'll be damned."

"Well, wasn't gonna let your boy get killed like that without a little vengeance," Kaiden said, nodding to Marlo.

The demolisher snorted. "Wish I could've done it, but I'll certainly take the comeuppance." He looked at the spot where the bird had been before it vanished. "It could've stayed a minute longer. I wanted to kick it, at least."

Kaiden started to feel better. He could feel the pain subside rapidly and his muscles relax. He looked over to see Amber moving a device over him. "That's a nice trick."

"Battle medic, remember?" She finished and held the device up, a white gun-like apparatus with some vials of green liquid. "Stim Ray. A battle medic never goes into the field without one."

"Works pretty good, but talk with Doctor Soni in the med bay. She's got this blue stuff that is *amazing*."

"I'll look into it." She chuckled.

"Not bad, I must say." Kaiden looked over to see a man in dark green medium armor and a wide visor like his but with a full helmet with spikes protruding from the back. He was followed by three others—a large fellow with heavy silver armor, another with blood-red medium armor, and another with camo light armor. "My name is Jaxon. This is my team—Luke, Cameron, and Raul." He gestured down the line. "Nice to see another ace in action. I think I've seen you in the workshops."

"Yeah. I keep to myself mostly, but you're right. I don't see too many other aces."

"Not too many have what it takes—like taking down a Devil Bird by yourself. Not really normal criteria, but I would say it counts."

"That was pretty damn vicious," Kaiden heard another voice say as he felt a hand clap onto his shoulder. "Good show, too. Call me Silas." Kaiden turned to see a man in brown and green medium armor and a full-face mask and visor but nothing in the back, revealing long dreadlocks.

"Nice to meet you, but if you could let go for a moment, that spot isn't healed quite yet."

"Oh, right," Silas said and stepped back. Kaiden turned, and Amber continued to run the Stim Ray over him.

"This is my partner, Izzy." Silas motioned to a woman walking up to them in dark purple light armor.

"Isabella. Nice work on the Devil Bird. Probably gotta lot of points for it, huh?" She offered her hand.

Kaiden shook it. "I sure as hell hope so," he stated dryly.

"Damn straight you did. Got thirty-five thousand for the monster! We're at forty-six thousand total. Pretty safe to say we're probably in the lead so far."

"Bitchin'," Kaiden answered. "Guess all we gotta do is get to the end…which is where now? Kinda got off course."

"About three miles that way." Izzy pointed west.

"All right then." Kaiden took his Raptor out of his holster and looked back at the ground behind him, "We're close to the end, guys. Let's bring it home," he yelled, earning more cheers as the others walked toward them.

"Feeling all celebratory, now, are we?" Chief asked.

Kaiden smiled under his mask. "No reason not to be. We're almost to the end with plenty of time to spare, and there's like thirty people here. Looking like the end of the road."

"The game is still going. You should stay on your guard."

"I guess, but for once, I don't feel like there's anything I gotta worry about."

Kaiden felt a rumble, then heard the loud crack of a laser. He heard screams from behind him as an explosion went off, knocking him and the group around him back.

He cursed as he slammed into a tree, then scrambled hastily to his feet as the light from the sun went dark. The rumbling continued. Kaiden looked to see at least a dozen soldiers disappear. He heard what sound like the humming of an energy core and felt the tremor of impact. Bewildered, he looked over the thicket to find out what was coming as the others recovered.

His eyes widened as he saw something knock the trees down and enter the clearing.

"What the hell is that?" Chief yelled, astonished.

Kaiden loaded another clip of ballistic rounds, his last.

"Chief…activate Battle Suite."

CHAPTER TWENTY-NINE

"What is that machine?" Sasha asked, watching the chaos unfold onscreen.

"I think I have an idea." Laurie sighed, looking at Wulfson who simply continued to down the bottle of scotch.

"Did you design it, Professor?" Sasha inquired. "I certainly don't remember it from any previous tests."

"I did, but I wouldn't implement it, certainly not for a test," Laurie stated. "It was a droid based off old Asiton designs. I made some modifications—improvements—and added my general flair. It was supposed to be a defensive unit, built to deter opposition and give us an edge if any... galactic issues arose."

Sasha raised an eyebrow. "A World Council contract, I assume?"

The professor nodded. "Until they shut me down—or rather, the Academy Board did. But since the Council wanted the project secret, I had to play along and sent the prototype away to be disassembled at a different facility. I did, however, keep a digitized copy for use in the Animus, to continue testing…until I got bored and left it in one of my folders to collect artificial dust."

"Then why is it here now?" Sasha growled, annoyance creeping into his voice.

"Ask the giant drunk." Laurie huffed and pointed a thumb to Wulfson.

"It seems hypocritical to call me a drunk, narhat," the officer scoffed.

The professor flicked the hair out of his face as he got up to return to the bar. "At least I have the decency to pace myself."

"I'm a giant, remember? One bottle at a time is pacing myself," he joked, polishing off the bottle.

"Why would you have the droid's file in your possession, Officer Wulfson? And how did it get into the test?" Sasha asked.

Wulfson placed his legs on the table top and leaned back in his chair. "It was part of the deal I struck with that long-haired idiot with the silver spoon shoved up his ass. I was going to use it for personal training to see how well I fared. Never got the chance before I got a request from the head monitor for any potential ideas for implementation in the Soldier's test."

"They asked for your help? Guess they didn't have a room full of monkeys and typewriters, so they settled on one gorilla with an Animus directory," Laurie jeered, rinsing his glass.

"You gave them access to this…Galactic War Droid?" Sasha guessed, folding his arms.

Wulfson stretched before folding his arms behind his head "I gave them the option to use it. I said it came from my personal files, that I got Laurie to whip me up a few killer robots for me to test my mettle."

"At least you know how to cover your big ass." Laurie snickered, pouring some wine into a glass.

"Too much of that stuff will kill you, Laurie—or, at least, running your mouth under its effects will." The giant sneered.

"They haven't used it before now. I wonder if no one simply came across it or if there's another reason." Sasha spoke his thoughts aloud.

"The head monitor said that they probably wouldn't use it—too much for first-years. Maybe this batch is doing so well that they decided to…how would you say it? Give them a bonus level?"

"That or add another obstacle," Laurie suggested, taking his seat once again. "It has been a while since a Devil Bird was taken down during a test, and certainly never by one initiate."

"Perhaps…" Sasha continued to watch the initiates run through the forest, the giant machine barreling after them. "But are they testing the whole group?"

Marlo fired another fully charged shot at the head of the machine. It connected, knocking it to the side for a moment before a turret on its side activated. It aimed in his direction and fired a cascade of plasma bolts his way.

He dove to the side as Silas brought out a grenade

launcher and shot a thermal at the turret, destroying its base and sending the gun tumbling down the side.

"Thanks for that, buddy," Marlo called.

"Thank me when we get the hell out of here," Silas yelled back. "We need to move."

He helped the demolisher up, and they went deeper into the jungle as the machine began charging another powered shot from its main cannon. A beam tore through the forest, obliterating anything in its path.

"This is bullshit," Cameron screamed, firing at the massive body of the machine, only for his shots to be absorbed by a barrier.

"Energy projectiles ain't gonna do shit to the body. Go for the head," Jaxon ordered.

"Nobody but the heavies have anything that can scratch that thing," Flynn yelled, using his sniper to take out the small guns on the side of the massive droid.

"How come *his* shots are getting through?" Cameron complained.

"I'm firing metal rounds. The barrier doesn't protect against those," Flynn answered.

Cameron leaped away from turret fire, looking over to the group after he landed. "That's stupid. Who would design a barrier that way?"

"It's a holobarrier—less strain on the power core while still giving it good defense," Izzy explained.

"That means we can— Oh, *hell*. Luke, get back," Jaxon shouted to the titan, who hammered away at the underside of the machine. He clearly hadn't seen one of its legs raising over him, blocking the light.

As he looked up, the leg came down, smashing him into the ground. His body disappeared.

"Stim Ray won't fix that..." Amber winced.

"Damn, how many are we down to?" Raul asked.

"Well, those of us around that Kaiden guy seem mostly intact. Some of the others who weren't fried by the laser joined in along with a few who came in the aftermath." Silas took position with Marlo and fired another grenade.

"Unless we get a hell of a lot of heavies firing at the head all at once, I doubt it will do much good," Flynn stated grimly.

Jaxon fired a few more rounds before lowering his weapon. "Best chance is to actually get on that thing and try to destroy the core."

"I'm guessing you've yet to take a course in team morale, Ace," Izzy jeered. "Or at least coming up with a plan that seems plausible?"

"Not a lot of choice," Raul muttered. "We could all die, but this thing is between us and the end zone. We're either going to have to take it down or find a way to get by it."

"Guess we'll see who the fastest sprinter is pretty soon," Cameron muttered.

"Well, that's bullshit." Marlo groaned.

"Wait, speaking of Kaiden, where the hell is he?" Flynn asked.

Kaiden blinked for a moment before lifting himself to his feet. He looked around as he felt the ground shake but didn't see any of the soldiers or the giant droid.

"What happened, Chief?" he asked, rubbing the side of his head.

"Ya got blown into next freakin' Tuesday is what happened," the EI snarked.

"I died?"

"No. Almost, but you leaped out of the immediate blast radius and your body sailed way the hell over here. The fighting is about four hundred yards to the south-east."

Kaiden hissed as he tried to take a step. "My body feels like it's gone through a meat grinder. I could really use that blue stuff right about now."

"I'm starting to think you've got a problem."

"I can quit any time I want…right after the next hit…" Kaiden slumped over, holding himself up against the trunk of a tree.

"You got that health injection from that lockbox. I would recommend using it."

"Good call." Kaiden reached into his supply pouch, removed the syringe, and looked at his arm. His gauntlets were mostly destroyed, and most of his flesh was seared or torn. He stabbed the needle into his flesh and pressed the plunger down, feeling the effects almost instantly as his strength returned and the pain dulled.

"Won't fix the armor, but at least you'll have a little hop to your step."

"It'll do for now," Kaiden said. He looked around and saw a device in the distance. "What's that?"

"Touch it and see."

"That's a phrase that usually indicates nothing good will come of this," he muttered and walked over to the device, an orb floating over some sort of base. Tentatively, he placed his hand on it, and it glowed green. His display lit up.

Checkpoint Reached.

"At least we don't have to worry about getting shot back to the beach."

"I could use a day at one after all this," he decided. Another tremor rippled, and Kaiden turned back to see a flash and an explosion in the distance.

His short-term memory kicked back in. He remembered seeing a giant machine, the head long and curved with some sort of glowing device in the center that projected the power laser. It stood on four massive legs, a white metallic body with an oval design and ports holding turrets, plasma cannons, and rocket launchers. One of which had launched right at him, he recalled, knocking him away.

"Good thing you got that battle suite online. Probably wouldn't have reacted so quickly otherwise."

"Turned it off almost right away too. You blacked out for a little while there."

"So it's still available?"

"Yeah, but I doubt it'll do much good against whatever the hell that thing is."

Kaiden thought back to the beginning of the test, going over the glossary. "That was probably the unidentified hostile."

"Safe Bet."

"You still have no clue what it is? Even though we got to see it up close?"

"Based on appearances, it looks like an Asiton droid. Can't say it's ringing any bells, though. Don't have

anything on file that looked like that thing," Chief admitted.

"Means we don't have a game plan, huh?"

"Sure we do. Get the hell out of here," Chief stated acerbically. *"That thing is distracted, and we're only a few miles away from the end zone. Safe to say we got this in the bag."*

"What about the others?"

"What about the others?" Chief snickered. *"Their sacrifices won't be in vain and all that stuff...whatever makes you feel better. It's not like they're actually dying."*

Kaiden thought it through. It was true. He probably had the lead, thanks to taking down the Devil Bird, and he would probably get a bonus too for being one of the first to get to the end. This was a test of individuals, after all.

He saw another blast, the trees along the line of the beam disintegrating. He looked between the battle zone and the way toward the finish line and sighed.

"You're going back, aren't ya?" Chief asked.

"Can't pass up a challenge," Kaiden admitted with a shrug. "Besides, if we don't know what it is, no one's destroyed one before. I get to put my name in the history books and all that junk."

"True enough, but if that's the case, you'd be excited. I can read your vitals—no adrenaline pumping or heart rate increase," Chief noted, his avatar popping up in front of Kaiden. *"Come on now, buddy, what's the real reason?"*

He walked over to where he initially woke up, Chief hovering beside him. His Raptor lay on the ground a few feet away. He picked it up and dusted it off, checking the barrel and what remained of his ballistic rounds.

"I did the whole live-to-fight-another-day thing before.

It's not as victorious as they make it sound." He primed the gun and snapped the lever "I keep remembering something an old...friend of mine once said. His name was Jake."

"The guy I synthesized my personality off of?" Chief asked.

"Yeah, though that wasn't really my choice. You kinda made an assumption there." Kaiden huffed belligerently, looking back at the EI's avatar.

"You told me to make the process speedy. Out of all the options you went through, it was the only one that caused a positive reaction. Just as much your fault as mine," Chief pointed out haughtily, his color changing to a slightly annoyed red. *"Besides, it's not one-to-one. I'm not exactly like him, I'm my own...artificial character."*

Kaiden chuckled. "Yeah, for better or worse, I can certainly tell the difference." He slung the shotgun on his back and turned to the EI. "You've been a pain in the ass, but you've made this fun so far. I ain't complaining."

"Well, if that doesn't warm my little cyber heart," Chief said sarcastically, but that didn't stop him from turning a slightly delighted pink.

Kaiden walked over and looked at the battle in the distance. "Something he said a long time ago keeps echoing in my head since I got here. Never settle." He pulled Debonair out for a moment, checking it for damage. "A pretty simple phrase, but damn, if it doesn't get my blood boiling. Like he was looking down on me at the time." He placed his pistol back in its holster after he was satisfied. "But, the more I think about it, the more I think he meant it differently."

The floating orb hovered around until he hung in front of Kaiden again. *"I think I get it."*

"Do you now?"

"He meant you can always do better," Chief elucidated. "Take it from one whose ideas you keep bucking. Most of the time, I think nothing of it. You'll die or get beat-up, I'll laugh, then you'll learn and follow instruction. But you have somehow been getting by on that stubbornness of yours."

Kaiden shrugged. "Helps that I'm almost always right."

The orb began to contract and expand, and a laughing noise erupted from the EI. "Ha! Not even almost—barely would be closer, and that's being generous."

"For a minute, I thought you were trying to have a moment there." Kaiden scowled.

"Can't let that ego get too big, or you might do something terrifyingly *stupid*."

Kaiden chuckled. "Maybe. It would probably be pretty fun though, right?"

Chief's eye looked off to the side. *"Probably, but I'm also beginning to wonder if EIs can have aneurysms, so maybe keep it to a minimum?"*

"No promises."

Chief sighed before disappearing and reappearing in the display. *"Figured as much."*

Kaiden took a running stance before sprinting off back to the battle. "Shut the hell up. You love it."

"Luke is on his way back," Jaxon informed the group. "He's got another life to spare, but if he dies again, he's gotta try to get around."

"I'm sure we can find something for him to do," Raul

muttered.

"We got a plan yet?" Marlo asked, taking another shot that zoomed past the head. "Dammit!"

Jaxon took a few shots at the machine's head. "Like I was saying, we have to get on or inside that thing…try to get the core directly."

"Neat idea." Flynn clucked his annoyance, taking out another rocket launcher. "Got any recommendations on how we get up there?"

"Cameron has scorpion wire. It can bypass the shields and pull someone up to it, and they can climb up the rest of the way while the rest distract the droid." Jaxon didn't look convinced that it was a viable option.

"You want me to get on that thing?" Cameron asked, aghast.

"I said someone, not you," Jaxon retorted. "You probably don't have the firepower to do it, anyway."

"Then who should go?" Amber asked, stitching up Silas with her Stim Ray.

"Well, if we had that psycho who rode around on the Devil Bird, he'd probably—" Izzy broke off as they saw the head begin to charge up another blast. "Shit, this one ain't missing."

The group saw a couple explosions go off on the machine's head, stopping the charge and causing it to sputter. They turned to see Kaiden lower his weapon and give them a wave. "Sorry about that. Bastard got me pretty good. Can I help?"

Jaxon noticed that the others were all looking at him. Then, as one, they looked back at Kaiden with Flynn nodding his head. "Oh, hell yes, you can."

CHAPTER THIRTY

"So the plan is for me to fling my ass on top of the death-machine, find its core, and destroy it—assuming there's nothing blocking it?" Kaiden asked in mid-stride. He and the remaining soldiers ran through the jungle to put some distance between them and the killer droid. "I'm starting to think plans made on the fly aren't very well thought out."

"If you have an alternative, I'm all ears," Jaxon retorted. "Luke and the other heavy would snap the line with the weight of their armor, none us have any explosives left, and you seem to have a death-wish. It makes you a prime candidate."

"I don't have a death wish, I just really want things dead sometimes," Kaiden countered.

"I'm only working on the info I got."

"You've known me like five minutes."

"And in those five minutes, I've seen you ride on top of a Devil Bird, blow it up, crash on the ground, get hit with a rocket, and choose to come back to take down a weaponized engine of nightmares." Jaxon laughed.

"He does have a point, mate. I was gonna say you're quite brave, but suicidal tendencies also make sense," Flynn stated as he leaped over a fallen tree.

"At least you give me the benefit of the doubt."

"So, are we doing this or not?" Izzy asked, looking over her shoulder. "Because that thing is coming back, and it seems pissed."

"Good Lord, what did you think it was before?" Raul inquired, hauling his rifle out.

"Passive-aggressive?" Silas suggested, drawing his own gun.

"So what's it going to be, Ace?" Jaxon asked.

"You calling me that as a pet name or because we share the class?" Kaiden inquired, slowing his stride and turning to face him.

"Would it help if I offered to buy drinks if we make it out of this?" Flynn asked, prepping a smoke grenade.

"It's certainly added incentive." Kaiden looked back at Jaxon, "Who's got the wire?"

Jaxon turned to his teammate. "Cameron. Get over here."

The bounty hunter hurried over as missiles erupted around them. He pulled off his gauntlet and handed it to Kaiden. "Trigger on the side fires, button on top drags you up. The hook is magnetized, so just aim in the general area."

Kaiden nodded, taking the grappling gun as they dodged plasma fire. He slid next to Jaxon. "Got any idea where I should go?"

"Go for the top of the body. My guess is there's a hatch or hole that will lead inside. If there isn't, make one. I think we've gone beyond hurting its feelings."

Another volley of rockets erupted a few feet away, knocking them back. "Even so, I think it's overreacting a bit." Kaiden groaned, forcing himself off the ground.

"We'll cover you, but there's still a few turrets left, and they seem automated, so try not to get bullet-riddled before you get a chance to play hero."

Kaiden attached the gauntlet to his right arm. "Hero? Not too interested in that, but I'll certainly take the points for it."

"Hold up a second," Flynn said, pressing the side of his helmet.

Kaiden saw a message pop up on his display.

Flynn King invites you to join his party of 9.

Kaiden looked at Flynn and tilted his head. "What's this for?"

"So we can keep track of each other and communicate through our EIs, just in case."

"All of you are in a party?" Kaiden asked.

"We've been together long enough that the system did it automatically, but since you went flying, you didn't get in," Jaxon explained.

Kaiden looked to Flynn and Jaxon. "Doesn't that mean we have to share points?"

The two looked at each other incredulously for a moment, then turned back to Kaiden. "You're really going to bother with that right now?" Flynn fumed.

"I'm simply...curious," Kaiden said with a shrug,

"We'd share points anyway since everyone pitched in to

take this thing down—*if* we get it down. If it makes you feel better, you'll probably get a few extra points for dealing the killing blow," Jaxon grumbled.

"I'll take it," Kaiden chirped, giving them a thumbs-up and accepting the party invite.

"Super, now move!" Jaxon commanded, his tone acidic.

Kaiden leaped up and ran at the droid. His companions fired behind him, trying to keep the death machine occupied.

He fired the grappling hook at the top of the droid's body. It connected, and Kaiden took Debonair out as he hit the button to ascend. He fired at a turret trying to gun him down, the lasers hitting the barrier for a moment before he passed through, then hitting their mark and burning through the guns.

"I've made it," he called, only to see all turrets on the deck turn in his direction. "Oh, shit!" he yelled as he rolled away from the oncoming fire.

"Activate your barrier," Chief shouted.

Kaiden did so, placing the device in front of him. The barrier popped open as a curved shield, giving him some protection from the blasts.

"It's still damaged from the fall. You don't have long."

"Scan for a hatch or doorway," Kaiden commanded.

"Look down."

Kaiden glanced at his feet to see he was standing on a circle with a line through it. "That works too." He examined it and found a lever off to one side. Holding his breath, he grabbed it and twisted quickly. The doors opened, sending him down the hole.

"Well, this is an interesting development." Laurie looked amused rather than concerned.

"Why is there a hatch on a killer robot?" Wulfson asked.

"It was meant to function on its own or as transport. Plus, it would allow for easier internal repairs," Laurie explained. "There was supposed to be a barrier in place to block unauthorized personnel, but I never implemented it into the artificial version."

"It would appear that the soldiers have won, assuming Kaiden doesn't get lost in there or somehow trips and knocks himself unconscious." Sasha deadpanned, though a definite twinkle in his eyes betrayed his satisfaction.

"That would be a riot." Wulfson guffawed.

"It certainly would, but there are other things he should worry about," Laurie admitted.

The commander and officer turned to stare at him, both with a look of curiosity.

Laurie rolled his eyes as he placed his drink on the table. "It's the weak point of the whole design. I wouldn't simply leave it unprotected." He spoke reasonably, folding his hands as a rest for his chin. "Kaiden has a bit more to worry about than some wires on the ground, I can assure you."

"Damn, it's dark in here," Kaiden muttered, moving through the interior of the bot.

"*Activating night vision,*" Chief stated, Kaiden's display becoming green and his surroundings clearer.

He was in a bare hallway. A few sparkling lights shimmered on the wall, but nothing indicated a power source or weapon function.

"Hey, Flynn, Jaxon, anyone there?" Kaiden whispered.

"Speak up a bit, mate. Rather loud out here," Flynn answered.

"You in?" Jaxon asked.

"Yeah. Not seeing any power core, though. It's kinda barren in here, a little unnerving."

"You're probably on the top level," Silas stated. "It'll be further down, in the middle or toward the bottom. You need to—" His voice cut out.

"Is the connection spotty?" Kaiden asked, tapping the side of his helmet.

"Not in the Animus. He just took a plasma bolt to the chest and got reset," Jaxon informed him.

"Dammit." Silas cursed, coming back onto the comms. "I'm down to my last life."

"That's unfortunate," Kaiden lamented as he continued down the hall, looking for a ladder or another hatch.

"Don't risk it. Just try to sneak by," Jaxon ordered. "That goes for the rest of you. If you got a life to spare, get your ass back here. If not, we'll try to manage while you get around."

"Rather pragmatic of you," Amber chirped.

"If this doesn't work, it's all we got. We can't afford to play around much longer. Time is running low, and we still got ground to cover," Jaxon admitted.

"Well, if any of you make it to the end zone before me,

see if you can set up some streamers and confetti for my arrival." Kaiden chuckled.

He heard Flynn laugh. "Sorry, I didn't choose a party bomb as one of my gadgets. Maybe next time."

As Kaiden continued to laugh, he heard something tap against the metal. "I hear something… Going silent."

He turned the comms off as he put Debonair away and took out his Raptor. He aimed it down the hall, waiting for something—anything—to come out.

He was greeted with a shot to the chest, causing him to stumble back. He looked up quickly and fired several rounds, connecting with something before sparks flared up.

Kaiden paused for a moment, then lowered to a kneeling position, waiting for return fire. Nothing happened, and after a few minutes, he rose again and crept down the hall, where he found the body of some sort of droid—a round body with a blaster on top and four legs, like a miniature version of the massive machine he was inside.

"What the hell is this, Chief?" he asked, and a white scan line cascaded across his display.

"Defense drone, certainly not the only one. Be on guard. It'd be rather silly to get this far to die to one of these little bastards."

Kaiden looked up and down the hall and discerned a ladder leading down. He moved to it and slid down, his Raptor never leaving his hands. He was now in a larger room with hallways crisscrossing and boxes containing machines and tech littered about.

"Think it would help to take some of these out?"

"Nah, you'd have to use your ballistic rounds or thermals to

make a dent in those shields. Best to save those for the core or any more drones."

Kaiden nodded in agreement. "Can you scan for an energy reading or something? Tell me if I'm getting close?"

"Sure thing," Chief acknowledged, Kaiden saw a white circle onscreen spinning for a moment before a white arrow pointed downward. *"One more level down and we should be good."*

"That's something of a relief…" His voice quieted as he heard more tapping—a lot more.

"Seems you got their attention."

"For once, I'm good without it." Kaiden grimaced and ran down one of the adjacent halls.

"Can't tell how many there are, exactly, but it's enough to be a problem."

"Grand." Kaiden muttered a low expletive when he heard the drones move closer. "Hope the others outside are holding up."

"This is just the fucking worst!" Cameron roared his rage, taking shots at the small robots that had begun dropping from the belly of the gigantic machine.

"Guess it decided to answer our infiltration with some back-up," Izzy grumbled, walking backward and destroying a couple of drones.

"At least they are much easier to destroy," Luke shouted with a swing of his hammer, smashing a few and knocking others back. "And fun too!"

"Better than dealing with that damn laser," Marlo

growled, firing a blast from his Tesla cannon. "Speaking of which, it hasn't fired another shot since Kaiden showed up. Anyone know why?"

Amber finished healing Raul before switching to her sub-machine gun and firing at the swarm. "I'm not sure I care as long as it doesn't do it again."

"Best guess, his ballistic rounds caused it to malfunction for a while. Now that he's in there, it's probably juggling with interior defenses and dealing with us," Jaxon explained, venting his gun.

"Wonder how he's doing." Flynn lifted a finger to his helmet. "Hey, Kaiden, how are you faring in there?"

Kaiden's back was to a wall, constant streams of laser fire coming from both hallways next to him as the drones advanced.

He held two fingers against his helmet. "I'm fine," he muttered sarcastically. A rocket rushed passed him from the hallway on his right, slamming into the wall and cracking it.

"Oh, good. Rockets, that's fun." He sighed.

"Actually, that's helpful," Chief said.

"What are you thinking?"

"Look, the wall was damaged."

"Think it could be a way out?" Kaiden asked.

"Also a way down. How many ballistics do you have left?"

Kaiden looked at the auxiliary indicator on the side of his gun. "Five shots."

"That should be enough. Take out the wall, use the scorpion

wire to grab onto the side, and blast a hole in the side below. Should take us straight to the core."

"Better than being here," Kaiden shouted and fired an explosive round at the wall, blasting it apart and revealing the sky outside. He ran and jumped through the hole, firing the grappling hook behind him and holding on.

"Care to give me a target, Chief?"

"Onscreen. It'll take a couple shots."

Kaiden saw a blue 'X' appear on the side and about twelve feet below. He aimed and fired two rounds, busting through the exterior. Cautiously, he tried to swing over, but if he let go, he wouldn't make the jump. It was too sheer.

Kaiden activated the comms. "Cameron. How do I descend?"

"You have to hold down the drag button," he replied.

Kaiden pressed down on the button, the line loosened as he descended, and he began to swing himself over as the drones fired at him. He'd barely touched the new entrance he'd made, and the line disappeared. His foot slipped, but he caught himself on the edge, climbing up and moving out of the drones' line of sight.

"The grappling hook disappeared. What happened?" Kaiden asked over the comms

"Drones got Cameron. Since the grappling hook was his, it left with him. He's on his last life now too, and we lost Marlo as well," Jaxon said.

"Son of a bitch. You make it?" Cameron asked as he resurrected.

"Yeah, I'm on the level with the core," Kaiden answered.

He heard tapping on the exterior of the machine. "Are the drones walking along the side of the machine?"

"Yep, I take it you made those holes?" Flynn asked.

"You bet, but I didn't take into account that these things were climbers. I'm heading to the core." As he turned to run, he heard a loud whirring sound in the machine.

"Shit! The laser's back online," Jaxon shouted.

"Y'all git. I'll meet you guys in the end zone."

"Roger," Jaxon shouted as the line went silent.

Kaiden ran down the room he was in to a door in the distance. It didn't take long for laser fire to begin shooting past him. He serpentined through the room, blasting the door with a ballistic round to open it, only to be greeted by another group of bots blocking another door.

"Damn, there are a hell of a lot of these." Chief growled his displeasure.

Kaiden heard a rocket behind him and rolled. The thing passed over him and slammed into the other room, destroying the bots and opening the next door.

"Guess they have their uses, though," Kaiden jeered. He ran into the next room and stopped short at the sight of a giant cube, metallic and glowing blue, with a large number of wires and connections attached to it.

"This the core?"

"Good guess."

Kaiden heard a loud clack and turned to see a cannon activating on the ceiling. The drones entered the room and began to fire, and he dived behind a console as the lasers and rockets fired in his direction.

"Don't think we'll be walking out of here."

"We can at least take this metal bastard down with us."

He could hear the cannon charging up. Calm now, he took off his belt and activated the remaining thermals, tossing them under the core.

"Don't die just yet. If you die before the thermals go off, they'll disappear."

Kaiden looked up to the cannon and could see the energy form. He blasted it with his last two ballistic shots, shifting it to point up slightly. He dove as it fired, and it blasted him over to the other side of the room and directly into the path of the drones.

He winced as he turned to look at the grenades. He heard the final beep as they began to explode and the drones began to fire.

"Good thing we got that checkpoint, huh?"

"No kidding."

CHAPTER THIRTY-ONE

As Jaxon crossed into the end zone, he looked back at his party. One-by-one, they made it in, some cheering, while others slumped over in exhaustion.

He heard someone call out to them and turned to see Silas waving. "Good to see you guys make it."

Jaxon nodded before reaching his hand out for Silas to shake. "Thanks for your help. You been here long?"

"A little less than ten minutes," Silas admitted, taking the ace's hand. "Wish I could've been there with you when you took that damned thing down, but I saw it blow up from a distance. It was a wonderful sight!"

"Agreed." Jaxon looked over to see Cameron walking over. "I would never have believed seeing a virtual being blow up could be so satisfying."

"I also made sure to destroy the tiny drone that killed you, Cam," Luke said, lumbering over.

Cameron removed his helmet, revealing tanned skin and close-cropped red hair. He gave his titan teammate an annoyed look. "Thanks for letting that out into the open." He sighed.

"Oh… Uh…it's the thought that counts?" Luke asked sheepishly, and Cameron rolled his eyes.

"Marlo also got taken out by a rocket, and Izzy got caught in the final laser blast. They make it back yet?" Jaxon inquired.

"Right here," Izzy shouted.

They turned to see Izzy and Marlo hustling to the inside of the end zone, a few other soldiers entering with them.

"Oh, God, I've run a lot today!" Marlo groaned, taking a seat on the grass next to the group.

"Fortunately, my checkpoint wasn't too far back. I ran into the big guy on my way here," Izzy explained, resting on her knees for a moment to catch her breath.

"Good to see you've made it," Flynn congratulated them, walking over to the rest with Amber and Raul.

"Guess that means we're all accounted for," Amber stated before looking back at the jungle. "Except for Kaiden."

"Is he on his way?" Flynn asked, looking at Jaxon.

He shrugged. "Can't tell. He left the group."

"Maybe it's because we finished?" Flynn asked, crossing his arms.

"No, a little after the killer droid exploded. I guess when he resurrected."

"Maybe it was a mistake?" Silas suggested.

Flynn and Jaxon looked at each other, remembering one of their last exchanges with Kaiden before looking back at the group.

"Points, probably," they said in unison.

They heard a loud noise behind them and looked outside the end zone. A missile headed straight for them and slammed into the outside barrier of the wall.

"What the hell? Why are we getting shot at when we've crossed the finish?" Cameron yelled.

"I don't think they're shooting at us," Jaxon said. He pointed at the tree line a half-mile away from them. There was a soldier in camo light armor, a long jacket, and a wide-brimmed hat running toward them, followed by dozens of mercs and armed bots firing at him.

"Move your dumb ass," Chief roared as Kaiden dodged and weaved through the various shots and blasts coming his way.

"Positive encouragement only, Chief," Kaiden retorted, firing a few shots back with Debonair as he reached the limits of his running speed.

"You lost that privilege when you decided to go through a merc base on your last life."

"Thought I could get some last-minute points. Didn't think they would call in reinforcements. Or have a warehouse full of bots, either."

He heard a pair of rockets shoot his way and rolled to the side, staggering to get up as the blasts went off before continuing his sprint.

"Only a little over a quarter-mile till we cross into the end zone," the EI informed him.

Kaiden looked up to see a giant translucent green wall. "Think they'll stop chasing us after we pass through?"

"They should. Otherwise, we'll have to deal with a bunch of soldiers, all pissed off that you brought a battalion to their medal ceremony."

"It's more a horde than a battalion." Kaiden looked up to the ridge to see a line of said soldiers form along the edge of the end zone.

"Oh, good, a welcoming committee."

Kaiden scoffed. "Would be nice if they— Oh, shit," he exclaimed as he saw over thirty soldiers arm themselves and point in his direction.

"Hit the dirt."

Kaiden threw himself to the ground as he heard gunfire and projectiles fly by him in the direction of his pursuers. He heard pained yelps, cursing, and the sounds of singed and punctured metal behind him. It soon went quiet, except for the sounds of burning and static discharge.

Kaiden stood up and looked back to see that the mob chasing him was now quite thoroughly quelled. He began to walk over, waving as he recognized his group. "Appreciate that, guys."

"Consider us even now," Jaxon replied, holstering his weapon.

Kaiden looked back at the slaughtered hostiles and pointed. "Guess I don't get those kills?"

Flynn pressed a button on his sniper rifle, causing the barrel to shrink and the body and stock to fold into itself before placing it on his back. "Seriously, mate? You've got a problem."

"I've got several," Kaiden muttered as he crossed into

the end zone. He collapsed at their feet as they circled around him. "But for now, I'll settle for those drinks you promised if I took down that big mechanical dick."

"That honestly sounds pretty good right now," Flynn admitted.

"We've got a couple of days of downtime after this. I know a great place in town. I'll get us a feast," Luke declared.

"Food sounds fantastic too. Didn't think you could burn so many calories in the Animus." Kaiden groaned.

"Well, the mind does burn calories if used a lot," Amber stated, taking out her Stim Ray. "And you've technically been running a lot, at least in your head." She pointed the device at Kaiden and activated it. He felt his energy return.

"Oh, that feels really good." Kaiden sighed happily, taking a moment to relax before pushing himself off the ground into a sitting position.

"That was my last charge, but I don't think I'll be needing to use it again in the next fifteen minutes."

"So we're almost out?" Kaiden asked.

"Fourteen minutes, fifty-four seconds, and counting," Jaxon assured him.

Kaiden nodded before pushing himself off the ground and looking back at the jungle. The sun was beginning to set in the distance, and he could see more soldiers making their way to the finish.

He looked back at the group. "Any of you get that placement bonus?"

"Silas, Cameron, Flynn, Amber, and me," Jaxon replied. "Though the last three of us just got twenty-third through twenty-fifth."

"The four of us would probably have gotten the top places if that machine didn't show up," Cameron fumed at Jaxon before releasing a resigned exhalation. "But it's whatever. I still got seventeenth, and it was a pretty fun ride."

"Agreed." Silas concurred. "Wasn't exactly either my plan or Izzy's to have to deal with a walking war machine, but it was a thrill." He looked at Cameron and gave him a thumbs-up. "I got fourteenth."

"Met some…interesting people too," Izzy chirped as she placed an arm on Silas' shoulder and leaned on him.

Flynn looked at Kaiden. "Glad I didn't shoot you back when we first met."

Kaiden crossed his arms and shrugged. "You wouldn't have hit me."

"Maybe not." Flynn laughed, pointing a thumb toward Marlo. "But Marlo's big cannon might have."

Kaiden gave the Tesla cannon a once-over. "That would be…a safer bet, yeah."

The group went quiet as they watched the sun disappear and the last remnants of the testing group make it in. Soon, dozens of soldiers walked around and chatted easily among themselves.

They saw one last soldier hustle in. "That makes one hundred," Raul commented.

"Got six minutes left," Jaxon announced. "But since everyone is here, they'll probably port us out in a minute."

Just then, a loud ring sounded, and giant screens formed in the air. All the soldiers looked up to see Head Monitor Zhang onscreen.

"Congratulations, initiates, on not only passing your

test but being the only Soldier group so far to pass with all one hundred initiates accounted for."

"Damn, must have upped the difficulty this year." Silas sounded irritated.

"There's still time," Izzy added.

"We will begin de-syncing you from the Animus in due time, but first, your final scores."

Zhang disappeared from the screen, replaced by a scoreboard showing the bottom twenty-five positions.

Marlo placed his cannon on the ground and leaned against it. "I wonder who got first?"

Flynn looked over his shoulder. "Still feeling confident, Kaiden?"

"And cocky," he responded with a raised fist.

The scoreboard continued to climb until it reached the top twenty, showing five positions at a time.

"Hey, Marlo got eighteenth," Amber declared.

"Not too bad, I guess. I suppose those deaths cost me a bit." Marlo sighed.

"Oh, come off it mate, you did good," Flynn said, clapping him on the back.

The board changed again, fifteenth through eleventh.

"I got thirteenth?" Cameron spluttered.

"Hey, I got fifteenth," Izzy pointed out.

"I got eleventh." Silas folded his arms behind his head. "Not bad."

"Killing that death machine really boosted our points." Izzy looked at the group. "Good job, team."

"That means the rest of us got into the top ten," Luke noted.

"Let's see who's top dog." Cameron chuckled.

The board flashed, showing tenth through sixth this time.

"Sixth." Raul huffed his annoyance "Could be worse, I suppose."

The screen changed, showing the top five one position at a time.

5th place: Amber Soni 75,000 points

"I got fifth," Amber shouted, jumping excitedly in the air.

"You're Doctor Soni's kid?" Kaiden asked, looking over.

"Could be a different Soni," she pointed out wistfully. "But in this case, you're right."

Kaiden scratched the underside of his chin. "I see… About that blue stuff—"

"Look, it's changing," Izzy announced, cutting him short.

4th place: Luke Kruger 79,500 points

"Fourth," Luke declared, grinning broadly.

Raul whacked the side of his helmet. "Luke beat me? That is worse."

"That means the three of us are at the top," Flynn commented.

"Wanna place some last-minute bets?" Kaiden asked.

"I'm already getting the group drinks, so no need to burn more cash." Flynn snickered, "Besides, I only bet when I got a chance to win."

"So then, who do you think got it?" Kaiden asked. Flynn stared at him a moment before looking back at the screen.

3rd place: Flynn King 89,200 points

Flynn whistled. "Those turrets and drones must have been worth a dollar-pound."

"What the hell is a dollar-pound?" Kaiden asked.

"Next up is second," Silas observed. "They usually show the last two positions at the same time."

Jaxon tapped Kaiden on the shoulder. "Either way it goes, it was good working with you," he said with a salute.

Kaiden reciprocated, though his salute wasn't as formal. "Right back at you."

"Figures the top positions would go to aces," Amber said.

Kaiden knocked against his chest a couple times. "Hey, it's in the name."

The screen went dark for a moment before the scorecards burst onscreen.

2nd place: Jaxon Cage 101,900 points

1st Place: Kaiden Jericho 113,500 points.

"Holy hell," Flynn cried. The other soldiers in the test cheered as bursts of different color lights erupted in the sky and the screen declared, *"Congratulations, Initiates!"* in bright white letters.

"We did it, partner." Chief's orb popped up next to Kaiden, awash in a happy pink glow.

"You really need to stop being so pessimistic." Kaiden chuckled.

"Like I said, can't let you get too full of yourself."

"Will you let me gloat for a while at least?"

The EI's eye looked to either side for a moment before looking back at him. *"Within reason, but you've earned a little cockiness."*

"You know that was already there," Kaiden jeered.

"And it's worked out so far," Chief admitted.

"You two did amazing," Silas boomed. Kaiden looked

over to see the group huddle around them. "Both your scores are the highest anyone has ever gotten during these tests."

"The last high score was one hundred thousand even," Jaxon noted. "Feels nice to surpass it, even if I'm not the new high score."

"Like you said, probably got some extra points for dealing the killing blow," Kaiden responded. "But we'll have other opportunities to go at it. Nice to know I got some real competition in the aces. Might convince me to stick around."

"After what I've seen, I recommend it. Gives me some motivation too," Jaxon answered with a nod.

"Aw, is this your EI, Kaiden?" Amber asked, poking the pink orb. "It's adorable."

"Well, uh, thank you, darlin'," Chief said sheepishly.

"Pink is a pretty color on you," Amber chirped before walking off.

"It's...uh, not my natural color. I got this emotive skin thing... come back, please," Chief cried, floating after her.

"First time I've seen Chief flustered. Have to remember to use that on him," Kaiden mused aloud.

"So that's Chief, eh?" Flynn asked, walking up to peer at the orb. "Pretty neat. This here's Jeeves." He held out his hand to show a translucent kangaroo in a yellow color and tuxedo top.

Kaiden snickered. "I thought you told Marlo that stereotypes were a bad thing."

"Well, sure...but just look at this cute little bugger," Flynn cooed, holding the avatar closer to Kaiden as it hopped in place.

Kaiden gripped the marksman's wrist lightly and moved it out of his face. "Nice to know that a guy whose job it is to put bullets through skulls has a soft side."

Jeeves disappeared, and Flynn put down his hood and unlocked his mask, revealing sea-blue eyes, long blond hair, and a beaming smile. "I can be sentimental, sure."

"It's one of the things that keeps us sane in all this." The two turned to see Jaxon walking up, his helmet in hand. The dark blue skin, seaweed-like hair bundled into one long braid, and dark black eyes surprised him.

Flynn whistled. "A Tsuna, huh? Haven't seen too many of you among the Soldiers."

"Almost all have come to this academy for engineering, scientific, or medical purposes. I was chosen to represent the warriors of my species."

"Doing a pretty damn good job of it so far," Flynn assured him.

"Where's your, ah…" Kaiden motioned around his neck. "Breathing water circle thing?"

"My hydro insulator, as the device was called, is on me in the pod. I do not require it in the Animus."

"That's nifty." Flynn nodded.

"So I guess we're doing a big reveal thing here?" Kaiden asked, taking off his hat and unlocking his mask. "Don't be too amazed by what you see."

As Kaiden removed the mask, Flynn chuckled. "I don't think I'll have any feelings of inadequacy around you, Kaiden."

Kaiden gave him a pensive look. "Sassy Aussie bastard."

"Comes with the territory, although I would like to

know how you got that scar." He pointed to the line just to the side of Kaiden's left eye.

Kaiden traced it for a moment. "I'll tell you over those drinks later."

Flynn nodded. "I'll hold you to that."

Kaiden saw others begin to disappear in a flash of light. Chief popped back onscreen.

"Time to get out of here. You can initiate de-sync when you're ready."

"Gotcha," Kaiden acknowledged, looking at the others. "I'll see you all on the other side."

"Make sure you do." Jaxon tapped the side of his head.

Kaiden saw a prompt pop-up.

Jaxon Cage would like to network Y/N

"What's a network?" Kaiden asked.

"Oh, good idea, Jaxon," Flynn exclaimed, tapping his head too. Kaiden received another prompt.

"It's to keep track of each other in the Academy—set-up studies, partner up for tests or training, or keep social," Jaxon explained.

As Kaiden accepted the requests, more appeared from each of the soldiers he'd fought beside. He took a deep breath and accepted all of them.

"Guess we'll have our own battalion soon enough," Silas noted.

"We did pretty damn good here. They should probably split us up if they wanna challenge us," Amber declared.

"Don't give them any ideas now." Marlo chuckled.

"Besides, we're plenty dangerous on our own," Cameron added.

Jaxon pressed the side of his head again. "I'm heading

out. See you all at the ceremony." With that, he disappeared in a flash of light.

The others nodded and said their goodbyes before disappearing, leaving Kaiden alone for a moment. He looked over the island one last time, watching the sky darken.

"They'll kick you out automatically if you take too long," Chief informed him.

"I'm going. Go ahead and start the de-sync." Kaiden sighed. "This actually turned out to be pretty damn fun."

"The test?" Chief asked as Kaiden saw the island vanish.

"That too."

CHAPTER THIRTY-TWO

Kaiden flipped the circular medal in the air, catching it before looking it over one more time. The rank-up medal was a silver coin, no bigger than an archaic half-dollar coin, the Nexus academy symbol etched into it with a number 2 at the top.

"Hitting the big time now, huh?" Chief asked.

Kaiden put his oculars on. "Maybe not big time, but I'm a hell of a lot further along than before."

"And in less than a couple weeks. Way better than I initially figured you'd fare."

"Why? What did you think?"

"Honestly? Figured you might get held back a year," Chief admitted with a roll of his eye.

Kaiden chuckled as he placed the medallion on his capsule bed. He stood to put on his academy jacket. "To be fair, I was contemplating if I should even be here for quite some time." He picked the medal back up and put it on the collar of his jacket. "Guess it didn't turn out so bad."

"Wow, for once I was the optimistic one," Chief observed.

Kaiden zipped up his jacket. "Speaking of you, I'm surprised you didn't want me to get you one of those fancy new skins. Since I beat the high score, they basically let me choose my winnings. You could have gotten something real shiny."

"Maybe, but I'm feeling all right about my current look. Chicks dig it."

"Apparently."

"Plus, I saw that kangaroo in the suit and realized I could be a lot worse off—or that you could've gotten some rather horrible ideas."

"I won't confirm or deny that." Kaiden shrugged. He looked around the SC dorm, empty except for him.

"You finally gonna get out of this place?" Chief asked.

"I'm one of the last ones here, but yeah. While the space is nice and all, I'll be moving to the Soldiers' Dorm when I get back." Kaiden stated.

"Moving on up."

Kaiden shook his head as he started to leave the sleeping quarters. "Speaking of soldiers, you know why they had to tap their heads to talk to their EIs?"

"It's the device that they use. Tapping prevents EIs from taking unnecessary action or misunderstanding orders. Sort of a fail-safe," the EI explained. *"The typical soldier EI isn't as complex and astute as I am."*

"Well, aren't I lucky." Kaiden scoffed.

"Plus, I can read your mind."

Kaiden stopped in his tracks, glancing at the EI at the top of his lenses. "You for real?"

"Well, not in a creepy way. I can read neural functions. Add

that to normal EI readings of their partner's physical stats, and I have a better way of knowing when to follow commands or assist you."

Kaiden sighed before smiling. "I learn something new about you every day."

"I'm an artificial being of unique character and many talents," Chief declared proudly.

"There's at least a little truth to that," Kaiden admitted. He turned to look at the SC quarters again. "Might be that I'm a little resistant to change, but I think I'm going to miss this place a little."

"You don't have to leave. You're still an SC. But it would probably be a little odd that one of the best soldiers isn't staying with the others."

Kaiden left the sleeping quarters and closed the door behind him. "Well, that, and the Soldier's Dorm is a bit nicer."

"Yeah, but don't you get better quarters either way with the rank-up?" Chief asked.

"The SC Dorms don't have level two rooms, but the Soldiers' Dorm does."

Kaiden could see Chief roll his eye again. *"So now, things are fitting into place."*

"Hey, if they're gonna offer me fancier digs, might as well use them, right?"

"How pragmatic of you."

"It is a good thing that I am aware of your unique bond with your EI, or I might have to warn the psych ward."

Kaiden turned to see Commander Sasha making his way up the hall.

"Howdy, Commander, haven't seen you in a hot

minute," Kaiden said with a smile, offering his hand. "You come all this way just to see little old me?"

The commander took his hand in a tight grip, shaking it once before letting go. "I wanted to congratulate you on your success in the test. I had some business to discuss with Professor Laurie so I couldn't make it to the ceremony."

"I understand. I was surprised Laurie wasn't there—over-blown festivities seem to be his thing."

"Well, he is normally a recluse, if you recall, though your being here seems to have certainly made him more active in the last few weeks than he has been in years."

Kaiden rolled his eyes now. "I seem to have that effect on people."

"It's a special gift. Don't put it to the side too casually," Sasha advised, clasping his hands behind his back. "I heard you chose a rank-up as your prize for taking first place."

Kaiden nodded. "Got a small treasure trove of goodies too—some special skins for my armor, a few thousand academy credits, even a couple mods for my guns along with the one I got in the test." He leaned against the wall, crossing his arms. "Gotta say that y'all take care of the winners around here."

"The saying that success is its own reward may be true, but incentive certainly brings out more enthusiasm," he said, looking off to the side. "I hear that you've been training with Officer Wulfson?"

Kaiden let out a dramatic sigh. "I'm sure that's what he calls it for legal reasons. I would file it under assault or torture, but I guess I can't argue that I've gotten results, and ridiculously quickly too."

Sasha formed a small smile. "Wulfson's methods are a bit extreme, but trust me when I say that when it comes to physical prowess and survival tactics, I would put him up there with the best, in and out of the Academy."

"I won't argue. It works out, anyway." Kaiden unzipped his jacket, holding the left side open to reveal a silver gun in a holster on his side with a glowing blue line on either side.

The commander looked at the gun for a moment and then back to Kaiden. "I see you're already making use of your perks."

Kaiden zipped up his jacket again. "You bet, but while I didn't have to fill out those stupid forms and go through a waiting period and all that junk, I still have to check in with a security officer daily, so he can look over my gun and see if it's been fired. If it has, I have to fill out a report. I already mentioned this to the lady in supplies, but you guys are really pedantic when it comes to weapons in a military academy." He shook his head. "Fortunately, Wulfson doesn't give two shits and he's the head of security, so it works out for me."

"You do realize you're mentioning this to an Academy Board member?" Sasha inquired.

Kaiden lowered his oculars to give him a scathing stare. "Come on now, Commander, don't be like that. You're the one who brought me here. I wouldn't have figured you'd now change the score."

The commander let out a quick laugh, surprising Kaiden. "I suppose you're right, but be careful with that, if you would." He began walking past him but paused to look at him with a brow raised. "If something were to happen, I would possibly be considered an accomplice."

Kaiden grinned. "I'll be sure not to besmirch your good name." He pushed himself off the wall. "Me and some of the soldiers I met during the test are going to Seattle during the break for some drinks. Care to come?"

"A kind offer, but no thank you. While you may be on break, there are matters I must attend to." Sasha hesitated. "Though I am curious, why go all the way to Seattle? Bellingham has plenty of good bars and restaurants."

"Luke wanted to take us to one of those places, but I figured I would prefer to go to a place that has something I know I'd like."

"And where is that?"

"Well, I was only in Seattle long enough to learn of one bar."

The commander turned back. "So you're off to the Emerald Bar then? A bit of a full circle for you."

Kaiden tucked his hands into his jacket pockets. "I'm not that sentimental, but when I talked to Julio, he offered to give me some celebratory drinks. One of the other guys, Flynn, already offered to get me drinks and Luke offered food, so I figured I could get fed and buzzed and not have to pay a single credit."

"How pragmatic of you." Sasha deadpanned.

"You know, between you and Chief, I'm beginning to think that's an insult instead of a compliment," Kaiden noted dryly.

The commander turned away. "I suppose it all depends on your point of view."

Kaiden reached out and grabbed him by his shoulder. "Hey, Sasha?"

Sasha looked back at him. "Yes, Initiate?"

"I just wanted to say...thanks." Kaiden removed his hand, a little embarrassed though he'd never admit it. "Thanks for bringing me here."

"Nonsense, Initiate Jericho, I simply offered the opportunity," the commander reminded him. "You brought yourself here."

Kaiden sighed. "I would make a smartass remark about your little philosophical ramblings, but I getcha." He put his hands in his jacket again, turning the other way. "Besides, I've probably done better than even you would have thought," he jeered before walking to the building's exit.

"How do you figure that?" Sasha asked.

Without stopping, Kaiden called back. "I'm guessing that you probably didn't think I would beat your high score!"

With that, Kaiden exited the building, leaving Sasha in the hall alone. "At first, I certainly didn't," he whispered, placing a hand across his chest. "But considering what I've seen and where you come from, I began to think it was possible." He walked in the other direction toward the back exit. "Honestly, I have begun to hope you can surpass much more than merely a test score."

Kaiden left the building, and the light from the setting sun hit his eyes. He went to shield them with his arm as his oculars switched to shaded lenses.

"Appreciate it, Chief."

"Not a problem. Where are we off to now?"

"I wanted to see if we could find—"

"Good evening, Kaiden," a voice called.

Kaiden looked over to see Chiyo standing next to a tree near the entrance to the dorms. He waved as he walked over to her.

"Good to see you. Couldn't find you after the ceremony—congratulations on getting first."

"You too. I hope it has convinced you to stay in the Ace Class?" she asked.

"Only if your success has helped you move past your… inner demons? Would that be right?" he asked, tapping his fingers against his arm.

She raised a questioning eyebrow. "It…I suppose it would be accurate. And I'm a little more certain of where I belong, thank you."

"Hey, quid pro quo…am I using that right too?"

Chiyo smiled as she shook her head at his silliness. "Only if you answer my previous question."

Kaiden nodded. "Yeah, I'm gonna stick around. Met another ace during the test. He's a little dry, ironically, but he definitely has a better grasp of the whole leadership thing than I do."

"Are you gonna follow his lead?" she asked.

"Hell no," Kaiden scoffed. "But since I've been here, I've learned that people are gonna offer their stu…help, whether I want it or not, so figured if I at least listen to at least some of it they'll give me a break, and I can maybe gain some good advice now and then."

Chiyo chuckled. "How pragmatic of you."

Kaiden's eye twitched. "What the hell? Is that everyone's word of the day?"

"What are you talking about?" she asked, giving him a puzzled look.

"Forget it." He sighed. "Not what I was here for."

"What would that be?"

Kaiden held a finger up, telling her to wait a moment. "Chief, send the invite, would ya?"

Chiyo's eyes shimmered a moment. "A network invitation?"

"I learned about it during the test, figured I'd make the offer," he explained. "It won't let you do your little appearing mysteriously act as easily, but it'll make conversation way easier than us running into each other in moments of serendipity."

She stared at him for a moment before smiling and closing her eyes. "Kaitō, accept invite," she stated before opening her eyes and looking back at him. "Thank you."

"It's all good." He placed his hands against his side. "I would have done it sooner if I'd known. I sent one to Geno—or rather, Jaxon did, and sent me a link. Apparently, they know each other. Although I guess all of them do since there's only about thirty of them here."

"I should probably send him one as well," Chiyo admitted.

"You haven't? He seemed pretty fond of you."

"I think that's just his nature." She shrugged.

"He and Jaxon do seem rather different."

"Did you think they were all like that?" she asked with an accusatory look.

Kaiden raised his hands in defense. "Hey. I've never known an entire alien race. I thought maybe it was a hive-mind thing or a cultural difference or something."

She snickered. "I'm just teasing."

He lowered his hands. "Well, that's a nice change of pace. Not exactly comforting, but nice."

Her smile remained. "It is nice to have a little relief sometimes."

"I'm glad. Our little chats have helped me out quite a bit. I'm happy to help, even if it's at my expense," Kaiden added.

"You've been more than helpful, even not as a victim of a childish prank," she admitted, "Where are you off to?"

"Well, I was looking for you, but since that's done, I'm going to Seattle to join some of the others for drinks. Wanna come?"

She blinked for a moment, caught off guard. "I wouldn't want to intrude."

"You wouldn't be. A few of the others are bringing along other friends, and Geno will be there too. Figure we all blow off some steam from the tests. Who knows when we'll get another chance?"

Chiyo looked up at the sky, thinking for a moment. "Probably after the mid-year test."

"What's that?" Kaiden asked, "Whatever it is, it sounds like it's quite some time away."

"A few months. I'll explain more on the way," Chiyo said.

Kaiden pumped his fist. "So you're coming? All right,

then, we should head over to the carriers. Last batch is off in thirty."

"Twenty, actually," Chiyo corrected.

"All the more reason to get a move on," he retorted, turning and motioning for her to follow. "Shall we?"

She nodded. The sun had descended a little further, the beginnings of night appearing in the sky and a cool breeze blowing in.

"So is it safe to say that you're settling in?" she asked as they walked along the edge of the island. A cool breeze blew in, and the water crashed against the barrier.

"Into the Academy? Sure." Kaiden nodded. "But into the life? Nah, I never settle."

AUTHOR NOTES

SEPTEMBER 11, 2018

Thank you for not only reading this story but also these *Author Notes* here at the back.

So, the set of stories coming out has been in production (Michael Anderle Productions™ LOL) since mid-February, 2018.

I reached out to my collaborator and asked him if he had any desire to work on a project, and fortunately, he said 'yes.'

A little about me

Many of you might know what follows, but for many this might be a story you have never heard. When I was forty-seven, I decided that by God, I was going to make a stab at writing books and publishing. Half my reason was because writing and publishing something of mine was a bucket list item in my life.

I was closing in on fifty years old, and that was a bit

past time to get my ass in gear if I was going to cross that item off my list of things to finish before I was...finished.

The second reason is my oldest son, who wrote fan fiction back in Junior High, I believe, didn't want to try because he didn't understand all the pieces and how they fit together. I believed I could go first, and then tell him.

That didn't go so well, *until it did*.

A little about Joshua

He is my oldest son, a talented and funny writer but not very good at 'let me get out there and try this!' Even after I could tell him everything about publishing he would want to know, it took a LONG time to get him to sit down and craft a book.

Part of the problem was SIS (Shiny Idea Syndrome), where this story was fun as long as another story didn't take his attention. Another was the absolute effort to put 40k–60k or more words down in a manuscript.

He went through the whole process, and opened his own account on Amazon to publish the book.

Unfortunately, he didn't publish book two in time and the ranking dropped. Also, he is a bit more of a perfectionist than I am, and was pretty critical of his effort, so it was hard to push forward.

When I changed some of the strategies of my publishing company, I reached out to him and asked if he would be willing to write for me. (I fully expected him to turn me down, but I had to ask.)

Surprisingly, he agreed.

AUTHOR NOTES

Why ask him?

Joshua is twenty-five at the moment, turning twenty-six in a couple of months. He has been playing video games—a *lot* of video games—since he was maybe two or three years old. I wanted to create a universe that would work for LitRPG or GameLit. I needed someone to work the Universe with me, so I could direct it but not have to come up with all of the answers.

Plus, they had to write well.

Both of those requirements fit him very well. If you ask his opinion on games, be prepared to chat for a while.

Was the collaboration a disaster?

Fortunately, no.

In the beginning, we both rather tiptoed around trying to say, "I don't like that, you elitist Cossack." (Not that I said it, nor does it make much sense—even as a pejorative—but you get the idea.) We worked out the details of the world, then the characters, and then the beats for book one.

The beats for book one turned into three books.

I was adamant about including the Fantasy Football aspect of the story. Joshua tended to shy away from writing those aspects when I wanted them. I kept getting, "I'll get there…but it didn't work because <insert reason here>."

Finally, in book 03 (half-finished as I type this, and probably due out in four or five weeks at the moment) I received my glorious KABANG with the teachers and their betting pool/fantasy football.

Not that he didn't change some of my ideas there, too. I'm happy to say I'm a magnanimous collaborator and full of patience…

Yeah, I can't sell that. They were good ideas, and I kept them.

Books planned for this series

Right now, there are twelve books planned for this series. Three for each year of Kaiden at the Academy (*Animus, Co-Op, Death Match* are the first three.) Each trilogy (year of his time at the school), Kaiden is doing something a bit radical compared to the others. After the twelve books, our thoughts (assuming we do well enough to continue the series, your reviews help!) are to move Kaiden and his team he builds into the bigger Universe. However, if you, the readers, want to read about other students going through the Academy, we have plans to support more series in the Academy as well.

I hope you liked this book. If you did, or any book on Amazon, consider leaving a review. They help all of us Authors as we produce books to see whether you, our fans, like them (or don't)!

Ad Aeternitatem,

Michael Anderle / Joshua Anderle

BOOKS BY MICHAEL ANDERLE

For a complete list of books by Michael Anderle, please visit

www.lmbpn.com/ma-books/

All LMBPN Audiobooks are Available at Audible.com and iTunes. For a complete list of audiobooks visit:

www.lmbpn.com/audible

CONNECT WITH THE AUTHORS

Michael Anderle Social
   Website:
   http://kurtherianbooks.com/

Email List:
   http://kurtherianbooks.com/email-list/

Facebook Here:
   https://www.facebook.com/OriceranUniverse/
   https://www.facebook.com/TheKurtherianGambitBooks/

Printed in Great Britain
by Amazon